We hope you enjoy this book. Please return or renew it by the due date.

You can renew it at your local libraries or by using our free library app.

Otherwise you can phone 0344 800 8020 - please have your library card and PIN ready.

You can sign up for email reminders too.

D0588147

A Life without You

Shari Low

First published as an ebook in 2017 by Aria,
an imprint of Head of Zeus Ltd

First published in print in the UK in 2018 by Aria

9 7 5 3 1 2 4 6 8

A catalogue record for this book is available from
the British Library.

ISBN (PB): 9781788541893
ISBN (E): 9781784978259

Typeset by Divaddict Publishing Solutions Ltd

Printed and bound by CPI Group (UK) Ltd,
Croydon, CR0 4YY

Head of Zeus Ltd
First Floor East
5–8 Hardwick Street
London EC1R 4RG

WWW.HEADOFZEUS.COM

To J, C & B.
Everything, Always.

1

Jen

She would hate that it wasn't a spectacular occasion. Quite an ordinary day really. Not good enough. Not good enough at all.

A Sunday morning in January. Dull outside. The clouds a blanket of foreboding, a grey persuasion that staying inside, under a duvet, was the best course of action.

We didn't take much convincing.

Dee was on one sofa, wrapped in a blanket, suffering from aching of the bones, I was on the other, nursing a mild hangover. The accomplices to our lazy day were steaming mugs of tea, the remnants of our Christmas stock of Matchmakers, and a movie box set: *The Godfather 1, 2* and *3*.

My choice.

There were no ailments in the world that could not be cured by a young Al Pacino, even if the volume was a few notches louder than it needed to be, a strategy aimed at drowning out the thumping techno beat coming through the wall from the 24/7 party house next door. The neighbours had only moved in a few weeks before. Judging by the trail of people that went up and down their path, either they were exceptionally sociable, or dealing in products that had a high demand. I just hoped it was Avon, but I had yet to see anyone emerge with a flawless complexion, so I had my doubts.

Dee winced as she adjusted her position. 'God, my shoulders ache.'

'No sympathy at all,' I quipped.

'You're a terrible friend,' she countered, but her words were softened by her grin. Her smile was the first thing that everyone noticed. Julia Roberts wide. A natural spring of happiness that needed no encouragement and always lingered longer than it needed to, as if it just wanted to give a little extra to the recipient's day. And it was a cliché, but the wild tangle of red hair suited her personality perfectly: unpredictably, fiery, prone to escaping constraints at the first possible opportunity. 'It seemed like a good idea at the time,' she groaned.

'At what time? When you signed up for it? When you put the suit on? Or when you stepped out of a plane at three thousand feet and plummeted to earth, relying on a bit of flimsy fabric to save you from splatting your organs across a turnip field?'

She shook her head. 'Nope, it was a good idea when we were all at the pub on the Christmas night out and I came up with it after three glasses of wine and a packet of cheesy Wotsits. Besides, it was for charity. That's a good thing, right?'

That smile again. No one was immune to it, not even me. It got her into so much trouble and then got her right back out of it again. Always had done. We'd been friends since we were five and met on our first day at Weirbridge primary school, so that was... ouch, my head hurt when I tried to concentrate... around twenty-five years of being rescued from tricky situations by her toothy equivalent of a SWAT team. Although, for the sake of full disclosure, most of those incidents were caused by Dee's love affair with risk-taking in the first place, and I, the mousy, sensible, well-behaved, good girl was invariably in the wrong place, at the wrong time. The time she shoplifted two caramel wafers from the school tuck shop because we forgot our dinner money. She charmed everyone as she pleaded innocence, while I was caught with a wrapper and got detention. The time she persuaded me to bunk off school and a teacher saw me keeping watch while Dee snogged her boyfriend round the back of ASDA. I got marched to the headmaster while Dee snuck into Home Economics and won a prize for her Bakewell Tart.

Luckily, I don't bear grudges. I put it down to love, an aversion to confrontation and exceptionally high tolerance levels.

The door opened and my boyfriend, Pete, materialised, clutching a six-pack of Budweiser. He took in the scene in front of him, the two of us, prone, tucked into cocoons.

'I've just had an insight into what it looks like when whales get confused and beach up on the sand,' he observed.

'I'd throw something at you but my shoulders are too sore,' Dee muttered, then turned to me. 'Did I mention my sore shoulders?'

'Several times,' I answered.

Pete was already heading out of the door and only the very perceptive would have noticed that his gaze barely met mine. 'I'm heading over to see Luke,' he declared, telling us what we already knew. It was a familiar pattern. Dee and I worked together in our shop in the centre of Glasgow from Monday to Saturday, but still, every Sunday, she came to the house I shared with Pete, and we commandeered the TV, while Pete headed over to Dee and Luke's house to colonise the high-tech tech, optimum sport-watching, obscenely large, flat-screen there. It was the non-sexual, non-kinky version of partner-swapping.

Dee and Luke had been married for five years, but Pete and I had yet to follow them to the 'death do us part' stuff, despite the fact that our relationship had preceded theirs by a decade, the legacy of a lethal fourth year Christmas disco at high school that had served up the perfect storm of contraband wine and mistletoe. Making it official had never been high on our priority list. I'd always thought we were fine just the way we were. And mostly, that was the case. Mostly.

He backed out of the doorway. 'See you later. I'll bring dinner home with me, so don't worry about making anything.'

There was a loaded dig in there. My cooking skills extended to salad and anything that could be put in the oven at 220 degrees for twenty minutes – and that was on a good, non-hangover day. Dee, on the other hand, could look in my fridge, find several food items of questionable origin and age, and whip them up into an appetising meal. It was like some kind of Marvel superpower.

The door banged behind him and there was a pause until my very perceptive friend cracked.

'Things not any better then.' It was more of an observation than a question.

I shrugged.

They weren't.

I took a sip of my tea to deflect the question, but her raised eyebrow of curiosity made it clear Dee wasn't for moving on.

I capitulated. I'd have made a rubbish spy.

'He's just… distant. Preoccupied. I'm sure it's just a phase. A dip. You know he can be pretty distracted sometimes.'

That much was true. Pete was just like Dee – needed the constant amusement and focus of something going on – whereas Luke and I were perfectly happy to snap open a beverage, chill out and leave them to it. We'd lounged on beach chairs in Bali and watched them surf. We'd sat in a rooftop bar in Vegas and watched them shoot off the roof above us on a roller coaster. We'd stood on the sidelines cheering them on when they crossed the line at a marathon. I saw first-hand why that old cliché of opposites attracting could work out particularly well. If Pete were like me, we'd live life at non-adventurous, turtle speed. If I were like him, we'd probably be up a mountain right now, risking life and limb, getting friction rashes from Lycra.

I much preferred the sofa option.

'Do you want me to talk to him?' Dee asked, and I could see she was concerned.

'Nah, it's fine. He's adamant that it's all in my imagination and swears there's nothing wrong, so maybe I'm just being touchy. He says we should book a holiday. I keep catching him looking longingly at the brochures for the Maldives I brought home from the shop last week.'

Our shop – Sun, Sea, Ski – was a one-stop holiday and travel shop that sold everything from bikinis, to sun cream, to ski wear, to scuba suits, to gizmos that allowed you to take pictures underwater. We also booked hotels and excursions, activity breaks, group adventures and we'd even planned a couple of weddings. We'd opened it right out of college, on a wing and a prayer, and the Gods of Package Tours had delivered. We'd made a million mistakes along the way, but we'd stayed afloat and managed to build up a great base of regulars, and develop healthy online sales. Our partnership worked perfectly. I handled the business side of things and

Dee took care of the promotion and marketing, writing a travel blog, trying out the products, going to conventions and establishing links with hotels and entertainment outlets in popular destinations. We'd never be rich but we'd survived this long and were finally making a pretty good living out of it.

'And you don't want to go?' she asked.

I took a bite of my caramel wafer. The shoplifting incident hadn't put me off them and, besides, it was purely medicinal, with long-recognised hangover-curing properties.

'It's not that I don't want to go...' I said, in a tone that I realised absolutely suggested that I didn't want to go. 'But it's just... look, it's expensive. And completely over-the-top ostentatious.'

'And fabulous,' she added, not that she needed to. I'd just described the two essential characteristics for any trip Dee ever took.

I wasn't that person. I was happy at home. Maybe a week in a cottage somewhere up north. Or a fortnight in a villa in the south of Spain if I was really pushing the pedalo out. But a fortnight in the Maldives would be at least ten grand. We'd be home in two weeks and all we'd have to show for it would be fading tan lines and a large hole in the bank account. I didn't see the point.

'You have to go!' Dee exclaimed. 'It's a trip of a lifetime.'

The irony almost made me choke on my tea. 'Wise words, Obi Wan Travel Guru. So tell me, how many "holidays of a lifetime" did you rack up last year?'

It was our standing joke. Dee's excuse was that she had to try out our products and maintain the authenticity of our travel blog. The reality was that the mere whiff of Piz Buin had a crack-like effect on her, an addiction that could only be satisfied by throwing half a dozen of our top-selling Melissa Odabash bikinis into her Eddie Harrop travel bag and heading to Glasgow airport. Luke went with her when he could, but he had those trifling issues called work, commitments and financial responsibilities. Last year, she did a week in LA, a fortnight touring the Hawaiian islands, three weeks in Australia, five days in Fiji, two Spanish activity trips and long weekends in Monaco, Rome, and Venice. I had a couple of weekends up north and a week driving behind Pete while he cycled across France. And that suited me just fine.

The conversation was halted with a loud thud from next door. Dear God, what were they doing in there?

Raised voices. More banging.

It was difficult to tell if it was high spirits or a high chance of violence. I should probably have complained to some department or other in the local council about noise pollution, but I'd tried to adopt a 'live and let live' policy. And when that was wavering, the earmuffs I'd brought home from a ski weekend in Glencoe last winter solved the problem.

More crashing sounds and raised voices. We lived in a row of four terrace houses; I just hoped poor Mrs Kinross on the other side had her hearing aid turned off.

Dee groaned. 'Oh, bugger, I've left my phone in the car.'

'Just leave it,' I told her. 'It's Sunday. No one needs you urgently, and if Luke wants you he'll call my phone.'

'Can't help it. I'm a nomophobe. It's a registered medical condition. I should get special seats on public transport.'

She wasn't lying about the first bit – nomophobia: 'an intense, irrational fear of being without your mobile phone.' It really was a thing and Dee really did have it. Her handset was rarely far from her side, it beeped with irritating frequency, and in the last couple of months I'd noticed her compulsion to check it every few minutes was getting more and more prevalent. I, on the other hand, got approximately one call a week, and it was usually from our cleaner Josie, to say that Dee hadn't turned up on time when it was her turn to open the shop.

She was already stretching, stiffly, as she got to her feet, pausing as she caught sight of something through the window.

'Police have just pulled up. Bloody hell, it's getting like an episode of *Blue Bloods* around here. Not sure I can take this much real-life excitement at the weekend.'

We both knew she was lying. A SWAT team could charge through my front room and she'd be riveted by the action. Not that it would ever happen. Weirbridge was a small town about fifteen miles from Glasgow, and the odd theft of a Flymo and occasional pub disagreement were about as much as the cops ever had to deal with.

Thankfully, I realised, craning my neck to see outside, there didn't appear to be any riot shields, just two fairly relaxed cops in high-vis vests, calmly alighting from their vehicle, their eyes on the neighbour's front door. S'pose it was only a matter of time before someone objected to our quiet little suburban street having the decibel levels of an Ibiza rave.

Curious (or nosy), I went to the window and watched as Dee headed out to retrieve her phone, smiling at the officers as they passed on the parallel paths, knowing the restraint she must be deploying to prevent herself from asking what was going on and getting a vicarious buzz from the action.

A substantial fist battered the neighbour's door. Nothing. The cops stood back, looked at the windows, returned to the door, banged again.

Dee's car was parked on the other side of the road, in front of a green used by the local Ronaldos as the Weirbridge equivalent of Real Madrid's Santiago Bernabeu stadium. Right now there were four boys, somewhere between the ages of eight and ten, using two raised, stone-walled flower beds as one set of goals, and a pile of jumpers and an Irn Bru bottle as the other, so absorbed in the game they hadn't even noticed the arrival of the cavalry. I recognised all of them. Two brothers from across the road. The boy who came to stay with his dad two doors along at weekends. And Mrs Kinross's little blond grandson, Archie.

As Dee crossed the road, she fumbled in her pocket for her keys. When she reached her car, she opened her driver's door and the top half of her body disappeared inside for a few seconds.

Bang. Bang. Bang. The knocks next door were harder now, impatience obvious.

Dee unfurled herself from the inside of the car and stretched up, looking puzzled, her aching bones making her movements very deliberate.

'Police!' a voice of authority shouted. More raps on the door.

Dee moved around to the back of her car and opened the boot.

I heard the click of a lock as someone finally answered next door.

Back to Dee. She pulled her backpack from her boot, opened the zip, peered inside.

A flash of black, then yellow in my peripheral vision. It took me a moment. A guy, early twenties, jeans, black hoodie, noted my inner Miss Marple. He bolted down the path, the two officers in pursuit, one of them barking into the black walkie-talkie attached to his vest.

Oblivious, Dee tossed the bag back into the boot of her car, then reached in and pulled out her gym bag, and started rummaging in it.

The guy from next door was about fifty yards down the road now. He came to a dead halt when he reached a customised Corsa that I knew belonged to a frequent visitor to our rambunctious neighbours. I congratulated myself on my observation skills and decided I'd be great in a *Crimewatch* reconstruction.

As he opened the door, the noise made Dee turn, her expression puzzled. Her eyes widened, the beginnings of a smile playing on her lips. We'd be laughing over the fact that we had a police chase on our doorstep for the rest of the day. Oh, the scandal. Behind her, a couple of the young kids had stopped playing and were now watching the action.

A roar as the souped-up engine of the Corsa started up, just as one of the cops reached its door. His hand grappled for the handle, the Corsa shot forward, out of the parking space, into the middle of the road.

Dee had found her phone now, had it at her ear and I could see her lips moving. She was smiling, no longer watching the high drama, engrossed in the call.

A roar of the engine as the Corsa accelerated, the cops on the road now, giving chase as it came back towards our direction, towards their parked car. I'd give anything to see them doing one of those stunt rolls across the bonnet before climbing in and roaring off in pursuit.

Over on the other pavement, the noise made Dee turn, still chatting and grinning.

Fast and Furious was about to make a clean getaway, when suddenly, over to my right, another police car appeared, blocking his escape.

The two cops on foot stopped running, confident they had trapped their prey. I watched. Dee watched. The kids behind her watched.

The Corsa would have to stop. Brake. And for a split second, I thought that's what was happening, but then... It took me a moment to process... In one explosive move, the car shot to the left, towards the green.

The boys realised it was coming, and started to run as it careered in their direction.

Except one.

The littlest one, Archie Kinross, couldn't keep up with the others, despite the frantic screams of his pals.

Dee saw him too. Now she was running, sprinting towards him. The car roared as it raced from one direction, Dee from the other, a terrified little guy in the middle.

There was a bang as it mounted the kerb, the engine screaming now.

I started running too. Across the lounge, out of the front door, just in time to see Dee reach the little boy, lift him, throw him to one side. Yes! She got him! She saved him! She...

The bang was indescribable.

The aftermath wasn't.

Gut-wrenching. Horrific. Brutal. Dee flying high in the air, and then... slow motion.

From somewhere inside me, a primal, desperate scream. I was running towards her, she was still soaring, upwards, her hair fanning out like a red halo around her head. Archie sat on the grass, his eyes wide with disbelief. His fleeing buddies had stopped at the sound of the impact and turned, and now they stood, frozen to the spot, faces contorted in shock and horror.

The car engine grinding as it raced forwards, under her, heading into the distance. Dee was soaring, then she twisted, like a high diver, and began to fall.

Almost there. I could catch her. 'Deeeeeeeeee!' It was my voice, telling her I'm on my way. Wait for me. I'll catch you. I'll make it, Dee, just...

The thud was barely audible, yet somehow the loudest noise I'd ever heard. She came down, head first, hit the small stone wall that bordered one of the flower beds. Then she was still.

Screams. All mine.

The police officers got there first, but I darted between them, slid to my knees, threw myself on her, shielding her. Too late.

Someone's voice. Maybe mine.

'Dee! Oh, God, Dee. Dee!'

The gorgeous, adventurous, wild, hilarious, adrenalin junkie, utterly irrepressible Dee Harper replied with nothing more than a slow, unfathomable trickle of red from the side of her mouth.

On that oh-so ordinary, devastating day, my best friend died in my arms.

2

Jen

A crematorium, a room furnished with black fabric and tears.

I reached for Pete's hand, my trembling fingers wrapping around his. On the other side of me, Dee's mum, Val, stood, her blonde beehive high and proud, staring at the coffin in front of us, tears coursing down her cheeks.

Wiping them away would have seemed like an intrusion, so I didn't. I put my hand on her arm, felt her hand cover mine, then drop as if the effort of movement had sapped her last ounce of strength. My heart broke for her. And for her husband, Don, a mammoth of man in both personality and size, on the other side of her. Next to Don, a younger version of the same DNA, Dee's brother, Mark. Six years older than her, he'd gone backpacking to Australia when we were twelve, loved it there and never returned. He'd landed early this morning and his tanned complexion, and long, tied-back hair looked incongruous in this sombre setting. Next to Mark was... A sob escaped me. Luke. Yet it wasn't him. The real Luke smiled. He laughed. He sang songs after a few pints. He was on a mission to enjoy life and he was crazy madly in love with my gorgeous friend. But that gorgeous friend wasn't here anymore. She'd been tossed in the air like a rag doll by a drugged-up driver, sustaining fatal injuries at either the point of impact or when her head crashed against a stone wall. The postmortem wasn't entirely clear, and it didn't really matter.

Either way, she wasn't here.

And this empty, broken man bore little resemblance to that guy who had loved her so much.

A nod from the humanist minister conducting the service, and Luke stepped forward, his motions slow and trance-like, waiting to wake up from a nightmare more horrific than he could contemplate.

He climbed two steps to the altar… not an altar… because there would be no worship to any God that could allow this to happen. It was more of a lectern. A podium. Luke turned to face the crowd, the contrast between the jet-black curls of his hair and his deathly pale skin never more stark, his suit jacket suddenly slack against the broad shoulders that had filled it only a couple of weeks before. Before this…

'Dee would love this. All her favourite people in one place,' he began. An instant ripple of heartbroken smiles concurred. 'This is the second time I've stood up in front of you all. The first time was at our wedding, and I told you how incredibly happy I was that we were going to be together until the end of forever. I'm not sure I've got the words to say how devastated I am that forever came so soon.' He choked on the last word, then took a deep breath, and continued.

'Before my wedding speech,' he said, with a smile so forced another piece of my shattered heart broke for him, 'Dee warned me that there was to be a suitable amount of soppy stuff, but nothing too corny. I'm not sure that I got the balance right, because I said that day what an incredible woman my wife was. How she made me laugh like no one else. Except Ant and Dec.'

We laughed then because she'd have expected it of us, even though none of us felt like we would ever want to laugh again.

He went on. 'I said that she was the most beautiful woman in the world. Except Cameron Diaz.'

In my head I heard Dee laughing the loudest, which only made the well of sorrow even deeper.

'I said how she had the biggest heart, and loved her family, her friends, and me more than anyone. Except Gary Barlow.'

He paused, breathed, set his jaw, determined to finish, to honour his girl. It took a moment before he found his voice again, stronger this time.

'And I said that she made me the happiest man ever. Except no one.'

A breath.

'There was nobody like my wife. And she'd be furious at us for being sad. So please don't be. Because every single person in this room got to meet her, and love her, and laugh with her, and that makes us luckier than anyone else.' He looked skywards, including Dee in the conversation. 'I know, too cheesy,' he told her.

His gaze returned to the mourners.

'Thank you for coming to say goodbye to Val and Don's daughter, to Jen's best friend...' My throat constricted at the sound of my name. '...and to my wife. Dee Harper, we love you, my darling. We always will.'

He walked back towards us, head high, hugged Val, squeezing her tightly, then returned to his seat, right about the same time as my heart broke in two. I didn't want to live

15

in a world where there was no Dee. No one did. The pain caught in my chest, a sense of disbelief holding it back. This couldn't be happening.

Someone, somewhere took the cue, and music started, Dee's favourite song, 'Sitting On The Dock of The Bay'. It had been the soundtrack to everything we'd ever done. As sunburned, hung-over eighteen-year-olds, we'd played it on the balcony of a hotel in Ayai Napa on our first holiday without her parents. We'd sang it at the top of our voices driving down Santa Monica Boulevard in a red convertible on her pre-wedding hen holiday for two. It had been the first dance at her wedding. It was the song she played to cheer herself up or to celebrate great times.

It didn't seem possible that she would never play it again.

3

Jen

The wake was held in the lounge of Weirbank's only hotel, The Tulip. The name was a homage to the work of Charles Rennie Mackintosh, who had once worked in the area and whose designs inspired much of the old architecture in the town. The Tulip was the venue for most weddings, christenings, birthday parties and funerals in the town, as if it had the capacity for both joy and heartache carved into its foundations.

Pete and I travelled back in the official car with Dee's parents, her brother Mark, Luke, and her Auntie Ida, resplendent in her fur finery, wailing into her pressed hankie. Ida was never one for understatement of emotion. At Dee's wedding, she'd grabbed the microphone, sung a medley of Cilla Black hits, and was only teased off the stage when someone said the sausage rolls were almost done on the midnight buffet.

'I can't believe it. I don't know how I'll cope. How will I cope?' Ida wailed.

Val's eyes caught mine and no words were necessary. I knew what she was thinking. Val had lost her daughter, but of course, Ida was making it all about her.

Dee's dad, Don, rolled his eyes at his sister's performance, but Mark ignored her, continuing to stare out of the window at the landscape he'd left almost twenty years ago. The tension was only broken when the driver took a wrong turn and went around the same roundabout three times.

'Aye, our girl never did have a sense of direction,' Don mused, our saddest moment suddenly elevated with the feeling that somewhere Dee was watching us, her irrepressible laugh demanding that we get over ourselves and pull it together.

Ida didn't get the message. Her snuffles continued all the way to the hotel.

In the foyer, the staff were lined up, respectively sombre, holding trays with a choice of wine, whisky or orange juice. Ida took a whisky, for each hand, and headed into the function suite.

Val pulled me to one side, her tears dried, her shoulders pulled back, determined to be strong until the day was over. 'Jen, do something for me.'

'Anything.' There was nothing she could ask that I wouldn't do. My mum had died when I was twelve, cancer, and Val had stepped right into the shoes that her best friend left behind, easing the burden for my dad, allowing him to take a job working offshore, a month on the rigs, a month off the rigs but on the beer.

I could never replace Dee – but I could make sure that I did everything I could to make this easier for the woman who had effectively fostered a devastated teenager, taking me in and making me part of their family. She'd gained a surrogate daughter to feed and take care of, and I'd gained a network of people who cared. I got the better deal.

But, oh God, I just hoped she wasn't going to ask me to say something at the wake. Or share my memories of my friend.

Or tell her, yet again, second by second, what happened that day. The guilt was already crushing me. Why hadn't I banged the window, caught Dee's attention? Why hadn't I run out at the first sign of that fucker from next door and dragged Dee back in? Why couldn't I see what would happen, stopped it, screamed, done anything instead of just standing there, watching as some scumbag moron, high on booze and drugs, rammed his car right through my best friend?

'Anything at all,' I repeated.

Val gestured in the direction of the flapping double doors. 'Find Josie,' she said. When Dee and I had opened our shop, Val had met our cleaner, Josie and they'd been best mates ever since. The two of them were like Dee and I, only twenty years older. I had to clench my jaw really tight so that my lip didn't start trembling at the realisation we'd never become them, never get to be two women in their later years, still pals and making each other's lives better. It was just me now.

Val squeezed my hand. 'Find Josie,' she repeated, 'and I need you both to keep an eye on Ida. If she makes any attempt to make a spectacle of herself, take her down.'

I could see that the humour was her way of trying to keep it together and it should have made me laugh, but it was so reminiscent of Dee I had to bite back a sob. 'I'm on it.'

She hugged me, and went back to the door, to stand next to her husband, son and son-in-law and greet the mourners who had come to share their loss.

I liberated a glass of wine from one of the trays and headed through to the hall. A picture of Dee stood on an easel at the door, as if we needed any reminding what she looked like. This was how I wanted to remember her – not the broken, bleeding Dee lying on the cold, wet grass. I recognised the image. It had been taken on her wedding day, as she and Luke were heading out of the church, and a shower of confetti had rained down on them. Dee was looking skyward, arms outstretched, grin wide.

I had to look away. Priority number one, be here for Val, Don and Luke. There would be plenty of time to sob my heart out into a vat of cheap wine later.

'Hey, how are you bearing up?' Pete asked, appearing at my side.

'Val has put me on Ida-watch,' I told him, gesturing to the plumes of Ida's feather fascinator, now poking out above the heads of a few friends who had gathered around her as she continued to lament her loss. Dee would be rolling her eyes right now, pointing out that the closeness of her relationship with Ida extended to weddings, funerals, and sporadic cards at Christmas.

'Good luck with that, but you'll probably need backup,' he said, as a loud wail from the feathered one cut through the subdued dignity of the room.

'I know. I've to find Josie to help. Have you seen her?'

'She was talking to the minister last time I saw her.'

There were black circles under his eyes and, for the first time, I noticed lines etched on his forehead. He looked exhausted. He'd been a rock, not only for me but for Luke too. That first night, we'd stayed with Luke and we'd barely left in the two weeks since then. I don't think any of us had had more than a few hours' sleep a night. We'd sit up late, sometimes talking, sometimes in silence, putting off the moment that we'd have to lie in a dark room, sleep evading us, thoughts of loss and death filling our minds. Yet, it was the best option for all of us. I wanted to be there to support him, and to be around a world that had Dee stamped on every ornament, blanket and CD, her presence so vivid I could almost pretend she'd just popped out to the shops or nipped away on one of her many business jaunts. I also couldn't face staying at home, seeing the crime scene tape, the skid marks on the grass, the curious stares of passers-by who'd come to gawp, the mark on the neighbour's wall where the car had finally crashed after spinning around, and racing out of control, back towards our row of houses. I didn't want a reminder that the bastard who'd done this to Dee had walked away unscathed. I'd heard the landlord had turfed out his mates next door, but I didn't want to see for myself. So instead, we'd stayed at Luke's, ostensibly for him, but really for us too. I'd cooked, cleaned, cried... Pete had been the go-to guy, the one who made arrangements, sorted stuff out, got us to where we needed to be, shuttled us back and forwards to Val and Don's house. Yet, he was hurting too. He'd known Dee almost as long as I had. She was the sister he didn't have, and his running partner in crime, fiercely disputing my theory (shared by Luke) that Spandex was an invention of evil.

Pete and Luke had rubbed along happily for years, on a blokedom level. As soon as Dee had introduced them, they'd discovered a mutual addiction to watching any type of sport that had led to five years of West of Scotland male friendship. Although, I wasn't sure that they'd ever discussed anything more meaningful than the half-time results of a league cup decider.

We were a four. Two couples that would go through life together, share holidays, paint each other's new houses, throw parties at Christmas, eat together every week, raise our kids as best friends, then deal with empty-nest syndrome by developing a love for cruising, where we'd soothe our ancient bones in the sun before heading inside to show the young ones that – arthritis permitting – we could still swing our pants in the disco.

That had been the life on the horizon for us four. Not anymore. Now we were a three. It didn't fit. Wasn't how it was meant to be.

'How are you doing?' I asked him. 'I'm really sorry. I feel like we've just all been getting through this and this is the first time I've asked if you're OK. I'm a crap girlfriend,' I finished with a rueful smile, expecting him to come back with an objection.

He didn't.

The room was filling up now. I knew I should really go and find Josie, then talk to Dee's extended family, our other friends, make sure their drinks were full and point them in the direction of the crust-less sandwiches and coronation chicken vol-au-vents on the buffet table. But my feet were incapable of movement as I watched the tiny subtleties of movement cross his face. We'd been together for fifteen years, half our lives. There was nothing about this man, no gesture, no energy that I didn't recognise.

Except this one. I reached out and touched the black wool of his suit jacket, deciding this unfamiliarity was only natural. We'd never dealt with death together, never had someone we loved taken away from us. My mum had died before we'd met. This was a set of reactions and situations that was new to us both.

'Babe, I'm sorry,' I repeated. 'Let's just get through today and then go home and we'll talk.' Reluctantly, I'd already planned to go back home tonight. Luke's brothers Matt and Callum both lived in London, but had come back up this morning for their sister-in-law's funeral. I was glad for Luke that they were going to stick around for a few days. The

Harper brothers were a considerable team when they were all in the same place. Dee had adored them all.

My dread at going back to my own house was balanced only by a tiny, selfish pang of relief that I could go home, close the door, just be still for the first time since I lay on that sofa two weeks and one day ago, giggling with my best friend.

Pete hesitated and I immediately realised why. Even though Luke's brothers would be with him, he still didn't want to leave him. God, how sweet this guy was. He might not be the most communicative when it came to his feelings, but underneath he was the kind of man who stepped up when it mattered.

'Or would you rather stay with Luke? That would be OK.' I added, trying to make it easier for him, in case he was worried about hurting my feelings.

'No, Matt and Callum will be there so I'm going to give them space.'

Before he could say any more, I spotted Josie out of the corner of my eye. As always, she was dressed from head to toe in black, a shock of silver hair spiked up in a style that she called a semi-gonk. Josie was Val's closest friend, but she helped out cleaning our shop and was part of our extended, non-related family. I started to step away to go corner her before she disappeared off to talk to someone, then quickly turned back to Pete, 'Let's go home when this is over.'

I didn't get a chance to hear his reply as a familiar voice from the stage at the end of the room demanded attention. 'Ladies and Gentlemen, we're gathered here today to mourn the loss of my niece, Dee.' Ida paused to blow her nose on a pink hankie that she'd extracted from the cuff of her black cardigan.

Oh bugger! Panic rose. I'd taken my eye off the attention-seeking ball and now it was too late. I saw Josie's head swivel around in horror too as Ida continued, 'I just know that our lassie would have wanted us to mark her passing with a wee song. And since I was the closest to her, it's only right that I'm the one to do that for her.' Another loud blow of the nasal cavities into the pink hankie.

Oh dear God, how to stop this? Val would kill me.

Ida paused, cleared her throat, closed her eyes, and broke into the first verse of a song that I recognised, yet couldn't quite place. It took me a moment. Then I realised it was a slowed down, almost melancholic version of the Temptations song, 'My Girl'. Which sounds beautiful and apt and poignant. If she wasn't singing it with the warble of a pub crooner after ten vodkas and Coke. With actions.

I thought about pressing the fire alarm, but there was always the risk that she'd finish the song in the car park to the assembled evacuees. Better to hope that she got it out the way before Val came in and...

'I gave you one job, love.' Val. Right behind me.

Mortified, I turned to face her. 'I'm sorry, I misjudged her. I didn't think she'd make a play for the room so quickly,' I whispered, hoping for forgiveness. 'I'll find a way to stop her,' I added, desperate to make this right, but with absolutely no plan on how to do so.

A river of tears poured from Val's eyes, and she began to laugh, quietly, with just a hint of hysteria.

'Don't. She showed up at the hospital when I was having our Dee. The minute she came out, Ida started singing "My Girl". Imagine. I was affronted. But she sang her into this world with that song, so she's as well singing her out.'

And with that, we stood and watched as Ida finished and took her bow.

The irony wasn't lost that the one person who would find this absolutely hilarious was the one person who wasn't here to see it.

4

Val, 1997

'Jen, love, there are plenty of bananas in the fruit bowl if you want one. In fact, take a couple home with you for tomorrow.'

Our Dee rolled her eyes. 'Mum, you're obsessed with us eating fruit. Jen, please take them all and then maybe we'll be allowed to break the Jaffa Cakes out of the cupboard.' I pursed my lips, more to stop me laughing than to reprimand my stroppy twelve year old for her cheek. That was Dee. My fiery redhead. Always something to say. In many ways, the very opposite of her best friend sitting next to her.

'Thanks, Val,' Jen replied shyly, slipping a couple into the plastic bag she'd come with today. The sight of it had made me wince. Poor soul. God knows, none of us had much in the way of money, but that girl had been using a plastic bag as a school bag for the last week. What the hell was Bob Collins thinking, sending her out like that? Didn't he care that it was giving the other kids ammunition, marking her out as different?

Actually, that question didn't need answering, because Bob Collins didn't do much thinking or caring at all. He did drinking. And fighting. And being an arse.

Poor Janice would be mortified if she could see this. I raised my eyes heavenward, choosing to believe that she was probably watching us. I missed her.

Janice had been a great pal to me, even after she'd married that waster. Bob Collins had the looks and the chat, but he didn't have an ounce of integrity or commitment. And if he did, he pretty much drowned them in whatever drink came to hand. Played the big shot. He acted all Bobby Big Bollocks. In reality, he was insignificant and utterly useless. When Janice first found the lump on her neck, he wasn't interested, told her to ignore it. She didn't, but it was already too late. Secondary cancer. Spread everywhere. She didn't stand a chance. Only a few months later she was gone too soon.

In her last days, I'd promised her I'd look after Jen, and that's what I was doing now, a task made easier by the fact that she and Dee had been inseparable for years.

In the weeks since the funeral, I made sure she got a decent meal every day. Kept tabs on her homework. And now I decided to take a tenner out of my housekeeping money and buy her a new bag tomorrow. It wasn't that we were flush, but there was usually a little extra in the food budget now that our Mark had gone off backpacking to Australia. Imagine! The other side of the world. Still, it was what the young ones wanted to do these days and he'd saved up the money for his flight himself from his weekend and evening job down at the chippy.

The door opened and Don came in from work, his face weather beaten from another day on an exposed site. Putting the foundations in was always the worst bit. No shelter, endless rain, and way too much muck. He looked like he'd been rolling in it and I bit my tongue so I didn't moan about the boot prints he was leaving on my newly mopped floor. I figured I was doing well when that was my only complaint about the man I'd married.

As he washed up at the sink, I saw Jen checking her watch, noticed the flinch of tension around her eyes, a clench of her jaw. I recognised the expression. I'd seen it often enough on Janice, when she was heading back to her house, dreading what she'd find there. Would he be sober? Drunk? Mouthing off? It was so unfair that Jen was now showing the same signs but what could I do? Bob Collins was her father.

I gave her a tight hug before she left. 'Any problems, just come straight back now, you hear?' I didn't have to spell it out. Bob had never been violent or aggressive to Janice or Jen, but he was an obnoxious pain in the arse when he'd had too many.

Don chatted to her about her day, until I put his tea in front of him. 'Right madam, upstairs, homework, bath and bed,' I told Dee, and waited for the harrumph. Yep, there it was.

'I'll do it for two Jaffa Cakes,' she said tartly.

'You'll do it or you won't step foot outside that door this weekend,' I retorted, one eyebrow raised.

She shrugged, got up, and kissed me on the cheek as she passed. 'Gotta love a trier,' she chirped, leaning down to give Don a hug, then disappearing out of the door.

This time, I couldn't stop myself from laughing. The cheek of that girl. I'd brought her up to be smart, confident and independent, but the price to pay for that was a soon-to-be teenager who was way too sharp for her own good sometimes.

Don and I had dinner, watched a bit of telly, then headed up for an early night. I checked in on Dee and saw she was already sound asleep under her Backstreet Boys duvet.

When I climbed into bed, Don reached for me and wrapped me in his big, tanned arms. 'You ok?' he asked. 'You're quiet tonight.'

I sighed. 'Just a bit worried about Jen. That's no life for a young girl, Don.'

'Then bring her here,' he said, with that black and white logic he viewed life with. Not that I hadn't thought about it, of course. But Bob Collins was her dad, a man who had just lost his wife, and he deserved a chance to show that he could change and make a good job of bringing up his daughter. The plastic bag and the tense expression had me worried though. I wasn't going to let that girl suffer for a single second, so I hoped my fears were unfounded.

My thoughts were interrupted by a noise, one I didn't recognise, outside. Feet on gravel? A grating sound? On any other night, I'd have left it but I could see Don was starting to drift off and my mind was too busy to do the same just yet.

I slipped out of bed, pulled on my robe, and peeked out of the blinds. Nothing to see. No one around. Just a figure turning the corner at the end of the street, a youngster, maybe about the same age as our Dee. And the same height. The hood was up so I couldn't see the hair but I suddenly had my suspicions.

I flew next door and they were instantly realised. Her bed was empty.

'Don. DON! Wake up. Dee's gone.'

'What do you mean "gone"?'

I now understood the sound I'd heard. Feet siding down a pebbledash wall.

'She's climbed out the window. Jesus! That bloody girl!'

I was already pulling on clothes and Don was on his feet, hopping into his clean jeans that had been left lying on the chair in his corner.

'Where the bugger has she gone?'

I checked the digital display on my alarm clock. It was after ten. Youth clubs would be closed. So would the café on the High Street. Was she hanging about the streets? Meeting someone? A boy? Oh dear God, I'd definitely kill her.

I had absolutely no idea where she would be. But there was one person who might.

We jumped in the car and five minutes later pulled up outside the Collins' house. It was in darkness, except for the flicker of a television in the living room window. Don got to the door first and battered it with his fist, every protective urge he possessed taking over. He adored his girl and while I'd gone straight to fury, this big tough man had nothing but concern and worry written all over his face.

It felt like ten minutes, but was probably two, before the door opened just a few inches. Jen looked as terrified as Don.

'Sorry if I woke you, love,' I blurted, before registering that she was still in her school uniform, 'but do you know where Dee is? She's climbed out of the window and we don't know where she's gone.'

'No, Val, I'm sorry, I've no idea.'

My internal lie detector screamed. I was a mother of two. I could spot a good fib at fifty paces and this one was coming from someone who was neither practiced nor confident enough to pull it off. I tried to work out the timings. Dee had a head start on us, but she was on foot and could cut through the scheme, so it would have taken her not much more than five minutes to get here if she'd ran all the way.

'Jen, is she in there?'

'N-n-n-n-o.'

'Jen, Are you lying to me?'

'N-n-n...'

Suddenly, the door swung open, and there was Dee, looking for all the world like we were inconveniencing her.

'It's fine, Jen' she said with a sigh, 'There's no point resisting. She'd have worn you down and got it out of you eventually.'

Seriously? More cheek? Oh, this girl would be grounded until she was old enough to go off on her bloody backpack year to Australia.

'Look, Mum, I'm sorry, but there are special circumstances.' From the official tone, I knew she'd been watching NYPD Blue again.

'They'd better be good,' Don said, with more calm than I currently possessed.

Jen opened the door wider, letting us traipse into the hall.

'Tell them,' Dee prompted Jen, weary but insistent.

Jen stared at the floor and my stomach churned, softening my voice.

'Jen, what's up love?'

Nothing. Silence. Just a single tear dropped to the floor from her bowed head.

It was too much for Dee. 'Her dad hasn't been home in a fortnight and she has no idea where he is and she hates being here on her own because it's like, way spooky and cold, so I've been coming round at night and staying with her then sneaking back into the house in the mornings before you're up.'

'But why didn't you just come to our house?' I asked Jen, dumbstruck.

'Because she didn't want to get him into trouble,' Dee answered for her.

I actually wanted to throw up at the thought of my twelve year old being out at this time of night and then again in the morning with me knowing nothing about it. For a moment I wasn't sure that I was any fitter a parent than Bob bloody Collins.

In a split second, though, that doubt escalated to sheer anger, but Don got straight to the solution before me.

'Jen, love, go pack a bag and you're coming home with us.'

A potent mixture of relief and fear crossed her face.

'But my dad...'

'I'll have a wee word with your dad. Don't you worry now. He won't get into trouble.'

'Really? I can come...?' The words got stuck in her throat and a piece of my heart broke for her.

'Go now, love,' I told her gently, then, as she took the stairs two at a time, I turned to Dee. 'And you, Dee Ida Murray...' she got her full name when I was furious, 'get in that car and wait for us and you'd better start working on an apology that will stop us from grounding you for the rest of your life.'

My words were stern, but all the anger was gone now. She'd gone about it completely the wrong way, but how could I fault her for doing a good thing, for looking out for her pal? I wasn't going to tell her that though.

She responded with a petulant sigh and flounced past me, muttering, 'Bet Mother Teresa's mum didn't ground her for taking care of someone that needed help.'

I waited until she was out of the door before I reacted.

'Mother Teresa? We're going to have some time of it with that girl,' I told Don.

'Yep, but...'

I could see he was going to stick up for her as always so I stopped him by putting my hand up. 'Save it, Don. We've got bigger things to worry about right now.'

There was a noise at the top of the stairs and I turned to see Jen coming down, three plastic bags this time. Another piece of my heart snapped off.

'OK, let's get you in the car.'

Don drove us and we were back home in a few minutes. Only half an hour had passed since we left but so much had changed.

'You go on in,' he said, as we climbed out. 'I'll just go see if I can track down Bob for a wee chat.'

I didn't argue, not wanting to upset Jen any more. I took the girls inside and made them tea and toast, popped all Jen's stuff in the washing machine, then gave her a fresh pair of Dee's pyjamas. She could borrow Dee's spare school uniform in the morning. We'd sort it all out.

It took time, but we got there. Within a few days, Jen had her own bed in Dee's room, clothes in the wardrobe, a shiny new school bag and the absolute security of knowing that she was wanted here.

My strong, silent man hadn't said much when he'd come home, just that it was sorted. It took about a week for word to filter back to me on what that meant.

Apparently, he'd found Bob in a pub, steaming drunk, draped all over some woman he'd been shagging since before Janice had died. He'd all but moved into her house now and that's why he hadn't been home to check on his daughter.

According to the gossip, Don had lifted him right out of his seat, dragged him outside and put him up against a wall, then told him, in no uncertain terms, that Jen would be *staying with us now. How he stopped himself from beating Collins to a pulp, I'll never know, but he did, because Don was a hundred times the man that odious little shit would ever be.*

'You'll visit her, contact her, keep in touch, and if you don't, I'll be back,' Don had spat.

In the end, Collins had got around regular contact by getting a job on the rigs, so he was away every second month. It amazed me that his craving for alcohol could withstand the enforced offshore abstinence, but the money clearly made it worth it.

I didn't care that we never saw a penny for the upkeep of his daughter. All that mattered was that Jen was with us.

And that was where she belonged.

5

Jen

My own home. My own blanket, still lying on the sofa where I'd left it that day. Two mugs on the floor. One mine, one…

I picked it up. I couldn't bear to wash away the traces of her, the touch of her lips on the rim of the ceramic, the fingerprints, invisible to the eye, that she had no doubt left on the handle. Instead, I carefully washed out the inside then placed it on the kitchen windowsill, facing outwards.

This was the first time I'd been back here since that Sunday afternoon. Pete had come back and packed a bag for me, then he'd gone to Luke's and I'd alternated between Luke's house and Dee's old room at Val and Don's.

I'd warned Pete not to clear anything up, when he'd come back, because I knew that I wanted to see it exactly the way it was, unchanged, just that last moment of normal before our lives were ripped apart.

Everything had meaning now. The washing basket full of clothes that I'd last worn when Dee was alive. Towels that she'd touched. Bowls that she'd used. I wanted to preserve everything exactly the way it was, to keep every trace of her here with me, like having that stuff mattered.

Yet, I knew it didn't. It wouldn't bring her back.

I went upstairs, past a dozen mirrored photo frames that documented our lives. The two of us, cutting open the ribbon on our shop. Taking our first flight together. Wearing posh frocks for our twenty-first birthdays.

I looked away, kept going.

Pete was lying on our bed, fully clothed, eyes wide open, staring at the ceiling. His light brown hair, normally meticulously short, was longer than usual, after circumstances had caused him to miss his fortnightly appointment. His jacket and black tie had been cast aside, but he still wore the white shirt, open at the neck, broad at the shoulders and then tapering down to the point it was tucked into his suit trousers. If this was any other time, my thoughts would go to a place that would involve nudity, but not tonight. Instead, it felt like there wasn't enough air in the room to breathe, and what was there had some kind of tranquilizing powers. I now understood the meaning of the phrase 'bone-tired'.

I sat at the bottom of the bed, facing him, my back against the grey chenille footboard.

'Hey,' I said softly.

His reply was a sad smile.

'I know it's a cliché, but I still can't believe any of this has happened. I can't believe she's gone, Pete.'

I didn't cry. There were no tears left.

'I know. Doesn't feel real.'

A pause. The last two weeks had been the most devastating event in our lives and yet neither of us had the stomach to talk about it.

'You know, she'd hate us to curl up and stop living. The last conversation we had was her telling me to start making the most of life.'

'Why did she say that?'

'Because I was telling her that you wanted to go on holiday.'

'What holiday?'

No wonder he'd forgotten. It seemed like a lifetime ago.

'The one to the Maldives. I saw you looking at the brochure I brought home from the shop.'

A few moments of silence made room for a thought to come out of nowhere and blurt straight from my gob, without pausing at my brain's common sense or financial checkpoints for approval.

'She was right, Pete. We should go.'

Another silence. This was the wrong time. I knew that. I mean, who makes holiday plans on the night of the funeral of their best friend? I couldn't explain it, and I knew it seemed hopelessly insensitive, but it almost felt like a mission to honour Dee, like somehow, by doing exactly what she would have wanted me to, what she'd told me to do, I was doing the right thing.

I was so busy refereeing the conflicting emotions in my head that I almost missed his reply.

'I... can't.'

'Oh come on. Work will give you time off if you ask them. I know it seems weird, but it just feels... right.'

'It doesn't, Jen. Nothing about it feels right. I can't do this.'

He sounded odd. Not surprising. Our grief was undulating, swelling and surging like crashing waves.

'You're right. I'm sorry. Maybe next year.'

What was wrong with me? A crashing tsunami of guilt took down everything in its path. What had I been thinking? A holiday? I'd just buried my best friend. No holiday was going to change that. And how could I even think about making plans when all I should be doing was mourning my best friend?

He spoke, but in such a low whisper that this time I didn't catch it.

'Sorry?' I said gently, both an apology and a question.

'Not next year.'

I thought again how his face was etched with weariness and sadness, every line carved out by our loss. I immediately realised what he was saying. After what I'd just told him, about Dee saying we should go, we'd always associate the Maldives holiday conversation with Dee, so of course, going there would only bring sadness. We couldn't go there. Not ever.

'I get it,' I told him, starting to undo the tiny buttons on my black cardigan. I suddenly needed to be out of these clothes right now. I'd undone two when he spoke again.

'I don't think you do.'

'Do what?'

'I don't think you get it. Dee's d—' He paused, choking on the word. 'What happened to Dee, it's made me see that...' It was so uncharacteristic for him to be struggling to get his words across, but I didn't interrupt. 'I want to live a different life, Jen.'

'So do I. You're right. That's what I was trying to say. We can do that. We can change...'

He stiffened. 'Not "we".'

'What do you mean?'

'I can't do "we" anymore.'

I started to shiver, a malevolent shudder that spread from my gut as I began to see what he was saying, yet convinced I must be wrong. Fifteen years. You didn't last that long for it all to dissipate with no warning.

I realised I was trying to speak but no words were forming. Instead, my jaw jammed in a semi-open position as he climbed off the bed, picked up the jacket he'd dropped on the chair in the corner and headed for the door, paused, turned, spoke.

'I'm sorry, Jen. I didn't want to say this and especially not today. I was going to wait. But this just isn't what I want anymore.'

Then he kept on walking.

Gone.

And I couldn't actually grasp what was happening.

Had the love of my life just left me on the day of my best friend's funeral?

6

Jen

'He left me.'

The water that was gushing into the kettle started to overflow as Val stared, open-mouthed, waiting for a punchline to a really bad joke. It was a cold February morning, a week after the funeral and it looked like she hadn't slept since.

'What do you mean "left you"? Like, went for a run to cool off?'

'No. He left me. Came back the next day, packed all his stuff. All he would tell me was that he'd moved in with someone from work. I haven't heard from him at all. Tried calling him a couple of times but he doesn't answer.'

'Oh, love. Why didn't you tell me?'

I didn't need to reply. The answer was written all over her face. Her lids were swollen from a relentless onslaught of tears, her cheeks sunken because, usually no stranger to a home-cooked feast, she hadn't been able to keep anything down since the day her daughter died. Her skin was dry, her lips chapped from lack of nutrients. Yet, despite everything she'd been through, the frown lines between her eyebrows showed that she was worried about me. That was the kind of woman Dee had been raised by. No wonder she became the woman that she is.

Was.

That thought was all it took. A wave of grief twisted my gut and I had to fight the urge to buckle over, to howl, to scream with utter fucking rage that she wasn't sitting here, at the kitchen table, ranting that Pete was being a dick, fighting me for the last chocolate digestive. I'd always loved this kitchen, with its blue walls and cream units and chaotic collection of gadgets. Every gizmo ever sold on QVC now had a resting place somewhere on these oak counter tops. The omelette maker. The sandwich toaster. The coffee percolator. The one-cup kettle. The under-unit drop-down TV. The Soda Stream. The slow cooker. The portable grill. In past days, the Museum of Superfluous Technology would make Dee and I giggle.

Not now.

My heart hurt. It truly ached.

'You know the weird thing is, if anyone had told me a month ago that I'd lose Pete, I'd have said it was the worst thing in the world, but it doesn't even come close.'

I should be angry. Fucking furious. Distraught. Devastated. Raging at the brutality and unfairness of it all. How could he leave me after everything we'd been through, after everything that had happened? But somehow, mostly what I felt was numb.

Perhaps it was the fact that my heart was already shattered. Or maybe it was more that Dee's death had left me empty. Like the pain sensors had been charged so high they'd short-circuited and powered down.

None of it seemed real. Nothing. I just wanted her back. And then, when she was at my side, we could plot a cunning plan to sort out Pete and whatever aberration was making him act so out of character.

Val nodded, a sad smile playing on her lips as she put the kettle back on its stand and flipped the switch on. 'I know, love. She'd have given him a right bollocking for this.'

'She would have,' I agreed, trying to force some levity into my voice.

'I hate him so much.'

The venom in her voice caught me off guard, but I knew immediately who she was talking about.

She went on, 'He's due in court for the first hearing this week. The police liaison officer said it'll be months until the trial and he might get bail or remand until then. Depends on the judge. But the thought of him walking the streets is eating at my guts. I want to kill him.'

This was a Val I'd never seen before, a seething, brooding, tormented Val.

'He'll pay, Val,' I said softly, trying to comfort her. 'Dee will make sure of it,' I added, 'she never let anyone get away with anything.'

I saw immediately that it was what she needed to hear. The mention of Dee's name and the assurance of justice brought the anger down, until it morphed into something more positive.

A pause. 'You know, Jen, she'd have hated this. She's up there right now telling the two of us to get a grip.'

'You think?'

'I do. Especially now that Mark's home. You didn't half used to have a thing for him,' she added, trying desperately to lighten the mood.

I decided I'd give her that one. Mark had been my first crush, and when he'd gone off to do a gap year in Australia, he'd left a huge swirl of my almost-teenage hormones in his wake. A few months later, I was grateful, though, as it left a room free for Val to take me in when my mum died. The year stretched into two, then three, then six.

Working as some kind of diver, he didn't get home very often, but Dee and I had gone out to visit him a couple of times and Val and Don went out once a year. Thankfully, my crush had worn off the second I met Pete, and by the time I was twenty I could look at him without going weak at the knees and hearing Take That singing 'Love Ain't Here Anymore'.

'How long is he staying for?' I asked.

Val shrugged. 'I'm not sure. I've told him he has to get back to his life. Nothing he can do here. I'd actually told him there was no point coming back after Dee... you know... but...' Her voice trailed off. She didn't say it unkindly. Val was fiercely protective of both her adult children. She'd do anything to protect their lives from disruption and sadness. I suddenly realised there was no more 'both'. Just one now.

'He wanted to be here with you, Val.'

For the first time, her eyes welled up, but she blinked the tears away. She sat down opposite me and pushed a mug towards me. 'I know. And now Mark's here and Dee is gone. How does that make sense? I don't know what's happening anymore, Jen.'

'Me neither.' I wouldn't cry. Couldn't. Val needed me to be strong and together, and a comfort to her, not a snivelling wreck. Don't cry. Do not cry.

'Och, love,' she whispered, leaning in and enfolding me in a hug.

My resolve shattered. I cried.

'That Pete doesn't know what he's done. Our Dee said he was having an early mid-life crisis.'

'I wish he'd bought a motorbike and a bomber jacket instead,' I said, laughing despite the tears and snot.

'You know he'll be back, don't you? It's just some kind of overdramatic reaction to... to Dee...' She didn't finish. There were so many half-spoken sentences these days. It was like neither of us had the words to express Dee's death, and if we did we couldn't say them out loud. And while I wanted to believe she was right about Pete, I wasn't convinced. He wasn't one who was prone to drama, or emotion or knee-jerk reactions. He took days to make any decision, longer if it was an important one.

'I don't think so, Val. I think it's exactly what it looks like. I think, if I'm honest, I knew that he'd been unhappy for a while and Dee's... leaving... made him realise life's too short to stay where you're not happy.'

Saying that should hurt. It should eviscerate my heart. Yet still, all I felt was numb. It was like I was a casual bystander, analysing and objectively commenting on someone else's life.

Val took a sip from her pink ceramic mug, a Mother's Day gift designed by Dee that had a cheesy Mum poem on one side and a retro picture of Richard Gere, circa *An Officer and a Gentleman*, on the other. Wearily, she replaced it on the table.

'But running away doesn't solve anything. Surely you owe it to the people you love to stay and be there for them?'

'Then I guess he doesn't love me anymore.' The brutal truth.

'You're better off without him then, Jen. Because that's what you want. Someone who'll fight for you...'

Her words drifted off and I saw that she was staring out the window, her jaw set in rage, looking for all the world like someone who would fight until her dying breath for those she loved.

7

Jen & Dee, 2005

'You get the traveller's cheques, the beach towels, the toiletries and the adaptors – I'll get the Frisbee, the kaftans, the travel straighteners and that Piz Buin stuff that makes you look like an international supermodel. And everything needs to fit in one carry-on case and be under ten kilograms, because there's no bloody way I'm unpacking my bras in the departure terminal at Glasgow Airport... again. That's ritual humiliation right there.'

Dee's long mane of red waves was pulled up into a ponytail, she had no make-up on, she was wearing dungarees that had belonged in the eighties, yet I felt like the bland one.

'No problem,' I replied, pulling my Calvin Klein bag up on to my shoulder. It had been a graduation present from Val and Don – they'd bought both Dee and I the same leather messenger bags, in different colours: Dee's black, mine navy. I loved it. It showed someone cared about me, unlike my dad, who had been on the rigs on the day of my graduation, and had gone straight on a bender when he got back on dry land. Four weeks later, I still hadn't seen him. 'But it'll have to be later today. I've got that two o'clock this afternoon.'

Dee looked up from the copy of Heat. 'So you have! I completely forgot. Are you ready for it? Prepared to set their knickers alight?'

I was never going to set the world, or anyone's knickers, alight as a junior accountant at Davis McDougal but it was a start.

Pete popped his head around the back door. 'You ready to go?'

The sight of him made me smile. 'Just coming.'

'Good luck at the interview. You'll be fab,' Dee shouted to my back.

A few hours later, I realised that her confidence in me was somewhat optimistic. I wasn't fab. I was downright dire. Facing a panel of two middle-aged, very serious men and a woman with a headmistress demeanour who was deeply intimidating, I stuttered, I sweated and I blanked. And by the time I left, thirty-two minutes after I entered the building, I knew that despite having a degree in accountancy, the last thing I wanted to be was an actual accountant.

Bollocks.

Back at the Kelvinbridge flat I'd shared with Dee since our first day at uni, I opened the door, struggled into the kitchen, laden with bags, to see her standing there, clutching a bottle of cider and an expectant expression.

'We couldn't afford champagne so this will have to do,' she informed me gleefully, as I thought, for the gazillionth time since I met her, that there was no one on the face of this earth who possessed more optimism than my cider-clutching friend, and no one I wanted to see more when life went resoundingly tits up.

'Is it for celebrating or drowning sorrows?' I asked.

'Celebrating?' she said, with an edge of question.

I shook my head.

She immediately switched to the alternative. 'Drowning our sorrows?'

''Fraid so. Make mine a large one.'

I couldn't help but laugh. I'd just blown the only job on the horizon, yet suddenly, thanks to Dee, it seemed hilarious.

We were on our second glass, when Dee gestured to my bags. 'What's in there?'

'The stuff for our holiday. Talking of which, we really should get packing.'

'I didn't manage to get everything I needed so we might have to do a quick shop in the morning before we go to the airport,' she confessed.

'What didn't you get? We can live without a Frisbee.'

It took a moment and I recognised her familiar 'should I go with the truth, or make up a great lie' expression.

'Any of it.' She went with the truth. 'Sorry. I got caught up with... with... I've no idea. I started packing, then Jase stopped by...'

Ah, that explained it. Her boyfriend of the moment. He was the manager of the restaurant we both worked in – a dangerous situation given the contradictory nature of Dee's short romantic attention span and our need to make the rent every month.

'... And we got a bit distracted, you know what he's like...' I knew. It's was why I always chose to work on their night off rather than be home with them and their overtly intimate, overly loud PDAs.

So her pre-holiday tasks remained undone. I tried to remember what had been on her shopping list. Frisbee.

Kaftans. Straighteners. Piz Buin stuff that would allegedly make us look like international supermodels.

'I'll get up early and nip to Tesco. Should be able to get some stuff there, and everything else we'll get at the airport. Life would be so much easier if we could just get everything we needed in the same bloody place.'

Dee's drink stopped halfway to her mouth. 'That's what we should do.'

'Yeah, right – there's no way you'll get up early.'

'No, not that bit, the other bit. We should open a shop that sells everything you need for a holiday, all in the same place.'

'How much of that cider have you had?' I asked. 'We know nothing about shops, we're skint, and we couldn't even organise our own holiday stuff so we've no chance of organising anyone else's.'

I could see she wasn't listening. This was vintage Dee. She had an idea in her head and it was consuming every synapse of her brain.

'You've got your inheritance.'

That was true. I did have the five thousand pounds my mum had saved in an endowment policy. In fact, the only reason that my dad hadn't drank it away was because she'd been smart enough to put it in my name and it couldn't be accessed until I turned eighteen. And of course, I was too sensible to have accessed it, no matter how close we'd come to missing the rent, so every penny of it was still there.

Five grand wasn't going to get us very far, though.

Dee didn't even pause to register the doubt on my face. 'And I've got that money I saved for a car. Between the two of us we could maybe get together ten thousand pounds. My mum and dad would help with loans and stuff. Oh my God, *this is genius! It could totally work, Jen. My marketing and stunning personality, your accountancy and brains – it's perfect! Say yes. Aw sod it, I'll just feed you more cider. After three you'll say yes to anything.'*

8

Jen, 2016

Closed due to bereavement

Josie had put that sign up on the door. She'd called me as soon as she'd heard what happened and told me she'd take care of it. Josie was one of those women, the kind who stepped up and took on some cloak of super-strength when things went to shit. She'd originally worked for Mel, who used to own the lingerie shop along the street, and had come to 'do a nosy' before we opened. She saw we were in disarray, picked up a hoover, and had the place gleaming in no time. Josie and Val had met that night, and hit it off immediately. Afterwards, we'd begged her to stay, and she'd agreed, splitting her time between the two shops. A few years later, Josie's son Michael had bought the lingerie shop, and a beauty salon next to it, married Mel and they'd eventually sold up and moved to Italy. There had been a wobbly moment when Josie took that opportunity to retire, but thankfully, she'd discovered that being a lady of leisure, in her words, 'bored her tits off' and she came back to work. She was more of a friend than an employee – part of the collective of our hybrid family.

I paused on the threshold of the door, unsure whether I could do this. I had to. This was what we'd built and I would be letting her down if I let it crumble. I forced the keys into the lock now and pushed the door open. Located on one of the busiest streets in the Merchant City area of Glasgow, in a row of small boutique stores and salons, the shop had been a leap of faith that had – thankfully – resulted in a soft landing.

Sun, Sea, Ski. I can't remember if the title was my idea or Dee's but perfectly summed up our product range – all you needed for a summer or winter break. Our customer base was supported by Dee's travel blog, which now had thousands of followers who also shopped on our online store. After a tough couple of years as we got established and found our niche, it was paying off in a big way now. And yet, I realised, as I inhaled the scent of Josie's lemon polish, it had never seemed so pointless.

All those great adventures and promises of tropical dreams, and now none of them would come true for Dee. She wouldn't travel to Nepal. Or the Amazon. We wouldn't go on another girls' trip, or take Luke and Pete off for a weekend break.

We wouldn't celebrate another Christmas. She wouldn't have children. We'd never be those women who had kids the same age and took them to the park together. We wouldn't moan about hot flushes and then spend our retirement cruise-hopping and drinking tequila before noon. We wouldn't have another 'hello', or 'love you'. We didn't even get a last goodbye… The tsunami of grief swelled again. Coming here was a mistake.

I closed the door behind me, then leaned against it and fought for breath. The shop still looked exactly the same as always. Of course it did. Yet how could that be when everything had changed?

Over the years, we'd redecorated and updated the interior to reflect our increased cash flow and growing product lines and services. Back at the start, the walls were a pale yellow, the stock displayed on plain white shelves and rails. The floor had been laminate and a till had sat on a desk Dee's dad, Don, had made us in his workshop.

Now, glossy mahogany wood was beneath my feet and the walls were lined with a sumptuous pale blue, glistening paper, the colour of the Mediterranean Sea. The shelves and rails were satin chrome and there were two beautifully carved white doors, one on the back wall, leading to the office and storeroom, and one on the side wall, leading to a bank of three fitting rooms, gained a few years ago when we extended into the small vacant shop next door.

The left-hand side of the room was the sunshine area – bikinis, sarongs, flip-flops, sun creams, and every kind of technological gizmo ever invented for a hot weather break. On the right, the ski zone – salopettes and goggles, gorgeous fake fur hats and shrugs, and cashmere après-ski loungewear that Dee had first ordered in bulk after too many mulled wines last Christmas in Gstaad. Thankfully, word of mouth had brought the customers in their droves and they'd sold out in weeks. This was our third re-stock and popularity showed no sign of diminishing.

In the centre of the room, there was now a white circular control centre, where the till and two computers were situated, with four chairs around it that clients could sit on while we booked their next trip or activity.

It was perfect. A shop with everything. Except Dee.

I stood for a few minutes, trying to come to terms with being here, steeling myself to go into the office. I've no idea how much time passed before I pushed the door open, flicked the light on, looking around like a stranger in a foreign landscape, detached, unfamiliar. My tidy, minimal IKEA oak desk sat perpendicular to Dee's workspace, the original desk Don had made for the shop, disguised by a level of debris that resembled a landfill. I smiled. Every week for nearly a decade I'd suggested she tidy it. Every week for nearly a decade she'd ignored me.

The pain, when it hit me, was so strong I gasped. It was just a cardigan, pale blue, from the cashmere ski wear range, but it was Dee's and it was sitting over the back of her chair, just waiting for her to pull it on when the afternoon chill descended. When my lungs kicked back in, I leaned over, picked it up, inhaled. It smelled of her. My senses took over, sucking all the strength from every part of my body and I slid down the wall to the floor. No tears, none of the wracking sobs that had filled the first week without her, just catatonic numbness as I realised that I had no idea how to function now she was gone. We'd been together for almost every day of the last twenty years and I wasn't ready to be alone. Didn't know how to be.

I yelped with surprise when the office door creaked open. In my daze, I hadn't locked the front door behind me, and Dee must have disabled the bell that alerted us to customers again. It was one of her more common hangover-survival tactics. I hadn't even heard movement out in the shop. A shoplifter could have been away with half our stock.

In the office, sitting on the floor, the first things my gaze connected with were the trainers and my lungs sucked in air as thoughts collided. I knew he'd come. Mid-life crisis over.

Oh, thank God. Pete had come back and... My eyes reached knee level and I realised I was wrong.

'Hey.' Luke. But it still wasn't the Luke I knew. This Luke had a couple of weeks' worth of facial hair, bloodshot eyes and a complexion with a tinge of grey that said it hadn't seen enough daylight. I noticed for the first time how much weight he'd lost, maybe about twenty pounds, so the bones in his face looked more visible, sharper, jarring against the unruly dark waves of hair that were swept back in an unruly tangle.

'Hi,' I replied, a sad smile hijacking my words.

'Are you going to get up anytime soon or shall I come down there?' he asked.

I patted the floor next to me in answer.

Just as I had done a few minutes ago, he slid down the wall to join me and I took in the ensemble of running shorts and T-shirt.

'Jogging? Really?'

His smile was as half-hearted as his shrug. 'Gets us all eventually.'

'Traitor.' I teased.

Jogging had been Dee and Pete's thing. Off they'd go galloping around streets, across parks, half-marathons, full marathons, up hills, in all weathers, while Luke and I would point out that we might not be super-fit, but at least we'd still have our own knees at sixty.

'Started the day after the funeral,' he said. 'Didn't know what else to do. I bloody hate every step, but at least hating the pain stops me hating the fact that she's not here.'

His words took me aback. In all the years we'd been friends I'd never heard Luke talk about feelings in any depth. He did socialising. He did parties. He was a chilled out, laid-back guy, but he definitely did making the most of life.

He did not do introspection and emotional outbursts. Dee would be astonished.

'So what brings you here?' I asked.

'Val said you were going to be here this morning. I didn't mean to come – just ended up here.' The last word caught in his throat and he paused and stared straight ahead, but I knew what he was thinking. How many nights had we all – Luke, Dee, Pete and I – sat in this office after work, drinking beers, feet up on desks, hanging out while we counted the takings or made plans for our next trip? More than our homes, this had been our place, the centre of our gang of four. And now it was just us two.

'She told me about Pete. Jesus, that came out of nowhere. I'm so sorry, Jen.'

'You didn't know?'

He shook his head. 'Only seen him a couple of times since the funeral, but Matt and Callum were there so we just played a bit of pool, had a few beers.'

'Yeah, I can see how it would slip his mind to mention that he'd moved out of our house and left our fifteen-year relationship.'

Luke managed a rueful smile. 'We're blokes. If it doesn't involve twenty-two guys chasing a ball, there's no point...'

'... talking about it.' I finished the sentence. How many times had Dee chastised them with that playful accusation? Although, granted, there was a grain of truth in there. 'He told me on the night of the funeral. Left there and then,' I said.

That one was a conversation stopper. Luke didn't know how to reply and I didn't want to suck up the sympathy and make this all about me. Luke was the one who needed it more. We'd both lost our partners, but there was a chance that I could sort things out with Pete. Luke was never going to have that option.

'What are we going to do, Jen?' he said, eventually.

I sighed. 'No idea.'

A pinging noise from the iPad sitting upright on a charging stand on Dee's desk made both of our heads snap round.

'If she's sent us some kind of answer to that question I'm going to be totally freaked out,' Luke said. 'You look.'

I nudged his shoulder. 'You.'

Reluctantly, he stretched over, gently tugged the charger's flex to slide the iPad across the desk towards us, and then when it was within reaching distance, he lifted it from the cradle and returned to his seating position on the floor.

I couldn't look. Had to look. Eventually looked.

There were two lines of text on the screen.

Reminder: one month until you leave for New York!
You have three events booked.

Nausea and sadness fought for supremacy in my gut. I'd forgotten all about the New York trip. Dee went every year to a huge travel convention there, although in the last couple of years, she'd only spent a day or two at the convention and used the rest of the time to check out cool new places to stay. This time she'd organised a three-day stay in a boutique hotel on the Upper East Side, a freebie in return for a write-up on the blog, and she had talked about doing a couple of shows and seeing what the big stores were carrying in their spring line for ski wear.

'Oh God. She was looking forward to that trip so much. I'll cancel the flight and get in touch with the hotel to explain.' Every word was shredded on a blade of grief that was lodged in my throat.

As we sat there in silence, side by side, Luke's breathing suddenly grew heavier and erratic, I couldn't bear to look at him. I wasn't sure why, then I realised that I didn't want to see him crying. Somehow it was too raw, too painful. We had been friends for years, had seen each other drunk, sober, happy, sad, angry, laughing, and even once – thanks to an ill-advised skinny dip in a freezing Loch Lomond – naked. Yet, right here, in this tiny, confined space, I didn't want to see him cry because it would be like taking a brick out of a dam of grief that no amount of flood defences would be able to halt.

A few moments passed before he spoke. 'You should go.'

'What?' I'd heard him, but I just required clarification.

'You should go,' he repeated. 'Dee would hate it to go to waste. She'd be bloody furious. You know she would want you to go.'

This wasn't in the script. Dee went on the trips, I manned the fort at home. That put both of us in our comfort zones. It worked. I had no desire to change it.

'And besides, you need to keep the shop and blog going, so you need to know what's happening out there. You need new products, new ideas, new experiences to write about. You know how much this all mattered to Dee and how passionate she was about keeping on top of the latest trends and making sure her blog had loads of great stories.'

That was true. Dee's chronicles of her travels had over ten thousand followers and the click rate through to the store's website was a reliable addition to our income, generating over 40 per cent of our online sales. Suddenly, this was less of an emotional dilemma and more of a business one. He was right. The reason our business was so successful was because we never let anything get stale. Dee would be furious if I let that originality and innovation slip away. But still, I resisted…

'I can't. There's no one here to look after the shop.' Even as the business had grown, we'd resisted taking on new staff and, instead, kept it in the family. Sometime Val would help out, sometimes, on the weekends, Pete and Luke would pitch in. I couldn't even think about how that would now be so different going forward.

'I can take a couple of days off work and do it and Val will come in to help me. To be honest, it'll probably be good for her. She made Don go back to work and he's doing such long hours that she's left with too much empty time on her hands. She could do with a distraction.'

'I'm not sure coming in here would be a distraction,' I pointed out. Val had been a constant support, lending a hand in the shop whenever Dee was away, so I had no idea how she would react to being back in a space that oozed her daughter's presence from every joist and corner.

'Maybe that's up to her,' he said, firmly but not unkindly.

He was right. Maybe it was.

'I'll think about it.' I said. It was as much as I could concede right now. Just getting through the day would be a major achievement for me at the moment, let alone planning to cross the Atlantic. I wasn't ready for that. I needed familiar surroundings. Steady acclimatisation. Not a step into the unknown.

It was as if the universe heard my thought and answered.

Another ping.

Reminder: Remember to check if you can bungee
from any NY landmarks.

A bungee jump. That was Dee's favourite kind of step
into the unknown. But not one that I could even think about
taking.

9

Val

I still remembered the old days when a supermarket opened at nine in the morning and closed at six in the evening. Maybe an eight o'clock late opening on a Thursday if you were lucky. Now? Twenty-four hours our local ASDA was open and at three in the morning I was grateful for it.

I dragged out every step, going as slowly as possible. I had nowhere else to be and it was not like Don even knew I was gone. God love him, when he closed his eyes at exactly ten o'clock every night, it was more of a coma situation than a sleep. For the last thirty odd years, when he woke up every morning at six o'clock, a habit that was down to a lifetime of working on building sites, I was lying there beside him. I still was. But now, instead of greeting him with a kiss and a smile, sometimes I'd pretend to be asleep; sometimes I'd act like I'd just woken up. What I never did was let on that I'd been driving the streets and wandering around supermarkets half the night.

In the weeks since... since... well, anyway, in the time I'd been coming here, I'd realised that it was like a different world, a nocturnal existence that had been going on the whole time while I, safe and smug in my happy life, had been blissfully unaware of it.

I'd already started to recognise faces. In the canned soup aisle, I saw Karen. I've no idea if that was her name, but it was the one I'd given her and it suited her. She was here most nights – or rather mornings – about this time, in her nursing scrubs, so she must work down at the hospital. Maybe she was in A & E. Maybe she'd been on duty that dreadful night. Maybe she'd even ran to our Dee as they flew through the doors with her, already gone, but desperate to try to bring her back to us. They couldn't. Maybe that's why Karen had a haunted look, why I saw her sometimes, just staring at the shelves, not focusing on what was in front of her until she snapped back to the present, picked up a tin of Heinz lentil broth or spaghetti hoops and strode off.

Over at the bakery aisle, Harry was loading a couple of baguettes into his basket. Ginger, like the prince, and about the same age. That's where I got his name. And ex-army too, I reckoned. He had that ramrod-straight stance, the broad shoulders, the fearless bearing, none of which was diminished by the altered gait of his limp. I'd seen him a couple of times before I noticed the prosthetic on his left leg. He was one of the few that made eye contact.

The junkies didn't. These weren't the same kind of evil, arrogant drugged up bastard that killed my Dee. These were broken, emaciated, barely-functioning souls who were too busy scanning the place for the half-hearted security guards that patrolled the aisles. Some of the guys in the uniforms were trumped up with self-importance, others obviously just trying to pay the bills for the family they left every night to come here. Some of them, though, were kind to the homeless souls that wandered in for the warmth. They walked as slowly as me, the homeless ones, a depressed shuffle, with empty baskets that they left at the till on the way out, as if they'd been unable to find anything they wanted in a shop the size of a football pitch. Broke my heart. There was one, Maggie I called her, must have been in her sixties. Every time I smiled at her she turned away, never smiled back, but I still did it anyway. Maybe one night she would. What had happened in her life that she was left with no home, no family, just second-hand shoes and an all-night supermarket coming between her and hypothermia?

The bloke at the till was one of the regular two who sat there most nights. James. That came from his name badge, not my imagination. A student, I had decided, maybe twenty-two or three. He looked in my basket and I wondered if he realised... A sirloin steak, onion rings, thick-cut chips, a peppercorn sauce, a banoffi pie, custard. The same six things I bought every time I came. All Dee's favourite things. Every year since she was a teenager, I'd cook her a birthday dinner, and her request never varied. 'You know what I like Mum,' she'd laugh, throwing her arms around me and squeezing me in the tightest hug. 'I've been on salmon and vegetables for a month to get ready for it. Steak, onion rings...'

'Banoffi pie and custard,' I'd finish.

So now, I came here when the insomnia kicked in and I bought all her favourites, because if I was buying them, then my girl must still be here. Out there. Working. Travelling. Drinking wine. Jumping from a bloody plane. Laughing. Talking. Breathing. Just breathing. Not lying in the ground.

James looked up as I tried to cover the involuntary gasp of pain with a cough, then looked back down at the items he was scanning. If he was curious about the tears and the muffled sob, he didn't show it as he methodically put each item through the scanner, the beep of the till's acceptance almost hypnotic.

I climbed back into the car, and slowly edged out of the car park. I was more careful now, even at this time of the night, so much more aware of the carnage a vehicle could cause. One more stop on the way home. The food bank. Criminal bloody shame that people were relying on charity to eat in this day and age, and don't get me started on those incompetent fools running the country. I hung the carrier bag on the door handle and got back into car. I'd no idea if it would still be there in the morning when the staff opened up, but if someone swiped it before then, I just hoped that they needed it.

Don didn't even murmur or change position when I crawled back into bed. Even when he was sleeping, it seemed like the exhaustion seeped from his pores. He was a good man, my Don. A huge heart, decent, loved his family, and would have done anything for Dee. I knew he'd have taken her place in a heartbeat. Now, he was broken-hearted and I didn't know how to fix him. There was no fixing any of this. All we could do was remember.

I lay there, willing my body to sleep, my mind flicking through a photo album of Dee's life. It was another new habit. Like those supermarket junkies looking for a fix, as I lay in bed I would think about moments of Dee's life – her little scrunched up face on her first day of school as she shooed me off telling me she'd be perfectly fine, that summer on Arran when she ran into the freezing sea, squealing all the way there and back out again five seconds later, that morning when she came home pretending she'd failed her driving test, then made a paper airplane out of her test certificate and fired it across the room to me. I'd hope that if I drifted off to sleep thinking about her, a dream would follow and there she would be, real again for just a few hours. It never worked but

I couldn't bring myself to stop trying. I so regretted all those days and hours and minutes we weren't together throughout our lives, when we were doing other things. Now I'd give everything in life for another hour with my girl.

Don's arm flopped over me and I fought the urge to shrug it off. The closeness made me feel like I was suffocating, and not just here with Don. I could be anywhere, busy shops, streets, the train station, and I'd suddenly feel that everyone around me was too close, violating my space, and I'd have to push my way out of the situation I was in. I inhaled, counted to ten, tried to slow the galloping beat of my heart.

It was an hour or so later, six o'clock on the dot, when his alarm started ringing. He opened his eyes, I closed mine. I felt him leave the bed, then the room, wandering out into the bathroom. On the way, he picked up the hanger with today's clothes from the back of the door, prepared and left there last night so that he didn't disturb me.

Eyes still closed, I counted the minutes as I listened to the familiar sounds. The flush of the toilet, the patter of the shower, the buzz of his electric toothbrush, the snap of the laundry basket as he deposited his wet towel and the shorts he wore in bed last night.

For thirty-eight years of my fifty-seven on this earth, we'd eaten breakfast together, but not since... Not now. He didn't ask why and I didn't tell him. I suspect he welcomed it too, was glad of being able to start the day without having to pretend he was fine. I knew he wasn't. I'd lived with Don long enough to sense every one of his moods and emotions. We could pretend with friends and family and neighbours, but not with each other. So instead, we were doing this dance of avoidance, orbiting each other's lives without actually colliding. It was safer that way.

I waited until I heard the front door close before I got out of bed. I pulled on the robe Dee bought me last year for Christmas. Marks and Spencer's. She'd let me pick it out during an afternoon of festive shopping on the condition that I'd act surprised when I opened it in front of the rest of the family. She'd laughed her head off when I ripped open the paper on Christmas morning and laid it on thick about what a great choice she'd made. 'It's exactly what I would have chosen,' I'd said with a wink. She'd put her Bucks Fizz down and launched in for a hug. 'You'll never win an Oscar, Mum,' she'd whispered, giggling.

That was our Dee. Always laughing. Always wild. Always there.

Until now.

I stopped at the top of the stairs, wanting that feeling of her, that memory to last just a little longer. Only when my breathing returned to normal, did I plod downstairs.

I shoved a cup into the machine that spat out just enough water for a mug, plopped in a teabag and some milk, then sat in my usual seat at the battered but beautiful oak table in the middle of the kitchen. Six chairs were around the table, each one of them belonging to one of us. Don always sat at the end of the table, mine was to his left. Dee's to his right, Luke next to her. Jen sat next to me, in the seat that had been Mark's, before he left for Australia and Pete was on the other side of her. It was an informal thing, grown from years of habit. No one sat in Dee's chair now. No one ever would again.

My back was to the door when I heard it open and Mark came in. My reaction was automatic. I steeled myself, rearranged my face into something resembling happiness, forced normality into my voice. He had a gap in his work schedule so he'd stayed around since the funeral.

'Morning son.' I said, turning with a smile. 'Coffee?'

'Thanks Mum.'

The Dolce Gusto machine this time. I loved a gadget. Had dozens of them. I'd enjoyed them all immensely. Now, like so much in life, they seemed so ridiculously stupid.

I pushed the thought away and handed over his freshly brewed cappuccino. 'There you go, m'darlin.'

I resisted the urge to ruffle his hair, sticking up in ten different directions, the way it had always done first thing in the morning when he was a kid. Oh, the battles I'd had trying to get that hair to look smart before he went to school. Now he was kicking towards forty and it wasn't any different. It was almost a comfort that some things didn't change.

'So I've been thinking. If it's OK, I'm going to stick around for a while,' he said.

I slipped into my chair and lifted my teacup before I answered. It gave me time to work on the correct response. 'Of course it's OK. It's great.'

And it was. I meant it. In some ways.

If you'd have told me a month ago that Mark would be back home for a while I'd have been ecstatic. Now, though, and I'm so ashamed I'd never tell a soul, every time I looked at him I was reminded why he was there. He was a grown man, for almost twenty years he'd lived in Australia, but he was still my boy and he came as part of a pair with our Dee. My children. But now, I only had a child.

Nevertheless, my smile stayed on as I reached over and put my hand on his. 'I hope you're not just doing this for me, Mark. I'm fine. I really am. There's nothing that any of us can do to bring Dee back so we all just need to get on with life again.'

Thank God he couldn't see into my head and realise that I didn't mean or believe a single word I was saying. This was the way it had to be, though. What were the options? That I sit here weeping and wailing every day, bringing everyone down and making it all about me? No. That wasn't going to happen. This was my family and I had to be the one to support them, to get them back to their lives. That evil little fucker – God forgive my language – behind that wheel had taken my Dee but he wasn't going to take another thing, another moment of normality or happiness from my family. I'd make sure of it.

The noise of a key in the front door interrupted my internal rant, and before the kitchen door opened, I'd pulled out a mug for Jen. Don was at work, so she was the only other one who'd let herself in with a key. My heart was sore for the girl. Dee and her had been like sisters their whole life, inseparable they were. And she'd had such a rough start, what with her mum dying so young. Now that history of premature loss had repeated itself. Jen's mother, my daughter.

What a tragic hand that girl had been dealt. She'd lost her mum, her best friend, her dad was a waste of space, and don't even get me started on Pete. I'd always thought he was a nice enough lad, but to dump her on the day of my girl's funeral? Who does that? Needless to say he'd made himself scarce round here ever since. Fifteen years he'd been coming to this house and now nothing. I just hoped I'd bump into him so I could give him a piece of my mind.

I'd already put Jen's cup in the machine and pressed the button for her tea before she reached the kitchen.

'Hello love, I've put the kettle... Luke!' When she came in the door, I realised I needed two cups. Luke's usual mug was at the front of the cupboard, well-used over the last couple of weeks. I was so grateful that he still popped in every day. It would have been so easy for him to shut himself away and I'd

67

almost have understood if he had. I was about to ask him what he was up to when I noticed the outfit. Years I'd been telling him he should join our Dee with that jogging lark and by the looks of the shorts and training shoes, he'd finally got started. I didn't even need to ask him why. I had my supermarket, he'd obviously found his own form of distraction.

We'd been pleased as punch when he'd married Dee and he'd never given us a single minute of doubt. He'd been steady as a rock and they'd been so happy. Was it better or worse that our daughter had lived a wonderful life? Better. Definitely better. And I would always be grateful to Luke for his part in that. The minute he married Dee he became our son and it would stay that way, even now that Dee's chair was empty.

Jen gave me a hug that lasted just a little longer than usual, and then Luke did the same, before taking their seats at the table.

There was a pensiveness about Jen, a sadness and hesitation that caused a few seconds of silence. That was new. We usually had an outpouring of chat from the moment we got together. So it was going to be up to me then. I had to set the tone. Our Dee would expect it. She couldn't stand moaning and moping.

'Right then Luke, so what has the town done to deserve seeing your legs at this time of the morning then?' I joked. As if nothing was wrong.

'They just got lucky,' he replied, sharp as a tack.

'So. What's happening then?' I stuck with bright and breezy. I wouldn't crack. This lot needed me and I wasn't going to let them down.

'I just popped into the shop…' He tried, but Luke couldn't keep his voice from faltering. He recovered quickly, with a swift glance at Jen before he went on. 'OK, I'm just going to say this. Dee had some trips booked in the next few months and I think Jen should take them.'

My glance went to Jen, who was staring at her mug, shoulders slumped.

Luke went on, 'Someone has to keep up the blog and honour the deals Dee made to feature hotels and activities on the website. But Jen feels...'

He broke off and looked at Jen, still staring at her mug. I saw the tension in her jaw, her teeth clenched together. In her own quiet, understated way, she was a tough cookie – her upbringing had left her no choice on that. But I could see she was struggling. We all were. It just didn't feel right doing anything without Dee, much less stepping into her shoes.

The stabbing pain ripped across my stomach again and it took every ounce of strength not to fall to the floor.

'You feel like you can't take her place?' I said, softly.

Jen nodded, still staring at the mug.

I moved behind her, bent forward to wrap my arms around her. Only then did I realise she was trembling, her shoulders shaking under my hug.

'I think you have to do it, love. You both worked so hard to build up this business and you don't want to stop that now. Dee would be bloody raging.' I tried to inject some humour into the last line, but I'm not sure I pulled it off. I meant every word though. That company was Dee's dream, a huge part of her, and it was up to us to make sure it continued to thrive.

Finally Jen spoke, thinly disguised anguish in every word. 'But I need to look after the shop, so it's not feasible.'

I was just about to offer to step in, when someone else beat me to it.

'I'll do that.' Mark said. 'I'm going to stay around for a while and, to be honest, I'll go a bit stir-crazy if there's nothing to keep me busy, so I'd actually appreciate having something to do. I can work in the shop with you, and take care of stuff when you're not around.'

'But what about your job and your life back in Australia?' Jen asked. 'Don't you have to get back there?'

I'd been putting off asking the same question, not sure of my feelings. I desperately wanted him to stay. But at the same time, every moment he was here was another minute that I had to pretend I was OK, act like I was coping. Maybe that was for the best though.

'I'm not back offshore for a couple of months yet so it's no problem. And there's no one there pining for me to come back,' he added with the same cheeky grin he'd had since he was a boy. 'So it's no hassle at all for me to stick around.' He was speaking to me now. 'Is that OK with you, Mum?'

I smiled. 'Of course it is, son. It makes sense. Keeps you out from under my feet as well.'

He smiled, recognising a familiar saying from when he was a child. I was never one of those overprotective types. I'd send them into the garden, off to the park, down to the shops. 'Away and get out from under my feet. And take your sister with you!' I'd say, stopping the Hoover, or putting the mop down, or abandoning the washing machine to give them some change for an ice cream or a packet of crisps. Off they'd toddle, just the two of them together, happily exploring the world until it was time to come back for dinner. These days it's all that helicopter parenting and hothousing and mollycoddling. Everyone to their own, I suppose, but how are kids supposed to mature and become independent when their parents are always two feet behind them? Let's be honest, we can never protect them really. Our Dee had travelled the world, gone to all-night parties, climbed mountains and jumped out of bloody planes, and yet she was only five minutes away from here, watching telly on a Sunday afternoon when...

'So that's settled then,' I announced. 'When do you want him to start?'

Jen finally looked up. 'Tomorrow?'

Tomorrow. That was sorted then. And I knew that Jen and Mark would get along fine. Maybe having him around was going to be a really good thing for all of us after all.

10

Mark

It was pretty damn hard to put into words how much I didn't want to be there. The whole place felt alien to me now and, let's face it, I was a few years past being comfortable living back with my mum and dad. Going from an apartment at the beach in Cairns to an end terrace house in suburban Weirbank had been a bit of a culture shock to say the least. I'm not sure if I ever really fitted in here but I definitely didn't now, especially without my sister here.

Dee and I hadn't been particularly close as kids. I used to get totally pissed off being made to take her everywhere. But later, long after I'd moved Down Under, she'd visit me once or twice a year and we became good mates.

There was never any doubt that I'd come back for her funeral.

There was no good time to bury your sister, but at least the way the timing had worked out, I'd managed to get here and stick around to support Mum. If I was honest, getting away from my life on the other side of the world for a while wasn't a hardship after everything that had happened there. Not that I was going to share that information and all the details with my mother. The woman had a core of steel, but I wasn't going to do anything that could make her worry about me for a second.

The door dinged as I pushed it open and the first thing I saw was Jen, staggering out of a doorway at the back of the shop, carrying a cardboard box that was half the size of her. I rushed over and went to take it from her but she rejected the offer.

'No, no, it's fine. I've got it,' she said, her knees buckling as she crossed the room and dropped it at the window. She turned back to me. 'I'll show you around,' she offered.

I might not be the most emotionally intelligent of blokes, but even I could see that she wasn't gleefully happy to have me there. I thought volunteering to help was a good thing for both of us, but she clearly had a dose of the hump. Great. Just what I needed.

At least I wouldn't have to bug her with endless questions about how to do the basics. Back in the early years, I'd supplemented my diving earnings by working in the shop at the local beach club, so I knew my way around a stockroom and a till. I glanced around, feeling strange that this was the first time I'd been in my sister's shop. Not for the first time, I wished I'd come back before now, just for a holiday, just to keep in touch and play a part in her life. Too late now for regrets. And besides, Dee clearly hadn't needed any of big brother's help. This place was laid out really well and I could see why it had been a success. My sister was obviously a pretty smart girl. Jen must be too – although she was currently hiding that under a dark cloud of gloom. Not that I could blame her. She'd lost her best mate and apparently her boyfriend had done a runner too. That was a double mighty dose of heartache right there.

'Where do you want me to start? I'm at your disposal,' I told her, trying to chip away at the frostiness.

For the first time, her smile looked like it could almost be real.

'I'm just going to change this window display,' she replied. 'Dee…' A deep breath, before she went on. 'Dee did a great job with this one for the January ski wear, but we always change it after a few weeks. It's time to get our cruise theme going for the start of the Med sailings in March.'

The conversation was halted by the ding of the door and I made a mental bet with myself as to how long it would be before irritation overwhelmed me and I took the battery out of the bell.

In charged a woman in her forties, gold Gucci sunspecs despite the fact that it was zero degrees outside. In the corner, Jen briefly turned around and I saw a flicker of recognition before she went back to the window display.

'Well you're new,' was the woman's opening line to me.

'I am,' I agreed, smiling.

'Australian?' she asked, picking up on the hint of accent that had inevitably crept in after so many years in Oz.

'Half and half,' I replied. 'But I just got back here a couple of weeks ago.'

She leaned against the desk, flashed her perfect teeth. Strewth. She wasn't going to win any prizes for subtlety.

'Well, if you need some company to get reacquainted with this city, Dee has my number. Speaking of which, where is my favourite travel genius?'

Oh. Crap. I hadn't expected this. I've no idea why. Of course, there were going to be regular customers who would know Dee and want to speak to her. I should have known this was coming and had something prepared but… Oh. Fuck.

Rabbit. Headlights.

'Hi Delilah.'

Jen had stood up and turned around, coming into the customer's eyeline for the first time.

'Oh Jen, didn't see you there,' she said, with a definite edge of condescension. 'Where's Dee?'

'She's dead.' And with that, Jen walked across the shop, into the office and closed the door behind her.

'Oh,' Mrs Gucci said, looking, if I'm truthful, a bit put out. 'Well. It'll just have to wait then, won't it?' She turned on her fancy heels, those shoes with the red soles, and headed out the door.

Right then. There was complete silence for a few moments as I tried to work out what to do. The extent of my knowledge of Jen was a vague memory of her and my sis as kids, a couple of holidays and then half a dozen meetings in the weeks that I'd been home, all of them surrounded by other people, and almost invariably she kept herself to herself and barely said a word. She was like the quiet, unassuming presence in the background. Not that anyone could get a word in between my mum, Josie and Auntie Ida anyway.

I took the fact that no more customers had entered as a sign that I should go check on Jen. When I opened the door she was sitting at one of the desks, just staring at a poster of a beach on the wall.

'I'm sorry,' she said as soon as she realised I was there. 'I shouldn't have said it like that. I'm not sure why I did. She used to drive Dee bloody mad. She even hit on Luke once when we had an anniversary party for the shop. But that doesn't excuse me saying that. I'm sorry,' she repeated.

It was the most I'd ever heard her speak.

'It's OK. Brutal, but OK,' I added with a shrug.

That made her smile just a little, but the misery was still oozing out of her.

Under normal circumstances I'd probably think she was a bit of a downer and absolutely avoid her at all costs. The last thing I ever wanted or needed was negativity. That's why I liked the laid-back, life-enhancing, live-for-today attitudes back on the Gold Coast. Working out on the ships suited me. Two or three month stints at a time, two or three a year. I was one of a rota of divers that inspected and repaired the hulls of the drilling ships and underwater sections of stationary rigs out at sea. The downside was that I was out there for weeks or months with no contact with the rest of the world, but the plus side was that the money was great and it allowed me to spend the rest of my life just chilling and diving for fun, making my own life with no constrictions. Sometimes, I'd just take off down the coast, for a few weeks, other times I'd get on my bike and see where it took me. Dee always said we both had the free spirit gene and she was probably right, although she'd managed to get married and settle. I'd only ever come close to a committed relationship once before, and I couldn't see it happening again. Tara had that free spirit, enjoy life thing going on too. She'd come over from New Zealand and we met at the bar of the local dive club. She was the first person I'd had the slightest urge to consider any kind of future with, but neither of us were the type for rules or conventional ties and it ended so suddenly we never had time to find out if we'd ever get there.

No point dwelling on that now though.

'Look, where can we get something to eat and drink around here? Why don't I go get a couple of decent coffees and... when was the last time you ate?'

'When your mother force-fed us lasagne yesterday,' she replied.

'OK, so I'll go pick us up something.'

She nodded. I had a feeling I could have said, 'I've just won the lottery' or 'I'll go jump off a bridge' and she'd have reacted in exactly the same way.

Maybe this wasn't such a good idea after all. Perhaps getting on the first flight back to Australia would have been the smarter move. But then, what did I have to go back for? Sod all, except work and an empty flat.

Right now, two cups of coffee and a couple of bacon rolls were about as good as it was going to get.

11

Luke

They expected me to care, but it just wasn't happening. Sitting around the boardroom table, we'd just spent the last two hours of a Friday afternoon discussing tag line pitches for a new brand of kitchen towel. Seriously. Who gave a fuck about absorbency and core market and brand values? It was paper bloody towels! Humanity wasn't going to stand or fall on whether one sheet or two was needed to clean up…

'Don't cry over spilt milk.' I'd blurted it out before I'd even thought it through. Yeah, it was clichéd. Predictable. Way too twee. Shit. Dee would have rolled her eyes at my rank naffness.

Colin Medour, the head of the agency's FMCG division – that's fast-moving consumer goods to anyone not familiar with marketing bollocks lingo – stopped, thought for a minute. He was mulling it over like I'd just suggested a new cure for cancer. Eventually, he nodded, his face suddenly beaming with something approximating gung-ho excitement. 'I like that. Actually, I bloody love it. OK, Callie, Domenic, Luke, work up some ideas on it. Can you get some visuals for us by nine o'clock on Monday?'

It was phrased as a question but we all knew there was only one answer.

'Sure.' I said, ignoring Domenic's gritted teeth and Callie's raised eyebrows. When I say raised... she'd been at the Botox again so it was more of a mild shudder.

Everyone else cleared out, delighted they hadn't been seconded to the kitchen towel action group, so they might actually make it home before eight o'clock for a change. Staying behind didn't bother me. What else was I going to do? Go home, crack open a beer and ponder the word 'widower' for yet another night? Reflect on my day, and try to mentally count up how many looks of abject pity I'd received before lunchtime? Or even better, how many of my esteemed colleagues had averted their gaze so they didn't have to look me in the eye?

Not that it was a surprise. Marketing agencies weren't exactly renowned for their fluffy, cuddly approach to their workmates, and BRALLAN MMA (Marketing, Media, Advertising) treated death like ageing and disease – best to be avoided because then it wouldn't be catching.

Bunch of twonks.

I caught myself, feeling the creeping sense of irritation coming over me again. Every day since Dee died, it had happened, some days so many times I lost count. A sense that my nerves had moved to the outside of my skin and I was being scorched by some invisible force. I didn't get it. Dee was an irrepressible force of joy and positivity, but she had also always been the volatile one, the one in our relationship that got irked, or short-tempered or impatient. Now she'd gone I was the one left pissed off and easily annoyed. I hoped it would pass because right now the only thing that helped was to run until I felt nothing but the urge to black out or throw up. And despite the rank indignity, I still kept doing it because it was the only thing that calmed the screaming in my head down from a roar to an admittedly pathetic whimper.

As we headed to the 'conversation pit' – yep, my workplace is pretentious enough to need a chilled out, dipped-floor 'focus area' in which to have a discussion. I suppose I should be grateful that there weren't matching flumes and bean bags. Yet.

I tried to bring my irritation down a few notches. Get it together. It wasn't as if any of this was a newsflash. Many of my esteemed workmates had always been self-important, narcissistic pains in the arse. Truth be told, I'd always found it more amusing than grating. Dee did too. She'd be in hysterics when I shared their more ridiculous utterings and delusions. Now it took all my discipline not to recount their grand-scale delusions to their smug, superior faces.

In fairness, Domenic and Callie were two of the decent ones. I wouldn't call them mates, but unlike several of the others, they didn't make me want to bang my head on my desk until I was unconscious. They'd been on my team for a couple of years now. Domenic had an ego the size of the ludicrously large gym bag he brought to work every day, but he was a good guy at heart and his Monday morning stories of his weekend antics were priceless. Callie had my respect because she was usually the smartest person in the room. Half the guys in the office had a thing for her but she never took them up on it.

'So, thanks for that,' Domenic muttered, sliding into the pit. 'Tonight was sorted – gym, pub, hook up with a chick that looks like a Kardashian...'

'Which one?' Callie interjected as she sat next to him.

'The one in the High Street,' he replied.

She rolled her eyes. 'No, genius. Which Kardashian? If we're getting the details of your life, I just want to make sure we've got it right.'

Thank God the guy resembled Orlando Bloom on a good day, because he wasn't going to seduce anyone with his knowledge of quantum physics.

'Kendal.'

'Good choice,' Callie quipped. A sudden tightness crept across my chest as I listened to the banter. It was exactly the kind of conversation Dee would have had. Funny. Quick. One of the boys.

The familiar tightness spread to my guts, giving me that sickening feeling that I'd only ever had a few times in my life before Dee died. The one that happens when you hear devastating news and it feels like your stomach is going to collapse. Now, it happened dozens of times a day. Every time I thought about her. Every time something reminded me of her voice, her hair, her smile, or now, her sense of humour.

I fought the urge to climb up and run. So much for the fight or flight instinct, I had no more fight left.

'Look, mate, on you go. I'll cover for you. My fault for opening my mouth anyway,' I heard myself saying. That happened a lot now too. Sometimes it felt like I was somewhere else, not quite inhabiting this body that was walking and talking and functioning like any other normal person. Nothing was normal anymore.

Domenic looked at me as if he was waiting for a catch. 'You sure?'

'Much as we'll miss your valuable input on shite tag lines for kitchen towels, we'll scrape through without you.'

He held his fist out for a fist bump. I stared at it for a second. 'I'm going to pretend I can't see that because I'm not fourteen,' I told him.

He was still laughing when the door banged behind him.

Callie lifted a biro to make notes. 'OK, where are we going with this?' she asked, and I watched as she wrote 'spilt milk' across the top of a page on her A4 pad. I knew what she meant, but right now the prospect of sitting in this bloody 'conversation pit' any longer was making my teeth grind.

'Pub next door?'

'Don't need to ask me twice,' she replied, already curling her legs up and pushing herself up to a standing position. Like Dee, she was fit and athletic. Every morning she jogged into work and then showered in the communal changing rooms. Yep, communal. Another idea on the same scale of naffdom as the conversation pit and anything that had come out of my mouth so far today.

'You sure? You're not meeting Justin?' Her boyfriend. An accountant who did triathlons in his spare time. I'm not sure which of those aspects was most inclined to make me think he was a knob.

'Nope. Called and cancelled when you got us a crap assignment at six o'clock on a Friday,' she said, but thankfully she didn't seem too pissed off about it.

'Sorry about that.'

'Wine will make forgiveness come quicker.'

The pub was busy with the usual mix of Friday after work suits and early-out girls in stilettos they'd be carrying by the end of the night. That was me once. Out on a Friday night. Not a care in the world. Laughing and joking. It was only a couple of months ago and yet it seemed like years since I'd been that guy.

Now I was just an emotional wreck that really needed a beer and I was grateful for the noise. God knows, anything that wasn't the silence in my house had to be a good thing.

We found a table in the corner, and put together a few top-line ideas that I could flesh out tomorrow with graphics and spin. It was a shit idea and we both knew it would get bombed out by Monday lunchtime, so I wasn't going to spend too much time on it.

We were just finishing up our drinks when Callie's expression changed very slightly and there was another little shudder between her brows. I think she was trying to frown. Or maybe it was concern. Or irritation. Dee had always said I was pretty crap at reading moods on a woman, so trying to decipher the facial gestures of someone prone to cosmetic enhancement was like breaking the Enigma code.

'So how are you doing?'

I should have been prepared for it. I'd heard it so many times in the last month; I even had a few pre-prepared answers.

'Hanging together, thanks.' I wasn't.

'Good days and bad days.'

Only bad.

'Och, I'm OK. Just have to get on with it.' Why? Who the fuck came up with that one? Who said we needed to get on with anything when all you wanted to do was get stupefying drunk, howl at the moon or wreck a room just to have an outlet for the excruciating pain of it all.

Callie nodded. 'It must be... I don't know... I mean, it's not... Oh Christ, I'm not very good at this. But you know, if you ever want to talk... My sister died a few years ago...'

'Sorry. I didn't know.' I was surprised that she hadn't mentioned it, but then, I guess we'd always kept things pretty surface level in the office.

'It's not something I publicise,' she countered, not unkindly. 'But I know how hard this must be for you, so if you want to talk or rant, then I'm available for listening.'

'Thank you. I appreciate it,' I answered truthfully.

There was a silence for a few moments that neither of us filled.

'Sorry. I've made you totally uncomfortable now,' she said, lifting her glass of wine.

'No, it's just...' I shrugged. She wasn't wrong about the uncomfortable bit. 'Talking about it doesn't change anything.'

Sure, it was true, but it hid the more pressing truth. For the last ten years, the only person I wanted to talk to when anything good, bad, happy, sad or hell, anything at all happened, was Dee. Talking to anyone else, with Val, Jen or anyone else in the family, would feel like... I searched for the right conclusion to the thought... Wrong. Like a betrayal.

Callie and I had had drinks after work a dozen times before, when Dee was away on one of her trips, and it had never felt awkward or weird. Not like it did now. This was what mourning did. Made you feel shit. Made you act like the skin you were in wasn't yours. Made you forget what you would usually do in normal situations. Except...

'Another drink?' I asked. Wouldn't blame her if she said no and, actually, it would be a bit of a relief.

'Sure,' she said. Couldn't knock her for staying power.

I fought my way to the bar, ordered up beer, wine, and at the last minute decided to take the lead from the hen party that had congregated in the corner where their screeches were being drowned out by the massive speakers on the wall behind them. They didn't seem to have a care in the world. I wish I felt the same.

'What's that they're drinking?' I asked an unimpressed barmaid.

'Irn Bru vodka shots.'

Crazy. I'd be nuts to start on those.

'I'll have two,' I said.

Callie nodded thoughtfully when I carried the tray back to the table and she spotted the amber shots. 'Ah, right. This could all get very messy,' she said, her expression suggesting she'd enjoy that.

I had another pang of unwelcome familiarity. That was exactly how Dee would have reacted. What was I doing here? This was no place to be when I was feeling like this. I wanted space. Or people who knew me well enough to care and to spot that I was on the edge of punching out a wall. Fuck, I hated this. I put the drinks down on the table.

'I'm really sorry, I... I need to go.'

Callie's brow shuddered again. I think it was trying to shape into something that would indicate confusion.

'Sorry, Callie,' I apologised again. 'I'm just...' I didn't even finish the sentence. I just turned and marched to the door, pulled it open and staggered out. I leant back against the wall, hands on knees, trying to breathe, hoping to shift whatever it was that was stuck in my throat and making my heart beat like a drum.

'You OK, pal?' one of the door stewards in a thick black padded jacket asked.

'I don't know,' I said. 'I just don't know'.

I stood up, took the deepest breath my lungs could grab. And then I started to run.

12

Jen

'Hang on Val, I'll ask him.' I pulled the phone away from my ear. 'Mark, your mum is asking if you're coming home for your dinner or going to the gym?'

I chose not to relay to Val that he was now rolling his eyes, laughing.

'Going to the gym. And can you tell her that I'll be home later, I've got a key, and I'm thirty-eight?' he asked.

I didn't need to pass that on. Val heard every word and retorted with some well-observed insults before ringing off.

'What did she say?' he asked.

'That you're a fabulous son and she cherishes every bit of you,' I lied breezily. I wasn't getting in the middle of this one. 'Any chance of getting a mobile phone so I'm not the go-between for you two?'

Mark stopped counting the day's takings. 'And have a direct number that my mother can get me on? No way. She'd be on the phone every two minutes. I'll stick to my Australian mobile, thanks.'

'But that doesn't work over here!' I protested.

'Exactly,' he replied, triumph written all over his best innocent face.

'Don't you have anyone at home that would want to call you?' That seemed odd to me. Surely there must be someone?

'Nah, my mates know they see me when they see me. Occupational hazard.'

'And no girlfriend?'

He shook his head. 'There was for a while. Tara. But she had to head back to New Zealand last month when her mum got sick. We had a pretty good thing going for a while but I'm not great at commitment or long-term plans. I'm a live for the day kind of guy,' he said with a playful smile that reminded me so much of Dee. That was exactly what she'd been like. I'd been so shocked when she married Luke, not because he wasn't perfect for her, because he was – but because she'd always said she never wanted the whole 'until death do us part thing'.

I felt a sudden kick in the solar plexus. Who knew that 'death do us part' would come so soon?

If Mark noticed me wobble slightly, he didn't say anything. Having him working here every day hadn't been as uncomfortable as I'd feared. After a bumpy start, when he'd got me on one of the days when it even hurt to breathe, we'd settled into a rhythm and seemed to roll along, keeping everything friendly and polite. He'd arrived in the UK on a cold January night and now it was almost Easter, and it felt like he was part of the furniture. He was great with the customers and he had picked up our systems and services really well and he did the coffee run twice a day. What wasn't there to like? It helped that we kept things on the surface. On a few occasions, he'd suggested hanging out after hours, but I'd resisted. Much easier to come to work, do what had to be done, go home. But even though we didn't scratch the superficial veneer, it was obvious that under the jokes and banter, Mark was struggling to adapt to living at home with his parents again. It couldn't be easy, especially when we were all functioning under a crushing blanket of grief. I was worried about Val. On the outside she was still being strong and keeping it together, but I could see she'd lost weight and there were dark circles under her eyes that no amount of concealer and blue eyeliner could hide.

The hand-carved clock on the wall, a souvenir from Dee's trip to Bali, chimed to mark the hour. Five o'clock.

'Why don't you knock off? I don't think crowds are going to storm in between now and closing.'

'You sure?'

'Absolutely.'

'Only I'm starting to get a complex. In the last couple of weeks I've asked you if you wanted to go out for dinner, down to the pub, and I even suggested a museum, in case you're one of those cultured types. My mum told me to keep you busy and I'm failing miserably.'

'Don't worry, I'll tell Val that you're doing a sterling job,' I promised. 'And thanks Mark, one of these days I'll take you up on the offers.' I didn't know that I would. I couldn't face the thought of sitting there, drinking, laughing, talking with her brother without Dee by my side. It wouldn't be right.

'I'll hold you to that,' he said, smiling, and I could see why many of our regulars had become even more regular than usual. He was surfer-dude perfect, with a whole dark-haired, David Gandy jaw, piercing blue eyes thing going on, the kind of guy that belonged on a billboard advertising Australian hair products for butch guys.

He popped into the office and reappeared with his kit bag. He headed to the gym most nights after work, and was constantly trying to cajole me to go with him. Right on cue...

'I'm happy to wait if you'd like to come with me?' he asked, but I wasn't swayed by his cheeky grin.

'No, I'm good thanks. I've got to finish packing tonight anyway.' In truth I hadn't even started packing, although my flight was first thing tomorrow. I'd been putting off even thinking about the New York trip ever since I'd agreed to go. I had a loose plan, and that was to feign illness and cancel at the last minute. I was thinking flu. Or an ear infection. Maybe a nasty bout of gastroenteritis.

I waited until he was gone, then headed into the back office. Almost two months after she'd gone, Dee's cardigan was still there, over the chair, waiting for her to come back for it. I sat in her seat and pulled it around me. I knew it was a figment of my imagination, but I still convinced myself that it carried her scent, that she was in the room. I put my feet up on her desk the way she did every night after work and wondered what she'd think of everything that had happened here? She would be proud of Mark for coming home and being with her parents. She'd be devastated to see Luke struggling without her. And I had absolutely no doubt that, right now, she'd be trying to come up with some ghostly way to acquire a baseball bat and go after Pete. The thought made me smile. 'Go for it, Dee,' I whispered.

I heard the front door open and was just about to go see if it was a customer when Josie swept in, a force of nature, armed with a Henry Hoover. She was in her sixties, but it seemed no one had pointed that out to her because she still looked and acted like she was thirty-five. Over the decade she'd worked for us, we'd realised that if there was a song, she'd sing it. A dance, she'd join in. A party, she'd be there until the end. A problem, she'd solve it. She was of the 'just get on with it' generation, built from positivity and medicinal caramel wafers. No moping, no martyrdom and no playing the victim, just a core of steel that came with a cigarette dangling from her mouth and a raucous cackle punctuating her every move. Her son, Michael and his wife Mel now lived in Italy, to be close to his daughters by his first marriage. Her daughter, Avril, was a brilliant make-up artist, living in London and working for a West End show. But she still had us here, her surrogate family.

'Jen, ma love, how're you doing?' she said, then quickly took in the fact that I was sitting at Dee's desk with her cardigan wrapped around me. 'One of those days, pet?'

'Every day,' I answered. I could be honest with Josie. No blocking things out because I didn't want to make things uncomfortable for Mark, or being calm for Luke or supportive for Val.

'You're dreading going to New York tomorrow?'

I nodded.

'Contemplating throwing a sickie and bailing out?'

I nodded again. Her psychic superpowers were incredible.

'I should have arranged to come with you. I can still try to get a flight...'

I blinked back the tears that had sprung up. Kindness was the killer. I could handle indifference and cold discussion, but the minute someone was kind and caring to me, I crumbled. 'Thanks, Josie, but I need to do this myself. I really do.'

She sighed. 'Probably just as well. I'm not sure if the arrest warrant is still out for me after that time I took out three tourists in Central Park with my Segway.'

My first genuine smile of the day. She was incorrigible.

'Want me to put a cuppa on?'

I shook my head. 'No thanks, Josie.'

She leaned down and hugged me. 'Right then, I'll get on and get out of your way. Shout for me if you change your mind about the cuppa.'

Releasing me, she opened the cleaning cupboard and pulled out her tray of sprays, cloths, and the overall she wore over her smart black polo neck and skinny jeans. If there was an award for stylish cleaners, it would be on her polished mantelpiece.

She only did an hour at the end of the night – and sometimes early morning before we opened – so when she was done she came back to the office and there I was, sitting in exactly the same position I'd been in when she started. She leaned on the edge of Dee's desk, facing me. This time, she just waited until I spoke.

'I don't understand any of this, Josie. It's like every day is just going by and I'm living someone else's life, just passing time until I can go back to mine.'

'I know how much you miss her, love. And what about him – have you heard from that spineless bastard?' Did I mention she was direct and took no prisoners?

'Nothing.' It wasn't for the lack of trying. I'd called his mobile. It went straight to voicemail. I'd emailed him. No reply. I'd even turned up on his sister's doorstep, to be told that she hadn't heard from him and, from her pitying expression and tone of voice, I believed her. They'd never been close, only seeing each other one or twice a year.

'Jesus Christ. It's like one of those true stories on the Crime Channel where someone disappears off the face of the earth and then you discover that they were a ruthless drug baron who'd been living in the witness protection programme. Or a serial killer. Or dodging bailiffs that want to take his telly back to Argos.'

I couldn't help but laugh. 'Our telly was fully paid up, Josie.'

'So not that one then. I'm going for serial killer.' She pulled a cigarette out of the packet and lit it. 'You know my offer still stands to pay him a visit.' She sounded like a Mafia don. On forty cigs a day.

I smiled, gratefully. 'Thanks, Josie, but I couldn't afford the bail money.'

'Well, if you change your mind... I've got Book Club tonight but I could wipe him out afterwards.'

'Good to know. Thanks,' I told her.

She picked up her stuff and with another hug she was off, leaving a whiff of Marlboro and Febreze.

It was time to go, but I was still struggling with the destination. For the last month there had only been two options. Number one – go home. Drink coffee. Maybe wine. Practice my 'not feeling well, think I'm coming down with something' face. And then watch trash TV until I slumped into sleep in the early hours of the morning. Tempting.

Number two – go to... Oh God, I couldn't. Not again.

I rested my head against the back of the chair, eyes fixed on the ceiling.

'So what do you think then?' I asked Dee, whispering. 'It's crazy, right? I'm not doing it anymore.'

Silence.

'No, really. I'm not going. It has to stop.'

More silence. But this time, I took it as a lack of agreement.

'Oh, bollocks.' I got up, lifted my bag, set the alarm and dashed outside.

The city centre was dark, cold and crowded, packed with office workers emptying out for the day. I jumped in a cab, gave the driver the address and fifteen minutes later I was sitting in a coffee shop across from Pete's office. He worked in computer software. Highly ironic given that he could never fix my laptop when it was buggered. His company was one of those achingly trendy ones that allowed flexi-time and he preferred to go in late and stay late. I checked my watch. Seven o'clock. He'd normally still be inside.

I sat. I watched. I'd counted up the windows to the eighth floor. The light was on, but at least a dozen people worked in his office, so it could be any of them.

The waitress, one of two or three that I'd seen here on previous visits, approached and smiled. 'Black coffee, right?'

Damn. What kind of crap stalker was I that I not only became a familiar face in my stalking hangout, but they actually remembered what I drank. It would make great testimony for the prosecution.

'Yes, thank you,' I said, making a mental note to leave a good tip, in the hope that she'd remember me for that reason, not the fact that I sat here every night staring at the building opposite. Two weeks now I'd been doing this and I didn't know why. I'd called the office a couple of times, but the secretary in his department had said he was on holiday every time. I'd had to stop calling because after all these years, she recognised my voice and I couldn't stand the awkward pity that laced her words.

What had he told them?

Oh Jen? Nah, didn't work out so I cut her loose.

Mutual agreement. Just not right for each other.

Settled down too young. Time to spread my wings.

Or the truth. *I just told her it was over on the day of our friend's funeral and walked out. Haven't seen her since. No explanation given.*

No doubt they'd laugh, assuming he was joking, but no, it was true – no explanation had been given. Not to me, not to Luke, not to anyone else in the circle we'd lived in for fifteen years. Nothing.

The waitress put my coffee in front of me and retreated, off to serve the couple that were holding hands at a corner table. I felt an urge to blurt out some warning about how he'd dump her one day when she was least expecting it, but I managed to hold it in. It was bad enough being weird stalker lady without adding weird crazy lady to the description.

The coffee scalded my lips, and I was so distracted by the pain that I almost missed him. He came out of his building, and my heart cracked at the sight of him. He looked exactly the same as the man I'd slept next to every night of my adult life. Tall. His hair was back to his usual short style, cut every second week so that it was cropped around the sides and back, but longer, swept back, on the top. He hadn't shaved but it only made him look better. He was wearing the coat he'd bought when he revamped his wardrobe just a few months ago. That shopping expedition had been a bit of a surprise, but at the time I'd thought it would cheer him up, knock him out of the weird mood he'd been in. I'd gone with him, picking out clothes, egging him on. In fact, I'd picked out the navy three-quarter length coat he was wearing, as he stood there... Laughing.

Yep, laughing. How fucking dare he? He'd shredded our relationship, walked out when I needed him most and disappeared off the face of the earth. It might look like Pete, but it couldn't be. My Pete loved me. Made promises. Spent fifteen years with me. Who was this guy? He was like a stranger. Standing there, like he didn't have a care in the world.

Only then did my gaze move to the side and I saw he was walking with a woman I recognised as Arya, a Londoner who had transferred up to Glasgow the year before. We'd chatted at the Christmas party. Nice. Breezy. Tall, blonde highlights, a plummy accent, with that kind of natural confidence that came from growing up in a stable, affluent world. I'd liked her. I think I'd even mentioned to Pete that we should have her over for dinner since she was new to the city, but we'd never got around to it.

Only the cold blast of air told me that I was out of the coffee shop, the beeps of the car horns told me I was crossing the road, the surprised look on his perfect bloody face told me he'd seen me.

Arya melted away – I've no idea if she even said goodbye, my eyes fixed only on Pete, my ears hearing only my voice.

'I think we need to talk, don't you?'

13

Val

The smell of the lasagne I'd cooked for Mark's dinner, on top of the stove, was beginning to turn my stomach. I covered it with cling film and put it in the fridge. He could heat it up when he got home. Don was working late again. He'd never worked so much overtime in his life as he did now. I didn't ask. If work was going to keep him distracted, I wasn't going to complain. He'd only get under my feet anyway.

I grabbed today's paper and sat at the kitchen table to do the Sudoku. They used to be my relaxation, but now all they did was focus my brain on something other than the urge to scream. But not tonight. The walls were closing in on me and I knew I couldn't sit here any longer. Not that there was anywhere I wanted to go. Josie had been trying to talk me into going away for a week or two. At first, she'd suggested going over to see her son and his family in Italy. I loved them all, but how could I watch another young couple, with their children, and know that I'd never see Dee with my grandchildren? I know it sounds selfish, but that was the truth. Josie had realised it straight away and suggested a dozen other places to go, but I'd refused. I wasn't leaving

Don and Mark, and I couldn't face leaving Dee's old room, her teenage stuff, the mug she used when she had a cuppa here, the photos of her on the wall. I needed every connection to her that I could find.

The blue light of the kettle flicked off to show that it had boiled but I couldn't even remember switching it on. Lately, a lot of the stuff I did was just going through the motions. Put the kettle on, get the cup, add the teabag, the milk, and only when I was stirring it did I realise I didn't want the tea at all. Or I'd go through the process of making a slice of toast only to shove it in the bin because the first bite stuck in my throat.

When would this get better? Would it ever? If this was it, then I'd be better giving up now thanks very much, because it wasn't a life.

My mobile phone rang. Damn thing. The ringtone played 'Stand By Me'. Dee had set it and every time it rang I thought of her.

Josie's name flashed up on the screen. There was no point ignoring her, as she'd just keep calling back. We'd met when the girls opened the shop ten years ago and she'd fast become a brilliant friend. Although, right now she was with the rest of the world on the list of people I was trying to avoid.

'Hello love!' I said. False cheeriness. It had become my specialty.

'It's me, pet. I'm just on my way home from the shop and just checking you're still on for Book Club tonight.'

I had to laugh. Book Club. A group of eight of us, all in our fifties and sixties, had been meeting every second Wednesday for years, and we'd yet to crack open anything resembling a romping good read. It had been Josie's idea to give it a name that sounded like we had a highbrow purpose.

'Beats the "Let's drink gin on a week night and gossip about everyone we know" club,' she'd said at our first gathering. It was a fair point.

'Don't want you bailing out at the last minute again,' she said, a pause in the middle of the sentence telling me she was having a puff of her ciggie while she spoke.

'Wouldn't miss it,' I answered, trying to sound like I meant it.

My words were met with something between a snort and a cackle.

'I think you said that last week. And the week before. And for the umpteen weeks before that. Right before you didn't show up.'

The words sounded harsh, but they were softened by years of trust. I knew she was just trying to help. Didn't mean I had to like it.

'Aye, all right Josie. I'll be there, OK? I need to go, Mark has just walked in the door and I need to make his dinner. Cheeribye.'

All lies. You wouldn't believe how easy they came these days. Every time I wanted to ignore something or someone. Every time anyone asked me how I was. 'Fine,' I'd say chirpily. They chose to believe me.

If for no other reason than it would get Josie off my case, I decided I'd definitely go tonight. I'd known the rest of the girls for the best part of ten years too and we'd been through everything from divorce, to affairs, to illness and, yes, death, so I was pretty sure I could hold it together for a few hours.

I gave up on the Sudoku and flicked over the page. I didn't actually read any of the paper anymore. Couldn't stand the sheer misery. Murder. Destruction. War. Pain. I was living permanently on the edge of crumbling into a mess and the slightest thing could tip me over, so I avoided other folks' tragedies. I had enough of my own.

I was just about to give up and go and get ready, when I zeroed in on a small headline halfway down a page.

COURT DATE SET FOR WEIRBANK KILLER DRIVER

The air went right out of my lungs and suddenly my spine couldn't support me. I buckled forward, grabbed on to the table.

It couldn't be, could it? Surely if something had been arranged then the police liaison officer, that nice woman who'd visited after... well, anyway, she'd have let us know.

I scanned the page and then saw the name. Darren Wilkie. It was like someone had poured ice through my veins and I felt the bile rising. Darren Wilkie. That was him. He killed my Dee.

Trial set for June 30th. Three months away. Darren Wilkie. 59 Ranes Drive. Glasgow. Death by dangerous driving. The charge had been dropped from murder, because it had, they said, been an accident. The fact that he was off his head on some kind of drugs didn't even come into it. What were they called? Legal highs. Why the hell were they legal when this was what they caused? Not that they absolved Darren Wilkie from the blame. Bad wee bastard.

It took me a minute before I could concentrate over the sound of my heart beating out of my chest. I scanned the report, wondering again why I was finding out about this by reading it in a newspaper. So much for the justice system looking after the families of the victims.

Victims. We were the bloody victims and I couldn't tell you how much I hated that we'd been forced into having that label by some snivelling, little bastard.

I knew I should phone Don, but what good would that do? It would just get him all wound up at work and that wouldn't help anyone. Instead, I grabbed the car keys, and headed outside, forgetting to even grab my bag.

I drove. I had no idea where I was going, so I just drove, trying to keep my mind so busy it wouldn't explode. Indicate. Turn left. Speed up. Slow down. Indicate. Turn right. Speed up. Slow down. I'd been doing it for a while before I noticed the yellow light on the dashboard. Bugger, I was almost out of petrol. Looking around, I saw that I was in the south side of the city, and it was only then I realised that I didn't have my purse or a credit card to refuel, or a phone to call anyone. God dammit. I pulled over. Stuck. Lost. And for the first time since the funeral I cried. Great big sobbing howls of pain that felt like they came from deep inside my body, making me tremble and…

There was a tapping at the window and I looked up to see a policeman, eyeing me with curiosity. The sight of him made me shake even more as I wiped away the tears with the cuff of my cardigan and rolled the window down.

'Are you all right there?'

No, I clearly wasn't all right. I was clearly all bloody wrong.

'Yes, I'm… I'm… fine. Just realised I've almost run out of petrol and I'm away without my handbag.'

'Ah. Can I call someone for you?'

Dear God, no. That was the last thing anyone in my family needed. I racked my brain for a way out. Then I saw where I was. Josie. Her house was only a mile or so away.

'No, it's fine thanks. My pal lives not far from here and I've got enough to make it to her house.'

'Are you sure?'

'Yes. Thank you. She's just up in Ratho Drive.'

'OK, well I tell you what – we're heading that way anyway, so we'll follow you in case you break down.'

No, no, no, no. I didn't actually want to go there. Look at the state of me – I didn't want anyone to see me like this. But what else could I do?

'Erm, right then. Thank you.'

I waited until he climbed back into his car before I indicated and pulled back on to the road, and yep, sure enough he followed me. There was no choice but to do what I'd told him.

I drove as slowly as possible, figuring he'd think I was conserving fuel, but actually hoping he'd get called away to some emergency and I could just pull over, ditch the car, and grab a taxi back to the house. I was sure the driver would wait until I'd run in for the money. Why hadn't I had that idea when I was talking to the officer? Bugger.

I turned into Josie's street, pulled up outside her Victorian semi, and got out, giving the cop a thumbs up and a wave. Maybe he'd drive away and I could bid a hasty retreat before Josie saw me.

'Well, you don't see that every day. When did you start getting a police escort? Or is he just really bad at covert surveillance?'

I turned to see Josie, standing in her doorway, arms folded, cheeky grin on her face, her grey hair a spiky, dramatic shock against her standard uniform of black polo neck ('covers my droop', she'd say) and black jeans ('useful colour if I ever need to adopt a career in burglary').

'I... I...' I tried to come back with a witty retort, to play along with the joke but it got stuck in my throat and – oh Lord, the embarrassment – I burst into floods of tears in the middle of her front path. 'Oh Josie, I was driving and I realised that bloody heap of junk was running out of petrol and I didn't have any money and the police stopped so I told them I was coming here and I'm... I don't know what I'm doing, Josie. I just don't know.'

She was already out of the house, arms around me, trying to steer me inside but I resisted.

'I can't Josie. I'm going somewhere.'

'Going where? We're going to Book Club later, Ma darling.'

Suddenly the plan was kicked from my subconscious to the front of my mind and I realised where I'd been heading all along.

I needed to go there. I needed to see.

'I'm going to his house,' I blurted.

'Who's house?'

'Darren Wilkie.'

That shocked her. 'But, Val, isn't he in jail?'

I shook my head, spitting the words out between sobs. 'Out on bail. Can you believe that? Out on bloody bail. He killed our Dee and he's out and living his life and my Dee is in the ground. How is that fair?'

A few feet away, the curtains on the window of the neighbour's house were twitching, but I didn't care. I wanted to tell the world anyway. Shout it from the rooftops. That evil bastard was walking the streets and my Dee was dead.

'I know, love. It isn't fair. It's so wrong.' Josie was still trying to pull me towards her, but I wasn't shifting. I stood absolutely still and my body went rigid. I knew if I went inside she'd try to talk me out of it and I wasn't changing my mind.

'Don't, Josie. I have to go. But I just need to borrow a tenner for petrol. Just enough to get me there and home again.'

Her arms slackened and she turned so her gaze met mine. 'What are you going to do when you get there?'

That stunned me. I hadn't thought that far ahead. 'I've no idea. Don't worry, I'm not going to confront him or do anything daft. I just want to see where he lives. I don't know why. I just need to go.'

She pondered that for a moment. 'OK, just wait right there.'

She left me on the path and disappeared inside, returning only seconds later, jacket on, bag over her shoulder. The door banged behind her.

'What are you doing?' I asked her.

'If you're going to do this, I'm coming with you,' she said. 'And don't try to argue because we'll be here all night.'

I couldn't help smile at the accuracy of that statement. The only person on the face of this earth who was more stubborn than me was the woman who looked like the long lost granny of Annie Lennox and Billy Idol.

All the fight went out of me and I physically slumped. 'Thanks Josie.'

'No probs. But if there's tyre slashing or bricks through windows, so help me God you'd better not take me down with you.'

Right then I realised how glad I was that she was coming along. There was no situation that wasn't made better by Josie's company. Even this one.

'Oh and Val…?'

'What?'

'Can we stop for chips on the way because I was just about to have my dinner when you and your police escort arrived?'

With that she turned and gave her twitching neighbour a cheery wave, and jumped in the car, as if there was nothing at all odd about the scene that had just played out at her front door.

We stopped at the petrol station, filled the tank, nipped into a chippy on the same street, then headed to the address that had been quoted in the paper: 59 Ranes Drive.

It was a long row of sixties semis, most of them with neat gardens and painted gates. I don't know what I expected but it was a nice enough street. Normal. Not in the areas that were notorious for crime, drugs and deprivation. In fact, it was disturbingly similar to our street. Counting ahead, I worked out which one was number fifty-nine. Red door.

I pulled into a space on the opposite side of the road, about twenty yards before we reached it, between a Fiat 500 and a Ford Mondeo, and pulled the handbrake on.

'Now what?' Josie asked.

'I don't know.'

'OK, well while you're thinking about it, here's your chips.'

She plumped a brown paper parcel into my lap, but I didn't open it. Nothing was getting past the huge lump that was back in my throat.

'Bugger. I forgot to get vinegar,' she said. I knew she was just trying to diffuse the situation, but it wasn't working.

God help me, I'd never struck another person in my life, but I wanted to storm across that road, batter the door until it was answered and then wring that little bastard's neck. I wanted to squeeze every ounce of life out of him. I wanted someone else to feel the pain that I was feeling.

I felt Josie's hand gently rest on mine and give it the slightest of squeezes.

'I'm here, love,' she said gently.

I nodded, tears threatening to spill again, heart beating out of my chest.

'But you know going in there isn't the answer. I'll stay here with you as long as you want, but we can't go in there. You getting arrested won't do Don and Mark any good at all.'

'I know,' I whispered.

'Besides, the lazy feckers can't cook a thing for themselves so they'd starve in no time.'

If it was meant to jolt me back to reality, it worked. Don would go crazy if he knew I was here. I'd never done anything like this in my life. Reliable Val. Mum. Wife. Liked the occasional night out and any excuse to meet up with my pals. At no point did 'irrational stalker' ever come into the equation.

'I think I'm actually going mad, Josie.'

She nodded, her gravitas only a little diluted by the rustling of her chip bag. When she spoke, it was quiet, uncharacteristically solemn.

'Probably. But it's only to be expected, love. It doesn't get any worse than what happened to you. So you go right ahead and be as crazy as you like, for as long as you need to be, and I'll stick right by you and make sure you don't get injured or arrested.'

There were no words to describe how much I loved her.

I took her at her promise and we sat there as the night grew darker and colder. There was no sign of anyone entering or leaving the house, or movement inside. I put the engine back on. At some point Josie put the radio on low, to break up the silence. Smooth Radio. Hits of the sixties and seventies. There was a comfort in the familiar tunes, but not enough to unfurl the knot of rage that was twisting in my stomach.

Josie rolled her window down, letting a cold blast of air into the car. 'Sorry. Smell of chips was near killing me,' she said, before fishing her phone out of her handbag and typing a message. 'I'm texting the book group to say we won't make it because we're on a stakeout.'

'Josie, don't...' I blurted, horrified that she'd share this. Too late I spotted the glint in her eye.

'I'm joking! You know I'd never betray a confidence or embarrass you. I've told them we can't make it because your piles are playing up.'

Her cackle was infectious, but it stopped abruptly when, at exactly the same time, we both saw the light going off in the window of the house, then the red door opened.

14

Jen

Rabbit. Headlights. 'Jen, what are you doing here?'

'Seriously? You think you get the first question?' I asked, full of attitude, not giving a damn that he must think I'd completely lost it. I was soaked, bedraggled, I'd just crossed the road like a stuntman in an action movie, and now I was treating him with full on, don't dare bloody question me, fury.

'No, but I...'

'You move out, disappear for weeks, won't take my calls and you think you get the first question?' I demanded again, my voice dangerously approaching a tone that would be lethal to the eardrums of dogs.

Oh bollocks, I was on a roll and I couldn't seem to stop. This wasn't the cool, calm way I'd imagined this conversation going the thousands of times I'd planned it in my head. In those scenarios I was firm, composed, as I got to the bottom of the problem, while displaying all the poise and confidence of a grown up. True, depending on my mood, those imaginary premonitions did end with him either begging my forgiveness and telling me he couldn't live without me, or with me strangling him with a pair of his Lycra running shorts, but the important thing was they never started with me ambushing him in the middle of the street and shrieking at him in front of passing commuters.

I sagged a little. 'Look can we go somewhere and talk?' I asked him, aiming for conciliatory but probably just sounding a bit needy.

'I can't, I...' he started to object.

That was all I needed to step straight back over the 'stroppy and confrontational' line.

'Look, Pete, we either do this now or I keep turning up here and you'll live in fear of leaving your office for the rest of your life.' It was meant to be said with a bit of humour, but if there was a jury present I could see that they'd have a fair case for a guilty verdict on threat and intimidation.

He shrugged, seeing no way out.

'We could go back to the house,' I said. Bad move. His horrified expression told me that was the last thing he'd agree to. 'Or there's a coffee shop across the road...'

As I gestured over to it, I saw three waitresses, including the one who'd served me, standing in the window watching us. I was mortified. Clearly we'd become entertainment to brighten up a boring day. They saw that I'd spotted them and scurried back out of sight.

'Yeah, OK,' he agreed. 'Sure.'

I stopped myself from blurting out some sarcastic comment, even though they were piling up like cannonballs in the forefront of my brain, just waiting to be fired. *Oh, only if it's not too much trouble. I do understand that after fifteen years together, it's a bit much to expect an explanation when you dump me and disappear. No really, it's fine if tonight doesn't suit. Just let me know when you'd rather do this. When hell freezes over? OK, I'll look out for sudden drops in temperature and cross my fingers.*

I hated him. And I loved him so much I just wanted to thread my arms inside that sodding three-quarter length navy coat and lose myself in his chest. But still I hated him.

The bell dinged on the door of the café as we entered, and the waitresses tried to act nonchalant, as if we were just any other customers that had wandered in off the street. I sat back down at the table I'd been at a few moments earlier, gratified to see that my handbag was still hanging on the back of the chair. That would have been the icing on the crapola cake – tracking down my long-lost boyfriend, seeing his obvious aversion to my presence and losing my bag containing all my worldly goods.

'What can I get you?' the waitress asked, as chirpy as ever, picking up my previous cup and giving the table a quick wipe.

'Just a coffee please,' I answered, grateful that she made no mention of the fact that I'd already been there, right before I'd sprinted across the road to accost my target. Thankfully, Pete didn't notice it.

'Skinny cappuccino,' Pete added. A pang so strong I almost gasped. Every time we were out together and Pete ordered that, Dee would howl with laughter and tease him for his metrosexual ways. Breathe. Breathe. I tried to fight down the tsunami of desperation and loss. I needed her here so badly. Breathe. Breathe.

Cheery waitress backed off, her blonde ponytail swinging behind her.

'Look, Jen, I'm sorry...' He paused, and I didn't rush to fill the silence. Let him struggle with this until he found a way to explain what had happened. Didn't he owe me that, at least? 'I should have called. Or come to see you. I know I've been totally shit.'

No arguments from me – just surprise that an articulate guy I'd spent half my life with, a man I'd plan to stay with until the end of time, was now struggling to string a sentence together. This was surreal. Completely bizarre.

I couldn't help pitching in. I had so many questions and judging by his current level of eloquence, I couldn't see him volunteering the answers.

'Where are you living?'

'I'm staying with Mike from the office. He had a spare room he was renting out. West end. I'll text you the address… so you can send on any mail.'

I saw the tiny muscle in the side of his jaw throb and I knew he was hating every minute of this. He didn't want to see me. Wow. It shouldn't have been a surprise, but somehow, when the thought landed, it was like I'd been emotionally tasered.

'Have you been there the whole time?' I tried to keep it level and controlled. I wanted to reach over and touch his face. Or slap it. I wanted to hold his hand. Or break it. Most of all, I wanted to roll back time to just a few months ago, when we were happy and normal and in love, and I woke up every morning curled into his body and then kissed him when he opened his eyes. He'd touch my face, and smile, and I'd think how lucky we were.

Were. Past tense. I'd slipped so far into the past, it took his reply to jolt me back to where we were now.

'Pretty much. I went to Lanzarote for a couple of weeks. Club La Santa,' he said.

Of course. I should have known. It was a sports resort that he visited at least once a year, usually in the winter, because it was the closest place that was pretty much guaranteed weather good enough to cycle, swim and run until his heart was content. A few times I'd gone with him, a couple of times Dee and Luke tagged along too. Luke and I would lie in the shade drinking Sangria, while our athlete partners hiked up a hill or did a ten-mile jog before lunch, for fun.

'With Arya?' I don't know where that came from, but from his astounded response, I was relieved to see I was off the mark.

'No, of course not. On my own. Just need some time to think.'

I bit my tongue. He needed time to think, but he hadn't pitched up at our door the minute he landed back on Scottish soil, so it was fairly obvious his thoughts didn't extend to missing me and wanting me back.

'And what conclusions did you come to?'

He was given a couple of moments extra to think about it because cheery waitress arrived back with our coffees. We fell silent until she'd retreated.

'Jen, I'm sorry,' he repeated. 'I know my timing was crap, and I didn't mean it to happen like that, but come on, you must have known things had been heading that way for a while?'

This was like talking to a stranger, one who was describing a situation that I absolutely didn't recognise.

'I didn't.' I replied, honestly.

'Really?' His turn for surprise.

'I mean, I knew things weren't great and you seemed a bit... distracted... but I just assumed you were going through a fed-up phase. I asked you so many times if something was wrong and you always said everything was OK. What was I supposed to take from that? How was I supposed to know that

"I'm OK" actually meant, "I'm unhappy in this relationship and I plan to bail out at the first opportune moment? Or the pretty crappiest moment ever, as it turned out."'

I must have raised my voice because the couple who'd just sat down at the corner table a few feet away both turned at the same time to look at us. Bugger.

Pete didn't notice. He just took a sip of his skinny bloody cappuccino and put the mug back on the table before he spoke again. 'I just didn't know how to tell you.'

'Tell me what?' Jesus. This was like having a conversation where the other person was speaking a completely different language and you didn't know what they were saying but you had a fair idea they were trying to ask for the nearest exit.

He sighed. 'Tell you that I didn't want to be with you anymore.'

Wow. Just wow. I mean, he was stating the obvious but wow, it hurt.

It took me a moment to recover. 'Why?'

He was just staring at the froth on his cappuccino now. 'So many reasons.'

Ouch. Really? And I'd spotted none of them.

He went on, 'Come on, Jen, we'd been together since we were fifteen…' Once more, I noticed the past tense. 'That's half our lives. And it wasn't working anymore. We'd lost that spark and we were in a rut. It was all so mundane, and predictable…'

I thought it was familiar and wonderful.

'…and boring. We were totally stagnating, Jen. Didn't you see that?'

'No. I didn't.'

If he heard the words I'd managed to squeeze out, he didn't acknowledge them. It was as if he'd warmed up to his subject all of a sudden and had found his voice.

'Didn't you ever wonder if there was something else out there for us? If we'd settled too soon? If there was more to life than just staying in the same jobs, living in the same house, doing the same things over and over…'

I flipped from wanting answers to not being able to listen to any more of this.

'No,' I objected. 'You make it sound like we had some terrible, tedious life, but we didn't, Pete. Yes, so we'd been together since we were fifteen and I get that relationships that start that young don't usually last the course, but I just thought we were lucky. Found the right one. And I thought we'd move house, keep doing new things, going new places, I thought we'd do it all together. I thought the next step for us was kids and we'd grow and change, but we'd last a lifetime. I really did. You used to say that's what you wanted too.'

He did. This wasn't all on me. To the couple at the nearby table, the waiting staff and everyone else that was trying to pretend that they were not listening, it would seem that I had totally misjudged our whole relationship. Hell, even I was beginning to think that was the case. I needed to remind him, to show that this hadn't been a one-way deal.

'Pete, only last year when we were in Florida you said you wanted to bring our kids there. We picked out names, remember? And yes, it was all a joke, and we would never have actually called them Epcot and Pluto, but don't tell me there wasn't a grain of reality in all that…'

'There was!' he said, defensively.

'So what changed? How did we go from that to this? When did you start feeling…'

'Trapped,' he added, helpfully.

'Trapped? Pete, we were in love! It wasn't a bloody siege situation.'

He took another sip of his coffee and then fell silent again.

I struggled for words, still completely bewildered by the whole thing. There had to be more. Something else. You didn't just go from loving someone so much you spent fifteen years together and picked out Disney-themed names for your children, to feeling like you had to escape their clutches. There had to be something else he wasn't telling me. Was he ill? Did he have some kind of life-threatening condition? Had he won the lottery and didn't want to split the cash? Had he embezzled money and he was just waiting to get caught? Or was I clutching at wild theories because the truth was something far more obvious…

'Is there someone else?'

'No.' Everyone else in the shop would absolutely believe the denial. It had been quick. It had been unequivocally firm. But I saw it. There it was. The flicker of his eyes to the right. The little vein in the side of his jaw, beating even more rapidly than before. The coffee cup lifted to his mouth to distract from the thing he didn't want me to see. He was lying. I knew he was lying.

'Arya?' I probed, ignoring what he'd said. I realised I'd already asked but in every good cop show interrogation they return to the same questions over and over in the hope of tripping up the offender. The chummy scene I'd witnessed earlier was evidence for the prosecution. 'It's Arya,' I declared, having convinced myself in approximately three seconds.

He put the cup down again. 'Jen, there's no one else.' Lie number two. I could feel it.

Behind the counter, cheery waitress had even stopped pretending to be wiping her tray with a cloth, completely entranced by the conversation.

'I haven't been seeing anyone.' Lie number three.

Something crumbled inside me. That was it. Despite his denials, I knew I'd got it right. Someone else. In truth, it didn't actually matter who it was. It could be Arya. It could be someone at the gym. It could be cheery flipping waitress. All that mattered was that he'd felt enough for someone else to walk away from me. And much as I wanted to tell him we'd get through this, that we could still make it work, I'd be wasting my breath.

I wasn't even sure I meant it. I still loved him, of that there was no doubt. Despite what he'd done, I still couldn't imagine a future that he wasn't in. But none of that was enough, because although he was sitting in front of me, he was gone. Out of my life. Disconnected from us.

Not once had he asked me how I was. How I was coping without Dee. How Luke was, or Val or Don. The people we'd been around, who were like family to us for the last fifteen years. He hadn't said a single thing about our lives together, other than to tell me the reasons it wasn't right.

I'd no idea how that could happen, how a steel door could just snap down and cut off a whole existence, blocking out every relationship that had been there before, but it had.

'I'll stay at Mike's for a while, and we can sort out the house when you're ready. I don't mind if you want to sell it or buy me out. Whatever's best for you.'

Best for me? None of this was best for me. It was distinctly not bloody best for me. I hadn't even thought about the house. My house. I'd loved it. It was the only one I'd ever owned, but in truth, I could no longer walk up the front path without seeing Dee lying there, leaving us. In the days before the funeral I'd considered selling it, but I'd thought it would be a joint thing, Pete and I picking out somewhere new, somewhere to start a new chapter together. Since then, I'd been too stunned by his leaving to give it a second thought. Until now. He wasn't coming back. He'd never live in that house again.

'So that's it?' I whispered. 'It's just over?'

'It is.'

15

Val

Every nerve in my body shot to the surface of my skin and Josie put her hand on my arm, a safety precaution in case I opened the car door and bolted across the street. I couldn't have done that even if I wanted to because I knew my trembling legs wouldn't carry me.

The street light a few metres along the road illuminated the house and I focused on the black-clad figure that was now locking the door, turning, walking down the path and...

It wasn't him. The shape and height gave it away initially, but it was only when the figure reached the end of the path and opened the gate, that I could clearly see that it was a woman. His mother? An aunt? Older sister? Much older, I could see now, probably about my age.

'Think that's his mum?' Josie wondered, before answering her own question, aping my thoughts. 'Must be. Too old to be a sister.'

Closing the gate behind her, the woman turned right and headed along the street, away from us, head down, walking fast. I had no idea what to do. I glanced back at the house. It was in complete darkness now so there was obviously no one home. I could stay and wait to see if he came back but he could be anywhere. Staying somewhere else. Out on the town. Back in jail. Dead. The last one slipped in. I hoped it was true.

'What do we do now?' Josie asked.

I started the engine. 'Let's go home.'

'Are you sure?'

'I am. You've indulged my madness long enough. Thanks Josie.'

She leaned over and squeezed my arm again, this time from a place of love as opposed to crime prevention. 'You sure?'

'Yep, let's go home.'

'Thank God. My arse is numb and I'm dying for a pee.'

I indicated and then waited until the car I could see in my wing mirror passed, before pulling out. The street was 30 mph, speed bumps every few yards, so I took it slowly. Going home was the right thing to do, although I couldn't deny I was curious.

'You've got to wonder what she's like though.'

'Who?'

'The woman. His mother. I mean, what kind of person raises a scumbag like that? How does that happen? Does she even care? Does she really give a flying toss about what he did to my girl?'

'Don't torture yourself, Val,' Josie replied. I knew she was saying it for my own good but it didn't make me feel any better.

'I want to know what she's like. I want to tell her how my Dee died, what our family has lost, what her son did and see her face when I do it, see if there's even a hint of care.'

I stopped at the give way, my indicators flashing to signal that I was turning left, heading back towards Josie's house.

To the right, I could still see the woman, a few yards up ahead. I pressed the accelerator, went straight ahead.

Josie pointed out the error. 'Pet, you were meant to turn left there.'

'I know, but I just want to see where she goes.'

'Oh bloody hell, Val. Come on, love. Did we not have a wee moment back there when we decided the madness was done for the night?'

'We did, but I just need to see where she goes. Humour me, Josie.'

'Unless I want to exit the car while it's moving, I don't have much bloody choice, do I? Christ almighty, this is turning into an episode of *Cagney and Lacey*. And I don't remember one where Cagney ever peed her pants while chasing a suspect, so you'd better cut this out and get me to a loo pronto. My bladder isn't what it used to be.'

'She's turning the corner,' I said, ignoring Josie's objections.

'That takes you on to the main road just along from Tesco. There's a load of bus stops there. She's probably catching a bus and I tell you, Val Murray, I am not chasing public transport across Glasgow and neither are you. We're going home, I'm making a dash for the loo, and then we'll have a cup of tea and discuss all the reasons this can't happen again.'

I was still ignoring her.

Wilkie's mother walked past the first bus stop, then the second, then just before she got to the third, she cut down a path to the right and headed into Tesco. Bit late to be doing her shop, but fair enough. Maybe she worked shifts, or didn't sleep, or was just nipping in to get something she needed for the morning.

Without even thinking it through, I indicated and swung round to the right, into the car park, just as she disappeared into the store.

'Tell me we're not going in after her, only I swear to God my bladder won't stand up to sneaking down the frozen food aisle.'

'We're not following her,' I said, archly.

Josie raised an eyebrow of doubt.

'Didn't you say you needed the loo? So here's the nearest one. I'm not having you ruining my seats. They're genuine PVC,' I told her, aware that she wasn't convinced for a second.

'And you're just going to wait here for me?' she asked, the question loaded with suspicion.

'No, I'll come in. Need to pick up a loaf for Don's sandwiches tomorrow.'

'I want you to know that I don't believe a word of it, but my need to pee is greater than my need to call your bluff.'

She opened the door and half walked, half ran to the door, with me striding to keep up with her. What the hell were we like? Two women of vintage, on a stake out, following people, and now stalking them in supermarkets. Or at least, one stalker, and one endlessly loyal pal caught up in the madness and along for moral support. I was really beginning to think I needed help. A sudden thought pinged into my head – under different circumstances, Dee would think this was hilarious. It was just the kind of thing she'd do and, if she was here, she'd be right with us, giggling somewhere between the kitchen rolls and the quilted Andrex.

Inside, the choices were a left turn for the café, a right turn to the tills and the toilets or straight ahead into the store. Josie immediately veered right to the loo and I just kept on going, through the fruit and veg section, up to the deli on the back wall. No sign of her. I turned right into the soft drinks aisle, nope nothing. I strode on, walking at a normal pace so that I didn't look out of place. At the bottom of each aisle, I'd look along the length of the tills to make sure she wasn't already checking out, but no sign of her.

The tinned veg and sauces aisle. Nothing.

Pet food. No sign.

Household goods, then dairy, then meats, fish, and, finally, frozen foods. Where the hell was she? How could she have just vanished into thin air? She had definitely come in here, I was sure of it.

It came to me like a lightning bolt. The toilets. She must have nipped in there first. Bloody hell, Josie could be washing her hands next to her right now.

The young girl serving an elderly gent at the till looked at me with interest as I dashed past them and through the checkout without stopping. There was every chance she was about to signal the security guards that I was a possible shoplifter, so I got in first.

'Your toilets over there, love?' I asked her.

She nodded and gave me a faint smile. Hopefully she now just thought I was a woman in a hurry as opposed to a woman with three tins of corn, a packet of salami and a pair of American tan tights under my coat.

In the toilets, my eyes struggled to adjust to the blue tinged light. I'd read somewhere that the reason for the blue bulbs was that it stopped junkies being able to see their veins well enough to inject. I'd no idea if that was true but it was a pretty depressing thought that someone could be so desperate they'd mutilate themselves in a supermarket toilet.

The doors on all three cubicles were closed, but I could see that only one of them had the engaged sign showing.

I pushed open the first two just to be sure and they both swung open. Must be the third, but surely that would be Josie, unless I'd missed her and she was currently scouring the milk and bread aisles for me.

I squatted down, and craned my neck towards the floor to see if I recognised the shoes under the gap at the bottom of the door, and of course she picked that moment to swing it open.

'I swear to God, you're going to get us arrested,' Josie announced.

'Oh, shut up and help me up. My knees have seized.'

'Lacey never said that to Cagney,' she retorted, scooping one arm under mine and hoisting me up.

'Thanks.'

'Did you find her?' she asked.

'Nope. That's why I was looking under the door. I wondered if she'd come in here.'

Josie was washing her hands in front of the mirror. 'I haven't heard anyone else in here so I don't think so. Hey, I look ten years younger in these blue lights. Think I might invest in them for my whole house.'

I waited until the hand dryer had switched off before pulling open the door, defeated, depressed, crushed that I hadn't found her.

'Home?' she asked.

'Home,' I agreed. What else could I say? Tonight had been a horrendous explosion of emotions, of grief, of desperation, but I'd achieved nothing except torturing myself even more. And Josie was right. What was the point? There was nothing to be gained. Dee was still dead. That wee prick was still not. And I was just going to have to accept it. What did it matter where he lived, or what his mother thought, or what

I wanted to say to them – I wasn't going to do it and even if I did, I'd be the one to come off the worst. They'd probably end up getting me done for harassment and where would I be then? No, behaving like this was letting them win, letting them take even more from us, from me, and I'd be damned if I'd let that happen. I needed to go home. Home. To my Don. To my son. To the rest of my life. Yes, it would be without Dee, but I'd just have to find a way to live with that.

We walked towards the exit, tills to our right, concession stores to our left, all of them closed up now. A pharmacy. I remember the days when they were called a 'chemist'. An optician. A travel agent. That immediately made me think of Dee.

Josie slipped her arm through mine. 'Oooh, look at that. A week in Tenerife, all inclusive.' A pause. 'Why don't we do that, Val? You could do with a break and I never say no to a week of factor fifty.'

She was still at it, trying to persuade me to take a break, but I couldn't. Don't get me wrong, I could see the sense in it and Don wasn't due any time off until the summer, so he wouldn't mind me going away for a few days with Josie. In fact, I think he'd be relieved. That didn't mean I could do it though. I tried to steer the subject away from me.

'It's Jen that needs the break. Poor lass. Her world's imploded,' I sighed. 'I'm glad she's going away for a few days. It can only do her good.'

I could see the worry in Josie's eyes as she replied. 'Aye, she was looking awful when I left her tonight. She's lost without your Dee.'

I didn't doubt it. Those girls had spent almost every waking hour together since they were kids and now that had been snatched away.

Josie continued, 'I was going to call her later and see how she was doing.'

I stopped abruptly. We'd reached the front doors of the shop to our left, but what had stopped me in my tracks was what was straight ahead, in the coffee shop area. There were about twenty tables, but only two of them were taken. At one sat the elderly man who'd been at the checkout when I passed on the way to the loos. At the other, a couple of teenagers, holding hands and staring into each other's eyes. Neither interested me. What had caught my attention was the woman who was clearing debris off the other tables, loading up her tray, wiping down the Formica. It was her. I was sure of it.

'What's up?' Josie asked, unaware as to why we'd stopped.

There was no way I was telling her. I didn't want her worrying about me and checking up on me every two minutes to see where I was and whether I'd ventured back over this way.

'Nothing. Just realised I forgot to get that loaf for Don's packed lunch tomorrow.'

'Want to go get it?'

'No, it's fine,' I assured her, as convincingly as I could. 'Let's just head back to your house. I can always pop back here and get one later.'

16

Jen

Most of the seven hours over the Atlantic had been spent staring at the same page of my book, replaying every detail of the conversation with Pete. Then I'd tried Facebook, Twitter, Instagram, but he'd never been in the least bit interested in social networking and as far as I could see that hadn't changed. Nothing. Verging into stalking territory, I'd eventually found Arya's Facebook page but it was private and there was nothing to see.

How could I not have known any of this was coming? I'd heard of things like this before, where one half of a couple thought they were happily married until their partner went off with his secretary, or announced she was living a secret life as an escort, or they discovered their other half had another family, a wife and six kids, in a different town. I always thought it was down to careless naïvety, that there must have been signs, clues along the way.

I guess there had been with Pete. He'd been a bit withdrawn. A little detached. More low-key than usual. But not for long, maybe a few months or so, and not to the extent that it was overly worrying. I hadn't taken it seriously, and Dee and Luke, who spent almost as much time with him as

I did, hadn't thought it was cause for concern either. I so wished now that I'd taken Dee up on her offer to interrogate him and get to the bottom of it.

Another lost wish. I wished she were here. I wished she hadn't gone to the car that day. I wished we were all exactly the same as we were three months ago. Too many wishes, all of them meaningless now.

My stare had now moved from my book to the window, but I still wasn't taking anything in. I liked New York, but I didn't love it as much as Dee, who made it her mission to get here at least three times a year. For me, it was too busy, too chaotic, but I was going to have to suck it up and get on with it. It was time for me to step up. No more wimping out. We needed new stuff for the blog, new experiences and ideas. We'd lost a few subscribers lately and I knew it was because the content had dramatically dipped without Dee's input. She'd worked hard to get every one of those followers and she'd be mad as hell if I let it slide. No choice then.

Traffic from Newark was as busy as ever, so what should, distance-wise, have been an hour's journey, took almost two. The hotel, just off Times Square, was a favourite boutique one Dee had stayed in before, but it had been refurbished, so she had wanted to come back and cover the relaunch and renovation. Yet another thing she never got to do.

The receptionist was in her twenties, with flawless dark skin and cheekbones that looked like they'd been carved out of bronze.

'I have a reservation – it should be under Dee Harper from Sun, Sea, Ski.'

She checked the screen. I was just about to explain the change of name when she said, 'Ah, yes, here it is. And I have a letter for you here also.'

She fished in a drawer and pulled out a white envelope with Dee's name on the front. Probably tickets for one of the events that she'd booked.

'Thank you,' I said, shoving it into my bag.

'I can see that our marketing department has discounted your room by eighty per cent, so all I need is your passport and your credit card for the incidental charges.'

I handed over my Sun, Sea, Ski business credit card, and waited until she ran it through the machine, before handing it back with a blinding white smile. I was just about to hand over my passport, when a group of Japanese tourists poured through the door, filling the whole hallway area with chatter. I saw the mild anxiety on the receptionist's face as she stuck my passport in the photocopier, pressed a button, retrieved it and handed it back to me without glancing at it. Again, I was about to explain the name change on the room, when she signalled to the concierge and said, 'Bill will take you to your room, and please don't hesitate to let me know if we can do anything for you. Have a great stay.'

Bill stepped forward and took my case, just as the first of the tour group started to speak to the receptionist in halting English. This was no time for confusing the issue with name changes and explanations of Dee's death, so instead I decided to come back down later.

The room on the third floor was obviously newly decorated, with a thick charcoal carpet, high-gloss cream furniture and crisp white bedding with a thick silver fur throw across the bottom third of it. It oozed simple class and luxury. Good choice, my friend. I like your style.

My mobile rang. Luke. 'Hey how are you doing?'

'I'm OK. Just got here and checked in. Dee arranged a doozy of a suite – it's beautiful.'

'She always did like a bit of class.'

'I was just thinking the same thing,' I told him, smiling, yet sad. 'Feels weird though. Like I'm walking in her shoes. It should be Dee who's here, Luke, not me.'

'I know, Jen, but if there was anyone else she'd want to be checking into her five-star suite, it's you. Thanks for doing it. I kind of feel like as long as the shop and the blog and some of the things that mattered to her are still around, then we've still got a bit of her here.'

'You're right. Are you OK? Having a quiet night in?'

'Yeah, I'm bushed. Just going to head to bed shortly. I'm a pretty exciting guy these days.'

I laughed. 'So I see. OK, I'll drop you a text tomorrow. If I survive whatever it is Dee had in store. She just had places and times in her diary, so I'm not quite sure what I'm in for. I didn't pack a bulletproof vest or a parachute. Do you think I'm doomed?'

'Definitely.' It was good to hear him laugh. He had always been the most live for the moment, life's a blast, kind of guy – I wondered if he'd ever feel like that again.

I wondered if I would either. 'Right, I'll report in tomorrow. If the line is bad it's because I'm in ER.'

He was still laughing when I hung up and it made me feel a bit better. I should have told him about meeting Pete last night but I was glad I hadn't. He had enough on his plate. The last thing he needed was to listen to my woes too.

Right, enough feeling sorry for myself. I could almost hear Dee screaming at me to get a grip and get out there.

I decided to have a quick change and head straight out. I checked Dee's Google calendar. I'd ported it over to my phone, to make sure I didn't miss anything. 'Westside Jazz Club, 8 p.m.,' was the only entry for the rest of the day.

I pressed on the link and it took me to the address. Ever efficient, our Dee.

I threw the phone on the bed and it was only then I noticed the beautiful bouquet in the alcove by the window, a small white card popping out of the middle of the blooms.

The marketing department were definitely trying to woo her. It wasn't a huge surprise. For the price of a well-picked bunch of flowers and a discount on a room that might be lying empty anyway, they could get a review that would reach thousands of potential travellers. I believe it was what Dee used to call a 'win-win kerching moment'.

I missed her. Again.

I kicked off my boots and padded over to the window, my toes sinking into the plush pile of the carpet. I opened the card.

Welcome back. I missed you... x

I read it again. I didn't understand. I missed you? Missed who? This didn't sound like something from the marketing department and it didn't make any sense. As far as I knew Dee didn't even know anyone in New York, let alone someone that would buy her flowers and 'miss her'.

Logical explanations began to pop into my head. They must have been left for the person that was in the room before I checked in. Maybe that person hadn't even noticed them and the cleaners hadn't cleared them away, so they were still there. Or perhaps they'd been delivered to the wrong room. I looked again at the note. It didn't say 'To Dee.' Of course, it had been a mix-up. Mistaken identity. I'd raise it with the receptionist on the way downstairs and ask her to relocate the flowers to their rightful owner.

I jumped into the shower, letting the water soothe away the aches from the flight. It couldn't do anything about the pain caused by every flashback to the conversation with Pete. I was convinced he wasn't coming back. This was more than some early mid-life crisis. It was more like a finality. A closure on a door that I wasn't ready to close. Before I knew it, tears were mingling with the water from the shower.

I stayed there way too long, the jets blasting away every hope and dream I had for the future. Eventually, my body pummelled and my fingertips wrinkled with moisture, I turned the shower off. The towels were thick and soft, and I wrapped one around me as I went back into the main room of the suite. Maybe I could just extend my stay here. Have a break. Wasn't that what everyone had been telling me I should do? I needed time to figure out how to begin to make myself feel better again because I knew I couldn't go on like this. The misery was killing me, bit by bit.

I sat down at the dressing table, took a comb out of my handbag, and ran it through my hair, before taking the hairdryer out of the drawer and blasting my hair dry. I pulled it back, plaited the bottom half around to the side, and tied a bobble on to the end. It wouldn't win any prizes for style, but it was as good as it was going to get.

I threw the comb back in the bag, and was just fishing out some moisturiser when I noticed the letter I'd been given at reception. I ran my finger along the seal and pulled out a note. Headed paper. The Waldorf Astoria. Dee had stayed there last year and I remembered how she'd raved about it.

The words were written with handwriting that I instinctively knew was male.

My darling Dee, Usual place. Usual time. Can't wait x

What the...? For the second time in the last hour or so I didn't understand what was going on.

My darling Dee? It sounded intimate but there had to be an innocent explanation. Of course there was. Dee would never cheat on Luke or do anything to hurt him. Sure, she had a real thirst for life and loved anything that got her adrenalin going but if she was doing anything untoward, I'd have known about it. She trusted me with all her secrets and she knew she could tell me anything and I'd never judge her.

There was another story here. Maybe just someone with an overenthusiastic line in endearments. A friend. Someone she'd met before. Loads of the PRs were like that – it was all 'darling' this and 'sweetheart' that. All air kisses and effusive hugs. That was it. For sure. Nothing to see here. Time to move on. Except...

I took the letter over to where I'd left the card off the flowers and compared the two.

Identical handwriting.

But what did that prove? Nothing, other than that it was the same excitable, overfamiliar PR person who'd written them both.

I checked the Google calendar again, even though I knew what time her first entry was at.

Yep, Westside Jazz Club 8 p.m.

Then there was one entry for tomorrow night. The Bar at the Baccarat Hotel, 9 p.m. I looked it up – it was a gorgeous, upmarket bar in a hotel on West 53rd Street.

The final entry was the morning after that, before I headed to the airport to fly home. All it said was 'Breakfast at Tiffany's.'

So. As well as the travel expo at the Jacob Javits Convention Center tomorrow, she had planned to go see a jazz band, visit a swanky bar and have breakfast at Tiffany's. It all sounded like the kind of stuff that Dee loved to do on these trips, giving her material that she would then spin to make a great review or article for the blog and give our followers great suggestions for a fun, sexy New York experience. Nothing obviously suspicious there. Nothing untoward. I gave myself a shake and told myself to get a grip. Dee was coming here on company business and it was time I got on with fulfilling her plans. Grabbing my coat, I headed out, leaving the notes behind.

Despite the cold, I decided to walk to the jazz club, picking up a hot dog from a stand at the corner of Times Square on the way. It wasn't that they were a particular favourite, but they were one of the things Dee looked forward to most in the city. She'd land, get a cab to her hotel, then head for the first hot dog stand she could find. After that she'd have at least one every day she was here. It felt right that I did the same.

The wind was whipping up a storm and I was glad I'd brought a beanie and boots. Dee and I had the same pair, Hobbs sale, mine in black leather, hers in brown. How many times had that happened over the years? We'd bought the same stuff, turned up in similar outfits, picked out the same place for dinner. Luke used to joke that we shared a brain – a brain that now kept going back to those messages. Why? I'd already decided there was nothing illicit about them. Hadn't I? As I walked on, again, I found myself rationalising them. It was impossible that anything untoward was going on. Absolutely out of the question. Although, it did raise the point that I hadn't actually gone through Dee's contact lists and informed everyone she'd passed away. Of course, all our friends knew and I'd told all the regular customers, although not in the kind of blunt manner I'd used with Delilah, my least favourite customer of all time. The way I'd told her still made my toes curl, but I guess emotions got the better of me that day.

Anyway, I'd also responded to Dee's business emails, telling some that I knew she had a personal relationship with that she'd died, and just letting the others know that I'd be the new point of contact, but not giving an explanation as to why.

News of her death had been in our local newspaper but it hadn't made the nationals and we were grateful for that. Val absolutely didn't want it to turn into a media circus. She'd banned us from mentioning it on Facebook or any other social networking sites and we were only too happy to agree. It had been one of Dee's big bugbears. She hated it when someone died and suddenly their Facebook and Twitter pages were full of woeful comments of loss and regret from people they'd met once at a bus stop. Her words.

'When I cop it, don't you dare let that happen to me. No eulogy. No false, patronising crap,' she'd proclaimed. 'And if Danny Jones from school posts a single message of sadness, write back that I still think he was a complete twonk for two-timing me in first year.'

I'd dissolved into giggles. 'What makes you think I'll still be here? You're bound to outlive me,' I'd countered.

'How do you work that out?'

'Dee, you run three times a week so you've got the cardiovascular system of a racehorse. I do no exercise whatsoever, so I have the cardiovascular system of a geriatric donkey on twenty fags a day.'

'True,' she'd accepted. 'OK. So I'll sort you out then. Who do you want postmortem messages of revenge delivered to?'

I thought about it. 'You can tell my dad he was crap, but that's hardly a newsflash. Other than that...' I pondered some more. 'Nope, I've got nothing.'

She'd sat back, stretched, then twisted her hair up and stuck a pencil in it to hold it in place. I'd seen her do that a thousand times before and it still made me smile 'Jen, you really need to get a bit more excitement in your life. By your age there should be a few more grudges. Get out there. Live dangerously. Take a few risks. Do some stuff you're absolutely not supposed to do. Piss people off,' she'd gone on, enjoying the theme.

'You're right,' I'd said, knowing absolutely for sure that she wasn't. All those things were Dee's domain. I'd settle for stability, contentment and predictability. That was my comfort zone. A psychologist would have a field day with that. Losing my mum at an early age. A father who had zero responsibility and cared for nothing except himself and where his next pint was coming from. I didn't ever want to play the victim card because I was lucky – the fact that he was so useless had compelled Val and Don to swoop in and take care of me and make me their own, which was a much better deal than living with my dad, even on the rare occasions that he was home and sober and he remembered he had a child. However, I'd be naïve to think my childhood didn't shape my need for security, just as Dee's unwavering surety that her mum and dad would support everything she ever did, and always be there to catch her if she fell, gave her the confidence to take crazy risks and occasionally live on the edge.

My mind went a full circle now. Was that what she'd been doing here? Taking a risk and living on the edge?

No. She wouldn't play fast and loose with Luke's heart and their marriage like that.

'So tell me, Jen...' Another conversation came back to me, this time on our sofas in my lounge on a Sunday afternoon. 'Hypothetically... If you could have a wild night with someone, say... Matt Damon... and you absolutely knew there was no way you'd ever get caught, would you do it?'

I'd laughed. 'Yeah, because Matt Damon is lying in bed in the Hollywood Hills right now thinking, "I need to fire up the jet and get to Scotland because I'm dying to shag that Jen chick who works in Sun, Sea, Ski."'

'You have no powers of imagination at all, do you?' she'd retorted, feigning disgust.

'None at all,' I'd agreed. 'But no. Not even Matt Damon. I'd be too self-conscious about my cellulite. What about you?' I carried on the hypothesis because it was making us laugh in between chocolate Hob Nobs. 'You can't have Matt Damon in case I change my mind; it would be weird for us to sleep with the same guy...'

'Yes, that's what would be weird about this scenario,' she'd said, giggling.

I continued, unperturbed by the sarcasm, 'If you could sleep with... Ben Affleck without getting caught, would you do it?'

'In a heartbeat,' she'd replied. 'Did you see him in *Batman*? Would need some amount of talc to get that suit off though.'

I pushed up on to one elbow so I could face her. 'You'd honestly sleep with another guy?'

'It's not any normal guy. Batman has superpowers,' she'd said.

I had an urge to probe deeper. 'And if it wasn't Batman? If it was just some gorgeous bloke that you met and you knew you'd never get caught. Would you?'

She was going to say no. Of course she was. Absolutely. I'd put my life savings on it.

'I don't know. Situation has never arisen.'

Just as well I didn't actually have any life savings.

She'd answered my question, but not with a definitive 'no', and now, as I traipsed through the streets of the East Village, I couldn't help wondering two things. One, why hadn't I got a bloody cab – this place was much further than I thought. And two, was that what was going on here? Had she found herself in a scenario that she felt she could get away with having a fling and gone for it?

I had an involuntary shudder and not just because of the cold.

Nope, I wasn't buying it. She wouldn't. For all the reasons I'd mentally listed earlier, the biggest being her love for her husband, she absolutely wouldn't.

'Evening ma'am.'

Thank God. A large guy with a bald head, shoulders the width of a sun lounger and a southern accent greeted me at the door to the club. He showed me inside, where a beautiful black woman, hair parted in the middle and flowing down her back, flashed her perfect, gleaming smile. The one I returned was somewhat substandard. I made a mental note to look into teeth whitening when I got home.

'Hi, I think I have a reservation under the name Dee Harper?'

The maître d' checked her iPad. 'You do indeed. Let me take your coat and then if you'd like to follow me.'

She checked my coat in at a small desk, then led me into the club. It was dark, and not yet busy, still early for the Friday night jazz scene to have got into the swing of things. The club was like the old speakeasies I'd seen in the movies. Dim lighting, just little lamps on small round tables, maybe thirty of them in the room. Deep red walls and a black carpet beneath my feet. On the stage at the front, bordered by red velvet curtains, was a lone guy with a saxophone, fingers moving like they were dancing across the notes.

I was shown to a front table at the far right of the stage, where a waitress appeared almost instantly. 'Hi, my name is Candy and I'll be serving you tonight. What can I get you to drink?'

'A vodka tonic please.' I rarely drank, but tonight it seemed like it was the right thing to do.

'Of course.' Candy headed off to the little bar I'd noticed at the back of the room, while I scanned the other tables, curiosity getting the better of me. Two tables had older couples sitting at them. I could make out the faces of the lady and gent closest to me, probably in their late seventies, both swaying almost hypnotically to the music. I noticed they were holding hands and immediately tears sprung to my eyes. What the hell was going on with me? I rarely cried, but lately I felt like I was a wailing mess every two minutes. I didn't even know why I was bloody crying. Actually, I realised, I did. I thought that would be Pete and I one day. Sitting in a café or a bar, in our seventies, still holding hands. Now that wasn't ever going to happen and I didn't even have my best pal here to make it better. And then I was bloody crying again. Dee would love this place. Had she been here already or was this her first time? I'd never heard her mention it, and as far as I knew she'd never blogged about it, but she'd been to New York so many times over the last decade that I wouldn't have been surprised if she'd been and just forgotten to mention it.

Focus. Don't wallow. Stop feeling sorry for yourself.

I cast my gaze around the room again. It was the kind of place where I felt I should be smoking an exotic cigarette, even though the one time I'd tried it I'd vomited into Val's cabbage patch and forced her to scrap that year's crop. Two tables had single guys at them. Nope, make that three. I caught the eye of a tall, suited guy who was being led to a table near mine by the beautiful maître d'.

Our connection lasted a split second and then he turned his attention to the waitress who'd appeared beside him and didn't give me another glance. Two other single blokes, one in his fifties, the other maybe a similar age to me, were eyes front to the stage, engrossed in the music. Further along the front row, a woman, wearing a silk jacket that was a kaleidoscope of colour, tapped her red-painted fingernails on the table in time to the music.

The waitress brought my drink and I sipped at it while mentally collecting snippets for the blog that I'd write up when I got back to the hotel. The décor, the vibe, the people, the music. This was a quintessential New York night. That was the headline. Dee would have come up with something better, but I wasn't as good at the creative stuff as she was. Maybe Luke could help until I got into the rhythm of it.

I could see Luke and Dee here. I thought again how this was her kind of place. To be honest, I wasn't much for jazz, but she'd love the music, the ambience, and the hint of decadence about it all.

My drink seemed to have evaporated so I ordered another one. The room was starting to fill up now and the sax player had been joined on stage by a double bass and a trumpet. All three were playing a bluesy tune that seemed brand new and recognisable all at the same time.

The second drink appeared on the table, then a third, and I realised halfway through that third drink that either my body or the room was starting to sway. I kind of liked it, but

I knew what that meant – I was about one more drink away from a cabbage patch situation and a hangover that would render me useless all day tomorrow. Time to head for my New York home. I had enough to write about and the club was getting pretty busy so they could probably do with my table back.

Outside, I got lucky and jumped into a cab vacated by a man who had just alighted. He held the door open for me and did an exaggerated bow. 'After you.'

'Thank you very much,' I said. It might have been slightly slurred but hopefully he didn't notice. No wonder Dee always said I was such a lightweight in the alcohol stakes. I'd had what? Three vodkas? Maybe four? Yep, four. Although I couldn't remember having ordered one of them – the waitress had just brought it over unbidden. Or did I order it? I must have. Actually I had no idea.

Back in my room, I dropped my clothes on the floor, an act of recklessness for me, drank a glass of water, and slid under the sheets. What a weird day. I was in New York. Alone. I was doing Dee's job. I was lying in bed, more than a little drunk. There were flowers in the window that came with an odd note. A strange letter in the same handwriting addressed to my departed friend. And I had absolutely no idea what was going on.

I wish she was here...

That was my last thought as I drifted off to sleep and the next thing I knew there was a drilling sound in my head and I was prising my eyes open. Oh dear God, the noise. It was deafening. That's what happened when I drank too much. I pushed myself up to a sitting position, swayed a little, then realised that the noise was all too real. Groaning, I padded over to the window, looked out, and yep, there was a guy with a jackhammer at the building site across the road. I hadn't noticed that when I arrived yesterday. I checked my watch. Eight in the morning. Crap, I'd overslept. Even though the next thing in the diary wasn't until noon I should be out by now, checking out cool places to go.

OK, time to get my act together. In a minute. Not quite yet. I sat back on the bed and lifted what was left of the night before's water. That had been a first. New York. Solo. A jazz bar. A little drunk. Dee would be proud, though.

Dee. I thought back to the weird stuff yesterday and decided that without a shadow of a doubt, it must be an overfamiliar, overenthused PR that had left the notes.

I chided myself. Nothing was going on. Of course it wasn't. I was a bit ashamed of myself for even contemplating that there could have been anything else to it.

I raised my eyes skyward. 'Sorry Dee,' I whispered. I could almost sense her pursed lips and see the arms folded across her chest in disapproval. 'Don't look at me like that,' I added for good measure.

Time for a shower. I got up, wobbled a little, thanks to a head rush, and crossed the room, and only then did I spot the envelope that had been slid under the door.

The words were in the same handwriting as yesterday's note. Of course they were.

My heart thudded a little faster and I just hoped it was a bill or a notification that some bloke would have a bloody jackhammer outside my window at eight in the morning.

Dee... Where were you? xx

I cast my eyes heavenward again. 'Care to explain this?' I asked.

17

Luke

Catch 22 situation. I pull on a pair of jeans and they fall off my arse. That's what all this running did to you. Then I decide to go shopping for better-fitting replacements. The thought of spending a day in a shopping centre looking for new clothes makes me want to hit my head off the wall. So I go for another run. And lose more weight. And my jeans fall off my arse again.

I had no idea how women did it. Dee would shop for new clothes at least once a month. Me? Same jeans for years, new T-shirts and jumpers at birthdays and Christmas, anything else, Dee picked up for me. I'm not proud but it's the way it was.

Only since she was gone did I realise how much she did. She paid the bills, she ordered the groceries that got delivered every week, she planned the trips, she bought the clothes. She didn't clean the house, because Josie popped by and took care of that once a week, but everything else was pretty much on her.

Sure, I did the DIY, a bit of decorating and kept our cars up to scratch, and yeah, I'd sometimes plan stuff for the weekends, but that was it. How crap was it that I only appreciated how much she did now that she was gone?

The other current issue on the crap scale? It was Saturday and I was headed into work for a couple of hours. We had a Monday deadline for a presentation to a new client and I just wanted to make sure everything was on point. I jumped in the car, and headed for town. The traffic wasn't as bad as weekdays, so I'd probably make it in under half an hour, then maybe I'd head to the gym. Or not. It was costing me way too much in jeans.

I pressed a couple of buttons on the hands-free set and connected to Sun, Sea, Ski.

Mark answered on the first ring.

'Hey mate, fancy heading to the gym when you're done for the day?'

'Let me consult my hectic social schedule,' Mark replied. I'd only met Dee's brother once before he came back for the funeral, when we went out to Australia on our honeymoon. He'd seemed like a pretty good guy, chilled out, laid-back, but I hadn't made an effort to keep in touch. It didn't matter though. Turns out first impressions were spot on and we'd slipped into a routine of going to the gym, heading to a sports bar, just kicking back and passing time. It suited him because he didn't know anyone here, and it suited me because I was a recently widowed sad bastard whose life had been obliterated by some screwed-up karma.

'Yep, turns out I'm free,' Mark said.

'Great, I'll swing by and get you at six.'

My shoulders relaxed a bit. OK, so I had plans for a Saturday night. It might only be the gym and a bar for a couple of pints, but at least it wasn't sitting in the house staring at all the reasons the past was so much better than now. Or hitting clubs, like some thirty-year-old saddo.

Which reminded me... I called another number on the hands-free, fully expecting it to go straight to voicemail, but to my surprise he picked up.

'All right mate?'

'Well, well, well, the invisible bloody man,' I countered.

A hesitant laugh. At least he had the self-awareness to sound embarrassed. There was no doubt Pete and I had initially become mates through the girls, but we'd rubbed along pretty well. After the funeral, my brothers stayed for a couple of weeks and Pete had hung out with us a few times but I'd barely seen him after that, and not at all in the last couple of months. I couldn't give a toss that he'd been a shit mate, but he'd really done a number on Jen, and if I was being honest, that's why I was calling. I'd known the guy for a long time and some insight into why he was acting like a prize dick would be useful.

'How you been?' I asked, trying to sound as normal as possible.

'Yeah, OK. Luke, I'm sorry that...'

'Don't worry about it,' I cut him off. I didn't need his apology. No use to me now.

'It's just been... Obviously you know Jen and I split.'

'Didn't see that one coming,' I told him honestly.

'Yeah, well...' That was it. Clearly I wasn't getting anything else, at least not on the phone. 'Look, why don't we grab a beer and a game of pool one night this week?'

'Yeah, sounds good. I've got a lot going on at work but let me give you a call when I know what night is good.'

'Sounds like a plan.'

I pressed the button on the steering wheel that disconnected the call. I'd bet my last tenner I wasn't going to hear from him.

The barrier in the office car park rose as I pulled up and I drove into my usual space.

OK, one more call. My daily fix. The same one I made every single morning when I arrived here. This one, I expected to go to voicemail; it always did.

'Hi this is Dee at Sun, Sea, Ski. Sorry I'm probably up a mountain, or below the sea, or lying in the sun, or avoiding work in some other way, but if you leave me a message, I'll call you back, I promise!'

You could hear the happiness and the gorgeous craziness in her voice and I knew that even if I hadn't been married to her, I'd have loved the way she sounded. And as I listened, I liked to tell myself that she was lying on a beach somewhere, or skiing down a black run, and she'd get back to me, as she always would, just as soon as she was able. It took me a few moments to shake the melancholy.

I switched the engine off and headed inside. There would usually be a couple of directors in on a Saturday, and I could see the lights on in their offices as I walked down the corridor on the way to the open-plan section I worked in. 'All the creative divisions gathered together in one large think tank' was how they pitched it. The truth was they'd probably read somewhere that the open-plan environment increased productivity because the endless stream of passers-by left no room for sitting all day playing Pacman or scanning Facebook on your laptop.

Callie saw me before I saw her. 'Hello there, didn't expect to see you today.'

'And I thought I was the only sad git who wanted to come in and check Monday's presentation,' I said, laughing.

'Guess not. And I was here before you so I think that makes me officially sadder than you.'

'Fair point,' I agreed.

'Great. Glad we had this chat. I feel so much better about myself now,' she said, joking. At least I think she was joking. Dee always said I was about as perceptive as mud when it came to other people's feelings. Maybe that's why I'd never sensed any annoyance from Callie after I ran out on her that evening in the bar. Since then, she'd been completely normal and we'd kept it all completely surface-level. Yep, I knew it was a cop out and I felt a bit crap about that. She'd opened up to me about losing her sister and I'd never mentioned it since. When she asked me how I was, I said 'fine'. It was all I could do for now. If we got into a situation where we were sharing our losses, I knew I couldn't be trusted not to fall apart and start wailing on her shoulder. Not a prospect I relished. Much better to keep this business. Cordial.

I switched on my Mac and waited for it to boot up. 'So how come you're in here on a Saturday afternoon? Is Justin The Wonderman Accountant off training for his next triathlon?' Safer ground. I'd been making fun of her boyfriend's reported perfection for years and she always entered into the spirit of it.

'Don't know,' she shrugged. 'We're not seeing each other anymore.'

Christ, I couldn't say anything right.

'Sorry, I didn't know. I wouldn't have mentioned it if... Oh, shite. Sorry.'

Only then did I notice she was laughing. 'My choice,' she said. 'I'm bearing up. Haven't ram-raided the ice cream freezer at Waitrose yet.'

'Good to know.'

My computer was up and running now and I opened my presentation and started working on it. I was engrossed in it for a few moments when I noticed she was smiling at me.

'What have I done now?'

Giggling, she shook her head. 'Nothing. That's the point. You are such a bloke. I'm the last one to play the gender card, but if you were a female colleague, there's a pretty good chance you'd be grilling me right now on every detail of the break-up and we'd be comparing notes on all our previous relationships. Not "Oh, you've chucked him. Fair enough then." Women aren't wired to stop that conversation at that point.'

'I prefer plausible deniability. Or maybe I just think that it's none of my business.'

She rolled her eyes like that was a bad thing. 'I'll never understand men,' she muttered.

'OK then, so why did you split up?'

There was a definite flicker of mischief in her eyes. 'Not telling you now.'

'And that's why I'll never understand women,' I countered, enjoying the banter. I didn't have enough of it in my life anymore.

We spent the next couple of hours sorting out the presentation until it was pretty much perfect, then another hour or so chatting about office politics. Or rather, Callie chatted, I listened, jaw dropping ever wider every time a new nugget of scandal was introduced. It seemed like half the agency was sleeping with a co-worker and the other half were conspiring to launch a managerial coup. It was like the employment equivalent of a reality TV show.

'How could I not know all this?' I asked, taking the coffee she handed over.

'Because you come in, do your job, leave, and don't gossip. It's very admirable but it means you miss all the best stuff.' She took a sip of her coffee. 'So, where you off to when you've finished here?' she asked.

'Just going to pick up my brother-in-law, then heading to the gym. I'm so rock and roll.' My brother-in-law. As I said it I realised it was the first time I'd referred to him as that – and technically the title no longer applied.

'And after?'

'Don't know. Probably a couple of pints at Oscars,' I said, naming the semi-trendy sports bar we occasionally popped into after a workout. 'He's over here from Australia, came back for the...' The word got stuck. It was the first awkward moment of the day. I cleared my throat and went on, '... funeral. He doesn't know many people so he's always happy to be dragged to a pub by my saddo self.'

'Is he single?'

'Erm, yeah.' Actually I had no idea. I knew he wasn't seeing anyone here, but I'd never asked if he had someone back in Australia.

'Good-looking?'

'Erm... Yeah, I guess. If you like fit surfer guys who look like they've just left the set of *Point Break*.'

She thought about that for a moment. 'My pal Lizzy and I are going out in the West End tonight, so we might just drop by and check out fit surfer guy. She's single. Got a thing for six-packs. Actually so have I.'

I didn't quite know what to say to that. And I had no idea if this would be cool with Mark or not.

She must have sensed my hesitation, because she seemed highly amused. 'Luke, I don't want to marry them off. We'll just stop by and have a drink.'

Something inside me sank. What the hell was wrong with me? It was just a co-worker, meeting up in a social situation, yet I couldn't seem to get my head round the idea that it was OK. Sort yourself out, Harper. 'No worries. Just didn't want him to think I was setting him up. I've a tendency to overthink things these days.'

'Well you should definitely stop that,' she said, picking up a grey bag and throwing it over her shoulder.

'Sometimes thinking is definitely overrated. See you later.' Huge smile, a wink, and then she was off down the corridor.

See, if I was overthinking things, I might conclude that she was flirting with me. And flattering as it was because she was pretty gorgeous, smart and funny, that might scare the crap out of me.

I got to Sun, Sea, Ski just as it was closing. There was a welcome party waiting for me.

'Luke, ma love, how are you doing?' Josie greeted me, crushing me in a bear hug. 'Dear God, are you wearing those magic pants or are you fading away?' she asked, pinching the area of my sides where my love handles used to hang proud. The irony didn't escape me that Dee would love the shape I was in now.

'Magic pants. Definitely. Mark wears them too.'

'Yup,' Mark agreed, pulling the door shut and listening until the alarm stopped beating.

'Good grief! That mental image will keep me amused for a long time,' she cackled, as she jumped into her purple Volkswagen Beetle and roared off.

'She's crazy, but I think I love her,' Mark said. 'Don't tell me all the ways that's wrong.'

'Nah, she's some woman.'

Mark held up a phone. 'By the way, I gave in and bought a mobile. My Oz one doesn't work here and I needed it in case my head office was looking for me. I'll text you my number. What's yours?'

I gave it to him and he stored it, then my phone dinged to show it had received a text.

Congratulations, you are now the fifth person to be granted my phone number. Use it wisely.

'Who are the other four?' I asked, laughing.

'Work, my mum, my dad and Jen. I really need to get out more.'

'You and me both. Shop busy today?'

'Yeah, not too bad. Mum came in for a while to help out, but she was knackered so I said to her to go home. She reckons she's coming down with something but she still tried to hang around. Think she's worried about us being short staffed.'

Irritation crept up the back of my spine. 'Yet another way he's a dick.'

Out of the corner of my eye, I saw Mark turn to stare at me, and I realised I'd said that out loud. 'Who's a dick?'

'Sorry, mate. Talking about Pete.'

It took Mark a minute. 'Jen's bloke? The fella who dumped her? Yeah, he sounds like a walking douche. But what's he got to do with the fact that my mum is crook?'

I'd learned enough Oz-speak on my trip there to know that meant sick.

'At weekends, or if Dee was away, or if Jen had accounts to file, then me or Pete would come in to help out. Can't get over the fact that he's just walked away and left her, dropped her right in it.' I turned to him said, deadpan, 'Thus, this is another way in which he is, in actual terms, a dick.'

'No argument from me, mate,' he said, grinning.

Jen said a few of the customers in the shop had major hots for this guy and – not that I'm an expert on these things

149

– but I could see why. He was like one of those blokes off billboards. He didn't have the appearance of someone who had a fondness for a pie. In fact, his six-pack showed through his T-shirt. It had been bad enough hanging out with super-fit Pete the dick, but Mark was in a whole other league. I might have lost a few pounds with this running lark, but I wasn't going to win any Action Man lookalike competitions any time soon. Not that I minded. My ego could take it.

We talked about football on the way to the gym, a conversation that then continued through the workout, and on the drive to the pub. I pulled into the car park, a secure area that I could leave the car in if I decided to have more than one pint. I'd be happy to just have a couple and head home.

It was only when we got into the pub that I remembered what Callie had said earlier; I'd yet to fill Mark in that we'd be having company.

I carried our pints across the packed bar, and over to the high table we'd managed to snag in the corner. Bruce Springsteen was playing on the sound system, but not so loud that you couldn't have a normal conversation. There were a dozen huge screens suspended from the ceiling around the U-shaped bar, each one of them showing a different sports channel. From where we were sitting we had basketball on the screen. NBA. Local derby, Clippers versus Lakers. I watched J.J. Redick take a shot from just outside the three point line. It swished straight in.

'Listen, I hope it's OK with you but I mentioned to one of the girls I worked with that we were coming here tonight and she said she might drop by.'

Mark's pint paused on the way to his mouth and he looked at me.

I immediately went on the defensive. 'Nothing like that. Look, mate, I know we've never really discussed it but your sister was pretty much irreplaceable and I can't see that ever changing.'

Mark finally got the beer the rest of the way and took a drink, before answering. 'I know it's a pretty weird thing to say, but I didn't know Dee that well. I left when she was twelve and, after that, only saw her for short times, but I think I knew her well enough to have a fair idea that she wouldn't want you to mope around forever.'

I didn't know how to answer that and, to my total embarrassment, I felt my face begin to flush and my throat begin to close. This is why I didn't have conversations like this with my mates, let alone my dead wife's brother. Too uncomfortable. Too near that place that felt like someone was holding a hot poker to my chest.

Until a few months ago, I'd never cried, never had a panic attack, never felt anxious, rarely got angry. Now it happened when I was least expecting it, ambushing me when I really could do with just feeling fucking normal for one fucking day.

Jesus, I missed her. Missed our lives. Missed holding her at night. Missed her brilliant cooking. Her laugh. Her constant drive to enjoy herself. Her wild side. Her soft side. I missed everything.

It took me a while to trust myself to answer, without dissolving and embarrassing us both. 'Maybe, but not yet. I couldn't even imagine how that would happen.' Change the subject. 'What about you? Seeing anyone back in Australia?'

'That story might take a few pints,' he said, taking another sip of his beer.

Even I could detect that his answer sat somewhere between pissed off and bitter.

'Hit a nerve?' I asked, pointing out the obvious.

'Something like that. My job doesn't make it easy – I'm away for a month or two at a time. Makes it hard to keep a relationship going. I'd been seeing someone for a year or so. Tara.' He pulled out his wallet and showed me a picture of a blonde woman, maybe about thirty-five, tanned, walking towards the camera with a surfboard under her arm, her smile wide as she stuck her tongue out at the camera.

'She's a cracker. What happened?'

He shrugged. 'She was from New Zealand, worked at a dive school teaching tourists and kids. We'd hook up whenever I was onshore. I'd been thinking for a while about asking her to move in with me when I got back onshore last time, but her mum got sick and she went back to Christchurch to help her out.'

'So that was it?'

He nodded. 'Bit of a free spirit, Tara. Just stick with it as long as it felt good, she always said. I guess it stopped feeling good because I haven't heard from her since she left. Before I came back here I texted a couple of times but she didn't reply. Guess it's one of the reasons I'm still here. Next contract doesn't start for another few weeks and there was no point going back to nothing. Thought my mum would rather have me here but, to be honest, I'm not so sure now.'

That didn't make any sense. 'Val? She's made up that you're back. If she's acting a bit off it's just... you know. Her and Dee were really close. Must be so hard for her.'

Mark nodded. 'I get that. And don't get me wrong, she's not falling apart or anything. She just seems... empty. Jesus, this is all a bit deep, isn't it? Can we go back to analysing the defensive strengths and weaknesses of every team in the league?'

'Absolutely.'

'Excellent. I'll get the pints in.' He picked up his almost-empty glass and headed to the bar, returning ten minutes later with two fresh pints.

This was more like it. No complications. No hassle. Just football, basketball, and a bit of surface level chat with a bloke who was my brother-in-law, but not really.

And then Callie and her mate, Lizzy, arrived.

18

Jen

I read the note for the tenth time.

Dee… Where were you? xx

My dearly departed pal wasn't giving me any clues.

Two kisses. OK, didn't exactly confirm that this was a romantic thing. I put two kisses on the end of texts I sent to Val, or Josie.

Actually, there was a thought. Perhaps these notes and flowers were from a female friend, someone Dee had met and clicked with. Yes! That was it! Scandalous affairs and subterfuge happened in the movies, not to shop owners from Weirbridge, so that had to be the innocent explanation.

Or maybe it wasn't. I'd have thought she'd have mentioned meeting someone like that to me. And if that was the case, why hadn't she received any email correspondence from the person? I'd have noticed and replied, given that all Dee's emails were forwarded to me now. Half were work, almost the same amount were spam, then there was the occasional one from an old friend. Other than that, not much else. Our circle was an unusually tight group. We worked together, socialised together, went on holiday together, and if we needed to contact each other we texted or phoned.

The whole thing was making me homesick. I picked up my phone and texted Val.

> Just thinking about you. Wish you were here. Love
> you xx

Send.

See! I'd done two kisses without even thinking. And bollocks, I'd forgotten the time difference. It was three in the morning at home.

To my surprise she replied straight away. Damn. Hope I hadn't woken her.

> Not the same without you here luvly. Hope you're
> having a great time. Love you xx

If I could have half the strength of Val Murray, I'd be forever grateful. I knew her heart must be aching every second of every day, but she'd never shown it, never wavered in caring for everyone else. If ever there was a lesson in motherhood, Val Murray was it.

I was about to toss the phone on the bed when I realised there were two more texts that had come in while I was asleep, one from Luke and one from an unknown number. I swiped to open Luke's first.

> Pete is a dick. X

In spite of myself and the huge Pete-sized whole in my life, that made me laugh. I'd no idea what had happened to inspire it, but, immature as I was, I appreciated the moral support.

I opened the next text.

> This is Mark. You wore me down so I bought a phone.
> And I agree with Luke. X

I texted them both back the same message.

> Just woke. Hangover. I'm clearly not fit to be a
> responsible adult. And I applaud your perceptiveness
> re. ex-boyfriend's character. x

Bugger! Forgot the time difference again. I just hoped their phones were on silent and I didn't wake them. Or that they were out somewhere, living it up in a club. Strike that. Neither of them were the type. Mark was heading for forty, and he'd told me his clubbing days were long behind him, and Dee and I always had to drag Luke and Pete to a club if we fancied a dance, and then they only came under protest, much preferring the laid-back vibe of any bar with several large flat-screen TVs showing sport.

A knock at the door made me jump. When I answered it, I saw a tray with a silver cloche covering a white china plate, and a pot of coffee and some pastries next to it.

I had a vague memory of filling in a room service form when I got back the night before, and ticking the box that requested the tray be left at the door. I must have had a premonition that I'd look like something from the *Night Of The Living Dead* this morning. I caught myself in the mirror. Correct assumption.

I couldn't face the pancakes but I nibbled on the bacon and had two coffees in between showering and getting ready for the day. Right. Forget the notes. Forget the flowers. There was absolutely no point in speculating. I had no idea what was going on but I knew my friend and I trusted her and that was all there was to it.

Time to attack the day. I threw on a pair of jeans and a sweater – Dee used to say April in New York was like the Glasgow version of summer. Sunny, sometimes windy, and just warm enough that you could leave home without the trusty support of thermal knickers.

I jumped in a taxi to the convention centre, right at the end of West. 34th Street, next to the Lincoln Tunnel and overlooking the Hudson.

When I arrived, I pressed the ticket I'd printed off from Dee's email against the scanner and headed on through into a vast hall packed with stands and people. How to do this? Dee had these things down to a fine art, knew exactly what to spend time on and what to avoid. I was a rookie in an expert's world, so I wandered up and down every row, taking leaflets if something looked interesting, occasionally chatting to someone if they were too persistent for my insistence that I didn't need more information, and generally winging it.

For six hours, I browsed, until my feet ached and my head was splitting, but weirdly, it was a soothing experience. No one knew me. I didn't have to pretend. Or be overly polite. Or explain. I was just one person in a hall full of complete strangers, none of whom gave a toss that my life had disintegrated to dust and I had absolutely no idea what I was doing there.

I wandered some more. I learned about yacht charters, and concierge services, exclusive islands and private jets. I found out there were hundreds of unusual ways to get married, and a couple of interesting ways to die. I sampled gadgets and gizmos, all designed to make a trip easier, more relaxing, more fun or, in the case of the personal security travel sprays, more likely to end in the arrest of an attacker. I saw what the rich indulged in and how far a budget could go, and somewhere along the line, blogs started to form in my mind. I pulled my phone out and started dictating ideas and by the end of the day I had a dozen or so vague concepts that I was sure I could, with Luke's help, shape into really interesting travel pieces. I wasn't loving the experience, but I was certainly enjoying it more than I thought I would. This assault on the senses was Dee's world. But I could, for the first time, appreciate a little of why she adored the buzz of it.

On the way back to the hotel, I stopped off in an Irish bar for a drink and something to eat. It wasn't the kind of place that took reservations, so I slid into the one table that was free. It was like countless other Irish bars in countless other cities around the world. Memorabilia on the walls. A fiddler in the corner. Guinness on tap. But it also had a real old New York feel about it, and it was packed out, so I decided that while I was there, I may as well write up something on it.

As soon as the waitress with long red hair and a Boston accent had taken my order of a large coffee and a plate of stew, I pulled out my iPad and typed up pointers for the blog – the décor, the menu, the staff, the customers, the music – and took a couple of snaps of the pub and the menu on my phone.

It was late, almost eight o'clock, by the time I got back to the hotel. All I wanted to do was put my feet up and rest my weary bones. I almost succumbed, but I remembered the entry in the diary.

The Bar at the Baccarat Hotel, 9 p.m.

Reluctantly, I slipped on a simple black dress, pulled my hair back into a ponytail and headed out for a cab. The concierge had one waiting for me before I even reached the door. I climbed in, gave the address and then watched the city go by as we drove down streets that were still packed with traffic.

The journey was like a one-way ticket back to the past. Dee and I had first come to New York when were twenty-one and I could remember every exclamation, every laugh, every wild thing we planned to do. And every single one of those wild ideas came from Dee. More and more I was realising that she was the one that made the stars, and I just polished them. I was so, so grateful that she did. A crushing pain twisted my stomach, a wave of grief so strong I had to hold on to the door beside me.

Tears came next, tripping down my face, and I turned, looking outwards, so the driver wouldn't see. I was a woman, in a cab, breaking her heart because too much was gone and there was no way of getting it back. Pete was as dead to me as Dee was. I'd never understand it, never comprehend what went wrong, but I was absolutely sure there was no way back. Yet, if he appeared at my door – our door – and told me it was all a mistake and he wanted me back I'd forgive him in a heartbeat. Dee would be furious about that. She'd tell me to man up. Have some self-respect. She'd say he didn't deserve me. Yet we both knew he did. At least, he did back then.

The taxi veered to the left, and stopped in front of a glass building fronted by huge topiary balls in black square planters. I quickly composed myself, and while the driver was sorting out change from a twenty, touched up my foundation. Couldn't go charging into a suave hotel looking like I was suffering from a debilitating allergy.

Inside, the foyer was elegant and classy, but it didn't prepare me for the sumptuous magnificence of the bar. The black and white tiled floor, the deep red of the walls, the exquisite beauty of the chandeliers. This was so far from my usual hang-out destinations, but again so perfectly Dee. She would love every inch of the glitz and glamour.

I swallowed a sudden wave of sadness and took a seat at the bar. Come on, Jen. You can do this. I ordered a gin and tonic, looked around, taking snapshots of the room so I could recreate them in words for our readers. All the while, strangely, searching for something familiar, a reason to be here. That's when it struck me. Why had Dee put set times on her visits to the jazz club and here? I'd just assumed the jazz club opened at 8pm, and that's why a time had been noted, but a hotel bar like this one would be open from early evening at least. So why 9pm? Was she meeting a friend? I checked my watch. It was five minutes past. I scanned the room again. Almost every seat was taken by an impeccably-dressed reveller. Many people were standing, deep in conversation, laughing, whispering. I knew no one. Recognised not a soul. I stayed for an hour, enjoying the buzz, but all too aware that I was an incongruous sight, sitting alone, in an epicentre of social interaction. No one spoke to me. No one gave me a second glance. No one offered the slightest hint as to what my best friend in the world would have been doing here. Not meeting a friend then. Another explanation for the pre-determined time occurred to me. Perhaps she'd just heard that's when the bar was at its atmospheric best. Yep, that must be it. And she'd have been right. It had been an interesting experience, but I had all I needed now to write it up.

I paid my check, and headed back outside, where a uniformed man held a cab door open for me once again.

I hadn't wanted to come on this trip but maybe it had happened for a reason.

Or maybe this all belonged to Dee, and by being here, carrying out her plans, doing what she loved, all I was doing was walking in my best friend's shoes. And I wasn't sure where they were taking me.

19

Luke

There was a train thundering past my window. Had to be. Except, I didn't live near a train track. It must be thunder. I forced one eye open and all I could see was darkness. Shit. Where was I? And what had I been drinking last night? I tried to unstick my tongue from the roof of my mouth and realised my beverage of choice must have been superglue.

I tried to press the rewind button. It was fuzzy but eventually it kicked in like a movie I was seeing for the first time. Mark and me in the bar. Callie and Lizzy had arrived. I remember thinking it was weird seeing her in civvy world. At work she was all smart suits and power dresses, and even on work nights out she dressed sharp, but both she and Lizzy had been wearing skinny jeans and T-shirts, Callie's black, same colour as her leather jacket, Lizzy in blue jeans and a red T-shirt, with a short white jacket. They both wore heels that would give you altitude sickness.

I'd made the introductions and we pulled over chairs.

'What can I get you to drink?'

'I'll come with you,' Callie had offered.

The first round had been beers. Then tequila. Then shots. More tequila. I remember laughing. Lizzy was a nurse and had endless stories about the bizarre happenings in A & E. Callie held her own by taking the piss out of everyone we worked with, and doing it in a way that was funny even if you didn't know them.

At one point Lizzy had headed outside for a cigarette and Mark had gone to keep her company. Callie had asked if I was going to do a runner again like I had last time we'd gone for a drink. Shit. So she hadn't forgotten about that. I'd assured her I didn't even know where all the exits were and she'd laughed at that.

Mark and Lizzy came back. More tequila. More shots. His arm was around the back of her chair and there was no distance between them at all. Every now and then she'd lean into him and he didn't move away.

More tequila. More shots.

Closing time at the bar.

Mark's phone buzzed. Val, asking what time he'd be home. The girls had thought that was hilarious.

'I live not far from here,' Callie had said. 'You're all welcome to crash at mine.'

I pressed stop on the rewind. My heart was beating faster. What the fuck had I done? Dee would kill me for staying out all night and... It took a moment to remember and then the reality check sucked my lungs dry. My wife was dead. My wife was dead. My wife was dead. Oh God. I felt a tear slide down the side of my face from my eye to my ear. I didn't wipe it away.

The rewind button went down again. Mark had texted Val back, saying he was staying at my house. More hilarity. More ribbing over the sad truth that he was nearly forty and lying to his mum about where he was spending the night.

We'd walked, stopped for burgers from a snack bar that had probably been warned by the council for breaking every hygiene law known to man, then we'd got back to Callie's home. A flat. One of the new ones on the waterfront. All minimalist and leather and glass.

More tequila.

Mark and Lizzy had gone out on to the balcony. Callie and I were in the kitchen.

Panic rose again. Oh God, Dee, I'm sorry.

We were talking.

'You never asked me about what we were discussing earlier,' she'd said.

'What were we discussing?' Right then I had trouble remembering my name.

'The demise of Justin The Wonderman Accountant.'

'Ah, yes. So what happened then? Come on, I'm getting in touch with my feminine side. Look at this interested face,' I'd said, carrying on the joke from earlier. Clearly that one synapse of my brain wasn't swimming in tequila.

'I was attracted to someone else,' she said. 'So I decided that Wonderman wasn't for me. The Lycra shorts didn't do it for me anyway.'

'So what does?'

'What?'

'Do it for you?'

Jesus Christ, what had I been thinking? Nothing. It hadn't meant to be a come-on. Just a natural progression in a drunk man's brain, from one sentence to another.

'You,' she'd said.

Fuck. I lost the power of speech right about then.

'I know you've been through a terrible time and I know it's too soon, but when you're ready to think about moving on, you know where I am. Three desks along from you.' More giggles. All hers.

I remember thinking she was beautiful. And I remember thinking I wanted to hold her, and feel someone else. Even if that was all it was. Just to hold someone.

'I really, really want to kiss you,' she'd said next.

Bloody hell. Seriously? I was a messed-up, psychologically damaged, grieving mess, and she was flirting with me?

My drunken self wanted to hold someone, but that was it. I hadn't kissed another woman since the day I met my wife. Dee Harper was my wife. And yes, she was dead, but I was still her husband and there was nothing I wanted to change about that and, oh fuck, the pain. The room began to spin as I panicked, my head suddenly hurt and my stomach churned.

'S'cuse me, I...'

I'd staggered out of the kitchen, found a bathroom, threw up, then staggered back out. Callie was in the hall.

'I'm sorry,' I mumbled, mortified.

I expected irritation, maybe embarrassment, but instead, she looked at me knowingly, like she understood somehow.

'You can sleep in there,' she said, softly, pointing to a door. 'The spare room. You'll be quite safe.'

A smile from her, then a grateful one from me.

I'd gone in, crashed on the bed, fade to black.

That was it. I pressed stop on the rewind button once again.

The relief was all-consuming. I hadn't touched anyone else because I knew I couldn't. I belonged to Dee. Touching someone else would mean she wasn't there anymore, that she wasn't coming back, and I wasn't ready to make that a reality. How could I? I didn't even remember a time that I didn't love her.

Another thought, pushing those ones out of the way.

I wasn't ready now, but I couldn't live my whole life like this. At some point I would need to make changes. To think about other things. To get some kind of life back. There was going to come a time to let go.

But not yet.

20

Jen

My case was packed and ready for me to nip back and collect later. I finished the coffee I'd ordered. Nothing else this time.

I had no idea what to expect from this morning but I was thinking that Breakfast at Tiffany's would almost definitely involve shopping. Dee loved the Tiffany's brand. Last time she'd been in New York, she'd treated herself to the eponymous heart-shaped stud earrings. The time before, the bracelet in the same style. Before that, a trademark chain with the heart and toggle. She had at least five or six pieces from the collection. No doubt she'd planned to add another trinket on the morning visit.

I pulled out my iPad and double-checked the opening hours and address. I knew it was Fifth Avenue, but I wasn't sure of the exact number. I clicked on her entry in the Google calendar. Ninety-seven Greene Street. I was sure it was Fifth Avenue. I checked again. It definitely said 97 Greene Street. A quick Internet search gave me the explanation. There was another Tiffany's at Greene Street. I had no idea. I checked the opening time – 11am. I had plenty of time to kill, so I decided to walk. It would take around an hour, but at this time in the morning, even on a Sunday, a cab probably wouldn't be any quicker.

At almost exactly eleven o'clock I rounded the corner, strolled down a cobblestone street, past Dior, Louis Vuitton, Anna Sui, and there it was – a beautiful cream façade, planters outside bursting with greenery, awnings in Tiffany blue reaching out over the windows.

I perched on the edge of one of the planters and watched as people went by, some on their way to work, but most just out strolling, papers or iPads under their arms, walking dogs, holding hands, jogging, sometimes in pairs, his and hers running tights. They were probably wondering why I was smiling, but it brought back a random memory of last Christmas, when Luke and I had decided, in a moment of conspiracy, to buy Dee and Pete matching running tights. The first time they'd met up to go for a jog, I'd let Pete answer the door to Dee, and it had taken them a moment to realise there they were in co-ordinating outfits. Luke and I had thought it was hilarious and they'd been good enough sports to go out like that. They'd done ten miles looking like something from Barbie and Ken, Olympic edition.

It took a few moments before I could bring myself back to the present. OK, Breakfast at Tiffany's. I was where Dee planned to be, but breakfast? I scanned the street and that's when I saw it. A hot dog stand was already set up and serving about twenty yards down the street. Of course. One hot dog a day in New York – her Big Apple rule. The thought of a hot dog for breakfast, or brunch, didn't appeal, but still I headed over, bought one, lathered it with ketchup and mustard, just the way she loved it, then I found a shady spot in a doorway, and ate it slowly, making sure that if she was watching me, she got to savour the moment. When it was done I looked heavenward, as I did a dozen times a day, and smiled.

I hoped she was looking down and I hoped she wasn't too pissed off with me over the notes and flowers. Before I'd left this morning, I'd called down to ask reception if they knew who'd sent them. I drew a blank on both. There was a florist's number on the bottom of the card, so I'd called there too, only to be met with a brick wall of 'client confidentiality'. What the hell was going on? Was it a huge mistake or... I'd stopped. Enough.

I wasn't sure if Dee would be laughing at my ludicrous suspicions, or horrified that I could doubt her for a single second. I hadn't really. Sure, the thought had flashed through my mind, but I'd immediately dismissed it. Dee loved Luke. All this strange stuff that had happened would have a totally innocent explanation, and maybe one day I'd find out what it was. Maybe I'd discover who sent them and why there were no emails or calls to find out if they'd been received, no names or numbers left, no further attempts to contact her some other way. Or maybe I'd never know. All that mattered was that I was here and doing what she would have wanted me to do, keeping her legacy alive. Perhaps in a way, me being here was Dee's way of forcing me to keep going. Maybe.

I got up and wandered back the way I'd come, passing Space Nk, then Tiffany's. I'd done breakfast, so now I was ready for the second part of the task. A description of the interior of the store would be great for the blog, but I had no intention of making a purchase. I wasn't much of a shopper. Or a jewellery person. I always wore the little diamond studs Val got me for my twenty-fifth birthday, never taking them out. My mum's wedding ring was on the third finger of my right hand, a tiny part of her that I loved to keep close. And around my neck, a gold chain Pete had bought me last year for Christmas. I should probably have that melted down now. Or at least replace it with something that meant a little more than a tribute to a guy who walked away.

As I reached the door, I realised my timing was perfect, as it was held open by a tall, dark-haired man who was leaving.

Inside, a handsome guy in a smart suit was behind the counter. 'Morning, m'am,' he greeted me, with a smile that showed his parents had invested in a great dental plan. 'What can I get you?'

I had absolutely no idea. Instinctively, I touched the chain around my neck. 'I was just thinking about replacing this,' I said.

'A necklace? Certainly. Let me show you a few.' He guided me around the shop, pointing out chunky silver toggle chains, gorgeous wishbones, beautiful curved bows, regaling me with the stories of the collections in each case, Return To Tiffany, Tiffany Infinity, Keys, Atlas, and even stunning leaf-inspired pieces designed by Paloma Picasso. Every item in the shop had beauty and a distinctive class, but nothing spoke to me until... I saw it, in the glass display that held the 1837 range, a fine silver chain, with two interlocking circles, one silver one gold. That was us, Dee and I. One silver, one gold, different but connected in a way that couldn't be broken.

If the lovely chap serving me noticed the tears that sprung to my eyes again, he didn't mention it. Instead, he boxed up my necklace in that perfect little blue box, tied a bow around it and popped it in a blue gift bag.

I handed over my credit card, not caring that this was more money than I'd ever spent on any single item except my house and my car.

He handed me back the card and the gift bag at the same time, and I managed to get back out on to the cobbled street before two tears fell. It was strange. We'd only ever been to New York together once, over a decade ago, and it wasn't a place that held huge sentimental value for me. Everything and everyone we loved was back home. But standing here, I'd never felt so close to Dee, to the point where I could almost feel her beside me.

Eventually, I dragged myself away and retraced my steps back to the hotel, collected my stuff, then headed to the airport. Traffic was light so I made good time, and the flight left right on time.

As we hit cruising altitude, I reached into my bag, took out my little blue box and removed the chain. I took off the necklace that Pete had given me and replaced it with one that signified love instead of betrayal.

I lay back, closed my eyes and worked my way back through the trip. It had been sad, confusing, lonely, interesting, fun. The old Jen would have hated it, been desperate to get home to Pete, or to beg Dee to join me. The new Jen knew she didn't have that option and in some ways maybe it was good to move forward. Maybe I needed to let go of the past. Dee would have demanded it. It made me smile as I thought how much she'd have loved the last few days. I know I didn't do it justice – she'd have been out every waking hour, exploring and experiencing everything she could find. I just hoped she was proud that I'd stepped up and carried out her plans. I'd gone to the travel expo she attended every year, and then I'd visited the places in her calendar.

The jazz club... Boozy, decadent, the strangeness of sharing such an intimate environment with a collection of strangers I could barely see in the darkness.

The Bar at the Baccarat Hotel... Grand, beautiful, like an elegant throwback to a bygone era.

Breakfast At Tiffany's... I reached up and put my fingertips on the two adjoining rings. Dee and I. I tried to imagine what this morning would have been like if she'd been there. We'd have walked arm in arm from the hotel to Greene Street, and she'd have bitched the whole way there about the fact that taxis were invented for a reason. It was one of her great contradictions. She would run for ten miles but she wouldn't walk anywhere if there was another option. We'd have bought those hot dogs, and sat there in that doorway people-watching, making up identities and backstories for the people who passed by. Then she'd have pulled me up, teasing that it was time for me to restart the diet, before linking her arm through mine again and steering me into Tiffany's. She'd...

My daydream paused the moment that door to the jewellery emporium opened.

The guy who had been leaving when I went in. We'd passed in the doorway, and at the time I was too caught up in the spontaneity of the moment to register him, but now I realised there was something familiar about him. I racked my brain. Home. Work. Customers. Nothing. A celebrity? Someone who'd been in the press? Still nothing.

New York. Stood to reason that it would be someone I'd already seen there, but what were the chances of meeting the same person twice in a city that size? Pretty slim to none.

I ran through the staff I'd encountered at the hotel, the workers in the places I'd visited, even the hot dog vendors.

Aaaargh! This was beyond infuriating.

The drinkers in the Irish pub. Nope, nothing. The shadowed faces in the audience at the jazz club. Nothing there. Then… Bingo. There he was. I was waiting for a taxi as I left the jazz club, one stopped, I stepped forward, and he got out, held the door open and did a jokey bow. 'After you,' he'd said.

I'd climbed in, said thanks and he'd smiled before heading towards the club door.

It was the same man I'd passed leaving Tiffany's. I was sure of it. Not 100 per cent, pick him out in a line-up sure, but positive enough.

How could that be? What were the chances of bumping into the same man, twice in two days, in one of the busiest cities in the world?

Coincidence. It had to be.

But…

I had a feeling the odds would be up there with me winning the lottery while stuck in a lift with Matt Damon.

So. Maybe not a coincidence? A whole new set of unanswerable questions began to ricochet through my head.

Was he there, at the club, and then at Tiffany's, looking for Dee? Did they have plans to meet? Was he a business contact? A friend? Something else? Something… more?

Why had she never mentioned him? Was it because there was nothing to tell? Or was there something she felt unable to share? I paused before the next escalation of that train of thought. I didn't want to go there. I felt hopelessly disloyal even contemplating the possibility. But was there even a tiny sliver of a chance that Dee was meeting him because she was doing something she shouldn't?

And how could I possibly know for sure when the only person who could tell me was no longer here?

21

Val

Don's snoring was like the rumble of a train as it trundled through a stretch of line with many tunnels. Loud, quiet, loud, quiet. Once upon a time it would have driven me mad and sent me storming off to the spare bedroom. Now I lay right next to him and barely registered it. It was there, in the background, almost comforting. Not that I'd ever admit that to him of course. I still gave him a dig in the ribs every now and then, when the volume was getting so loud the neighbours might start to worry that the street was being invaded by marauding bears.

I caught the time on the digital alarm clock as I slipped out of bed. 3.16 a.m. I'd been dozing off and on for a couple of hours but I wasn't going to get back to sleep now. I looked in on Mark as I passed his room. He'd been sound asleep in bed all day after coming home looking rough as a badger's arse from Luke's house. I was glad for them that they got on so well. They were good for each other. Though the irony wasn't lost on me that our Dee's brother and husband only really became friends when she was no longer here to see it. Where was the sense in that?

I went downstairs, stopping at the pile of clothes I'd ironed in the afternoon, pulling out a pair of jeans and a long, thick jumper. Comfort clothes.

Silently pulling them on, I tried to tell myself that I wasn't going anywhere. Strange how we can try to fool ourselves into believing something to be true. I was like the alcoholic that slipped a bottle of gin into the toilet cistern but told myself I wouldn't drink it.

Of course I was going out, and of course I knew where I was going. It had started because those aisles were the only place I could keep my mind busy, where I didn't have to think about anyone else or put a brave face on it, where I wasn't trying desperately to keep the blind bloody fury at bay, to stop the anxiety from choking me and hold back the screams of rage.

That was then. Now it was all about him, the one who had caused this, taken my girl from me. I wanted to bump into him, to know him, to see his evil face. But I couldn't find him, so for now, this would have to do.

I crept down the stairs and closed the door silently behind me. We lived in an end of terrace house and had to cut down a path, past the other houses in the row, to get to the car park area, so when I switched the engine on, I knew that I was too far away for the noise to wake the sleeping menfolk I'd left behind.

It took me longer than expected to get there and I nodded to the security guard as I passed him at the door. Up one aisle. Down the next. Up one aisle. Down the next. I went as slowly as possible, making every moment last, stopping to stare at products I had no intention of buying just to drag the time out. Eventually, I got to the till. An older gent rang each item through.

A sirloin steak, onion rings, thick cut chips, a peppercorn sauce, a banoffi pie, custard.

'Looks like you're going to have quite the party there,' he said with a wink.

'Looks like it,' I agreed. I wouldn't tell him the truth. I'd learned it made people uncomfortable. Better to just smile and nod. Smile and nod.

Bag packed, I paid cash, then headed towards the exit. Only, I wasn't leaving. Of course I wasn't.

I carried on past and headed to the café, because this wasn't my usual store. It was her store. Darren Wilkie's mother. I had no idea if she'd be here, didn't even know if the café would be open. Most of them weren't at this time of night. But I'd come anyway because I'd become so consumed by anger and a need to know about her family, that it was impossible not to.

As I reached the first table, I saw that it was open and it already had customers. A bloody priest, or maybe a vicar, sat at a corner table speaking to a young woman, maybe nineteen or twenty. They didn't look up. If I was religious I might see the man of the cloth's presence as a sign of some kind of divine intervention, but any religious notions I'd had died when my girl took her last breath. How could any God do that?

Unable to answer, I went to the deserted counter, picked up a mug, put it on the chrome tray of the machine and pressed the button for a black coffee. The noise must have alerted the night worker, as I heard footsteps coming from the back area.

It wouldn't be her. Of course it wouldn't. There must be a whole team of staff that ran this place. But even as the thought ran through my mind, I knew it would be.

She looked tired. Maybe a little frazzled. Her burgundy hair, straight out of a bottle, was pulled back in a ponytail and there was a whole lifetime of weariness etched in her face. The edges of her fingers were yellowed with nicotine and she had the skeletal frame of someone who lived on cigarettes, vodka and not much else. I hated her on sight. No wonder she'd raised a vile piece of scum that killed my girl. Had she even tried to teach him right from wrong? Had she ever instilled in him the importance of making good decisions and treating other people with respect?

The liquid in the cup began to ripple and I tried desperately to steady the tremors of my shaking hand.

'Can I get you anything else?' It was her. The mother of the boy who killed Dee. She was talking to me, her voice tired, raspy, but softer than I expected. I shook my head, not trusting myself to speak.

'That'll be £1.50 then, please.'

I've no idea what she thought about why my hands were shaking. Or the fact that I seemed incapable of speech yet was looking her straight in the eye. I'd thought about this moment so many times and yet now I had nothing to say. This wasn't the place or the time. I wasn't sure, didn't know enough about her or her wretched family.

I managed to give her the exact money, took my cup and my bag of groceries to a table and sat down. For the next half hour I watched her when she wasn't looking. I saw her clean tables, wipe down the glass-fronted cabinets, mop the floor and refill the salts, peppers, sauces and sugars.

And I hated her.

With every bone in my body I seethed and cursed her, because if she hadn't given birth to that monster then my Dee would be alive today.

There was so much talk now about feelings after something like this happened. About 'moving on' and 'letting go' and 'gaining closure'.

There would be none of that for me.

My daughter was dead and I was angry and bitter and I made no apologies for the fact that I couldn't imagine ever letting that go.

22
Jen

May 19th. It would have been Dee's thirty-second birthday. We met at the cemetery at 10am on a morning that was as overcast as our moods. Don and Val. Josie, Luke and me. Mark had flown back to Australia to join his boat, but he'd announced on the day he left that he was going to head straight back here after his stint was over at the end of June. He said he wanted to support Val during the court case, but I wondered if it had anything to do with Lizzy, the girl he'd met on a night out with Luke, and dated a few times before he left. I wasn't sure. He'd said it was just a casual thing.

I turned to Val. It was hard to believe that the woman standing next to me was the same woman who had danced on tables last Hogmanay doing a jig to celebrate the New Year. That she had been bright and boisterous, full of life and absolutely irrepressible. This Val, four months after her daughter had been killed, was several stones thinner, almost shrunken, in size and in personality. Beside her, Don was showing the effects of the last few months too. He'd aged ten years, his eyes sunken and his cheeks hollow. In the old days, they'd hold hands, they'd bicker, they'd flirt and they'd laugh, but now it was like they just coexisted. Not that Val would admit that. 'Och, we're fine love,' she'd say when I asked. 'When you've been married as long as Don and me you learn to just get on with it.'

Luke was another one who'd dropped a couple of stone. His dark wavy hair fell down over the collar of his shirt and he was smarter than I'd ever seen him in the suit we'd gone shopping for last weekend. I knew Dee always loved him in a suit, but his old ones were falling off him now, so he'd asked me to go with him to the gents department of a big swanky store to pick a new one out.

'Special occasion?' asked the bright, fifty-something woman with the dark red, chin-length bob who served us. 'No wait, don't tell me, I can always guess...'

Oh God. Please don't.

'It's... It's...' she'd worked up to it, as if the ether was in the process of delivering some vital piece of information. 'You're getting engaged!' she'd announced triumphantly, waiting for us to marvel at her powers of perception.

'Sorry. Way off,' Luke had said with a kind smile, happy to leave it at that. Unfortunately, Betty the Suit-Selling Psychic didn't get the message.

'You're going to a wedding.'

Blank looks.

'A christening? A birthday?' She must have registered a flicker of change in our expressions. 'See! Although, I have to say, I usually pick up on it long before the fourth guess. So whose birthday is it then?'

'My wife,' Luke said. I had absolutely no powers of intuition, premonition or psychic talent, but even I knew what was going to happen next. Just our luck to get the chattiest shop assistant in the city on the one day we'd have appreciated a monosyllabic paragon of disinterest.

Right on cue, she turned to me. 'Oh, that's lovely. Is he taking you somewhere nice? I hear the restaurant in that Blytheswood Hotel is an absolute treat.'

'I'm not his wife,' I told her, hoping her dodgy psychic powers would pick up the subliminal message I was sending her, along the lines of, 'Stop, please, in the name of all that is holy, stop right now.'

'Ah I see. Working today is she?'

Luke decided it had gone far enough and threw in the ultimate conversation stopper. 'She passed away.'

'She... Oh.' Poor woman had been mortified. She'd hastily picked up a tie Luke had been considering. 'I'll just see if I can get this in blue.' And off she'd bustled, face the colour of the scarlet tie in her hand.

'Do you think Dee set that up to totally mortify us both?' Luke had said.

'I do indeed,' I'd replied. That's how we talked about her now, like she was still here, still a part of us, involved in everything we did.

I wondered what she was thinking now as she watched us lay flowers, white roses, in front of her headstone.

After a few moments, Josie, Val and I moved back to sit on the bench that they'd had installed in front of her grave. Don and Val came here every Sunday, Luke and I every few weeks.

'In the name of God would you look at that!' Josie said, gesturing a few graves along to the left. It was the opposite direction from the way we'd come in, so we hadn't noticed it, but now I realised that satellites in space could probably see the apparition. A huge stone, with gigantic feathered wings attached to the back of it and flashing lights decorating the top of it. Yes, they were flashing. Either they were solar-powered or this was a case for those ghost-hunters off the telly.

'Feel a bit bad now that I only brought our Dee a bunch of roses and a bamboo plant,' Val said, making the three of us giggle. We weren't being disrespectful. Dee would have been gutted if that scene went without one of Josie's caustic comments or Val's razor-sharp retorts.

I watched as Luke stepped forward, gently touched the headstone, and then came back to join us and I could see the effort it took for him to hold it together. Birthdays were a big thing in our group. The celebrations usually lasted a whole weekend and Dee's usually involved some death-defying activity. Skydiving. Go-cart racing. Tank driving. Paintballing. I still had the scars.

'Right then, are we off?' Luke asked, rubbing his hands together to heat them up.

Don and Luke walked in front of us as we headed back to the car. My arm looped through Val's, as I realised something else. This was the first time in fifteen years that Pete hadn't been with us on Dee's birthday. I wondered if he'd even remembered today was her birthday? Did he care?

Val must have been reading my mind. 'Have you heard from Pete?'

I shook my head. 'The papers arrived from the lawyer yesterday for me to buy him out of the house. It'll all be finalised within the next few weeks.' I couldn't keep the resignation from my voice. All the fight to hold on to whatever we had was gone and now I just wanted to break the last ties with as little pain as possible.

'Are you going to sign them?' she asked.

I shrugged. 'I'm not sure. At first I wanted to stay where I was but now... I'm thinking that maybe it's time to move. Too many memories,' I told her and I knew she understood.

Val was still curious. 'And have you seen him again since that time you stalked him?'

I shook my head, smiling as I rolled my eyes. 'I prefer "casually bumped into him",' I clarified. 'But no. I guess it would be different if we had kids or, you know, maybe a hamster, but there's been no reason to meet up and he made it clear that we were done. I can't believe I've loved him half my life and now he's like a stranger. I'll never understand it.'

'I do. Spineless. Fecking spineless. If ever there was a man who deserved a boot in the bollocks, it's that one,' Josie piped in.

Val didn't argue. She'd always had a soft spot for Pete, but the minute he'd betrayed me it was over. That was Val. The most loving, caring person, until you crossed someone she loved.

The table at The Tulip, the Mackintosh-inspired hotel and restaurant where we'd held Dee's funeral, was ready for us when we arrived, a red velvet semicircular booth around a table with a crisp white cover. It might seem odd returning to a place that held such sad memories, but the happy ones overruled it. Dee was christened here, we had our graduation party here, our twenty-firsts, she got married in this very room, and almost every birthday and anniversary in the Murray family had been marked by a trip here. It was their favourite place. We belonged here. The only thing that felt strange to me was that Dee wasn't here too. I pushed the thought from my mind.

We ordered mojitos, Dee's favourite drink, ignoring the quizzical look from the waitress who probably didn't get too many people asking for cocktails on a Thursday at eleven in the morning.

As soon as they arrived, Don proposed a toast. 'To my girl. The craziest, most beautiful, kind-hearted, and bloody untidy one that there ever was. Happy birthday DeeDee.' His voice cracked on the last word.

'Happy birthday!' the rest of us piped in.

Luke's turn. 'And to my wife, who I miss every day. And who, if she was here, would probably tell me to man up and stop being pathetic. Happy birthday, my darling.'

The rest of us laughed.

'Cutting, but true,' I teased him.

'Right then smart-arse, your turn,' he said.

I thought about her every day, yet I didn't know what to say.

More than anything I wished I could speak to her, even one last time, to tell her I loved her, that I missed her, and to ask her the questions that had been going over and over in my mind since New York. Despite doing my best to dig for information, I still didn't understand what had happened. I'd searched the friends' photographs on Dee's Facebook page for any sign of the guy I'd seen but there wasn't one. I'd gone through her phone and the camera she used to capture images on her trips but he wasn't in there either. Other than going back and interviewing the staff at the jazz club and Tiffany's, I was all out of ideas. Besides, there was still the possibility that it was a complete coincidence, or that the guy was just a business acquaintance that she'd promised to meet up with. I knew nothing of the facts of the situation, so I'd decided to put it all down to one big strange unsolvable mystery, and forget about it. Only, that was easier said than done. Especially on a day that was dedicated to honouring her in all her crazy, funny, unpredictable glory.

'Happy birthday to Dee, who was never short on love, laughter, surprises, or really daft ideas that got us into no end of trouble,' I toasted, to another rousing cheer from the others.

We turned to Val, and for a moment I thought she was going to crumble, but she took a deep breath, sat up straight and held her glass aloft. 'To Dee Ida Murray...'

'Ida?' Josie asked, gobsmacked.

'It was the only way I could get her to stop singing bloody "My Girl" in the delivery room the night our Dee was born,' Val explained. 'It was that or Don was going to have to press the fire alarm.'

'True,' Don nodded, deadpan. Luke, Josie and I were in stiches.

'To Dee Ida Murray Harper,' Val proclaimed, 'who gave me grey hair, a few too many wrinkles, and thirty-two years of loving every moment of being her mother. Except that time she got wrecked on Pernod and blackcurrant at the school disco and I had to bin my white shagpile rug.'

The memory made me choke on my mojito. Dee had sworn we'd be so cool at the fourth year disco with our illicit alcohol in our Ribena bottles and we absolutely were. In fact, that was the first night I ever snogged Pete. Unfortunately, we weren't so cool a couple of hours later when Dee was vomiting like something out of *The Exorcist* and Val was there with the Marigolds and the Dettol, trying to get the large purple stain out of her rug, while threatening to ground us until middle age.

Finally it was Josie's turn. 'Happy birthday to that messy lass Dee, who was clearly brought up to think the cleaning fairies would walk around after her, picking up her stuff.'

Val interjected. 'She was indeed. I blame Don.'

Back to Josie, glass aloft. 'My job is much easier since you've been gone... but I'd work all day long for ever more to have you back.'

I gave her a hug as we toasted. Yet another large slug of mojito on an empty stomach was beginning to make me feel a bit light-headed so I was glad when lunch came.

A sirloin steak, onion rings, thick-cut chips, peppercorn sauce, a banoffi pie and custard. To outsiders we must have looked like a happy family having a celebration, making toasts and being raucous.

We ate, we talked and we reminisced, and it was many hours before we were ready to leave, every mortifying story told, every disaster rehashed, every wonderful event played out again for us all to cherish.

I hugged Val, Don and Josie in turn before they climbed into their taxi for the ten minute ride home, and then waited with Luke for our cab. Our houses were only a few streets apart, a situation Dee had decreed would make complete financial sense on occasions just like this. 'We can share taxis – we'll save a fortune,' she'd proclaimed when she and Luke had decided to buy a house so close to the one Pete and I owned.

'Your house first or mine?' Luke asked, as we waited.

I swayed against the pillar outside the grand mahogany door of the hotel, the cool air a welcome reprieve from hours of tequila hot flushes.

'I don't mind. Yours is first, so probably makes more sense.'

Just at that the taxi came round the corner and he held open the door as I climbed in. As I gave the driver Luke's address, I spotted the time on the clock.

'It's only six o'clock,' I said, more out of surprise than anything. It was still daylight, but it felt like we were heading home after a night out.

'What's that?' Luke asked, climbing in the other side of the back seat.

'It's only six o'clock. Feels like later.'

'Yeah, guess it does,' he said, exhaling.

I put my hand on his. 'You did great today. Val and Don wanted a celebration of her life and that's what we had.'

'We did. So what do you reckon? Would she have approved?'

'Absolutely. Although she'd be trying to drag us all to a club right now to continue the celebration. You and I were always the lightweights.'

'Yup, that whole "opposites attract" thing, wasn't it? Me and Dee, you and Pete.' He cut off to speak to the driver. 'This next one on the right here, please.'

The cab pulled in to a stop.

'Want to come in for a nightcap?'

I knew exactly what he was thinking. He didn't want to go home to an empty house and, to be honest, I didn't either. Especially not that house, especially not tonight.

'Sure,' I agreed, climbing out. I looked heavenward. 'Are you watching, Dee?' I whispered, while I waited for Luke as he was paying for the cab. 'Sometimes we're not complete lightweights after all.'

23

Val

He'd had way too much to drink, my Don. It was a long time since I'd seen him like this. Don't get me wrong, he wasn't wrecking the house or ranting or singing, he was just looser, more like the old Don than he'd been since the day our Jen called us from the hospital.

The taxi had dropped us first, then went on into Glasgow with Josie in the back, singing 'My Girl' as she went. It was one of those songs, wasn't it? Got stuck in your head and you ended up humming it for days. Bloody Ida.

'Want a cup of tea, love?' I asked him when we got indoors.

'Not for me,' he said, then he surprised me by taking my hand. We'd barely touched in months, and certainly nothing more passionate than that. I'd used the excuse that it was because Mark was here but we both knew it wasn't.

He pulled me in tight and wrapped his arms around me. Those big, solid arms that had spent so many years on a building site and still had the strength of a man half his age. There had never been anyone but Don for me. Still wasn't. Problem was, I didn't feel anything for anyone anymore.

That wasn't true. I felt pure, unadulterated hatred for Wilkie and his family. Thought about them constantly, ruminated over what I wanted to say to them when I got my day in court, face to face, not over a counter in a supermarket café. But that scum aside, my feelings seemed to have been switched off at the tap.

Don was swaying now, holding me tight in the middle of the kitchen, moving to an imaginary song he could hear in his head. Probably bloody 'My Girl'.

We'd done this thousands of times before over the years, just him and I, when everyone else had gone to bed or gone home after a party, he'd put a bit of Frank Sinatra on the cassette player and we'd sway around the kitchen just like this and I'd think how lucky I was to have him, how blessed I was to have the life that I had.

The bitterness almost choked me.

'Right, come on, love, I'm tired,' I told him, breaking off, and to my shame, not even acknowledging the flash of hurt that I saw cross his big handsome face. It wasn't even seven o'clock, but I couldn't face watching TV or sitting at the kitchen table trying to think of things to say to each other. I wasn't completely lying. It had been so long since I had a full night's sleep that I permanently felt like I was existing in a state of pure exhaustion. Maybe an early night would help.

I locked the back door and headed up for a bath, killing another hour before going to bed. Don had stayed downstairs, watching a bit of TV, but came up when he heard me come out of the bathroom. I got to bed first, pulling on my pyjamas while Don headed to the loo. I hoped sleep would come quickly. I'd had too much to drink today to go out for a late night drive, so I was staying here whether I wanted to or not.

Five minutes or so later, Don climbed into bed, but instead of turning the other way, as he'd done every night for months, he pulled me into him, the way he'd done for the first thirty-seven years of our lives together.

'I don't know what to say to make this better for you, Val,' he said, his voice low and sad.

I don't know if it was shock or surprise, but it certainly caught me off guard. Don wasn't one for talking about emotions or feelings. For the last four months we'd barely had a conversation deeper than what we were having for tea, and I didn't blame him for that. It was as much as I could manage too.

'I don't think anything can,' I said honestly, the darkness swallowing my words.

'I know. And I feel the same. But, love, we've already lost Dee – and I think the day that she went, we lost each other too. I love you, Val. Every bit of you. And I'll miss our Dee every day of my life. But we have to start living again, Val. Just tell me how I can help you see that.'

I couldn't answer him, couldn't get the words out. The pillow was wet with tears, and I don't know if they were his or mine, but I did know that he was right. And I knew that I had to find a way to lift this pain, this rage at the bastard who had destroyed my family, otherwise one day it would finally dissipate and I'd discover that there was no one left.

Wilkie had taken Dee. I had to find a way to stop him taking more from us, but I just didn't know how.

24

Jen

The balcony was my favourite part of Dee's house. Luke's house. Funny how I still thought of it as being Dee's first. It was a townhouse, with bedrooms on the ground floor and the open-plan kitchen and living area on the first floor, to make the most of the views overlooking the hills in the distance. When Luke and Dee moved in, Don had replaced the lounge window with doors, and added a gorgeous semicircular balcony. It helped to have a dad that was a builder. The décor was all Dee, though. Silvers and greys, plush pile carpets, velvets, leather and crystals, a blingtastic combination that looked like the inside of one of the five-star hotels she'd visited on her travels. Unfortunately Dee had always lived like she had a five-star hotel housekeeping service too. Thank God for Josie.

'Josie doesn't come in anymore,' Luke said, making me laugh. 'Coffee, wine or beer?'

'I was just thinking about that. And beer.'

He pulled out two bottles from the fridge and handed me one. After all the mojitos, I couldn't face more spirits, but I wasn't in the mood for coffee. Dee wouldn't approve of the party being over yet.

We took the drinks out on to the balcony, grabbing a huge thick fur throw that Dee kept by the door, before slumping into the two wicker armchairs that sat side by side.

'Hang on, back in a minute,' Luke said. 'Just going to grab a sweatshirt before hypothermia sets in.'

A few moments later he was back, his suit swapped for jeans and a thick jumper. He handed me a sweatshirt I recognised immediately. Abercrombie & Fitch. Another purchase from Dee's last New York trip. She'd bought it for me, then borrowed it one night and I'd never seen it since. The thought of that made me smile. I pulled it on and rearranged the blanket around my legs. There was a comfortable silence for a few moments, both of us lost in thought, processing the day.

Luke spoke first. 'Do you ever look back and think that life was great, and wonder why it all went to crap?'

'Every day,' I said ruefully, but trying to keep my tone light. 'At least a dozen times. And that's before breakfast.'

That made him smile.

Another few moments of silence, each of us pulling our thoughts through a well of way too many mojitos.

'You know, sometimes I used to wonder if I was enough for her. I've never told anyone that before.'

I turned to look at him, surprised. 'Of course you were enough. Why would you think that?'

He shrugged. 'Because it's true. I'm not feeling sorry for myself or being maudlin, it's just the way that it was. I think we were lucky that she had a job that added a bit of excitement and variety. She needed that. Needed to always be planning something, doing stuff. It was like she could never just be content with what we had, always had to be planning the next thing, researching the next trip, looking for that rush.'

It was strange. I'd known Dee for most of my life and I knew all this to be true, but I'd never realised that it worried Luke.

'We had a fight that morning,' he said, almost a whisper.

'Really?' I replied, surprised. In my mind I skipped back to that day. I'd replayed it a million times in my mind, but only from when the police arrived to deal with the noise from next door. Before that we were on the sofas, laughing about sore bones and her hangover. 'She never mentioned that. What did you fight about?'

'Kids.' The weariness in Luke's reply made me want to hug him. 'We'd been talking for months about whether it was time to start a family... Actually, scratch that. *I'd* been talking for months about whether it was time to start a family and she'd been telling me all the reasons that it wasn't.'

I would have bet my last pound that Dee told me every single thing about her life, yet I knew nothing of this. 'I don't know if I'm more shocked that she didn't want to start a family or that she didn't tell me you were discussing it.'

Luke smiled. 'You know what she was like – didn't ever dwell on the tough stuff.'

That was true. It was one of the things I loved most about her. That ceaseless optimism and determination to live for the moment, never let anything bog her down.

'I thought she wanted children though?' I asked. 'We used to talk about how we'd bring up our broods together.' That memory brought another flash of pain.

'She always did and we were going to start trying but then one day she just changed her mind and started to come up with a million reasons why we should wait. Her job. She wanted a bigger house. More money in the bank. It would stop us travelling. We weren't ready to settle down. She had loads. A whole list of reasons why we shouldn't and nothing on the list of reasons why we should.'

'What did you do?'

He thought for a moment. 'Just hoped that she'd change her mind. I didn't get it. Then I started thinking that she'd changed her mind about me too and maybe we were in trouble, but she said I was overthinking it and she just wasn't ready. Soon, but not yet, she said.'

'And that's what you argued about that morning?'

He nodded, sighing. 'I brought it up again that morning and asked her to give me a timeframe, but she wouldn't. So I got pissed off, asked her if she could really ever see herself having kids with me...'

'Of course she did!' I jumped in, heart breaking for him.

'She said she didn't know anymore.'

'No way!'

I could see his face in the light from inside and the anguish was in every crease and furrow of his brow. I couldn't believe what I was hearing. Why didn't she tell me any of this?

He went on, 'Then she left to go to your house and that was it. And sometimes I get so pissed off with her. I know that makes me a fucking horrible person, but it didn't have to be like this. If she hadn't changed her mind about kids, we could all be here now. Me, Dee, our baby. Maybe two. I'd still have a wife, and a family and it would all have been so fucking different.'

I tried to form words but nothing was coming out. I was stunned. Completely shocked. It was a few moments before I recovered the power of speech. 'I'm sorry Luke. I really am. I had no idea. We talked about everything, or at least I thought so, but she didn't tell me any of this.' I didn't mention that a few things about New York had been a bit of a mystery too. Instead,

I went on, 'I would have helped if I could. Not that it would have made a blind bit of difference because it would have taken a better woman than me to change her mind about anything.'

That part was absolutely true. Dee had the confidence, the stubbornness to remain completely resolute and steadfast in what she wanted. Always had. It was that bolshiness that got our shop opened, that grew our business, and that made our lives as full of adventures and experiences, even the ones we didn't particularly want.

'I don't think anyone has that kind of superpower,' he said, shaking off the sadness. 'Christ, I'm sorry, Jen. This is what happens. One minute I'm holding it together and think I'm fine and the next I'm rocking back and forward being battered to death by a big stick of regret. I just wished I'd kissed her that morning before she left, you know? Told her how much I loved her.'

'She knew.'

'Yeah, I guess.'

He got up and disappeared inside and came back out with two more beers. When he sat down, he pulled the huge blanket over a bit so it covered his knees too.

'Why are we subjecting ourselves to frostbite out here?'

I pointed upwards at the one and only spot of light in the sky. 'Because it's beautiful and we can see the stars.'

'That's a plane coming into land at Glasgow airport,' he countered.

'This is why I work in a shop and not in astronomy,' I conceded, before going on. 'You know, I'm beginning to wonder what the hell is wrong with me.'

That surprised him. 'Why?'

'Was I in some weird trance for that last couple of years? The two people closest to me, Dee and Pete – no offence,' I said, when I realised I'd excluded him from the list, 'both had stuff going on that I knew absolutely nothing about. Dee was having this whole dilemma over starting a family and didn't say a word. And Pete was slowly sinking into a pit of misery so deep he upped and left me. Jesus. I really need to work on my people skills. Is there anything about you I should know now? Please speak up and get it out of the way. Emigrating this weekend? Cross-dresser? Shagging Jennifer Aniston.'

'Definitely that one,' Luke said, the mood lifting thanks to my rant.

'But really, how could I have been so blind to everything?'

'Because you just like to see the good in everyone? Bugger, that was lame. Sorry. Best I could do on the spot.'

I leaned over and flicked his ear, feigning irritation.

'Talking of being clueless, I'm also guilty as charged. I had no idea what a tosser Pete was. Have you heard from him again?' he said, asking the same thing Val and Josie had wanted to know earlier.

'Not a word. Josie has threatened to have him exterminated. I'm thinking of taking her up on it,' I joked, with just a tinge of bitterness.

He put his feet up on the table in front of us. 'You know, it's strange to me. We were mates for, what? Five years? I mean, it's one thing dumping your girlfriend of fifteen years, but you'd think he'd miss me more. We went through five league championships and several cup finals together.'

The glint in his eyes told me he was kidding, but I went with it. 'You're absolutely right. Maybe you two could try some kind of mediation service. There must be one. Buddies Forever. Or the Bromance Breakdown Service. I'm just glad you have me and Budweiser to see you through this difficult time.'

'And Callie,' he added, with a cheeky grin.

'Of course! And Callie! Is she still lusting after your body?' It felt weird saying that to my friend's husband. At first the thought of him with another woman had made me feel slightly nauseous, but he assured me the feelings were only one way, so that made it easier to joke about it. 'Mark said she made it pretty clear she wanted to seduce you. Do people still say seduce? I've been out of this dating thing way too long.'

'They do but only in TV shows set in the 1800s.'

For the first time in months I could feel the knot of tension easing across the back of my shoulders. This was the first snatch of normality in so long, the first conversation that felt like the old days. For a moment I could almost believe that Pete and Dee were out for a jog, and Luke and I were sitting, passing the time with a couple of beers until they got back.

I knew it wasn't true, but I had a high enough alcohol level in my bloodstream to go with it just for a little while.

'OK, so what do they say now? Get jiggy?' I asked, giggling.

'Since we're not fourteen, I'd have to say no to "get jiggy".' He was properly laughing now too and it was so good to see. 'All she said was that she'd like to go out some time. A date.'

'Are you going to go?'

He sighed, bringing the mood down. 'I can't see it. Every time I think about it the only person I see with me is Dee. I can't imagine being with someone else. Just wouldn't feel right.' There was a twinge of relief when he said that. I wasn't ready to face the possibility of Luke meeting someone else and building a different life.

I nudged him. 'God, we're a couple of sad gits, aren't we?'

'Indeed we are. But the fact that there's two of us makes me feel better about it. I'd hate to be the only pathetic git around here.'

I held up my beer and he clinked the bottle with his.

After knocking back another large gulp, I checked the time on my phone and saw it was after eight. 'I'd better go. Work in the morning. Val said she'd pop in and help for a few hours. I really need to think about taking someone on permanently, or at least until Mark gets back. He reckons he'll be here for three months next time. I hope so. I kinda got used to having him around.'

'Yup,' Luke agreed. 'He was my Pete-replacement. I just hope he doesn't desert me too or my new friends at the Bromance Breakdown Service will start to think it's me. Bollocks, it's freezing!'

The last exclamation was in response to the fact that I'd whipped the blanket off and stood up. Time to go home. It had been a long emotional day and I was glad it was over. Every day hurt, but the important ones were worse somehow.

Luke held open the balcony door for me. 'Thanks for coming back, Jen. The house is way too quiet without her.'

'And mine's way too quiet without Pete,' I answered reflexively. It was true. 'I'm starting to dread going home at night.' I was walking ahead of him now, folding up the blanket and putting it back in the basket in the corner of the lounge.

'Stay here.'

I paused, turned. 'What?'

'Stay here. Come live here for a while until you decide what to do. The spare room is empty, it never gets used, and didn't you help Dee decorate it anyway?'

All of this was true, but still... I couldn't. It wouldn't be right. This wasn't an episode of *Friends* where everyone just swapped apartments when their circumstances changed.

This was real life and I couldn't just up sticks and move in here. It would be wrong, wouldn't it?

'I think the beer has got the better of you, my friend. This is one of those decisions, like stopping for a kebab, when you wake up the next morning and really wish you hadn't done it. But thank you,' I leaned into him and gave him a hug. He was such a good guy. He didn't deserve any of this.

'Come on then, I'll walk you home.'

And suddenly the thought of going home on my own, in heels, walking back up that path, seeing where Dee had lain...

'I'll stay.'

Why did I feel weird saying that? I'd slept over here dozens of times before. I even had pyjamas and toiletries in one of the drawers in the spare room. But on every one of those times, Dee had been here. Now she wasn't and it just didn't feel right. But then, nothing felt right anymore.

'You sure?' Luke asked. 'I didn't mean to go for the sympathy vote.'

'I'm sure. Just for tonight. I don't want to be on my own either.'

I could see the relief in his expression. 'Thanks Jen. Can we watch crap telly and drink more beer?'

'Absolutely.'

It was one night. Just two bruised souls keeping each other company. What harm could it do?

25

Luke

Ishouldn't really have been surprised that it was Josie who found out first.

It was thanks to a rookie mistake – I hadn't asked her for the keys back when she stopped coming in to clean twice a week. It was amazing how little mess one person made. Dee always argued that she wasn't untidy, but over the last few months it had been proved otherwise. Not that I ever wanted to be proved right on that one.

God, I missed her.

Actually, that was what I was thinking when I put the key in the door on a Thursday in early June. When would I stop expecting to hear her voice when I got home? When would I stop picturing her there, in the bath, waiting for me wearing a big smile and nothing else?

Instead it was a whole other image that was waiting.

'Hey Luke,' said the voice the minute I closed the door behind me. Josie. Dressed in her standard colour of ninja black.

I think I actually physically jumped. My tough guy credibility just got wasted by a septuagenarian brandishing a Henry Hoover.

'Josie! You scared the crap out of me.'

'Yup, that's the effect I go for with men. I find it stops them from obsessing about my good looks and charm.'

I gave her a hug, taking in the spotless house.

'I know you don't need me anymore but just thought I'd pop in maybe once a month and give the place a good going over. You know, get into all the nooks and crannies.'

That's when I detected a slight air of disapproval and immediately realised why. Bugger. Of course she would have seen the signs. Jen's stuff was lying on the table, her breakfast mug in the kitchen, her toiletries in the bathroom. We hadn't been expecting the investigative cleaning equivalent of Inspector Morse to stop by.

Maybe Josie wouldn't ask.

'So out with it then? Who is she? I mean, I know it's none of my business and you're a grown man, son.'

She didn't get the irony in that statement.

'And I'm not one to judge...'

That one did actually make me fight to suppress a smile. Josie judged, juried, and executed at every available opportunity. It was part of that barely disguised charm.

'... but I mean, it's only been five months. Five! What kind of woman does that? Waltzes right in and parks her fecking slippers when Dee is still in the very bloody fabric of this house. And like I say, I'm not one to judge, but I've already heard all about that Callie one at your office and let's just say anyone that forward needs to have a good think about the way they're behaving. I mean, a married man! Just widowed! And...'

'It's not Callie.'

That stumped her. It took her a moment to regroup. 'Oh for the love of God, Luke, don't tell me you've started using those dating websites because, let me tell me you, you don't know where they've been. They get their photos up on that Internet, showing off their bits and...'

I almost wanted to let her keep going. This was the most entertainment I'd had in ages – even if there was every possibility it would lead to assault with a deadly Dyson if I didn't de-escalate it within the next few seconds.

'Josie! It's not an escort.'

'Well who in the name of...'

'It's Jen.'

'It's... no. Oh suffering Jesus.' She was absolutely aghast, making me spill out everything I said from that point on in one panicked, unpunctuated ramble.

'It's not what you think she's just staying here for a while and we didn't say anything because we didn't want anyone to read anything into it or take it the wrong way it's just because she was struggling to live in her house and I was grateful for company and don't look at me like that because I'm telling you the truth and if you don't believe me go check the spare room and you'll see the bed's been slept in and that's because that's where Jen sleeps it's totally innocent Josie it really is.'

Christ, the CIA should have this woman on their side. The first sight of Josie's raised eyebrow of cynicism and they'd fold like a weak-willed duvet.

'I haven't been in the spare room yet,' she conceded, but I could see that she was climbing down off the moral high ground.

'Come on, I'll make you a coffee,' I offered.

'Better put a vodka in it – the shock near made my blood pressure explode.'

She sat at the table in the kitchen. Dee had found it at a police auction for furniture that had been seized by the 'proceeds of crime team'. Some bloke called Killer Ken was probably languishing in jail right now completely unaware that the police had flogged off his prize possessions and his dining table was making a lovely statement in my kitchen.

'Jen never said,' she stated the obvious.

'I know. We just didn't want anyone discussing it or jumping to the wrong conclusions, and doing something nuts like coming storming in here with a vacuum cleaner.'

Josie didn't even blush.

I went on, 'She's had a crap time of it and so have I, so it just made sense. But we're friends, Josie. That's all it is. Like you and me. When you're not shouting at me,' I said, still trying to talk her down from DEFCON 1.

A riled up Josie wasn't to be taken lightly.

'How long has she been here then?' she asked, peeved that she knew nothing of it.

'About three weeks. Since Dee's birthday. It's just a temporary thing though. She's decided to sell her house and then she'll buy somewhere else and move in there. It was hard for her going back there every night, seeing where Dee died, and then with Pete gone too.'

'Arse,' she spat.

I assumed – and hoped – that referred to Pete.

I ploughed on, 'So this just makes sense. We're keeping each other company. Makes it a bit easier.'

She seemed to be accepting this, but came back for clarification. 'And you don't think you two will... you know.' She made that gesture that people over sixty make when they're referring to sex.

Oh Christ. I cut her off right there. 'No. Honestly. We're too alike, Jen and I. Besides, we'd never get anything done.' It was the standing joke between us. Pete and Dee were definitely the go-getters in our respective couples. Without them driving us to do stuff, Jen and I would barely manage to wrestle ourselves from Netflix. That was, however, why we worked perfectly as housemates. 'Plus, you know...' the conversation took a more serious, soul-baring turn, 'I couldn't imagine being in love with anyone that wasn't Dee.' The truth of that hit home for both of us.

'Och, son, my heart breaks for you, it really does,' she said, full of emotion and sympathy.

We had a moment. If it were a poetic novel, it would say our eyes connected and it felt like she was looking into my soul. But then they moved somewhat south on the anatomy.

'And can I just double-check that you're not just using her for your physical pleasure either, because then I'd have to kill you,' she cackled, an infectious laugh that was the one brilliant consequence of a lifetime of twenty fags a day.

'She's in the spare room, I promise you! And Josie, do me a favour – don't mention it to anyone. Not even Jen. She's so worried that someone will get the wrong idea and I wouldn't want her moving back into that house and being miserable just because she was worried about what people think.'

She pondered that for a few seconds and obviously it passed some kind of test. 'Aye, I can see why that would worry you. I'll keep it to myself. Unless I need material for a blackmail situation.' And there she was, off again, that barking laugh.

She headed into the kitchen and came back with her jacket on and her bag over her shoulder.

'Right, love, that's me away. I don't have time to do the spare room today, but I bet Jen has it spick and span anyway. I'll pop in again next month and just give everything the once-over. Try not to surprise the life out of me again. At my age, I haven't got many shocks left in me.'

I gave her a hug. 'Yeah, right. You'll be around forever. Marlboro would never let anything happen to you.'

This time the cackle lasted until after the door was closed.

I climbed the stairs, unbuttoning my shirt as I went. My bedroom looked exactly as it did when Dee left the house that morning. Her wardrobe door was still slightly ajar because she'd crammed too much stuff in it. Her dressing gown was still hanging on the back of the door. Her phone charger still sat on her bedside table. Her phone had been smashed in the crash, but I'd kept the bits, in a plastic evidence bag, in my bottom drawer.

The book she'd been reading was next to the charger. James Clavell. *Noble House*. She'd picked it up after a trip to Hong Kong, because she wanted to get an idea of what it was like at the time of the story, which was set in the sixties, when it was still a British territory. I'd read it, cover to cover, a couple of times now, wondering what she thought of it before she put it down and went to sleep for the last time. That was something I thought about all the time now. Tomorrow could be our last day. Maybe the day after. Dee had no idea that she'd never come home that Sunday. I'd never given death a second thought, but now it seemed like it was on my mind all the time and my reaction to it swung like a pendulum. Sometimes I'd think all that clichéd shite, like 'live every day like it's your last.' And other times I'd think 'what's the point of starting anything or planning anything because it could all be taken away in a heartbeat.'

I sat down on my side of the bed... What was I saying? They were both mine now. I pulled my shoes off, one by one, and lay back on the bed, reaching over to Dee's bedside cabinet for the other thing that lay there. A photo. Her and

I. Our wedding day. Laughing at something – I can't even remember what.

'I always loved that photo.'

Jen, in the doorway. I hadn't even heard her come in.

'Me too.'

She came over, kicked off her shoes and sat on the bed, back against the pillow, legs stretched out and crossed.

'Rough day?'

'Nah, it was fine,' I replied, putting the photo back down. 'But there was a bit of a situation when I got home. Josie was here. Still had her key and came in to give the place a spring clean. She saw your stuff.'

'Oh bugger.' Jen's head fell back and rested on the headboard. 'What did she say?'

'She thought it was Callie's and basically said she was a slapper.'

Jen brightened at that. 'Excellent.'

'But I told her it was yours.'

'Great.' Her sigh made it clear that it wasn't.

'It was actually fine. Once she stopped having murderous thoughts about me, I explained what was happening and she totally got it.'

'You think?' Jen asked, unsure.

'Yep. She believed me. I'm fairly sure she swept my bed for traces of your DNA to make sure you hadn't been sleeping there. She's probably on her way to a lab somewhere to get them analysed right now.'

I could see Jen was starting to relax. 'I hope she understands,' she said quietly.

'I think she does. I asked her not to mention it to anyone.'

'Good. I know Val would understand too, but I just don't want to give her anything else to think about just now. She's trying to hide it, but I think she's in bits over the court case. I'm glad Mark is due back this week – she needs him around. Be good to have him back in the shop too. Honestly, you've no idea how many of the clients ask for him and then look woefully disappointed when I say he's not there. Clearly my high levels of customer service and industry knowledge don't quite stack up next to the surfer dude David Gandy lookalike.'

'Who's David Gandy?'

'Oh my God, I'm dealing with amateurs here.'

She whacked me with a pillow and I thought again how glad I was that she was there. Dee would have approved.

'So. What's on for tonight? *Cold Feet* box set or *Homeland*?'

I thought about it before coming to the obvious conclusion. '*Cold Feet*. I can't watch the new series because I didn't watch the original episodes years ago, so I need to catch up. Besides, I think *Homeland* would give me flashbacks to Josie's interrogation.'

26
Val

My first thought when I woke up and opened my eyes. Sixteen days. Sixteen days until I see that evil little bastard across a room and I can look him in the eye and tell him what he took from us. I didn't care if I got dragged from that court, I was going to let him know. Him and his whole rancid family. Sixteen days.

Having the date to focus on was all that was keeping me going. I had to be strong. Had to make sure I was there to get justice for my girl. I felt like I couldn't mourn, couldn't grieve, couldn't start to think about the future until I saw that scumbag destroyed. I'd never have thought myself capable of hating someone the way that I did that boy. He had to pay. It was that simple. And maybe then we could start to heal, Don and I. I hated myself for the fact that I still couldn't be a wife to him, couldn't love him, take care of him, but every time I saw his face I remembered what we'd lost. Our daughter. Our girl.

Rage rose again.

Sixteen days.

But I had to get through today first.

Don was already in the shower, so I pulled on my dressing gown and slipped my feet into my slippers, then went downstairs. The postman had already been so I gathered up the mail and took it through to the kitchen. Didn't know where you were with the post these days. It either came at the crack of dawn or when you were getting ready for dinner. Not like the old days. Two deliveries a day. First thing in the morning and then another in early afternoon. When she was tiny, Dee used to sit watching for the postman coming so she could dash out to say hello.

'What are you smiling at there, love?' Don asked, wandering in and snapping me from my thoughts. For a moment I was irritated. Nostalgia was all I bloody had. Looking back. Replaying the past. Feeling snatches of happiness because for a moment I could make myself believe I was back there, not living in this hell of a life we had now.

'Och, nothing. Just daydreaming,' I told him. The memory was mine and I didn't want to share it. I know that makes me a selfish cow but it was how I felt and there was nothing I could do to change it. Instead, I busied myself, flicking on the coffee machine, putting some bacon on the George Foreman grill, buttering the rolls. That was our normal Saturday morning regime and I did it almost automatically now.

I heard the front door opening and Jen and Luke came in. I was glad those two still spent time with each other. Dee had been the common denominator for both of them so they could easily have drifted apart, but as far as I could see that hadn't happened.

Jen gave me a tight hug and I kissed her on the cheek.

'How're you doing this morning?' she asked.

Right Val, come on, I told myself. Big smile. Positive attitude. Get it together. It was one thing Don knowing that something inside me had died with our Dee, but apart from that one day when I pitched up at Josie's in bits, there was no way was I going to burden anyone else. That wasn't what they needed. Poor Luke, left without the woman he thought he was going to spend the rest of his life with. And Jen, she'd practically lost a sister and best pal at the same time. They'd lost so much – and I wasn't going to have them worrying about me too.

'I'm grand, m'dear. Grand. Bacon rolls will be ready in ten minutes.'

Luke took a seat at the table, and handed over a newspaper to Don, keeping one for himself. They both turned to the back pages like they did every Saturday morning. It was the little routines like this that got us through. They'd spend the next hour talking about the football that was being played today. Jen would have her roll then head off to open the shop. I'd get the house cleaned then pop over and give Jen a hand for a few hours. We were a team. We pulled together. I wasn't going to be the one that let us down.

Jen poured herself a coffee and made one for Luke, then took a seat.

'Val, Luke's going to come in and help in the shop today,' Jen said. I was glad Luke was getting back into his routine of working in the store for a few hours on a Saturday. I knew it must have been tough for him. Jen was still talking. 'So if you fancy a day to yourself or taking this man of yours out for a boozy lunch, it's no problem.'

I couldn't think of anything worse. I didn't even look at Don, although I could see from the corner of my eye that he'd raised his head from the paper and was watching me. 'Och, no, you're fine,' I said with a laugh and a wink. 'Sure, you can get too much of a good thing.'

Don put his head back down into the paper and didn't say a word. I wanted to say sorry. I wanted to explain how

I could act like my old self for the others but just couldn't manage it for him. It was because I had to. They needed me. I couldn't crumble and let them down. And God knows, if I could keep it up twenty-four hours a day, I'd do it for Don too, but it just wasn't possible. Short bursts. From the minute I was with one of the others, they got strong, positive, back with the old banter Val. Sixteen days. I just needed to get the court case over and it would all start to get better. It would.

'Up to you,' Jen said, smiling. She was such a pretty lass. Didn't have the confidence or the drive of our Dee and I always thought that was what made them good for each other. Dee spurred Jen on, and Jen calmed our Dee down and kept her grounded. It was a perfect balance. A bit like Dee and Luke too.

As I handed over her roll, Jen reached up and gave me another hug.

'Thanks for everything you're doing to help out, Val. I really appreciate it. Mark will be back soon and then you can put your feet up.'

'It's no bother at all. You know I like to keep busy. And yep, another week or so until he's back. I haven't heard from him since he left, but then I never did. They're not allowed anything but emergency calls out on the ship.' I didn't say that the only time that had happened was when Don had called him to tell him about Dee.

The chat flowed easily enough while we ate our rolls. Surface stuff. The shop. Luke's latest campaign. All of us avoiding the subject that was on all our minds.

Jen finished her breakfast and put her cup and plate in the dishwasher. Luke immediately got up and did the same, which was a bit odd. In the past, when he was working in the shop, he'd usually stick around for a couple of hours and keep Don occupied, then pop to work mid-morning, when it was starting to get busy.

'You off just now?' I asked.

'Yeah, we came in the same car today. I was up early so I, erm… swung by and picked Jen up on the way here.'

That made sense. The price of petrol these days was shocking.

'All right, then, love, well I'll see you both later. I'll come in about noon. Give you both a chance to go grab some lunch.'

Don didn't say a word and I was glad. I wasn't getting into a discussion about what I was going to do with my day. That was my bloody business, not Don Murray's.

Luke leaned over and gave me a kiss on the cheek and then they were off.

I cleared the rest of the dishes away and had almost finished wiping down the worktops, when I noticed the pile of post. It gave me something else to do, so I sat back down at the table, and opened the letters one by one. A gas bill. A letter from Childline, asking me to increase my monthly standing order. I'd do that. Great work they did. A reminder that my boiler was due a service. An appointment card from the hospital for Don's annual health check, part of an insurance plan Dee had insisted we both buy. 'Don't want either of you two popping your clogs before you've had a chance to blow my inheritance,' she'd said, her best cheeky grin in place. The pain of the memory almost made me gasp. If only we'd known she'd go long before us, I'd have taken every penny we had and moved us all away, a million miles from that drugged-up bastard that killed her.

Sixteen days

I tossed the appointment letter to one side and that's when I saw the postmark on the top right-hand corner of the final envelope. Office of the Crown Prosecution Service.

Why would they be writing to me?

My heart started to hammer in my chest and the breaths stopped coming altogether as I broke the seal and took out the paper inside.

Dear Mr and Mrs Murray,

I'm writing to inform you that the date for the court appearance in the matter of the court versus Darren Wilkie has been postponed until 30th October. We regret any inconvenience this may cause. Should you...

I stopped reading, the page blurring as white rage consumed me. How could they? We were nearly there and now they'd gone and moved the bloody goalposts. Suddenly my breaths were coming thick and fast, my heart thudding even harder.

It was supposed to be sixteen days away, and even that felt like forever. I couldn't wait until October. I couldn't feel like this for another four months. And what if they decided to postpone it again? I couldn't wait. I needed some resolution to this and I needed it now.

27
Jen

He was waiting for me on the step of the shop and I couldn't be happier to see him. 'Mark! I thought you were getting back tomorrow?'

'We docked early. There was a major storm brewing so it was safer to cut the trip short and come onshore, so I just jumped on an earlier flight and landed last night.'

'Is this where I pretend I actually understand what you do?' I asked him, laughing as I put the key in the door and then quickly switched off the beeping alarm.

'I'm an inspection diver on an R&D ship for an oil company. They are looking for drilling sites. My job is mostly underwater, inspecting the ship for faults and damage and then organising, sometimes doing the repairs.'

'And yet I have to cajole you into going out for the sandwiches if it's raining,' I pointed out, as we reached the back office and dumped our bags.

He had the grace to look sheepish, which still somehow made him look impossibly handsome. His face was tanned again, like it was when he'd first arrived, and it made his blue eyes, exactly the same shade as Dee's, look even brighter. His deep brown hair was falling over his face, that messed-up look that he totally pulled off. No wonder he'd been such a hit with our clients. I should really put a sign up saying 'Please do not objectify our staff. It's wrong. Unacceptable. But yes, I get that he's gorgeous.'

We both automatically slipped into the routine we'd established when he'd been here before. I got the till drawer with the day's float out of the safe, he flicked the kettle on and then switched on the rest of the lights and the sound system. 'Club Tropicana' started playing out in the shop. It was our summer soundtrack. That had been Dee's idea too – different soundtracks for the seasons – and she'd spent weeks making them all up herself, putting together several playlists for winter, spring, summer and autumn, so we didn't start to go stir-crazy listening to the same tracks every day. It worked a treat. I carried on chatting while I got the rest of the pre-opening tasks sorted out. We'd had a delivery late yesterday afternoon of a new Piz Buin factor fifty mousse, and I hadn't had time to put it on display, so I decided to do that now. I reached for a pair of scissors and sliced the box while we caught up.

'Did you get a chance to go home, to your place in Australia, I mean?'

He put my tea on the coaster on my desk. If he noticed that Dee's cardigan was still over the back of her chair, he didn't mention it. 'Nah, nothing to go home for. Jeez, that sounded a bit pitiful,' he said, grinning. 'What I meant was, I knew I was coming here anyway, so no point in going home for a couple of days and unpacking and packing again. Easier just to come straight here.'

'Bet your mum was glad to see you.'

His brow furrowed. 'Can't believe the trial has been delayed. Think it's hit her pretty hard. I think my mum and dad need the closure. Guess we all do. Anyway, sorry to bring the vibe down. What's been happening? What have I missed?'

Poor Val. As if she hadn't been through enough. She always had a smile on her face, and a hug for everyone but this had to be hard on her. He obviously didn't want to dwell on it so I didn't.

'Erm, nothing. Actually, something. I decided to sell the house.'

'Wow, what brought that on?'

I decided to go with the truth. Not the whole truth. Just most of it. I didn't want to mention that I was now firmly ensconced in Luke's spare room. It was only a temporary thing until I got my own place, but it felt so much better not having to go home to that empty house every night.

'It's got too many memories, good and bad. Great ones of my time with Pete, until he sat on our bed and told me he was leaving. And great ones of Dee until…' The tears sprang to my eyes and I swallowed them back. That happened less often now. In the early days, it was every couple of hours, they'd just well up and the next thing I knew I'd be wailing. Now, I could go a couple of days, a week maybe, perhaps two, and then something would ambush me and it would be like she'd only passed away yesterday. This time, I held it together, thanks mostly to the fact that he switched the focus of the conversation.

'Still no explanation from Pete?'

I shook my head. 'Nope. He hasn't said anything to Luke either, in fact they don't see each other anymore. It's like he just cut us out of his life completely. I'm meeting him next week though. It only took me about forty five texts and the threat of turning up at his work to get him to agree. Dee had organised a trip to Barcelona for next weekend and I'm going to go on it so we've got some stuff to update the blog with, but I wanted to see Pete before then. I just want to tell him face to face that I'm selling up. And I guess I want to have another go at getting answers.'

A text interrupted the conversation.

'That'll be him cancelling,' I said, but when I picked my phone up, I saw there was no notification of an incoming text.

'Mine,' he said. 'Lizzy.'

'Ah, so how is the romance of the year going?'

'It's going,' he said, a little offhand.

'Ooooh, do I detect trouble in paradise?'

He sighed. 'Not trouble. Just maybe a difference in perception. We just kind of fell into dating, and I had a bit of time to think about it while I was away and I reckon I should probably call it a day. She already knows that I'm only here again for a few months, and that I'll be heading back to Australia and my old life, so no point in starting anything up here, is there?'

'Probably not.' I admitted, experiencing a pang of regret at the reminder that he would be leaving. It had been great getting to know him and there would be a real hole in my life when he'd gone. I didn't want to think about that right now though, not when we had crucial things like his love-life to sort out. 'Just break it to her gently and please make sure she doesn't show up here.' I added.

'I hardly think she'll bother. She's a great girl and we were never exclusive – she was dating a couple of other guys too.'

I put my hands over my ears. 'No, no, no, no – don't tell me this. I don't get the whole modern dating exclusive-non-exclusive-thing. It terrifies the life out of me. Pete and I met when we were fourteen and back then you snogged a guy behind the school shed and that was it. Exclusive. I'm never going to be ready for the dating world. I'm going to be single forever and end up living alone, still working here, a dried up old husk surrounded by Heidi Klum bikinis.' I was joking, but there was definitely a truth in there. Dating. The very thought of it made me want to lock the door and stay on the sofa watching *Cold Feet* until the end of time.

'Aw, Jen, it won't happen like that,' his words oozed sympathy.

'You think?'

'Yeah. Some other brand of bikini will be trendy by then.'

I'd walked right into it and his cheeky smile was irresistible. I was still laughing when the door beeped outside to signal the first customer of the day.

'Glad we had this chat. You might want to work on your counselling skills though.' I said, trying to replace amusement with sarcasm but not quite succeeding.

I was almost past him when he put out his hand and caught mine.

'I'm kidding,' he said, 'and you know it. You're going to find a great guy, one that deserves you and makes you happier than you ever were with that dickhead.'

'You reckon?'

'I know it,' he said.

Something in the way he said it, with such surety and conviction, made me believe him.

28

Val

I'd come to hate the dance of avoidance Don and I did when we were going to bed. I'd go up first, get ready, climb under the sheets. Then I'd hear him coming up after me, going into the bathroom, then he'd come round the other side, under the covers, and he'd spoon my back. I suppose that was something. Until we'd talked after Dee's birthday dinner, there was a chasm between us that neither could breach. At least now there was a bit of contact. At least physically. But emotionally and intimately, we'd never been more disconnected.

I kept hearing that old Pink Floyd song that I used to love without really relating to the lyrics. 'Wish You Were Here', it was called and there was a line in it... Two lost souls swimming in a fishbowl. That was us. Don and I. He didn't know what to do with the love he used to feel for Dee and I couldn't love him when I was so consumed with unadulterated anger. Two lost souls.

Since I opened that letter, my rage had reached an all-time high and it was all I could do to contain it. It had been incredibly difficult not to race right round to his mother's house, to rage and rant. I'd even got as far as my front door, but I'd stopped myself just in time. I had to. I couldn't go round there in the state I was in. Much as I wanted to face him right now, to make him pay, to punish him, I wanted to be calm, prepared, to be thinking straight when I faced him.

The new trial was three months away and sometimes I wondered if the pain inside me would kill me by then. Or maybe it would be the strain of trying to keep it hidden that would get me. Josie was making it her mission to keep me busy. Book Club. Lunches. Popping over most days for a cuppa, always looking at me for signs that I was going to have another meltdown. I assured her I wasn't. I was fine, I said. Getting through it. Staying strong.

That was my story and I was going to stick to it no matter what. This pain was mine and I wasn't for sharing.

I felt Don's body curve into my back and realised that I welcomed it now.

I heard him murmur, 'I love you,' and it jolted me. For thirty-eight years we'd been married and every night those words were the last thing I heard, until Dee died and he fell silent.

Tonight was the first night since then that he'd said it aloud, exactly the way he did before, and I didn't know whether to be grateful or devastated. Did this mean he was getting over losing her? Getting back to normal? Didn't he know there was no normal anymore?

He must have felt my body tense. 'I'm going to start saying that to you again, Val, because I do, love – no matter what's happened.'

I heard the catch in his voice and realised he wasn't getting over her.

He wasn't a talker, never one for vocalising his feelings. In all these months, we'd talked plenty about Dee, but never about how we felt about losing her. I knew he was hurting, but what did it say about him that he was trying to reach me? He was a bigger person than me. This was his way of taking small steps back to me. Touching at night. Telling me he loved me.

'I know,' I said, hating myself because I wasn't giving anything back. I couldn't. There was nothing to give.

After a few minutes I heard his breathing change and felt his arms relax and he slipped into sleep. For an hour or so, I watched the red digital numbers on the white alarm clock on my bedside table change and I knew I couldn't stay here.

I hadn't left during the night for weeks, doping myself up with sleeping pills, knowing that I wouldn't drive if I'd taken them. It was the only way, because if I'd gone out there, I knew where I'd go and I was scared of what I'd do when I got there.

Now Mark was back, though, I didn't want him to see me taking them or being groggy in the morning. Instead, I lay here at night, tossing and turning, fighting the urge to get up. Until I couldn't.

Don let go of me altogether now and rolled on his back and I waited for what I knew would come next. Yep, there it was. Deep, guttural snores. Quiet at first, then louder as he found his rhythm. I felt the rage grow inside me and I knew it was either get up and go, or suffocate him as he slept. I'd had enough mourning this year so I got up and silently left the room.

As I passed the closed door of Mark's bedroom, I was telling myself I'd just go downstairs for a cuppa, but I knew I was lying. I took a pair of thick black leggings off the pulley that hung in the utility room, and from the folded pile to my left, picked up a long, thick, grey, roll-neck Arran jumper that didn't need ironing and slipped it on, then pulled on my black leather boots that were lying by the back door. I was out of the door in less time than it took to boil a kettle, my footsteps not making a sound as I walked down the path, past my neighbours' houses, until I reached the car park, then closed the car door gently so I wouldn't wake anyone.

The feeling of freedom when I pulled away was like shedding a skin of stress. I drove on autopilot, deliberately not thinking, not planning, because that way I didn't have to admit where I was going and stop myself. But of course I knew.

Twenty minutes later, I passed the shop she worked in, but kept going, around the corner, I didn't want to see the mother – I wanted to see him. I pulled into a space in the street across from their house, and turned the engine off. Every window was in darkness, as I suppose it would be at three in the morning, and that made me even angrier. Was he in there? Sleeping? Playing on some daft PlayStation or Xbox? Was his mother in bed, able to sleep despite knowing what an evil bastard her son was? Or was she round the corner at work, laughing with colleagues, pitying the unfortunates that came to the late night café, in denial about the fact that as that killer's mother, she was the most unfortunate of all?

I stayed for maybe half an hour, then turned the ignition. Despite my earlier decision not to go there, five minutes later I drew into an empty space right at the door of the supermarket.

The doors made a swooshing sound when I entered, and every nerve in my body was screaming at me to turn left, go to the café and see if she was there. But not yet.

I turned right, took a basket, started walking, up the first aisle. Fruit and veg. Turn. Crisps and sodas. Turn.

Breads and cakes. Turn. And so on, up and down every aisle, drawing it out because although the anticipation was killing me, the reality of getting there and seeing her was even worse. Christ, I was a mess. But at least I knew it. That had to count for something.

The bloke at the till didn't even look up as he rang it through and I was glad. The chatty ones were the worst.

A sirloin steak, onion rings, thick cut chips, a peppercorn sauce, a banoffi pie, custard.

He added on five pence for the bag I was packing it in and I paid with my card, then started walking, slowly, an invisible force pushing me, while another tried to stop me taking my next step.

I turned in to the deserted café and my heart sank. It wasn't her behind the counter. All I could see was the back of a head, but the hair was short, grey, almost cropped to the scalp. A man. How could I be filled with both relief and disappointment at the same time?

I should go home, but my hands were shaking and I didn't trust myself to drive on this much adrenalin. One tea. Ten minutes. Just long enough to settle myself.

Only when I reached the counter did the person turn around and I froze. It was her. The same person, yet not. Gone was the dark red bob, and in its place was hair that was not much longer than stubble around the sides and back, a bit longer on top. Same face though. Same person.

Our eyes met and I looked for a hint of recognition. None.

'What can I get you?' she asked, a forced smile.

'Tea,' someone said. There was no-one else here so it must have been me.

'It's just in front of you, there,' she said.

Of course it was. I knew that from last time and from every other supermarket café I'd ever been in. With shaking hands I lifted a cup, then a teapot and teabag. I opened the silver lid, put the bag inside, then placed it on the chrome shelf of the machine, pressed a button, and watched as the water came out, desperate to focus on something other than the woman across the counter who had now moved a couple of feet along to the till.

'One pound fifty please.'

I took a fiver out of my purse and handed it over. Only then did I have a chance to look at her and I saw that she had black circles under her eyes, sunken cheeks, and her hands shook worse than mine. If she was anyone else on the face of this earth, my heart would go out to her, yet I felt no pity. Not a shred.

She handed back my change and this time our hands touched and I had to steel myself not to recoil. Those hands had touched her son, held him, fed him, probably soothed him when he was a boy and he couldn't sleep at night. Did she wrap them around him when she went to collect him from the prison, when he'd got out on bail after killing my girl? Did they hand over money to him so he could go buy a couple of cans and a few more pills to get high? I hated her.

'Are you OK?' It took me a moment to realise she was talking to me and that I'd been staring at her the whole time. Bitch, feigning concern.

'Yes. Long night,' I replied as if that explained or excused it.

'Do you want me to take that to a table for you?' she asked, gesturing to the cup that was rattling against the teapot because my hands were trembling. The thought of her touching it made me want to vomit.

'No,' I said, not caring if she thought I was the rudest cow she'd ever met. I thought she was the worst mother and her spawn should be exterminated. Rude didn't even come close.

I wanted to stare at her, scream at her, tell her exactly what I thought about her and her thug son. I wanted to reach over and grab what hair she had left and pull her head down and bang it against the counter until she was unconscious. Rage. Pure seething rage. But I didn't do any of that because I'd never struck another human being in my life and she wasn't going to be the first. I hated her, but I hated her son more and I wanted to face him, tell him what he'd done, scratch my fingers down each side of his face until he bled.

She half shrugged and I turned away, took a seat at a table in the corner. I took two sips of my tea, and realised I couldn't drink it. I got up, picked up my bag and walked out, not giving a damn if she was looking at me, or thinking I'd lost the plot.

My time would come. But not yet.

29
Jen

We'd arranged to meet again in the café across the road from his office. May as well give the waiting staff a bit more entertainment.

I arrived an hour early, because I couldn't concentrate on anything else anyway. I wanted to look serene and composed when he arrived, and I wanted to see who he left the office with. I'm not proud.

'Hello again,' said the same waitress who'd been there last time. No shock that she remembered me after the scene I'd caused.

'Hi. Can I have a cappuccino please?'

'Of course,' she said with a smile, then retreated, probably to inform the rest of the staff that I was back and they should tune in for the second episode of my life drama.

I'd barely sat down when, to my surprise, I saw him come out of his building, dressed in his running gear. That bit wasn't the surprise. He often went for a run straight from work, because he said that if he waited until he got home, he'd never go back out again. It was too far for him to jog all the way from the office to Weirbank, so he'd run for forty-five minutes, then nip back to work for a quick shower before driving home. His company had a gym and changing rooms on the ground floor, so he had all the facilities he needed.

No, the surprise was that he had his arm around Arya, all five feet eight inches of gorgeousness. Actually that wasn't it either. The real surprise came when he stopped and kissed her, full on, in the middle of the street. Pete hated public displays of affection. He thought they were naff and embarrassing. I once tried to kiss him at the top of the Eiffel Tower and he jolted his head up so quickly his chin caught my tooth with maximum force and I spent the next two days taking ibuprofen for the pain.

This time, as I watched him tenderly place his hands on each side of her face, I waited for the stab through my heart, but weirdly, none came. Four months ago, I'd have charged across there and confronted him. Now I was just happy that I knew.

'Ouch,' came the low voice, almost a whisper from a few feet away. I turned to see the waitress, standing still, holding my coffee, her stare going in the same direction mine had been, taking in Pete and his snogfest.

'Yup, ouch,' I told her, with a conspiratory grimace.

'Ex?' she asked, her tone friendly, with an edge of sympathy.

'That obvious?'

'Not this time, but it was the last time. You were like a stuntwoman tearing across that road.'

That made me laugh. 'Not my finest moment,' I replied ruefully.

And that could have been it. End of conversation. Case closed. If she hadn't gone on, 'Yeah, well, he's not worth it. Trust me. Goes through them like water.'

For a minute I thought I'd misheard her but she hadn't finished yet.

'There was you, then there's that one over there, then there was another one that he used to meet in here some lunchtimes. Of course, it could all have been innocent, but I doubt it. Enjoy your coffee.'

Enjoy my coffee? She'd just told me there was a very real possibility my ex-boyfriend was a serial womaniser and now I was to enjoy my coffee?

Chin on floor, I turned back to Pete, who was now holding Arya's hand as she said something to him, then he laughed and leaned over to kiss her again, before she went in one direction and he took off running in the other. I've never prayed so hard for rain.

What A Creep. What a complete arse. I realised right then that there was a part of me that had still been hoping he'd come back, that had been waiting for the call or for him to arrive at my door, *our* door, and beg me for forgiveness. I also realised that the reason I wanted to tell him I was selling the house face to face was because I was hoping it would jolt him to his senses. Of course, I knew it was crazy. He had already sent over the papers to buy him out. Somehow though that didn't seem as final as actually selling the place, moving on to something that didn't have a piece of us in it.

I spent the next forty five minutes alternating between feeling like a fool and hating him, until I saw him reappear around the corner and run back towards the building. I mean, sure he was gorgeous, and fit, and all those things, but really he was just a bloke in running tights with... he turned to go into the building... sweat marks on his arse. Somewhere in my head I could hear Dee screaming with giggles at that one and I knew if she was right here she'd be telling me to woman up (she always said the man-version was sexist) and get him chucked. She'd always thought he had a tendency to be a wee bit too full of himself anyway.

For the first time in the six months since he'd walked out, I knew with absolute certainty that if he asked me to take him back, I'd refuse. Wow. Empowerment, fuelled by the almighty shot of caffeine that was in the cappuccino, flooded through me.

No more.

Done.

What had I ever loved about him? I struggled to pinpoint what made us tick. We just motored along. There was no grand passion. No big fights. We'd been together so long, we just fitted, and a big part of what made our lives great was our group, Dee, Luke, Val, Don, Josie... we made the most of life together and in hindsight I wondered if that disguised the fact that there was something missing. Well, he was certainly making up for that now.

Twenty minutes later – nope, he couldn't even give me the respect of arriving on time – he waltzed in, freshly showered, and slid into the chair across from me. The waitress was at his side in a heartbeat, and even though he would be too much of an emotional fucknugget to sense her disapproval, I got it loud and clear and returned it with a subliminal nod of thanks for the solidarity as she took his order for a fresh orange juice. She was back with it in seconds, obviously unwilling to miss a moment of potential drama.

I said nothing until he couldn't stand the silence anymore and jumped in. I took childish satisfaction in the fact that he caved first.

'How you been?' he asked.

'I'm fine. Luke's fine. Val and Don are fine. Josie's fine. Oh and Mark's fine. I know you didn't get to know him but he's actually a great guy. We're all fine. Every single person that you used to share your life with, apart from Dee, is fine. And we'd all like to thank you for pissing off when we needed you most.'

This clearly wasn't the conversation he expected and he immediately flipped to defensive. 'Wait a minute, how dare...'

A collective sharp intake from behind the counter and I know the other waitress, the chef, maybe the cleaner, and anyone else in the vicinity was listening in.

For my sake – and theirs – I couldn't hold back any longer.

'I dare because you're vile. You really are. And I can't believe I didn't see it before.' I barely paused for breath because I didn't want to give him the chance to interrupt. 'Even if you wanted to leave me, how could you desert Val and Don? You practically lived at their house since we were teenagers, and look at everything they did for us. And Luke. He just lost his wife. He was your mate and you ditched him. Who does that? Ah, that's right, you do. So I just wanted to let you know I'm rejecting your offer to buy me out and selling the house. It'll go up for sale next week. If you want any of the furniture, you're out of luck, because I've donated it all to charity. Sue me.'

I was on a roll now and it was going all the way down the Retribution Highway.

'And by the way, I saw you and your girlfriend over there earlier. Nice show you put on. Don't bother with your nonsense denials, you two-timing big prick. Nope, don't start telling me the details of how it started because I do not give a fuck. I don't care what you do with her, with the others before her. You're not worth it. You're really not. Anyway, can you do me a favour and give her a message from me? Tell her she could do so much better than an adulterous arse who could walk away from everyone who loved him without a backward glance.'

With that I got up, summoned every ounce of dignity I possessed, and started to walk away. I almost made it without incident. Almost. It was purely, well almost, accidental that, as I walked past him, my hand strayed from my side and flicked his orange juice into his lap. He sprung to his feet but I kept on walking.

'He's paying,' I said loud enough for him to hear.

'Certainly. You have a nice day now,' the waitress retorted, almost weeping with the hilarity of it all. It was as close to one of those rom-com victory moments as I was ever going to get and I milked it. I swayed my arse as I strutted out the door, I jumped in my car, I played Beyoncé songs really loud all the way to Weirbank, then I screeched around the corner, stopped at the car park at the end of Val's terrace, stormed up the path, rapped on her front door because I couldn't stop to take the time to find my key, then ambushed poor Mark, who answered the door, with a furious outburst of 'It's done!', before taking one step inside the hall, closing the door behind me, and sprouting tears like a burst water balloon.

I never did do empowerment very well.

'Hey, hey, hey, what's wrong? What's done? What's happened? Oh shit, you were seeing Pete. What's the jerk done now?'

'Is Val here?' I wailed. So much for the strong, composed new me. I needed Dee. I needed Val. I really, really needed Val.

'No, she's at Book Club with Josie. My dad's working late. It's just me. Oh bugger, come here.'

He opened his arms and I stepped into them, tears soaking his T-shirt in no time, his arms around my heaving shoulders. This was all too much. Way, way too much.

'I'll call Josie,' he offered.

'No! She'll kill him. With her bare hands.'

He smiled his infectious smile and then that thing happened where you're laughing and crying at the same time and it's a toss-up which one will win the day and...

I don't know what happened. I really don't. Some cosmic force lifted me up on to my tiptoes and I kissed him, right on the mouth. Not just a peck. Suction. And then, to my complete shock, I realised he was kissing me back. He slowed it down so that it went from frantic to holy crap, this is amazing. It felt so good to be in someone's arms again, to feel wanted. All the tension went, my shoulders relaxed, then his hand went from my shoulders to the side of my face, cupping it and... A vision of Pete, kissing Arya, touching her face. I pulled away, the moment most definitely, absolutely gone, and I groaned, 'I'm so sorry. I didn't mean to do that. I really didn't.'

His hands went down to my sides now, holding me, so our faces were still close enough that I could feel his breath when he spoke.

'Trust me, you really don't have to apologise. I was definitely halfway culpable on that one.' He was teasing me, just being gorgeous, funny, flirty Mark, the guy that could make dozens of my customers blow two hundred quid on a cashmere jumper they'd hide from their husbands in the back of their wardrobes.

And I'd kissed him. Guilt and mortification were the first two emotions to arrive. What had I just done?

'I'm going to go...'

'Don't.'

I wasn't sure if it was him or the bit of me that wanted to kiss him again that said that.

Him. Because he said it again.

'Don't go.'

I nearly didn't, but this was messing with my head way too much. I didn't do spontaneous, or rash or wanton. I just didn't. I thought for a week before I bought a new pair of shoes. Two weeks if they were for a special occasion. This was the kind of stuff Dee did, not me.

Dee.

Oh God. I'd just kissed her brother. She would be horrified.

That thought came straight out. 'Dee would be horrified.'

Mark went for an incredulous, 'No, she wouldn't.'

This was one of those moments in life where there was a decision to be made and I felt woefully under-prepared to make it. On the one hand, hadn't Dee's passing shown us that life was short and had to be grabbed by the balls? Not literally. Kissing was enough to send my inner moral compass into a spin cycle. On the other, this was a really bad idea. Val and Don were the closest thing I had to parents and this was their son.

'I can't.'

'I'm glad you did,' he countered.

Was it wrong that part of me was too?

I backed up, opened the door. 'Sorry,' I said... and then I left, running to the car, in a completely different state than I was half an hour ago.

This so wasn't me. Dee had always been the wild one. I did predictable. Balanced. Stable. Measured. All of which were missing in bloody action right now.

My stomach was churning all the way home. Mark. Of course he was attractive, but he wasn't my type at all. My type was... Pete. That was it. I'd been out with one guy in my life so that was all I had to base my preferences on.

My car stopped and I saw that I was already outside Luke's house. I'd driven the whole ten minute journey on autopilot. I wasn't ready to stop freaking out over this. Why did we all have to live so bloody close together?

Please be out. Please be out. Please be out.

As soon as I opened the door, his head popped up from the sofa.

'Hey! I was getting ready to rustle up a posse of Josie and Val and come looking for you. How did it go?'

'Not as expected,' I whimpered.

He sat bolt upright, face full of concern.

'Why? What happened? I swear to God he's such a...'

'I kissed Mark.'

30

Luke

'You what?' I couldn't have heard that right. No way.
'I kissed Mark. Shit bollocking crap.'

She crossed the lounge, kicking her shoes off as she walked. Even that was out of character. Jen always took them off, picked them up, then took them upstairs to her room. I mean, the spare room.

Instead, she left them where they fell and kept on going until she reached the sofa I was half-sitting, half-lying on. She plumped herself down on the edge of the coffee table so she was facing me, and put her head in her hands.

'I have no idea what I'm doing, Luke. None at all.'

I was going to say something along the lines of 'none of us do', but she had more to say so I just kept quiet and let her go on.

'I feel like everything is out of control and I'm second-guessing myself. Should I sell the house? Should I not? Should I be living here?'

'Of course you should,' I replied.

'I know I'm so much happier than when I was at my house, but I'd hate to upset Val and Don, or anyone else who got the wrong idea...'

'They won't.'

'Maybe, but I don't want to risk it.'

I understood that. In truth, I felt the same.

'Until tonight I wasn't sure if I was really done with Pete,' she admitted.

That one took me by surprise. 'I had no idea there was any doubt. If I'd known, I probably wouldn't have called him all those names.'

That at least made her smile. 'They're all true.'

'Indeed they are,' I agreed, glad the two furrowed lines between her eyebrows had relaxed just a bit. 'So what happened?'

'I had to watch him making out with Arya in the middle of the street.'

'Pete?' I was incredulous. 'But he hates public displays of...'

'I know! He doesn't bloody hate them now. People were having to swerve around him while they stood there like the last scene in a bloody Hugh Grant movie. Honestly, it was unbelievable. Then the waitress more or less told me he was a serial shagger...'

'What?' he countered, astonished.

'Ok, well, not quite. But she did say he'd brought other women to the café. So when he eventually unhanded his latest girlfriend and he came to meet me, I told him he was a spineless, treacherous arse and I was selling the house, then I stormed out all proud of myself. Drove home listening to Beyoncé, decided to go see Val, got there, crumbled into pieces, Mark answered the door because Val was at Book Club and I kissed him,' she went on.

'Christ.'

I didn't know Mark that well, but from what I did know, he wasn't the kind of guy to take advantage of a situation. It struck me that Dee would be loving the drama of all this if she was here. This was the kind of stuff she thrived on. There wasn't a reality show she didn't watch or a piece of gossip she didn't want to hear.

I didn't possess the same skills. I had a sudden tightening around the chest area, completely unsure how I was supposed to react.

'I don't know what to say,' I blurted. 'This crosses over a line to stuff I'm not equipped to discuss.' I wasn't lying. I did surface level, irrelevant and sport. I'd been friends with blokes for years and not realised they'd married or divorced in that time.

'There's nothing *to* say. I'm just so glad I'm going to Barcelona tomorrow. I couldn't face him.'

'You're going to have to sometime.'

'I know. God, I'm hopeless.'

'You are.' I didn't mean it but it made her smile again and it was better than patronising shite. 'But Dee would be loving this.'

'I miss her so much, Luke. I'd do anything to rewind the clock and have her back.'

'Me too.'

I leaned over and gave her a hug.

'Careful,' she warned, 'apparently when men try to console me I instinctively kiss them. Who knew?'

'Don't worry, I'll be ready to duck,' I assured her.

'I'm a thirty-two-year-old woman. How can my life suddenly be so much of a mess, Luke?'

If I had the answer to that I'd have applied it to myself. Treading water at work. Welling up when I least expected it.

Living with a pal because I couldn't stand coming home to an empty house. I had no idea how to fix myself, never mind anyone else.

I might be rubbish at depth and emotional trauma, but I decided to give it a go. Dee would be proud. 'Because we've been pretty much pissed on by life this year. This time last year we knew where we were at and where we were headed but everything has changed and we're just swimming against the tide...'

'Drowning,' she interjected.

'Maybe. But we just need to stay afloat...' I broke off and changed tack. 'Am I using too many swimming references? Because I feel like I am. Sorry, I'm rubbish at this.'

Her smile was only slightly tinged with sadness. 'You're doing great. Thank you.' She got off the table and turned around so she was sitting on the sofa next to me. She put her head on my shoulder. 'What should I do about Mark? Is it going to be really uncomfortable now?'

'I'm sure he'll cope,' I told her, pretty positive I was judging that one right. He didn't seem like a guy to take things too seriously. He'd been seeing Callie's pal Lizzy on and off since that night in the pub, and Callie told me they'd agreed it would be a casual thing. I wasn't sure how that worked, but they both seemed cool with it.

'I need to go pack,' she said, but didn't move. 'Tell me we're going to get through this, Luke.'

'We are. And look, tonight was progress. You put Pete in his place and you know for sure that it's over, so you're moving forward. I hate that expression, but it's true. One step in front of another. One day at a time. OK, now I'm using too many AA-meeting clichés. Your romantic life will still be fucked but you'll never drink again,' I told her, making her laugh again.

'You are so, so bad at this,' she answered, feigning sorrow. She kissed me on the cheek. 'Don't worry, that was just a thank you. I appreciate it, Luke. Being here, having you. I think we just need to hold on until we come out the other side.'

'I think you're right. Good night luvly. What time are you leaving in the morning?'

'About five-thirty.'

'OK, so you'll be gone by the time I get up. Have a safe flight and text me when you get there.'

'I will,' she promised, climbing the stairs at the other side of the room. 'Maybe being away will give me some clarity.'

'Maybe it will,' I agreed as she disappeared out of sight.

I lay back on the sofa, staring at the ceiling. Clarity. How come I had an uneasy feeling that – to stick with my newfound emotional depth and swimming analogies – I was starting to be carried down an unexpected stream.

31

Jen

Looking out of the cab window, I saw the hotel long before I reached it. Ten minutes from the airport, in the L'Hospitalet area on the outskirts of Barcelona, The Renaissance Fira looked to be about twenty-five stories high, but what distinguished it from any other hotel I'd ever been in was that the windows were in the shape of trees.

As I entered through the glass doors, I automatically took mental notes of the surroundings for the blog. Marble floor, leather seats in the foyer, a bar over to the right-hand side. Polite check-in. This time I'd called ahead and changed the name on the reservations, so while it was still booked under Sun, Sea, Ski, they knew I was coming instead of Dee. I didn't explain why. I pushed down the memories of New York that were threatening to bubble to the surface. I'd closed that door. Shut. With a bang. There was no point revisiting thoughts or events I'd never be able to explain.

I was handed a key card and directed to the elevator lobby. Glass, chrome, black, but the strangest thing was the black trees behind the glass walls. As the lift rose, I realised the building was a hollow square, four sides, and in the middle, going right up through the structure, were jungle-like areas full of trees and bushes. I was detecting a theme.

The lift stopped at the twenty-third floor, and I exited, turned to the right, walked along the edge of the garden to my right, a black wall to my left, a few strategically placed neon pads indicating the positions of the doors. My key card worked first time, a bit of a rarity in my experience, and when I went inside I stopped to take it all in and commit it to memory. Unusual, for sure. Minimalist. Postmodern. And, especially rare for a hotel, all white. The tiles on the floor could have been marble or granite, I wasn't sure. White walls. To my left a white wardrobe, then a low shelf that ran the whole way along the wall to the glass frontage, a huge window that was opaque, apart from the huge leaf-shaped area in the middle which was clear.

To the right, there was a magnificent – I committed 'magnificent' to memory for the blog as it truly did sum it up – white bed, with voile curtains that could be pulled around it to give privacy from the seating area between the bed and the window. It was so beautiful, so romantic, that I found myself wishing for a second that Pete was here, before I remembered that Pete and romance definitely didn't belong in the same sentence any more. I wasn't sure that they ever did.

I checked Dee's iPad. This was a quick visit, flying in this morning and then home on the last flight tomorrow night. There was only one thing in the calendar and that was dinner tonight, at a restaurant about five minutes from here. I thought about going out now and jumping on the metro into the city centre, but Dee had done many blogs from Barcelona, and I'd come here a couple of times with her so I'd already experienced the tourist stuff. To be honest, I didn't fancy the chaos. What I did fancy, was relaxation, solitude, and a few hours respite from having to think about anything or anyone. Dee would marvel at my enjoyment of being alone and doing nothing, while I would watch in admiration as she refused to sit still for a minute, constantly chasing new experiences. Within ten minutes of arriving anywhere, she'd be talking to people; within a day, she'd have a gang of friends. I loved her for it, but it wasn't me.

I'd read on the website that there was a rooftop pool, so purely for research purposes obviously, I changed into a swimsuit, pulled on one of the white robes that were hanging in the wardrobe, and took the lift skyward. Actually it required two lifts to get there – one that went to the twenty-fifth floor and then another for the pool level above.

I pushed open the door from the corridor to the swimming pool deck and my eyes took a moment to adjust to the blinding light. When they did… wow. I understood now why Dee wanted to come here. The pool wasn't huge, maybe twenty metres long, but it was surrounded by a dark wood deck on three sides, lined with huge white leather double sun loungers. To the left, was a long bar. Behind me to the right, just around the corner, I could see a seating area under a white canopy. But what really sold it was the view. On all sides, I could see for miles, the city of Barcelona in front of me and to the left, the mountains in the far distance beyond the city, and way to the right, the port area and the sea. It was breath-taking. Just stunning. I realised the word 'magnificent' was in danger of being overused on this trip.

In the far corner, I noticed a lounger was free so I padded round to it, dropped my book and my sun cream, then went back to the bar for a towel and a drink. A gin and tonic and a black coffee. Dee's order. Her favourite combo. It seemed perfect for the moment. I was here, trying to live up to her unspoken wishes by carrying out her plans, so it was only right I gave it a twist of Dee authenticity.

Towel under my arm, I carried both drinks back to the lounger and put them on the table beside it, spread my towel and discarded my robe, then stretched out like a sleeping bag being unfurled after months in its carrier. The heat immediately warmed me and I pulled my sunglasses – Gucci, found in the office, so either Dee's or freebies we'd been sent as part of a summer package – down on to my face, and rubbed on the SPF 50. My Scottish complexion, fair with a tinge of blue, wouldn't stand up to the sun for more than a few minutes without a thick coating of cream or a duffle coat.

With the sunglasses on, I was able to surreptitiously scan the other loungers. This was definitely the 'beautiful people' set. Designer swimwear, beautifully toned bodies, deep caramel hues, buff nails... and that was just the blokes. On every set of eyes there were the signature styles of the most exclusive designer sunglasses. Just from where I was sitting I could see Chanel, Tom Ford and Prada.

I didn't belong here, but that didn't mean I wasn't going to make the most of it.

The stresses and strains, and thought of Mark's tongue, dissipated in the searing heat and I pulled out my book, Anna Smith's *Kill Me Twice*, and started to read, sipping my drinks and wondering why the hell I'd always taken a back seat on the windswept travel. Of course, I knew. I was just as happy at home, pottering about the garden or having lunch at Val's. As work went though, this definitely wasn't a bad shift.

My eyes flicked up as I turned the page, took in the view. I wondered what the two beautiful girls over at the bar, with golden tans in elaborately slashed swimsuits, were laughing at. I also wondered what their tan lines would look like when they took those cossies off. That should have been Dee and I – in more sensible outfits, naturally.

I smiled at the older couple in the corner, the man snoozing, the woman lying next to him reading something on a Kindle, their hands touching as if they just liked the reassurance of the other one being there. I thought that would be Pete and I.

The overwhelming sense of loss seeped into my pores. Don't cry. Do not dare cry. Do not be the woman in the corner, snivelling, making the people around you back off in case you suddenly decide to latch on to them and share your woes.

I closed my eyes, inhaled, fought back the tears, opened them...

He was there.

It was definitely him.

I sat bolt upright. Yes. Over by the door, in a T-shirt and shorts, scanning the area. The guy from New York.

I could see him holding open the door of the cab outside the jazz club. He was in clear focus as he passed me when I went into Tiffany's. And now he was turning, walking back towards the door.

I shot up, not caring that my blue-white flesh wobbled in outrage. This was a serene oasis of calm, so shouting or sprinting around the pool and causing an international incident was out of the question. Instead, I adopted the hip-swinging gait of an Olympic speed-walker, not caring that it made me look like I was in urgent need of getting to a loo.

Along one side, left turn, along the other side... people were turning to look now. Och, sod it. I burst into a run, down towards the door, through it... Lift or stairs? Stairs. I ran down the one flight to the floor below, where I'd changed lifts earlier. No one there.

There were five lifts in this lobby and I scanned the numbers at the top. Three were going down, one coming up, one was at this floor. I pressed the down button and the doors on the closest one flew open. I quickly jabbed the button to descend but it already felt hopeless. He could be in any of the three lifts going down, and he could stop on any floor to get out.

'Come on, come on...' My heart was racing. What the hell was going on here? Twice was a coincidence, but to see him a third time, in an entirely different country... There was definitely something untoward about all this. Was Dee in some kind of trouble? Was it a friendship? A fellow blogger she occasionally met up with? Was she... oh bugger, I hated thinking it again, but was she doing something illicit? No. She wouldn't.

The doors opened on the ground floor and I flew out and scanned the lobby, searching for his face amongst the crowd congregated at the door, the lines of people waiting to check in and out at reception, the group of guys sitting at the bar to the left, the security staff. Nothing. He wasn't there. Dammit. However, had I ever wanted to be centre of attention, now was my moment, because almost every set of eyes in the lobby were trained on the woman in the bikini who was standing there, blue-white flesh on show for the world to see.

Mortified, I backed up into the elevator area, grateful to see a gaggle of elderly ladies disembarking, all wearing large hats and pulling trolleys, no doubt on a stopover, before going to join one of the many huge boats that left the port, the fourth busiest cruise ship dock in the world.

I ignored their curious glances as I slipped around them, back into the lift to make my way skywards again. I conceded defeat. There was no way I was going to find him in a hotel this size, let alone this city.

Back on the roof deck, I ordered up another gin and tonic and took it back over to my lounger, letting the ice-cold sensation of the liquid cool me down and calm the throbbing sensation that had started in the side of my head, probably as a result of the combination of the heat, the exertion, the shock and the sheer bloody mortification at having flashed my thighs to a large section of the population of Barcelona. Dee would think that was hilarious. Resting my head back on the padded luxury of the lounger, I had a conversation with her in my head.

I wish you were lying next to me, drinking gin and laughing at the orange-hued bloke in the corner in Speedos. And I wish you would tell me what the hell you were up to. Come on, Dee, let me into the secret.

She didn't answer. However, a thought did occur to me. She had dinner planned tonight at a restaurant near here. On two out of the three bookings she had in her diary for New York, he was there. And I would bet my last drop of SPF 50 that he would be there tonight too.

32

Val

The cemetery was deserted apart from a group of teenage boys, maybe fourteen or fifteen, huddled in the little shed at the gate, with half a dozen cans of lager, a large plastic bottle of cider and a packet of cigarettes between them. There wasn't much to do in the town on a Saturday night for that age group, but still I wondered where their parents thought they were. I was never mother of the year, but I always knew exactly where my two were, who they were with and what time they'd be back.

And look how that worked out for me.

I kept Dee safe, all through her childhood and teenage years, protected her, helped her make good choices, and then, when my job was done, I let her out in the world and what happened? That's when she needed protecting most and I wasn't there to pull her back inside, to push her out of the way or change her plans for that day so she was nowhere near that piece of scum when he killed her.

As I reached the boys in the shed I could see that they were already well on the way to a drunken night. I stopped as I passed, and stared at each one of them in turn.

'Whit?' the smallest, therefore the one with the most to prove, asked. 'Whit ye looking at?'

'I'm just memorising your faces, son, because that way if anything happens to any of these gravestones, if there's a single flower damaged or a stone chipped, I'll know who I'm hunting for.'

That shut him up and the rest of them just put their heads down and reached for their cans. I kept on walking, past decades of death, until I got to Dee's corner. It was a bright, warm July night, and the white roses I'd planted along the front of her stone looked beautiful.

As always, the first thing I did was give the granite a clean with the packet of wet wipes I carried in my bag, talking to her the whole time in my head. 'Just me, love. Your dad's down the pub and I was at a loose end so I thought I'd pop up to see you. Our Mark's out with the girl he's been seeing. Lizzy is her name and I've not met her yet, but Josie has given me the rundown – sounds like a right character if you ask me. Non-exclusive, he calls it. What a load of nonsense. Wouldn't have happened back in the day with me and your dad. Never did go in for all that free love carry-on. What else? Oh, Jen is away at some hotel you'd booked in Spain. Poor love didn't want to go, but she's trying to keep everything the way it was with the shop and the website and make sure you'd be proud of her. I worry about her though. That imbecile Pete still hasn't shown his face. He'll get a piece of my mind when he does. Shameless, he is. Utterly bloody shameless. None of us have seen hide nor hair of him since he walked out on the lass. Not even Luke. I'm worried about him too. All that weight he's lost. Josie says she went over to give the house a clean last week and it was exactly the same as when you left it. You picked a good man there, pet. Solid and dependable, like your dad.'

Stone polished, flowers clipped with the pruning shears I always brought with me, a few weeds pulled up and put in a pile for me to take away when I was leaving, I parked myself on the bench we'd had installed right in front of where she lay and continued my one-way chat.

'I went to see her again. The mother. I know I said I wouldn't but I couldn't help myself. Still no sign of that son of hers. And wait until I tell you Dee, the police liaison officer told me the evil bastard plans to plead not guilty. Not guilty. I can't tell you how angry that makes me. If he was not guilty, then I wouldn't be sitting talking to you in a cemetery on a Saturday night. I hate him, Dee. I've never wanted to kill anyone with my bare hands, but I'd gladly squeeze the last breath out of that boy. No, not a boy. A man. Twenty-four, he is. Old enough to know better and be responsible for his actions, yet he's trying to squirm his way out of it by pleading not guilty. I won't let him get away with it, pet. I'll get justice and I'll watch him rot.'

I was suddenly aware of a presence right behind me and it wasn't of a spiritual nature.

'Is this a private party or can anyone join in?' he asked me.

'God Almighty, Luke, you scared the living daylights out of me. Thought it was one of those wee rascals that were boozing down at the shed. Had a word with them on the way in and I don't think they were best pleased.'

He had come round to the front of the bench now and I could see he was in his full running kit, his T-shirt, hair and face dripping with sweat.

'Did you threaten them with vigilante justice if anything got vandalised?'

'How did you know?'

'Just an educated guess,' he laughed.

He had a lovely smile, this man. No wonder our Dee loved him. I'd worried at first that he was too laid-back, too amenable, and our Dee would walk right over him, but to give him his due, he managed to hold his ground in most things in a calm, understated way. He was good for her and I was grateful.

'Wild Saturday night planned then?' I went on.

'Crazy. You?'

'Heading to the clubs as soon as I leave here,' I replied, keeping the banter up because I was determined to keep it together and not have him thinking that I was here because I was in some kind of sad, lonely state. Truth hurt. 'Josie's at home with her sequined knickers on just waiting for me to pick her up.'

He howled. 'Noooo. I may never get rid of that mental image,' and there was nothing to do but laugh.

There were a couple of minutes of silence as we both thought about the best way to ask the same question. I knew that because he went first.

'So what's brought you up here then, Val? Are you OK?'

'Of course I am.' I wasn't. 'I just like it up here…' I hated it. 'Because it's quiet and I can think.' I couldn't – unless it was about the vile ways I wanted Darren Wilkie to suffer.

Luke seemed to accept this though.

'What about you?'

He leaned back, sighed. I could see he was troubled. Who wouldn't be in his situation? 'Sometimes I think I just run up here to prove to her I'm out running and not comfort-eating myself into a blob.'

He was trying to joke himself out of it, but I wasn't for letting him.

'And other times?' I probed.

'I just don't know how I'm supposed to live my life without her. And I don't just mean without loving her. Since the day we met we spent all our time together, either Dee and I, or the four of us, with Jen and Pete. We went on holiday, did stuff every weekend, met up after work for dinner. And now, Dee and Pete are gone and Jen and me... well, we're just lost. I go out running, I go to the gym, but it's just existing. I don't know when I'm supposed to start living again, Val. And I don't know how I'd even start. I have no idea what makes me happy without her. Sorry. I shouldn't be unloading all of this on you.'

My heart was breaking as I listened to him. I was ashamed to admit I hadn't really thought about where he'd go from here. He was still a young man – too young to have given up on finding more happiness. Dee wouldn't want that. She really wouldn't. And much as it made the pit of my stomach ache with pain, I felt that I had to give him permission, for his sake.

'Don't you apologise. You can talk to me anytime about anything at all, Luke. You know, Dee wouldn't want you to carry on like this. Our Dee believed you should live for the moment, I don't have to tell you that. Even when she was a kid, she ran me ragged with plans and ideas, and madcap schemes. Don used to think it was hilarious, but he wasn't the one out roller-skating up and down the front path with her or sitting in A & E when she'd fallen off the rope swing for the tenth time.'

'She still had the scars,' he said, smiling sadly.

'She did. And she still kept on going. That's the point, Luke. It's OK to keep on going, to stop living in the past and start finding a new way to live. And I know it'll be hard if you meet someone else – God knows, I can't stand the thought of it – but you can't go through the rest of your life not being loved. When you're ready, your new life will come.'

I nearly lost it when he put his hand on top of mine and I saw his eyes were filled with unshed tears. Dee always did say he had a sentimental side, but I'd seen only strength and care for the rest of us since she passed. He'd been doing what we all had – fighting to keep our heads above water so we could keep each other afloat.

'Thanks Val,' he said, kissing me on the top of my head. 'I think I needed to hear it. I find it hard to contemplate the future, but when I do, I just can't get past the thought that I'd be disrespecting her if I go on to have a great life.'

'I think you'd be disrespecting her if you didn't.' Much as it hurt to me to say it, I meant it.

We sat like that for a while, both lost in our own thoughts. I've no idea where Luke's mind had gone, but mine was right back at Darren Wilkie and the things I told myself every day that I would say to him.

Without making a conscious decision to talk about it, I heard myself blurting out, 'Do you ever think about him, Luke?'

'Who?'

'That evil bastard who killed Dee. Darren Wilkie.'

I could see him mulling the question over, thinking about his answer before he spoke. 'Sometimes, when I see something in the paper or think about the trial. Other than that, I don't, because it won't change anything. He did it. As long as he gets what's coming to him, that's all I care about as far as he's concerned. Aside from that, I give him no headspace. He's not worth it.'

I knew he was right and I so wished I felt the same, but the twisting, gut-wrenching hatred I felt for Wilkie would just not allow it.

What a state we're all in, Dee, I told her, and I felt her roll her eyes and heard her voice telling me to get it sorted.

I will, love.

I will.

Just as soon as I've seen that bastard pay the price.

33

Jen

I was starting to make a habit of arriving early. The restaurant was a traditional little tapas place, maybe fifteen tables, and given the resemblance and ages of the staff, I made an educated guess that it was a family-run business: Mum, Dad, and two adult sons.

The walls were a deep burgundy, the floors made of mahogany slats that looked a hundred years old, and every particle of air was infused with the aromas of tomatoes and garlic and oils and spices.

It was the kind of place I loved. Nothing showy or flash, or over-the-top trendy. No customers taking selfies or fascinating people to gawk at. It wasn't the kind of place I'd expect Dee to choose. Unless she hadn't been the one to pick it…

When I was greeted by the welcoming chap I took to be the patriarch of the family, I asked for the table nearest to the door.

'But the back is much quieter,' he said, his words heavily accented. Normally, I'd have gone with his recommendation, but I wasn't risking having to charge out after that bloke for the second time today, so I wanted to be prepared, vigilant, and ready to pounce if he showed up.

Although, as a precaution, I had worn Stan Smith trainers with my pale blue maxi-dress, borrowed from one of the new ranges we were stocking in the shop for summer. With my hair up in a ponytail, and a bit of a pink tinge from the sun today, I was thinking that – lack of strappy high heels aside – I was nudging the presentable side of the grooming scale for once.

One of the waiters, a dark-haired, high-cheekboned beauty of a man, brought over the coffee I'd ordered from his father. It wasn't the normal pre-dinner aperitif, but the last thing I wanted was to have my judgement clouded by alcohol tonight.

Nine o'clock came. And went. A few more tables had filled up now and my heart jumped every time the door opened with more diners, but it was never him. It might be time to face the possibility that I had officially gone a bit mad. Made a huge mistake. Got carried away with the drama and made something out of nothing.

The waiter was hovering a little, so I ordered a tortilla and some chicken in a garlic sauce. It wasn't as if I'd be kissing anyone tonight.

Aaaargh, that thought took me right back to the night before. Mark. I'd been trying to avoid thinking about it all day. How could I? Seriously? How could I have done that? And while he didn't exactly put up an argument, that didn't detract from the mortifying truth that I led the charge. A tingling sensation spread across my stomach and I launched an internal battle against it until I was forced to concede that yes, it was flattering that he didn't want me to stop and seemed, in the moment, absolutely open to the exploration of oral cavities, but that was beside the point. Did I find him attractive? Absolutely. But then, I also found Adam Levine from Maroon 5 attractive and I'd yet to lunge at him with my tongue out. Although, in fairness, that theory hadn't been tested because I'd never met him. But still, what an embarrassment I was. If Val and Don found out they'd be horrified. Yes, I realised Mark was a grown man and was entitled to make his own relationship decisions, but I just knew that any kind of romantic relationship would be too close to home.

More deliberations. This was turning into a full internal moral investigation.

So if he wasn't Dee's brother, would I go there, I asked myself. Something deep inside, I think it might have been my ovaries, made it clear that I would and it was all I could do to stop myself laughing out loud.

The door opened and my stomach lurched... then fell. A couple, a tall, slender woman with tumbling caramel curls and a perfectly made up face, in a red bodycon dress and high shoes with pointed toes. Pure class. The man following her was older, but impeccably suited, his black hair swept back like a forties movie star. If Dee was here and we were playing our usual people-watching game, making up backstories for everyone who passed us, she'd be hissing in my ear right now. 'Wealthy couple, second marriage, great relationship, incredible sex, her on top.'

I watched the owner greet them with effusive hugs and kisses and show them to their table, and only when they moved away did I realise they weren't the only ones who had just arrived.

He was standing there, in the doorway, scanning the room. Before I could think it through, I'd jumped up and put my hand on his arm, woefully aware that I was making a habit of ambushing blokes.

'Excuse me,' I asked, voice trembling just a little. 'Are you looking for Dee?'

His surprise was obvious and for a split second I thought I'd got this completely wrong. Until he answered. 'Yes. I'm sorry, but do I know you? Did Dee ask you to come?' The accent was Australian. Perhaps this was a friend of Mark's. Of course, that was it. Maybe if I'd asked Mark instead of suctioning myself to his face, he'd have been able to explain it all, to laugh off my stupid suspicions and provide an entirely innocent, logical explanation for all this. I felt totally ashamed of myself for doubting her. How could I? She would have backed me up until the end of time and I'd thought the worst of her. And now I was going to have to break the news that Dee had died.

'No, she didn't. But I think there are some things you should know. Will you join me?'

34

Luke

Until half an hour before, I hadn't been planning on coming. I truly hadn't. That's why I'd gone out for a run earlier, and ended up meeting Val in the cemetery. A bit of a surprise, but I was glad it had happened. Some of her words of wisdom had hit home. Maybe it was time to get out and start making some kind of life again.

Until last year, I'd always been a shoo-in for a work night out, but since Dee died, I just couldn't face it. People didn't quite know how to play it. It was OK in an office environment, when they could have a quick chat, show concern, and then get back to their desk, but a night out was different. I was always afraid that they were worried about getting stuck in a corner with me, offloading all my woes. There's nothing quite like the fear of a crying man to make people avoid eye contact.

That was only part of it, however. The truth was, I felt guilty. How could I be out, laughing and dancing and knocking back beers, when my wife was dead? A couple of pints in the pub with Mark, and on that one occasion, Lizzy and Callie, was one thing, but a full-on, party-mode piss-up was something different altogether.

Yet, I was here.

Over six months after I'd buried my beautiful wife, I was here. And I wanted to turn around and go straight back out of the door.

'Well, would you look who's decided to join the party,' the voice said, and without even turning around, I knew it was Callie. She threw her arms around me and kissed me on the cheek. 'You came. I'm glad,' she said, smiling.

There was no denying how gorgeous she was, especially tonight, in a white dress that went from her neck to her knees, and definitely showed off her figure. Her hair was loose and wavy, her heels so high she was almost the same height as me.

'You don't have a beer! Let's fix that.' She led the way to a roped-off section of the bar, where a large bucket filled with ice and cold beers was already set up. This was par for the course. When our agency celebrated something, they did it in style, taking over the whole VIP area of a trendy West End club, champagne bottles on ice, beer in a cooler, all of it on the agency's tab. Tonight's party was in aid of the Don't Cry Over Spilt Milk campaign. Yep, that cheesy line had won us the campaign and then the national account, adding a cool ten million to our turnover. I'd get a big fat bonus and so would the rest of my colleagues, thus the urge to party in ostentatious style. Many of them were loud, they were borderline obnoxious, they had no lack of confidence in their own brilliance, but hey, nobody was perfect and at least they weren't boring, like the guy who, until an hour ago, was contemplating a night in with a rerun of *Top Gear*. I wasn't proud.

'I'll be right back,' Callie said. 'Just going to track down my drink and bag.'

I pulled out a beer, twisted off the top, and then got caught up talking to some of the other guys in the team, who all, admittedly, made full eye contact and didn't seem to be scanning the room looking for an exit plan to escape potential crying man.

Talking of loud and over-confident... 'Dude, you're here!' an inebriated Domenic yelled, holding his fist up to do the bump thing again.

'Still no, man,' I told him, repeating the same reaction I gave him every time.

He seemed to think this was hilarious.

'Kylie, this is Luke,' he shouted, blasting the eardrum of the girl next to him. I assumed this was the one he'd been seeing for months and remembered his claim that his girlfriend looked like a Kardashian. Actually, he had a fair point.

I held out my hand. 'Good to meet you, Kylie.'

She looked at it with obvious surprise before shaking it. Perhaps I should have gone with a fist bump.

'Hey, didn't your wife own a holiday shop?' Domenic blurted. So much for my colleagues avoiding the subject.

'She did.'

'See, told you!' he said to Kylie. 'He'll totally get you sorted with a discount for Ayia Napa.'

'That would be, like, dope,' Kylie responded. I think that meant I got some form of approval.

'I'll speak to the other owner and set something up,' I assured her, hoping Jen wouldn't be too pissed off.

'Oh yeah, 'cause your wife, like, died. Sorry about that.'

Yep, my wife, like, died. She did. The constant irritation and claustrophobia that I'd felt for the first couple of months after she passed got a grip of me again and I knew I had to get out of there. Baby steps, right? I'd come here. I'd socialised. Time to go.

'I'm just going to get another beer,' I announced, before backing up and bunking out. Navigating my way through the crowd took a few minutes, as I swerved the beer bar and the boss with equal success.

'Where are you going, Luke Harper?' I hadn't quite swerved Callie.

'Just heading off.'

'You just got here!' she exclaimed. I saw that she'd found both her bag and her drink. 'You can't leave yet. Come dance with me.'

She grabbed my hand and pulled me towards the dance floor. I'd rather have had my eyes poked out with kebab skewers. I was dancing on two beers. I had a strict ten-beer dance limit, and even then, only if there were shots too.

Right on cue, several waitresses swarmed around the dance floor, each of them holding up a tray of little cups. Vodka jellies. Dee loved them. I took it as a sign that she was encouraging me, looking forward to being amused by my shite dancing.

Callie took one in each hand, I did the same, we knocked them back, and it got me to the end of whatever Calvin Harris tune that was playing. I made a let's end this, throat-slashing gesture. She rolled her eyes and hung on to the back of my shirt as we edged our way off the dance floor. I finally found a safe place to stop, against the wall, in a corner, where we weren't getting jostled out of the way by enthusiastic clubbers. I remembered all too clearly why I despised nightclubs. I only ever went because Dee loved a dance, but even then, Jen and I would park ourselves on a sofa and talk nonsense to pass the time until Dee finally gave it up and returned from the seventh circle of hell, danced out, but totally buzzing.

'Right, you're not leaving yet,' Callie said. 'We finally got you out and we're going to make the most of it.'

'Yeah, but...'

She cut off whatever excuses I was about to come up with. 'Is it because of what I said last time?'

She was all big eyes and flirty now, a little bit drunk, crazy pretty and totally sexy. Yet, I felt a twinge of guilt even thinking that.

'Which bit?' I asked her. In my defence, I wasn't being coy. Sure, that night at her flat she'd come on strong, but I'd put that down to too much alcohol and a large pinch of pity, because the next day she'd breezed into work, as if nothing had happened and she hadn't mentioned it since. Hadn't we all said stupid shit when we were wasted?

'This bit,' she said, and then her lips were on mine, and her arms were around my neck... and I let her.

'Let's go,' she said, taking my hand.

I tried to tell myself I was just happy to have an excuse to leave the claustrophobia of the club, but as I followed her out, I knew it was time to start being honest with myself.

I'd known she would be here.

This was why I'd come.

My wife was dead for barely over six months.

And I was heading out of a club with another woman.

What kind of shit human being did that make me?

And why did I really want to hear Jen's voice tell me it was OK?

35

Jen

'I'm Jen, Dee's business partner.'

His expression changed, lightened, as if this made everything OK.

'She talked about you a lot,' he said, making him one up on me, who had never heard of him. I was still struggling to get my head around the fact that this guy even existed, that he was here, and that I was actually having a conversation with him.

'I wish I could say the same,' I said, trying to make light of it. 'I'm really sorry, but she didn't mention you and I don't even know your name.'

'Brad,' he said, his tone friendly. He'd obviously decided that he was at least intrigued enough to find out more, because he pulled out a chair and signalled to the waiter, who was on his way over when Daddy Restaurant Owner spotted my companion and bolted over.

Brad raised himself to his feet again and embraced him. 'Carlos, good to see ya.'

'Brad! So long, si?' He gestured to one of the waiters. 'Diago, wine for our friend!'

Clearly a regular then. While he was distracted with swapping endearments, I got a chance to take in his appearance. Early, maybe mid-forties. Smart suit, well cut, expensive cufflinks. He looked... suave. That was the word. Dark hair, short, swept back. Alpha male. His features not sharp enough to be handsome, but strong enough to be attractive. Even in the suit it was obvious he worked out. Wide at the shoulders, the jacket beautifully cut and moving with him like a second, very expensive skin. This was the kind of guy that ran a company or worked for himself, the kind that oozed confidence and was completely self-assured. He didn't sit at home with his girlfriend at night with his pyjamas on, watching *Cold Feet*.

I realised where I was going with this. He was the exact opposite of Luke. The pang of that realisation was like a physical blow. Luke. I've never been one for praying. Losing my mum so young and being saddled with a shit dad tends to erode the faith in all things bright and beautiful. Right now though, I said a silent prayer to anyone that was listening, to make there be some completely innocent explanation for all this, but a niggling voice told me otherwise. The truth was I could absolutely see Dee being attracted to this guy. She would love his charm, his easy confidence, and the little bit inside her that relished a bit of upscale glamour would be impressed by his obvious polish and expensive veneer.

At that, the door opened and Carlos bustled off to greet the new arrivals with much enthusiasm. The poor guy must be exhausted with this much exuberance every day.

'So where's my darling Dee then? And I'm guessing that the fact she sent you means you know our secret?' he asked, his expression open.

I really didn't like the sound of the 'secret'. Oh Dee, come on. Tell me you didn't.

Before I could answer him, the waiter arrived with a bottle of red, two glasses and my new acquaintance, Brad, tasted it, then signalled to the waiter to go ahead and pour.

Luke would just have popped the lid off a screw-top beer. Opposites.

'Salud,' he said, holding up his wine.

I was consumed with apprehension about how this was going to play out. Split-second decision. Head first. Get it out there.

'Brad, I'm really sorry to tell you but Dee is dead.'

A heartbeat. Then everything in his demeanour visibly slumped.

'Dead?' He put his glass back down as if he didn't trust himself to hold it. So she meant something, that was clear. This wasn't just a friendship or a meaningless fling. But I didn't have time to dwell on that because Brad was now looking at me like he expected me to reveal this was all a big, twisted joke and come out with some kind of punchline. Only, there wasn't one.

'She was hit by a car. The guy behind the wheel was high on drugs and trying to escape the police. He mounted a pavement, heading towards some kids, and Dee dived across to save one of them. The car hit her instead and killed her.'

He didn't speak, just slowly lifted the glass to his mouth and took another sip, his complexion greyed.

Even though I still had no idea what their relationship was, it was impossible not to feel sorry for him.

'When?' he eventually said.

'January.'

I watched as his features rearranged themselves into confusion, then realisation, then... sorrow. There was genuine feeling there, I could see it, but he handled it in a very composed way. This was a guy that didn't fall apart in a crisis.

It took him a moment to rewind to confusion. 'So how did you know about me then?'

'I didn't. I kept Dee's plans to travel to New York, followed the itinerary she had put in her calendar. The notes and the flowers at the hotel...?'

He nodded. 'Yes, they were from me. I didn't understand why she didn't respond. The hotel said she'd arrived...'

'That was me. Her name was still on the booking.' So it was him all along. Any hope that the notes and flowers had been harmless gestures from an over-enthusiastic PR person evaporated.

'Ah. That makes sense then. After the note went unanswered, I assumed there had been a complication, that perhaps her husband had joined her.'

'Luke,' I said, unsure why I had a sudden need to say his name and make him real for this guy. 'Her husband's name is Luke,' I repeated.

To the right, I saw the waiter approach again, presumably to take our food order, but Brad waved him away.

His brow was furrowed as he tried to join the dots, yet he still oozed pure, raw, masculinity. 'How could I not know? All this time?' He shook his head. 'I thought there had just been a change of plan. We had a very strict no-contact rule, no emails, no texts, no calls, no exceptions...'

The prospect of the truth was killing me but I had to ask. 'Because you were having an affair?'

Say no. Please, please say no.

'Yes.'

No. Oh Dee.

None of this was making sense to me.

'She never told you?' he asked.

I shook my head. Sadness. Anger. Irritation. Disbelief. There was a cocktail of emotions fighting for supremacy in my head and I couldn't untangle them.

'Will you tell me now?' I asked.

He took another sip of his drink, gave a sad sigh. 'What do you want to know?'

'When did you meet?'

'In 2011. She came over to Australia to see her brother...'

My mind whirred backwards until I sussed out the dates and blurted, 'But that would have been on her honeymoon.'

'Yeah. Timing sucked. I own several bars and restaurants along the Gold Coast and she just happened to walk into one when I was there, to do a report for her blog. Fate, she said.'

My rising anger was only contained by the fact that, for what it was worth, he seemed genuinely sad.

'And you've been seeing each other ever since?'

A rueful smile. 'It's what we do. I travel, looking for new investments, planning new hotels, clubs, bars. She travels. Travelled,' he corrected himself, then took a moment to breathe, to steel himself, before going on. 'And we met whenever, wherever we could. Always separate room bookings, no contact, everything pre-planned in advance, that way if one of us didn't show, the other knew it hadn't worked out and we'd just catch up at the next destination. That happened a couple of times. Last June... Paris...'

'Paris,' I said at the same time, remembering. 'I got the flu and she couldn't go. I remember not quite understanding why she was so pissed off at me. She only had to postpone it by a week.'

'I'd already left. I was there to check out a venue for a new club. Flying visit.'

How could I not know? How could she not tell me? How could she do this?

'So what was it? Were you planning to be together?'

He shook his head. 'I loved Dee, she loved me. But we both knew that we belonged elsewhere. I'm not one for commitments or ties. She had a life and a family in Scotland that she didn't want to leave.'

'And a husband,' I repeated. It was churlish but I couldn't help myself.

'Yes, and a husband,' he repeated, taking my point but not fazed by it in the least.

I noticed his expression changed. A question.

'I understand now that from the note and flowers you knew I existed, but how did you recognise me?'

'I saw you back in New York, at the jazz club. I was leaving as you arrived and you held a taxi door open for me. I didn't give it a second thought at the time, but then I saw you again at Tiffany's.'

'We always met there on our last morning.' There was a hint of nostalgia in his voice. 'It was our thing. I'd buy her something beautiful and she'd pretend to object.'

This was getting worse with every line of the conversation. All those pieces of Tiffany jewellery that she told me she bought herself...

'Were you at the Baccarat bar too?' I asked him.

He nodded. 'Yes. Another of our favourites. Dee loved that place.'

It gave me a pang of satisfaction that I'd already sussed that she would have adored the five-star luxury and glamour. I may not know all her secrets, but I did know Dee.

'I stayed, had a drink, she didn't show, so I left.'

He must have been one of the guys that had his back to me at the bar, otherwise I'd surely have spotted him.

'I didn't see you there. It was only when I was on the plane home and wondering about the notes that it struck me I'd seen you at the club and at Tiffany's. I still wondered if it was all a weird coincidence until I saw you this morning at the pool,' I said.

That surprised him.

'I tried to follow you. Ended up in the lobby in my bikini. Not my finest moment.'

His laugh, when it came, was low and brief and I took advantage of the moment to ask the obvious question.

'So can I ask, are you married too? Is that what it was? Two married people having something on the side to keep them amused?'

I really hoped he didn't detect the slight twist of bitterness that had sneaked into my words. I couldn't help it. I was getting more furious by the minute. How could she do this? And why would she want to? Didn't she give Luke a second thought? Was she so swept up in the glitz and excitement of it all that she just forgot about us? And why, for God's sake, had she never mentioned a single word to me about this? I couldn't even start to decide which of those questions hurt me most.

'No, never married. Not my thing. Like I said, the relationship I had with Dee was the very opposite of complicated. We met up, we had a great time, we went back to our lives until the next time. No strings, no ties, no demands. We both knew exactly what it was – pure enjoyment. We had a great time together and that was all it was ever going to be. She didn't want to divorce and I didn't want to marry so it was perfect. She was perfect.'

'I'm not sure her husband would agree with you right now.' I was finding it difficult to contain my anger.

'Dee said our relationship was what kept her and Luke together. Kept the excitement alive. I think she loved Luke and I in very different ways, and for very different reasons.'

I wasn't sure how to answer that. I couldn't even begin to understand how she could love two men at the same time.

My silence gave him the opportunity to open up a new path of conversation, moving it from the past to the present. 'Are you going to tell him?'

'I think I have to. Luke's a decent guy, a good man. Not telling him would be unfair.' I was thinking out loud now, going on instinct, despite the fact that there was not a single part of me that wanted to break that kind of news.

Putting his wine down, he thought about that for a moment. 'I think telling him would be unfair. I'd just be another ghost that he would have to live with.'

Snap. That was it. Pure fury, and I'm not even sure who it was directed at. The self-assured man in front of me? Or Dee, who had put this situation into our lives? Or myself, for not seeing it, not knowing my best friend enough to spot what she was up to?

I should have known. I couldn't believe I didn't.

Why, Dee? Why weren't we enough?

But the answer was right there in front of me. Brad and his glitzy life were about as far removed from our existence in Weirbridge as it could possibly be. Our life at home was never going to live up to Dee's thirst for excitement and adventure. In a twisted way, Brad was right. Having him probably sated her thirst, allowing her to lead a perfectly normal life at home with us, knowing that she had those carefree interludes to spice things up.

There was nothing I wouldn't do for her, but God, I felt sick at the thought of what she'd done. How could she? How could she? The question went round and round in my head, but I couldn't bring myself to vocalise it in front of this man. This stranger. A stranger who had loved my best friend all this time and who she had loved in return. I wanted to hate him, but right then all I felt was pity. He'd lost her too.

The compassion gave way to a gut-twist of anxiety and the surety that sitting here was somehow being disloyal to Luke.

Time to go. I didn't know everything but I knew enough.

'You're going now,' he said, calmly as I got up. It wasn't a question.

'I am. I'm sorry. It's just… too much.'

'I understand.' He reached into his inside pocket and took out a black leather wallet. Flipping it open, he slipped a business card out from one of the slots.

That's when I saw her face. A snapshot. That Julia Roberts grin, the waves of red hair, peeking from the folds of the leather. He kept her picture with him. If I needed confirmation that this wasn't meaningless, that was it.

'If you ever need to get in touch, here's my number,' he said, handing me a card.

I took it. 'I won't,' I told him, truthfully. I had nothing more to say to him and, even sitting here, felt like a betrayal of Luke. Yet another one.

'I know,' he replied softly. 'Let me walk you back to your hotel,' he offered.

He had manners. Two good men. Dee picked well – just one time too many.

'No, thank you. I really need to clear my head.'

He could see there was no point in arguing. I left him with his glass of wine and his thoughts. Another heart chipped.

The chill didn't even permeate as I strode towards the hotel. I just wanted to get back there, to pack, to call the airline and change my flight to the first one the next morning, to get out of this city where the memory of my best friend had been so tainted

The streets were still busy. The Spanish way. Eating at ten o'clock or later on a Saturday night wasn't unusual. No one gave me a second glance as I passed them, all going about their normal lives, completely unaware of the bombshell that had just detonated in mine.

At the hotel, the concierge pulled open the glass door and I thanked him, then crossed the lobby, took the lift up to my room.

Only when I'd closed the door behind me did my legs give way. I sank to the floor, spent, exhausted. How could she? Dee, what were you thinking?

Not since Pete walked out of the door, had I felt so utterly weary, so betrayed.

When I found some strength, I got up again, headed to the minibar and pulled out a miniature bottle of gin. I realised it wouldn't be enough, so I called room service and ordered three gin and tonics and a bucket of ice. I cracked open the one from the minibar while I was waiting, poured it into a glass from the vanity area, topped it up with a tiny can of tonic and then sat on the edge of the bed. Too wound up, too irritated, I got up and opened my case, then started packing, collecting my possessions and throwing them inside. I had so little with me, I was done in minutes. I pulled Dee's iPad out of the safe and went on to the airline's website. They charged me a hundred quid to change my flight. What a disgrace. It was blatant profiteering and totally shameless, but I'd have paid double if it meant I'd be home sooner.

Room service arrived and I tipped the guy ten euros. Someone may as well have a good night.

Picking up my mobile phone, I looked at the screen to check the time. One o'clock. That meant it was midnight in the UK. I unlocked the handset, pressed my favourites button, saw Luke's name and... My finger hovered over the dial button for a moment before I tossed it to the side. I couldn't just phone him and blurt it out. I had to think it through, come up with the best way to break it to him. Hey Luke, your dead wife was shagging someone else from almost the minute you were married.

He deserved to know, but I couldn't tell him on the phone. It had to be face to face.

I slugged down one of the large G&Ts that the waiter had brought, then lay on the bed and watched it spin. Lightweight once again.

'How could you Dee? How could you?' I challenged her aloud this time. 'And why didn't you trust me enough to tell me? How could you keep this a secret? How could I not know? Luke fucking loved you and you did this to him? Why? What gave you the right to do that?'

My memory threw me back to Brad's comment, saying Dee had been sure she didn't want to get divorced.

'Why not? Why not let Luke go and find someone that wouldn't cheat on him for his whole married life? What were you thinking? That this was OK? How deluded could you be?'

Even as I said it though, there was a part of my brain that was thinking it was classic Dee. Live in the moment. That thirst for excitement. Her love of the wild side, combined with a heady weakness for the flashy and finer things. Brad, with his suaveness and windswept lifestyle, would have been irresistible to her. I could see that now.

So why stay with Luke then? But I knew the answer to that question. She loved him. She really did. What they had couldn't be faked. The problem with Dee was that nothing was ever enough, no thrill or devotion could completely sate her thirst for more. If she went on a roller coaster it had to be the fastest. If she jumped from a plane, next time she had to go higher. If she was making money, she had to make more. I hadn't realised that applied to her husband too.

This would break Luke, but how could I keep it from him? He was struggling so much to find a way to heal. We both were. The only time we felt anything close to happy was when we were together, two damaged emotional wrecks supporting each other...

I must have dozed off, all hail the tranquilizing properties of gin, because the next thing I knew my phone was buzzing incessantly. I grappled around the duvet until I found it. Six o'clock was the time on the screen, right above the name LUKE. Just the sight of his name made me start to panic.

'Hi,' I croaked, my voice inhibited by the fact that my throat felt like it had swallowed a sandbag.

'I'm sorry, did I wake you?' he asked, and I could hear from his voice that something was wrong. Bugger, did he know? How had he found out? Had I called him when I was pissed off and a bit drunk? No, I hadn't. Definitely not.

'No, it's fine, I was just about to get up anyway. Are you OK? You don't sound...'

'I just got home.'

'But it's...' I struggled to remember if it was an hour forward or an hour back. '... five in the morning there. Wild night?'

He was fine. Just a bit drunk, maybe? He must have gone to the office night out after all. I told him he should, but he'd been pretty adamant he wasn't up for it.

'I went back to Callie's place,' he said. 'Spent the night.'

'Spent the night, as in slept on the sofa?' Please say yes. I beg you. I couldn't handle another shock right now. Not that I had any right to feel that way. Luke had every right to do as he pleased, especially after last night's revelations about Dee.

'No,' he sighed. 'Spent the night *with her.*'

My heart sank. Oh, Luke. Every word oozed such utter misery I didn't even need to ask how he felt about it. My stomach flipped and a wave of nausea started to rise from deep in my gut. How had I ended up in the middle of this twisted mess?

I threw the phone down, made the bathroom just in time before I threw up until there was nothing left in my stomach. Legs shaking, I tried to stand, just as the room phone rang. I'd never understood why hotels put phones in bathrooms – it wasn't a situation which I ever considered perfect timing to have a chat to a chum – but right now I was hugely grateful that they did.

I took the receiver off the cradle. 'Hello?' I stammered.

'Jen, are you OK? The phone went dead and I was trying to call you back but it wouldn't go through.'

'Sorry, I was just...' The sweats were taking over now. Chills sending water oozing out of the pores on my forehead, my hands, my back. 'I'm not feeling great. Think I drank too much last night.'

'Sorry I'm not there to help. Christ, what a pair we are.' He sounded almost melancholic. I wasn't quite sure how to respond.

Luke had slept with Callie. Was I supposed to berate him for being unfaithful to her memory? Or say 'Good for you!' and be happy that he was moving on? Or tell him that I really wished he hadn't? The last one was true. Yes, it was selfish and yes, I'd kissed Mark so I had no right to judge, but this changed everything. Before it was him and I, both piecing our lives together, relying on each other for support as the only two people who could really understand what we'd been through. Now that had changed. He had moved the pieces.

'And how do you feel?' I asked him.

I could hear the sigh, then the pause, then utter weariness. 'I don't think I've ever come closer to hating myself.'

His bereft tone, the palpable pain were like flashing, neon indicators that now wasn't the time to tell him about Brad.

36

Val

I'd been determined to stay home tonight. At least, that's what I told myself, but it was a lie, because I hadn't taken the sleeping pills that would have made me unfit to drive. Instead, I'd lain there, groundhog night, staring at the clock, listening to Don snore, until I could tell myself I'd given it a try, then I'd got up, dressed silently and slipped out. This time I went to the supermarket first, bought the same products as always, then went to the café.

She wasn't there. It was a man behind the counter, a wide, muscled, bloke with a shaven head and a smile that showed crooked teeth.

I didn't wait. I left, intending to stop at the food bank as always, hang the bag on the door and get back home.

This had to stop. I was driving myself insane. I needed to go home. To stop this madness. To get a grip.

Yet, here I was, turning into her street again.

I pulled into the kerb opposite the house, turned the lights off but kept the engine running, because even on this summer night it was chilly.

No lights on in the house.

I stared at the windows, each one in turn, wondering which room he was sleeping in, and wondered if I threw something through it would it hit him?

If only I had the courage to try.

I've no idea how long I'd been there when I was flooded with light from the car that was pulling in behind me.

Every nerve ending screamed, my heart started to race, panic, anger, fear and fury. It could only be him. Who else but a lowlife druggy or a demented, grief-stricken mother would be out here at this time of night?

A light. Different from the one on the car. This was a single beam, and I watched in my side mirror as it came towards me. My jaw set. Bring it on. Come right ahead, I dare you. Red mist descended. Fight or flight. I was staying and that no-good evil scum was finally going to get what was coming to him.

The shock of a knock on the window made me jump, but there was no fear. I'd been thinking about this moment for months, planning it, wondering how it would play out. Now I was about to find out.

I opened the window, adrenalin pumping, ready for him.

'Evening m'am, could you step out of the car please?'

The realisation hit me like a slap on the face.

I climbed out, and over the shoulder of a cop that looked about twelve and a half, I saw a light go on in the lounge of that bastard's house. He'd called the police on me? My overriding emotion flipped straight from dread to seething rage.

'Can I ask what you're doing here?' the officer said.

'I'm staring at the house of the scum that killed my daughter.'

That clearly took him by surprise, and his partner, the older man who'd been standing next to the bonnet of their car, observing, stepped forward.

'Ma'am, can I ask your name?'

'Val Murray.'

'And your daughter?'

'Dee Harper.'

Instant recognition. The older cop gave the younger one a subtle nod and then stepped forward to take over.

'I remember what happened to your daughter. I'm very sorry. Darren Wilkie was charged with it?' It was a question, but he already knew the answer.

'Yes,' I nodded. It didn't surprise me that they knew about Wilkie and his crimes. For all Glasgow was a big city, I knew Dee's death had been a talking point and it stood to reason that the cops who were responsible for Wilkie's area knew what he'd done.

'Mrs Murray, I'm going to have to ask you to step into the car with us. A complaint has been made that your vehicle has been seen here on several occasions. I do apologise, but we will have to fill out the necessary paperwork.' I could see the big cop was mortified at having to take this further. Just doing his job. I understood. 'We'll make it as quick as possible and there will be no need to go down to the station,' he added when I didn't move.

Even in my raging state, I could hear there was a message of compassion in his voice. We know this doesn't seem fair. Just come with us and we'll make it as painless as possible.

I didn't care. I'd never had so much as a parking ticket or speeding fine in my life, and nothing could be as sore or as devastating as what had already happened. I thought about Don, about Mark, and I knew they'd be beside themselves, probably even furious with me, but I didn't care. This wasn't about them, it was about Dee.

I was about to follow them when I saw a shadow crossing the road towards us, a figure in black. I tensed, the police officer sensed it and turned around to see what was behind him, his arm automatically going across me to protect me.

For a split second I thought it was Darren Wilkie, but no. Too small. Too slight.

When she reached us, her eyes took me in and immediately widened.

'I know you. You've been in the café.'

I said nothing, just met her stare. Her cheeks were even more sunken than the last time I saw her, her eyes sitting on top of black circles.

'You're the one that's been sitting out here?' she asked.

I didn't flinch. The cop stepped in to clarify, and it was obvious this woman was known to him. 'Mrs Wilkie, this is Mrs Murray.'

A blank look. She had no idea who I was. I decided to help her out.

'I'm Dee Harper's mother. That animal of a son of yours killed my daughter. So go on, do your worst. Have me arrested. It'll be nothing worse than what your family has done to us already.'

Her head recoiled like I'd slapped her and she was stunned speechless.

'We're just going to have a chat with Mrs Murray in our car and we'll take care of this. Why don't you go on back inside.'

My thoughts exactly. Go crawling back under whatever rock you came from.

'No,' she said. It was almost a whisper, until she found a stronger voice to continue. 'Can we just forget I called and let this go, Bob?' she asked, addressing the older officer. I don't know if I was more surprised that she knew his name or that she didn't want them to take me away.

After a pause for thought, he agreed. 'Aye. I think that would be the best all round, Margo,' he said, before turning to me. 'Mrs Murray, if you'd like to go on home now, we'll take this from here.'

His relief was obvious. Move along. Nothing to see here. But then she spoke again, this time to me. 'Can I talk to you? Properly. Not here,' she said, shocking me again. What did I have to say to her? There were a few home truths that I could deliver and my adrenalin was still pumping, so I heard myself agreeing.

'OK, but I'm not coming in there,' I spat. Hell would freeze over before I'd step foot in that evil bastard's house.

'Your car?' she suggested. I nodded and she turned to the police officers. 'Thanks Bob,' she said, her tone grateful, but it was obvious she was asking him to go now.

'We'll be in the area for the next hour or so,' he said. 'If either of you have any problems, just call 101. Mrs Murray, I'm sorry about your daughter.' With that, he gestured to his younger partner and they climbed back into their car and drove off.

Only when I was back in the driver's seat did I realise that my whole body was shaking.

The criminal's mother walked around the bonnet and got in the other side and for a few moments neither of us spoke.

'I called the police because I thought you were a drug dealer,' she finally said.

'That's rich,' I spat, still staring forward, not trusting myself to look at her, disgusted at the thought of having her in my car, sitting in a seat that Dee had sat in many times. The thought made me want to retch.

'I know. Darren owes money to half of the pond life in this city,' she said, 'and they turn up here looking for it. My house has been attacked so many times we've got the local station on speed dial. They don't even realise he's away.'

'Away where?'

'Inside. Been in Barlinnie for months. Nothing to do with what happened to your daughter. Drugs this time. Again. He's been dealing for years. Using for longer. If it's not the dealers that are raiding us, it's him looking for money for more stuff.'

I was incredulous that she was saying all this to me. This wasn't what I'd expected at all. I thought she'd be just like him, protecting him, but the disgust was in every word she spoke.

'Mrs Murray, there's nothing I can say that will make what happened to your daughter any less awful, but I'm so sorry. I really am. You must hate us and I don't blame you. There's nothing I can say to defend him because, the truth is, Darren didn't turn out right. His whole life he's been in one lot of trouble or another, right from when he was a boy. Special schools. Borstal. Care. Prison more times than I can remember. This is the only home he's ever had, but he's not been welcome here for a long time. There's a badness in him and that's the honest truth. We've tried everything to turn him around, but nothing worked. I could sit here all day long and tell you about the stuff that he's done to our family, to me, to my husband, God rest his soul, but I don't want you to think for a minute that I'm trying to share your pain. None of our other weans turned out like him. They're ashamed. We all are. I'm sorry for everything he's taken from you.'

She was suddenly racked by a hacking, crippling cough.

'Lung cancer,' she said. 'Five decades of fags. I'm not saying that for sympathy, just so you know.'

That explained the change from the burgundy dyed bob to the short grey crop.

Another coughing fit. 'The chemo is a bastard of a thing,' she croaked, trying to recover.

I'd have to have been made of stone not to have felt for her. Dear God, what a life. I had wished all sorts on Wilkie and his family over the last year, but not like this, not now, not on a mother who had so obviously been hammered by life.

Neither of us said anything for a while, until I finally found my voice. 'Our Dee was something special,' I told her. 'A big personality. She had a husband. Friends. A career. It's all gone. I'll never see her grow old and I'll never hold her children.' I was choking the words out, each one of them caught on a rock of grief that was rammed in my throat. 'He took that away from her. From all of us. I've never hated anyone more than I hate him.'

Her breathing was heavy and I saw that the windows were steaming up, creating a cocoon against the outside world.

'So you've been coming here to wait for him?' she asked. 'Because I've seen your car here a few times. That's why I called the police.'

'I don't know,' I said honestly. 'I really don't know what I'd have done if I'd seen him. I haven't slept a night since Dee was killed so I just drive. Here was one of the places I'd end up. And the café.'

'How did you know I worked there?' she asked.

'Was driving past here one night and I saw you leave and I followed you.' There was no point fudging the truth. 'None of this makes sense, I know that. Since the minute he got in that car and turned the engine on, nothing has made sense.' The fact that I was sitting here, as the sun was starting to come up, speaking to his mother, was testimony to that.

'He's going to be inside until the trial,' she said, 'and then for God knows how long. He deserves everything he gets – and it breaks my heart to say that about one of my own but it's true. I came to terms with that a long time ago. I understand you hating us. If this happened to one of my girls I'd feel the same.'

She had girls. I'd never given any other members of the family a thought, focusing only on her son. She buckled with another barking cough.

'The police told us he's pleading not guilty,' I said. 'So we'll need to sit through every detail of that day, relive it all, because he's not man enough to admit it. Has he not caused us enough pain? But I'll be there, because I want to see him in court and I want him to suffer.'

She nodded, everything about her defeated. 'That's fair enough. I'd do the same.' As she put her hand on the door lever, she paused. 'Just don't think that we support him and that my family are defending his actions because we're not. It's a sorry thing to say, but he was dead to us a long time ago.'

Her frail hand pulled on the door lever, and instinctively I reached out and touched her arm.

'I'm glad we spoke,' I told her, meaning it, all the anger gone now. 'I won't be back or bother you again.'

The sadness in her face told me that she already knew that.

I drove home, numb, replaying every line of the conversation in my head, one thought rising above the others – in some ways, her sentence was worse than mine. I'd lost Dee, but I had the comfort and pride of knowing that she was a good and decent person, that she never did harm, she loved and was loved back. His mother had also lost a son, for he was gone in almost every sense, but all he had left behind was a broken heart and shame.

It was proper daylight when I pulled into the car park at the end of our block, then walked slowly up to our door, and let myself in.

Don, his face purple, flew out of the kitchen and stopped dead when he saw me, then threw his arms around me like I'd come back from the dead. 'Jesus Christ, Val, where have you been? Me and Mark have been up half the night. We were just about to phone the police.'

His hug was so tight, his emotion so raw, that for the first time in a long, long, time, it felt good to have him hold me.

'It's a long story, Don. Come in and put the kettle on and I'll tell you about it.'

37

Jen

I hadn't given it much thought when Mark texted to say he'd be in late. If anything I was grateful for the reprieve from facing him again. I was tired, I was irritable and I could quite happily have shut up shop and not come in today. I'd done a fair amount of thinking yesterday. When I arrived back from Barcelona I'd jumped in a cab and headed back to my own house. I'd told Luke it was because the estate agent was bringing a viewer to see it first thing this morning and I needed to get it sorted out. It wasn't a complete lie. The estate agent was bringing a viewer this morning but he was showing them round because I couldn't face it. That aside, I'd made the decision on the way home from Barcelona that I was going to move back in until the house was sold. It made sense to be there to have it spick and span before each viewing. At least, that's what I told myself. The truth was, it was hard to be around Luke with Dee's betrayal at the very front of my mind, constantly torn over whether or not to tell him. He had offered to come and help, but I'd refused, saying that I was feeling crap, so would rather just get it ready and then catch up on sleep. Some hope. I spent half the night thinking that he might show up anyway, but thankfully he didn't. And yes, I knew that made me a rubbish friend, but I just didn't have it in me to console him and sympathise with the fact that he was feeling shit about himself. I had enough of my own crap to deal with at the moment and aaaargh! I was so bloody angry. I was feeling like the most put-upon, manipulated idiot that ever existed. Dee was a serial shagger, Pete was a traitorous adulterer and Luke was out getting his rocks off. Why had he done it? And why did I care? It was always going to happen eventually but I think I'd slipped into a comfort zone where it was him and I against the world and now he'd just stepped out of it and left me alone. I didn't need any of this. None of it. And frankly I was pissed off with the world.

I made my way into the shop an hour early so I could make sure everything was restocked and in order after my weekend away. Josie wandered in right behind me, a vaper hanging from her bottom lip. It was her latest attempt to quit the cigs. I'd completely forgotten she was coming in this morning because she'd missed her Saturday night shift. Something to do with a Book Club field trip involving Tom Jones.

I immediately resolved to act like nothing was wrong, otherwise I knew I'd get the third-degree interrogation.

'You look like someone stole your knickers off the line,' she observed archly, before going for a more direct, 'What's up?'

I obviously needed to do more work on my 'nothing's wrong' face. 'I'm fine. Just had a rough weekend.' Understatement of the year.

'Thought you were in Barcelona?' she asked, clearly confused about my misery.

'I was. It's a long story Josie, and unless you want to hear me wail, you're better off skipping right over it.'

She put her handbag on the desk, pulled up Dee's chair and looked at me expectantly. 'I don't do skipping,' she announced.

The dam broke. I should have kept everyone's confidences and kept the lies covered up, but I was just so damn weary that I told her everything. Dee's affair. Luke's one-night stand. Pete's cold indifference and new relationship. How devastated I felt about every single bit of it. I had to tell someone and if it was going to be anyone, Josie was the best person for the job. There was nothing she couldn't cope with, nothing would shock her and, more importantly, she loved every one of us. Except Pete. That love-horse had long since bolted.

After twenty minutes, she tossed aside the vaper and fished a packet of cigarettes out of her bag. After another ten, she pulled the chair over to the back wall, climbed up on it, opened the window that was closer to the ceiling than the floor, and leaned out so she could smoke. The woman was closing in on seventy and she was the most irresponsible person in any room.

She was also the best listener. All the while, she never commented, only asked questions for clarification.

'Och, that lass,' she said, when I finished the whole saga about Dee. 'She never could content herself. Val would be heartbroken if she knew.'

'I'll never tell her, Josie, and I know you won't either. You're the only person I've told.'

I'd thought about telling Val, thought about whether I had any right to keep such an important part of Dee's life from her, but in the end I knew I couldn't. It would break her heart all over again, tarnish her daughter's memory. She could never know. This was my, and now Josie's, secret to hold.

'That's a smart decision, my love. It's a big secret to keep but you're right to do it. What about Luke? Are you going to tell him?' she asked, as she closed the window, climbed down and then flicked on the kettle.

I'd thought about this almost constantly over the last twenty-four hours – at least, when I wasn't thinking about him sleeping with Callie – and I'd changed my mind every time.

'I don't know. On the one hand, I don't want to shade his memory of Dee and for him to doubt how much she loved him, because even although she did this, I know he was the love of her life.'

Josie nodded sagely.

'But on the other hand, what if he ever finds out and he realises I didn't tell him? He'd never forgive me. We don't keep things from each other.'

'Are you sure about that?' she asked. We always joked about Josie's right eyebrow raise of cynicism, but I didn't understand why she was deploying it in my direction. It took me a moment to get back on track.

'Yeah, of course. Why would you say that?'

'I know you're staying there.'

Ah. I was wondering when that would come up. 'He told me you knew,' I confessed. 'But I didn't tell you because I didn't want to talk about it while Val didn't know. I just felt weird in case she thought I was stepping into Dee's life. We just... I don't know how to explain it, Josie, but we were both lonely living on our own and it just helped us get through it when we had each other for company. God, it's all so complicated. I've moved out now anyway.'

She had the window open again and was standing back up on the chair, arm dangling out with another cig. It was a blessing we were on the ground floor otherwise there would be a serious risk to life, limb and lungs.

'Why?' she asked.

'Because... if he's going to be seeing Callie, I don't want to get in the way. Everyone needs to move on sometime.'

'And there it is,' she declared, but there was no triumph in her voice. 'You're lying to yourself and the two of you are lying to each other.'

My head was starting to really, really hurt again. 'Josie, what are you on about?'

She closed the window and climbed back down. No wonder she had the thighs of a twenty-year-old. 'I think you've developed feelings for Luke and he has for you too.'

'No, Josie, you're wrong. We've always loved each other, but it's not a romantic love. To me, he'll always be Dee's husband, whether she's here or not. And I'll always be Dee's friend to him.'

'I don't think so,' she argued gently. 'And you know something, it's OK. It's OK not to admit it to yourself and it's OK to take your time with it. It would be a big mistake to make if it's not right. But I think it is.'

No. She was wrong. Completely wrong. We were two drowning people clinging to each other in stormy waters. That was it. The doorbell pinged to signal our first customer, breaking the spell altogether, snapping me back to reality.

'Josie, can I point out you always guess the wrong ending when we go to see a movie?'

'I didn't say my insights were perfect,' she barbed. 'But I'm here if you need me, ma darling.' I failed to fight back more tears when she wrapped me in a hug, then wiped them away and composed myself to go and serve the customer.

Josie left after her shift and thankfully the rest of the morning was quiet – a saving grace because the banging in my head was getting louder and the lack of sleep was kicking in big time, while over and over in my mind, I ruminated over what she'd said, with varying degrees of conviction that she was way off base.

But the truth was, she wasn't.

That thought made me gasp. Oh my God, what kind of denial had I been living in? Every day, every night, for the last month, I'd only felt right when I was with him, only felt happy when I was hearing his voice.

But this couldn't happen. No way. No matter what Dee had done. I wasn't her, and I couldn't live with myself if I betrayed her like that. I couldn't do that to her. Besides, what would Val and Don think? What would Mark think? No. Nothing could ever happen between Luke and I, no matter what feelings I was having for him.

And while I was making definite decisions about my life, I had to clear up any ambiguity with Mark too.

When he eventually made it through the door at eleven o'clock, I was standing behind the counter and I was ready for him. I didn't even give him a chance to put his bag in the office. 'I just want to say I'm sorry about pouncing on you on Friday night. It's not something I make a habit of and you were just in the wrong place at the wrong time.'

That languid, gorgeous smile again. 'Don't know that I'd necessarily categorise it as "wrong",' he said, definitely on the flirtatious side.

My head thudded down on the desk. 'Dear God, make it stop,' I murmured, before lifting it again. 'Mark, hear the message. I'm a wreck. My life has fallen apart. I don't need complications. And right now I'm a heartbeat away from a one-way ticket to somewhere no one knows me and I can go back to having a normal, peaceful, un-bloody eventful life. No drama. No fuck-ups. No blindsiding occurrences. So please. Forget I kissed you, forget this conversation, let's just wipe the slate clean and act like it never happened. Can we do that?'

'Sure,' he shrugged.

I wasn't sure that I believed him, but I went with it.

'Good. Excellent. Let's start again.' I took a deep breath and put on a sing-song voice. 'Good morning Mark, how are you today? Having a good morning?'

He shrugged. 'Er, yeah. Bit strange to be honest.'

This wasn't in the script. We were no longer doing strange, shocking, tragic or dramatic. 'Really? Why's that?'

'My mum's been sneaking out every night to stalk Darren Wilkie and his mother.'

I put my head back down on the desk. So much for a normal, peaceful un-bloody eventful life.

38

Luke

Iremember the exact moment that I knew it was a mistake. Callie unzipped her dress and stepped out of it. Hot didn't begin to cover it. Athletic body, wide shoulders, incredible breasts, and once I got over the fact that she did the whole Hollywood thing, I stepped forward, ran my finger down the side of her face, leaned in and felt her breath on my face and slowly, softly kissed her... and thought about someone else.

Dee.

And then Jen.

Whoa, what had just happened there?

The sex had been OK. Callie was beautiful and sexy and the complete package and – bizarrely – she seemed to be attracted to a mess like me, yet as soon as it was over, it felt wrong. There was no real connection. No love. The claustrophobia set in and I had to get out of there, which made me the kind of bloke I'd never been. Not cool. Definitely not cool. After Dee had got over bollocking me for going near another woman, she'd definitely have had something to say about the sharp exit.

And Jen. What would she think? And why did that matter quite so much?

Christ, what was happening to me?

This was like one step forward, six steps back. Every time I thought I was turning a corner I ended up like this – talking to myself in clichés while feeling shite.

I went down into our bedroom – my bedroom – pulled off my jeans and shirt and threw on a pair of joggies and a T-shirt. What did it say about my life that I now spent most of it doing the very fucking thing I avoided throughout most of my marriage?

I pulled on my trainers at the door and stepped outside. I usually turned left to go to the cemetery, tonight I turned right. I broke into a slow jog, not bothering to limber up because quite frankly, a pulled muscle would be a welcome distraction. Save me from self-flagellation and bitter regret.

What an arse.

And what a hypocrite. I'd slagged off Pete for being a callous bastard and now I was even worse. I was the guy who screwed someone barely seven months after his wife died.

I had to stop and lean against a bus shelter until the urge to vomit passed, because I knew that wasn't the worst of it. The truth was much worse.

I arrived in her street before I even made the conscious decision to go there. I couldn't go up the front path, couldn't look at the spot where my Dee had died, so I ran around the back, flicked the catch on the gate, and opened it.

There she was, sitting on the back step, like she'd been expecting me to come.

Hair up in a messy knot, in jeans, a white T-shirt, and bare feet, a mug of coffee in her hands.

I walked up the path towards her and she smiled the saddest smile I'd ever seen. It was exactly what I expected to happen. She'd view me differently; decide I was like Pete, just another person that she'd known for years only to discover she didn't really know them at all. I'd expected this would happen and yet I'd still told her. I had a fair idea what that said about my stupidity.

'Hey...' I said, my breath taking a minute to slip into a rhythm that wasn't exhaustion or panic.

'Hey,' she replied.

I sat down on the step beside her. 'So are you sitting here, contemplating the fact that you're avoiding me because I made a major fuck-up?'

'Pretty much,' she answered softly.

She always did prefer to go with the truth.

'I'm sorry.'

'You don't need to apologise to me. I don't even know why I'm pissed off. It's your life, your grief, your heartache to manage. I've got no right to judge you, yet I am.'

'You're right. Actually you're a terrible pal.'

That made her smile again, not quite as sadly as before and that's when I knew I was going to tell her the stuff that I'd been struggling to admit to myself since Saturday night.

'I don't even know how to say this... I've stopped thinking of you as a friend. It's more than that now. My feelings for you... they're more than I should feel for a friend.'

'I know,' she replied, barely above a whisper, still staring forward, not making eye contact.

What? Was she psychic? 'How?'

'Josie told me.'

'Christ, she scares me.'

'Me too.'

Neither of us could pull the words together to go on yet, so we sat in silence until she beat me to it.

'She thinks I've got more-than-friend feelings for you too.'

OK, I hadn't seen that coming. I was fully expecting to be slapped down and sent off in shame. 'I'll probably regret asking this, but do you?'

'Yes.'

I closed my eyes to try to help my processing skills along a bit. This should make the situation so much simpler, but we both knew it didn't.

'I want to kiss you,' I told her, reaching over and turning her chin towards me, looking into her red, tired eyes for the first time.

'Don't,' she said simply. 'It crosses a line that I don't want to cross because I don't think I'd ever forgive myself.'

I shook my head. 'This is such bullshit. Don't we deserve to be happy? I can't believe Dee wouldn't want us to be OK, to make a life without her.' My voice was raising, exasperation running the show now. I could feel the irritation starting to twist inside me, not at Jen, but at this whole debacle of a situation. I never asked for this, and neither did Jen, but we'd been beaten and dragged down and damn near destroyed and I just couldn't understand any rationale that didn't allow us to recover from that and find new happiness.

'Maybe, but I couldn't live with myself if that life was the one she was supposed to have and I took it. I couldn't look at myself in the mirror in the morning or sleep at night. I just couldn't.'

'So we don't get a chance?'

'No.'

'Don't do this, Jen.' A weird mix of panic and resignation overtook me. Her reaction was so in keeping with her character. That was Jen. Do the right thing. No drama. No demands.

A huge tear rolled down her cheek and I leaned over and wiped it away.

She turned to me again, and this time I saw the pure determination in her features. 'We don't even know if it's real or if it's just because we've become this co-dependent, desperate pair. There's no good way out of this, Luke. If we tried and it worked, I'd hate myself every day of my life for stealing Dee's future. If we tried and it didn't work, I'd hate myself for destroying our friendship. There's no win for us.'

In my whole adult life, I'd never begged for anything, but the only thing stopping me pleading with her now was the look of devastation on her face. She'd been hurt enough. I couldn't hurt her any more. Fuck.

'So what do we do? Just pretend?'

'Yep. And then maybe one day we'll wake up and realise it was just a moment in time and it's passed. It is what it is, Luke. Don't try to change it.'

With that, she got up, went inside and closed the door... and I started running.

39

Jen & Dee, 1999

*D*ee *handed me a cigarette and I took a puff, then passed it back to her and she took one more puff, then tossed it into the toilet and flushed. Outside, we checked our hair in the mirrors, then headed back into the school hall, decorated by the art department to look like their interpretation of a Christmas disco. Glitter balls, streamers hanging from the ceiling and red fabric on the walls, a light box with two record players on the stage at the front of the hall.*

Robbie Williams' 'Millennium' faded out and All Saints' 'Never Ever' faded in. Dee shrieked and dragged me up to dance, our matching cargo trousers rustling as we moved. Khaki green trousers, white Adidas trainers, tight white T-shirts, huge hoop earrings. Val had told us we were gorgeous as we left the house, and for the first time ever I felt it. My mum hadn't been able to afford to buy me new clothes for the couple of years before she died, and my dad had drank everything away before and afterwards. When I'd arrived to live at Dee's house I had one case, and that was it. My whole life in one case.

Dee had shared everything with me. Her room, her music, her make-up and then when I turned fourteen, she'd got me a Saturday job in the hairdressers she worked in. 'Double trouble, you two,' Don would laugh, when we appeared downstairs, dressed to go out, wearing identical clothes, identical hair, identical make-up. And even though the truth was that everything looked better on Dee, I felt grateful because I'd become part of something. I was one of the Murrays.

When the record stopped and merged into Cher's 'Believe', we headed back to the chairs at the side of the room. Dee's boyfriend, Jake McGuinness, two years older than us and halfway through sixth year, came over with one of his mates, and asked Dee to go outside with him. Of course, she wanted to. Jake McGuiness was the second coolest guy in the school, only one step down from Ian McGuire, who held top rung position because he played football for Scotland.

'I'll be back. Cover for me.' And then she was gone, leaving me to chew my nails while Jake's pal Pete stood next to me. 'Do you want to go outside too?' he asked, when he could no longer stand the awkwardness. 'Sure.'

We found Jake and Dee in the corner of the sports pavilion, her sitting on his knee, his hands inside the back of her T-shirt. My first thought was that Val would kill her, my second was that Don would kill Jake.

'Jen-jen,' Dee giggled and I had no idea what was funny. 'Here, have some.'

She handed me a bottle of wine. Lambrusco. Screw top. Choices: say no, never live it down, or go ahead, and end up throwing up in a bush like last time she made me drink.

Of course, I took it, drank it, was completely wasted by the time we went back inside. I don't know who produced *the mistletoe, but Pete knew what it meant, leant down, kissed me.*

It was the first time I'd ever kissed a boy. I'd always been Jenny with the dead Mum. Jenny with the drunk Dad. Jenny that lives with Dee. Now I was Jenny that had kissed a boy.

I floated home, beyond thrilled with myself, stopping at the end of our terrace so we could spray perfume and pop a couple of Juicy Fruit to cover the smell of the wine and the cigs. Val and Don were on the sofa when we got in, same position as always, her head lying on his chest, his arm around her as they watched the telly.

'Good night, girls?' Val asked, scrutinizing us from head to toe. We must have passed the test.

'We're just going to go on up to bed,' Dee announced. 'Night Mum, love you. Love you too Dad.'

'Night girls, love you both back. With hearts on it,' Val said, same as she did every night.

We went upstairs, I pulled off my clothes, replaced them with my pyjamas and climbed into bed. I'd got off with a boy and a gorgeous one at that. Pete McLean.

'Told you he fancied you,' Dee giggled. 'You're totally going to go out with him again.'

I so hoped she was right. I'd been praying for it for weeks. It was only then I noticed she wasn't getting ready for bed. Instead, she was sitting on the windowsill, curtain open, watching outside.

'What are you doing?' I asked, completely puzzled and a bit annoyed. I wanted her to get into bed so we could lie awake and go over every detail of tonight, especially the bits that involved me kissing Pete McLean.

'Just... there he is,' She blurted.

'Who?'

'Ian McGuire. I told him to come meet me tonight and he's there.'

'But you're going out with Jake!' I reminded her.

She laughed. 'Jen, have you seen Ian McGuire?' she teased, sarcasm dripping.

The window was open and she was halfway out before I could say any more.

'I won't be long,' she said.

'Dee, you can't...'

'Of course I can,' she chuckled. 'But promise you'll never tell Jake. Promise me.'

Argh, she drove me nuts. Completely crazy. But I loved her.

'I promise I'll never tell.'

And I didn't.

Now, almost twenty years later, staring out of the front window at the spot where she died, I knew I'd keep the promise.

I'd never tell. And this time I didn't mean about Ian McGuire.

40

Val

The October wind was biting but I barely felt a thing. There was a man at the door with a camera, taking pictures like this was some kind of entertainment event. I put my head down and walked right by him, never looking at him. This wasn't a day that should have mementos. I didn't want any part of it captured for posterity.

In any other situation I might stop to admire the building, with its pale blond sandstone frontage and foreboding columns making up a grand, circular entrance. A Doric portico. I knew that was what it was called. Our Dee had done a project on Glasgow architecture in high school and this was one of the buildings she'd chosen to write about. The High Court of Justiciary. I'd brought her here to the Saltmarket area on a Sunday afternoon so that she could take a picture of it with her Polaroid camera. Now she was the only one of our family who wasn't here. Don, Luke, Mark, Jen and Josie surrounded me as we went through the door, following a police liaison officer who showed us through to the public gallery. I wanted to tell her we weren't 'public'. We weren't just here to pass the time and watch a show. I was here to get justice and see that piece of scum pay, to look him in the eyes and make sure that he knew that for the rest of his life I'd be wishing him a sentence of pain and suffering, just like he'd given us.

Don's hand was wrapped tightly around mine and our shoulders were wedged so closely together that I could hear the movement of his breathing. On the other side, Mark stared straight ahead. Three quarters of our family. That's all there would ever be again. The rage rose inside me, almost exploding out of me when we were told to stand and various people entered and then there he was. Darren Wilkie. An officer on each side of him, handcuffed, standing behind a wooden barrier. I recognised him from photographs, but what I hadn't expected was how utterly insignificant he would look. A wee, skinny runt, in cheap tracksuit trousers and a hoodie, not even the respect to dress appropriately for the court. Thin, almost skeletal, his head was shaved, his grey skin pockmarked with spots, his eyes narrowed, staring at his lap, where one hand was picking the skin from some unseen scab on the other. He was vermin. Rotten, stinking vermin.

Don's hand squeezed hard and now Mark's did the same, as if they were steadying me, stopping me from even trying to do what I'd thought about every day since the January afternoon he'd taken away the thing I loved most – climb over there and pull him down and then pummel him, beat him until he bled, eviscerate the bastard until he was nothing but a worthless pile of bile and waste. All those mothers I'd seen on the news and in the papers saying they'd forgiven the person who killed their child, well, that wasn't me. I didn't forgive him. Not even close.

Look up at me. Come on, you worthless bastard, look up at me.

He didn't raise his head. Not once.

The judge, a woman, spoke first, bringing the court to order and then it went on, conversations, declarations, voices that all merged into one because the white noise in my head cut out everything else. I didn't take my eyes off him for a single second.

Look at me. See me.

There was a sudden movement on either side of me, a flinch from both Don and Mark, and it jarred me enough to hear the murmur that was now rumbling in the gallery.

'What happened?' I whispered to Don, panic and anxiety flooding through me, fighting for space with the hatred and fury.

'He pleaded guilty.'

I didn't understand. They'd warned us that he was going to plead not guilty, take it to trial and we'd been told to prepare for the hearing to last a week, maybe two. And we'd have to sit there and listen to every detail of how it happened, relive it through the words of those that were there, see photographs of the crime scene and my girl's broken body, imagine every moment of her pain until she was gone.

He'd pleaded guilty.

The judge said something about sentencing in two weeks and that was it. The court came alive as people got to their feet and I looked from side to side. Jen was crying, holding Josie, her whole body shaking with sobs. Mark shook Luke's hand. My Don put his arms around me. 'It's over now, love. We can go home. It's over,' he said, in a voice that was so choked with emotion and relief that it chipped off another piece of my heart. It would never be over, but he was going to be punished and I'd go to sleep every night knowing the scum who stole my Dee's life was in a cell, rotting, unable to destroy anyone else's life.

Don released me as Josie and Jen reached my side. Jen reached out, took my hand. She was a good girl and she'd been through more than anyone should have to endure.

'Let's go,' I said, mustering as much dignity as I could manage.

'I'm proud of you, love,' Josie said, serious for once, 'you kept your peace.'

I didn't tell her that the only reason I didn't scream, shout, call him every name, lunge forward to gauge out his eyes, was because the liaison officer had warned me that if there had been any disturbances I could be barred from court for the remainder of the trial. That's how much I hated him. I was prepared to keep my silence to see him burned.

Now I didn't have to. No trial. It was done. I had no idea why he changed his plea but my family had been saved more pain, so it was the best outcome for us. It didn't make me hate him any less.

I felt Don gently pull on my hand as he led the way out of the row we were sitting in, then turned and started climbing the stairs, past the other rows, to the exit door.

That's when I saw her. Sitting in the back row, her posture stooped, the woman who was probably about the same age as me but looked a decade older. Her head was covered with a scarf, no hair visible around it, her cheeks even more hollow than before.

Our eyes met and the corners of her mouth rose in a movement that was almost as muted as the very slight nod of her head. That's when I knew she'd done it. I didn't know how and I probably never would, but she'd made him change his plea.

I let go of Don's hand and climbed towards her, watching as she rose unsteadily to her feet. Her face was blank, accepting of whatever I was coming to say, a woman beaten by life and by the son who'd caused her so much heartache.

I reached out to her, this tiny woman, and enfolded her in my arms and I held her. For her. For me. Almost a year of hatred and disgust towards the demon of her I had in my head was gone, and in its place was an understanding and a respect for what she'd suffered. She was a mother, one who was helpless in the face of the person her son had become, yet, even as she was being decimated by a brutal disease, she still found the strength to come here, to face his actions, to do the right thing. She was a stronger woman than me.

'Thank you,' I murmured. And then, slowly, I let her go, took my husband's hand and let him lead me, and my family, home.

Where we belonged.

41

Jen

It had started with three words I'd spotted a couple of weeks ago, when I flicked on to the month of November in Dee's diary. Written next to the 11th, was Mirihi Island Resort. It meant nothing to me. I'd checked her emails, but there was no booking, no other mention of it.

Of course, I had to Google it and when I saw it, even I, not one to be enticed by exotic locations or promises of luxury, fell in love. A thirty-minute journey in a seaplane from the main airport, Malé, it was a tiny private island, a boutique resort of private villas nestled in the clear blue waters of the Indian Ocean.

'Mark, what date are you leaving?'

'Twenty-fifth,' he'd said. 'Why? Want shot of me sooner.'

'Absolutely. It's been hell,' I'd teased him, defaulting to our standard relationship of loving sarcasm and affectionate insults. The truth, and we both knew it, was that I'd miss him horribly. In many ways, it was like having a piece of Dee still with me – that free spirit, adventurous soul who embraced life and had no desire to conform to what other people called normality.

Since he'd come home after Dee's death, he'd gone back and forth again to Australia, heading straight offshore for a couple of months, then coming straight back. This time was different. He was heading to his home on the Gold Coast for a week, to reclaim his old life, before going offshore for a three-month contract. After that, he would return to his Australian home, and the world he'd chosen when he'd left Weirbank two decades ago.

The whole family would be a bit lost without him around and I'd miss him. I'd miss his laugh. His laid back energy. And I'd miss the fact that he still never passed up on an opportunity to make fun of me for snogging him in my desperate moment of weakness. He thought it was hilarious and I'd come to see it for what it was. A temporary aberration that I'd never live down.

He'd also be missed by the three or four women that he was seeing on a very upfront, mutually agreed 'no strings, no ties, non-exclusive' basis.

The thought made me shudder. That kind of set-up wouldn't be for me, but I could see the benefits of knowing where you stood right from the start. I'd chosen to believe the mutually devoted, happy every after scenario and look where it had got me.

A plan was bubbling in my head. A holiday. A break from here. Time to heal, and think, and decide how to move on. I'd never been one for extravagance or swanky places, but the Maldives... it just felt right. Dee and I had discussed it on our last day together. Maybe this was a chance to bring things full circle.

'Would you be OK with looking after things here for a week if I went on holiday?'

I'd expected surprise and yup, right on cue, there it was. 'You? On holiday? Voluntarily? Are you stopping to pick up your personality transplant on the way?'

I threw a stress ball and he ducked so that it bounced off his shoulder and landed on Dee's chair. It was still exactly the same as when she left it. Same blue cardigan over the back of it, same riot of untidiness on the desk beside it.

'OK, OK. Yes. Unless you want me to come with you and lavish you with affection and sexual favours.'

'Tempting, but I'd rather have a bonkbuster and a pina colada,' I grinned.

'Your loss,' he shrugged with complete nonchalance, before going back out into the shop to meet the customer announced by the ding of the doorbell.

I'd checked the screen again. The timing worked perfectly. I handed over the keys to the house on the tenth, closing that chapter, starting a new one in the flat I'd rented by the river in Weirbank, just five minutes from Val and Don. I wasn't ready to buy somewhere else yet. I needed time to breathe, to find out where I was meant to be.

I think Luke had felt the same. He'd been gone for almost a month now, since the day after the trial, taken a sabbatical and gone down south to stay with his brothers. Before he went, we'd orbit the same people, have dinner at Val's house on a Sunday, he'd pop into the shop to see Mark, but that was it. No rehash of the conversation about us, no mention that it had even happened. The only consolation was that I was pretty sure Val and Don were so wrapped up in the preparations for the court case to notice that the easy friendship Luke and I had always had was gone.

It was all a blur of loss to me now. Dee. Pete. Luke. My pain receptors had long shut down, leaving me numb to all new incoming assaults. I hung on to the thought that it would get better.

And when I'd arrived at reception and been shown to my water villa, one of thirty that extended out over the lagoon, things definitely got better. Inside, polished wooden floors, simple but beautiful furniture, in muted neutral shades, brightened with flashes of orange and lime.

It was outside, though, that was truly breathtaking. A private deck, angled so that the only thing in view was the sky and the ocean, and perhaps a passing boat or two. Effusive descriptions were all too common in travel magazines, but I'd never known anything or been anywhere that was closer to paradise.

I had no idea how Dee had found it, but I was so grateful that she had. I could only assume that she and Brad had planned an island getaway. The notion made my gut twist. It had been a tough secret to live with. At least I had no fear of him arriving now and compounding the anxiety by telling me more about their relationship. He knew she was gone and I had a feeling that a guy like Brad wouldn't be one for solitary nostalgia. And I already knew more than I ever wanted to.

Standing against the wooden posts that supported the rope balcony, I couldn't help thinking how the person I'd been a year ago would never have done this.

Dee was always the explorer in our extended, hashed-together family. Crazy, irresponsible and, yes, occasionally selfish and thoughtless, single-minded and rash; she wasn't perfect but if I had a choice to take one person from this life to the next, it would be Dee. She fought our battles, created our excitement and added all the drama, while I'd been happy, truly happy, to take a back seat, content with what I had in life: my business, my home, my partner, my friends, my family.

A year later and the picture was completely different, like a snow globe that had been shaken in a storm.

I was bolder, stronger, more ready to step up and challenge life, rather than letting it slip right by me. And I was more battle-weary, sadder, too. Too many times to count, I'd wondered whether Luke and I could ever have found a way to be together but I knew I'd done the right thing. It was a moment in time. A desperate need for comfort. At least that's what I told myself. If I admitted anything more, it just took me right back to the truth – I'd never forgive myself if I took the life she had planned with Luke. No matter what he said about her reticence to start a family, I knew she wanted that. How many times over the years had we lain on my sofas on a Sunday afternoon, discussing the names we'd give our kids, and sure, Epcot and Pluto might want to change their monikers later in life, but at least they'd know they were unique. I stopped my mind from wandering. It was all moot anyway. Luke and I would never have a relationship, never mind a family or future.

I took a deep breath of sea air, then went back inside and changed out of my travel clothes and into a forties, retro style pale blue swimsuit and matching sarong from a new range I'd chosen for the shop. It had been a hit with the customers, one of several successes that had given me more confidence in my choices.

Feet bare, I walked along the narrow boardwalk that connected the villas to the land and decided to take a stroll along the beach, letting the waves roll over my feet so the hot white sands didn't burn them.

I passed two sun loungers in a shady nook to the left, a couple holding hands across the distance between the beds. In the water, another couple wrapped in each other as they kissed.

I swept away the brief tug of sadness that I was alone, because I knew that it really didn't matter. This was my choice, and I was going to savour every second of it. And anyway, in the distance I could see another solitary soul, a guy, sitting on the sand, facing out to sea, his head obscured by a hat, his body lean and paler than the others I'd passed so far.

Obviously not a local then.

Still walking, I turned to the ocean, letting the breeze cool my face while the sun radiated heat into my bones. It had been so long, since that first morning in Barcelona, since I'd felt heat on my naked skin.

I kept walking.

Dee would love this. If she were here she'd already have made plans to go scuba diving, kayaking, to eat under the stars and to dance until dawn.

I kept walking.

She'd have introduced herself to all the staff and won them over with her enthusiasm and unadulterated delight at being there.

I kept walking.

I turned back to see that the lone figure was still sitting there, on the sands, facing out into the water, waves lapping his legs, only a few feet in front of me now.

I stopped. Stared. Recognised.

Sensing me there, he turned, his hand at his brow to shade his gaze from the sun.

I didn't understand.

A voice. I think it was mine.

'What are you doing here?'

42

Val

'In the name of God, would you look at this,' Josie exclaimed, holding up one of the swimsuits that was hanging on the rail nearest the counter in Sun, Sea, Ski. At least, it was supposed to be a swimsuit. In reality, it was like three teabags, two at the top, one at the bottom, held together by an elaborate web of strings and ties.

'That's not a swimming costume, it's a gynaecological condition waiting to happen,' she declared.

I laughed so loudly Mark popped his head out of the office to investigate what was going on with his irresponsible temporary staff members. 'Unless you want to discuss thrush, you're as well staying in there, son,' I told him, chuckling again when he pulled his head back in, like a turtle going for cover.

'You'll miss him, Val,' Josie said, a mix of warmth and sympathy.

'I will, but he's got his own life to lead, Josie. I brought both of them up that way, to be independent and find their own paths. He's got to live for both of them now.' The words were melancholic, but they weren't said with sorrow. I meant it. It was time for him to get his life back. He'd given up almost a whole year to be with us, and, although it had been tough to adjust at the start, I was beyond grateful. I'd be selfish to expect him to stay here for ever.

'I've been thinking I'm going to come in here full-time to work after Mark has gone. Jen needs the help and I'll be at a loose end. I was fine at home before, doing Don's accounts and keeping on top of all his paperwork, but I think I need to be out and about more. Keep my mind busy. I'm best doing that in here until I decide what I want to do with myself.'

I knew Josie would understand. She kept on working because she liked to be busy and needed the interaction. I got that now. Semi-retirement had suited me once, when Dee and Jen were always popping in and out, and the lot of them, Luke and Pete too, were round for dinner a couple of times a week. After Dee died, I'd been functioning so poorly that all I could handle was a few hours every now and then, a bit of paperwork to distract my mind, a couple of shifts in the shop when they were short. Now, I was ready for more. Wilkie's conviction had given me some kind of closure, a will to move forward. The rage had subsided now that I knew he was being punished. Don't get me wrong, I still had my off days when I couldn't face lifting that duvet back, but the difference was that now when I forced myself up and into action, I didn't want to kill everyone in my path.

Don and I were better too. What did they call it these days? Reconnected. We laughed sometimes. Went out for dinner. I'd even put a bit of weight back on and I felt better for it.

I was still heart-sore without her, missed her every day, but I knew that I couldn't give up. She'd be so disappointed in me if I did. I'd find something else to occupy my time, something that I loved and that was just for me, but in the meantime, Jen could do with a hand here and I'd be happy to lend it.

I was worried about her. On the surface she was coping, getting ahead, and taking care of everything but the only social life she had now, as far as I could see, was coming round to our house for a bit of dinner and maybe going out for the odd drink with Mark. For a while, she was spending a lot of time with Luke, but that didn't seem to be the case so much now. In fact, they hadn't been round at the same time for ages. A thought struck me.

'Josie, our Jen and Luke didn't have a falling-out did they?'

'Don't know anything about that,' she replied completely sincerely, her face a picture of innocence. That's how I knew she was lying.

'What are you not telling me?' I said.

'Nothing,' she replied. Another innocent face. Definitely lying.

'Josie, don't make me prise it out of you because you know I will stalk you until you give in. We've already witnessed my skills in that department.'

It was strange but welcome that I could joke about that now. I hadn't seen Mrs Wilkie since that day in court, but I thought of her often, hoped that she was finding the strength to carry on.

Josie cracked as I knew she would. She loved my family like they were her own and she wouldn't keep anything from me if she thought I should know about it. Would she?

'OK, but Val, you've got to promise to say nothing. Swear to me.'

'I promise,' I said, my stomach beginning to turn just a wee bit with apprehension. Oh God, don't make it anything bad. We were just on the cusp of pulling ourselves off the floor and I wasn't for lying back down there.

'They're both denying it, but they got so close for a while there that I think they decided they were better backing off.'

I was stunned. 'What do you mean by "close"?'

Josie sighed and adopted a serious discussion posture, her elbows on the desk, leaning towards me. 'Right, don't get your knickers in a fankle, but Jen was sleeping in his spare room for a while because neither of them wanted to be on their own. No funny business though. Don't worry, I checked. I think it was Jen that decided it was a bad idea and moved back out. She was worried what people would think and maybe more worried about what it could lead to. Are you OK, Val?' she asked, looking at me with concern. 'You look like Barry Manilow has just walked in and smacked you with a shovel.'

That would have been less surprising, and definitely less confusing than the conflicting riot of emotions I was feeling. Luke and Jen? No. They couldn't. He was Dee's husband and Jen had no right to move on in there... Anger. And what was Luke thinking? Jen was vulnerable, the poor lass had lost everything and there he was taking advantage... Disappointment. But then, God love them, it had been so hard on them both... Sympathy. I'd had my Don to get me through it and I couldn't imagine what it must be like to do it alone... Understanding.

'I don't know how I feel about that, Josie,' I confessed.

'Well you don't have to worry yourself with it because, like I say, Jen moved out before anything happened and they've... what is it the young ones say nowadays...?' she pondered, before a triumphant, 'Moved on! That's it. They've moved on.'

Another fear popped up like one of those bloody whack-a-mole machines that our Dee used to love when we took her for day trips to Largs. Luke was down in London spending a bit of time with his brothers. If he'd had a fall out with Jen, what was to stop him moving down there permanently? What was to keep him here now? His parents lived in Edinburgh and his brothers were his only other family. Between Dee's passing and now this, maybe he'd decide there was nothing to keep him here.

Dread had taken over now. I'd taken Luke into my family and clichéd or not, he was a son to me now and I didn't want to lose him too. Too much loss. Too much.

'I'm away to put the kettle on,' I told Josie. Distraction therapy. It was a quiet afternoon, and there was no sign of a stampede of customers, so I needed to do something to keep my anxiety from running riot.

'There's caramel wafers in the cupboard above the sink,' Josie said, as I bustled off.

When I returned clutching two mugs, with a packet of Tunnock's wafers dangling from my teeth, Josie was posing in front of a mirror. I put the tea and biscuits down on the desk before I did someone an injury. 'What in God's name are you doing?' I asked, collapsing with hilarity. That woman was a tonic, she really was. She still had on her standard uniform of black polo neck and jeans of the same colour, but now she'd pulled the teabag swimming costume over her clothes and was rearranging the strings to make it fit her. Badly.

Tears of laughter were blinding me when the ding of the door interrupted the carry-on. Finally, a customer! A pretty blonde woman in her thirties, maybe, carrying a tiny baby in one of those papoose things, and credit to her, she didn't even flinch at the sight of Josie in that get-up. My maternal instinct was about to propel me closer to have a look at the baby, when she spoke.

'Hello, I wonder if you ladies could help me,' she said, a warm smile, the whitest teeth I'd ever seen and an accent, maybe Australian. Or Canadian. Sometimes I got them confused.

'I'm looking for Dee Harper.'

No matter how often it happened, it still took my breath away. Thank God Josie, in all her bizarre finery, stepped in.

'I'm sorry, dear, but Dee isn't here anymore.' She didn't go into detail. We'd learned over the months that it was best to leave it at that and not cause an uncomfortable situation for the customer or us.

To my surprise, the woman's face fell and she looked absolutely gutted.

'Is there something I can help you with?' I asked her, but she shook her head.

'Thanks, but it was Dee I was looking for. Is there any way I can contact her? It's pretty important.'

Josie came to the rescue again. 'Love, I don't want to upset you but I'm afraid Dee passed away.'

Her eyes widened and for a moment I thought she was going to cry. 'Passed away? But...' The sentence got stuck there. Going by her reaction, she was clearly more than a customer. Maybe a friend from Dee's travels? Someone she knew on that Facebook malarkey?

The baby yawned and this seemed to restart the young woman's thought process. 'I'm sorry,' she said, 'it's just that I was actually looking for Dee because I thought she might be able to help me find her brother. Sorry to have troubled you.'

'Wait!' I blurted, confused, as she turned to leave. 'I'm Dee's mother, Val.'

Her expression lit up like a fluorescent bulb.

'You're trying to find Mark?'

She nodded, but before I could say any more, Mark, maybe hearing his name, popped his head out the door again. 'Mum, did you shout...?'

His eyes went straight to the stranger.

'Tara?' he said with obvious astonishment, and I swear to the heavens I hadn't seen that face since the days that a wee boy would run downstairs and burst into the lounge and see his pile of presents on Christmas morning.

And, going by the lassie's delighted grin, she was feeling the same way. My gaze met Josie's wide-eyed stare and then we both immediately flicked back to Mark and... what did he say her name was?

'Hey,' she said, with an irrepressible smile that was so contagious, Josie and I were already jumping on the bandwagon.

Och, this was lovely. A pal of Mark's come all this way to see him.

Mark finally got his wits about him. 'Sorry, Mum, Josie...' He noticed Josie properly for the first time since he'd popped his head out and couldn't help but laugh. 'Josie, I'm not even going to ask what you're wearing. Anyway, Mum, Josie, this is Tara.' I watched as his gaze left her face and went downwards, to the tiny person strapped to her chest. 'And this is...'

Silence. Tara's hands went to the bump, cradling it as she answered Mark's question.

'This is your daughter.'

43

Jen

'Jen?' he stuttered.

I shared his overwhelming shock. 'What are you doing here, Pete?'

Even as he tried to shade them, I could see his eyes darted to the right. Searching for someone? Oh for bollocking bugger's sake, don't tell me that I'd managed to come halfway round the bloody world and end up in the same place as Pete and bloody bollocking Arya on their bloody bollocking honeymoon?

My gaze flicked skyward as I sent a silent message to my pal. Dee, if you did this, you have a sick, twisted sense of humour.

'Ah, shit. How did you know?' he asked, going somewhere between weary and defensive.

'Know what?'

'About here? Today?'

I didn't understand. What about today? Was it special? And... oh bloody bollocking not again – don't tell me he was here to get married and I'd just gatecrashed the party. This couldn't be happening. It just couldn't. It must be a hallucination. Maybe I didn't have enough fluids on the plane.

'What are you talking about?'

Realisation dawned on him, followed by an unmistakable flinch of guilt as he picked a pebble off the sand and launched it into the sea, spitting a tortured 'Fuck!' with the kind of vehemence I'd never heard before.

'What is it? Pete, you're seriously freaking me out. What's going on?'

I sank to my knees next to him and saw the raw, visceral pain in every line of his far-too-handsome face.

'Dee,' he whispered. 'I was supposed to be here with Dee.'

I froze, synapses of my brain exploding.

No.

This made no sense.

And yet…

The weariness was like a blanket of pure exhaustion lying on top of me, forcing me into the sands, removing every ounce of energy or free will. I was utterly defenceless and the most horrific thing was that, in that split second, I knew. He didn't even need to tell me, because it was all so crystal clear that I couldn't believe I hadn't seen it before.

Yet still… 'Tell me!' I demanded, while internally screaming that I didn't want to hear what he had to say. 'You were having an affair?'

He had the decency to hang his head.

'Pete, if what we had meant anything, you'd better tell me the truth now because anything else would be beyond cruel.' I saw a shift in his body language and decided to go on. 'For how long?'

The sands were burning my knees now but the pain barely registered.

'A few months,' he said, wearily, sorrow seeping from his words. 'But there had been something there for years…'

Years. I retched and he immediately stopped speaking. Bit late now for concern.

'Keep talking,' I spluttered.

'There had been something,' he repeated and I realised I was fighting the urge to punch him in that beautiful face. 'But we'd never acknowledged it. We spent so much time together...'

That was true. Dee and Pete were the sporty ones, the runners, the adrenalin junkies, while Luke and I were content to lounge in the background. It was a standing joke with us. Suddenly, it wasn't funny anymore.

'... and then a few months before she died we realised we couldn't ignore it anymore.' He paused. 'That's not true. *I* realised. It wasn't Dee.'

'But she admitted it too? She had feelings for you?'

Say no. Please say no.

He nodded. 'Luke was putting her under pressure to have kids and I think it freaked her out, and there I was, a diversion.'

Poor Luke.

'When did you sleep together? The first time, when was it?' I couldn't even scream or yell, my voice like the low, deadly demands of a stranger.

'We didn't. She said she couldn't...' My spirits spiked until he continued, '... while you and I were still together.'

'She knew you were going to leave me?'

There was a pause as he thought about what I'd asked him. 'Not really. We made a pact. Sounds crazy now. That we would both try to make it work. One year, we agreed. She would give it her all with Luke, and I'd do the same with you. We stopped meeting up...'

I heard the waitress from the coffee shop's comment in my head. There was another one, she'd said. 'You met in the café across from your work?'

'Yeah. How did you know that?'

For the first time since I'd met him today I knew more than him. Small victories.

'Doesn't matter. Go on.'

'We still ran and worked out together because if we stopped you might notice and wonder why, but other than that we didn't see each other alone.'

Everything about this made no sense, yet so much sense at the same time. My mind was reeling.

'So why are you here?' I asked, still not grasping the facts.

'Stupid dreams,' he said. 'I saw this place in a brochure and I told her that I'd bring her here, on my birthday, if we'd found a way to be together. I didn't mean it. It was a pipedream, but I couldn't stop thinking about it.'

His birthday. It was today. What did it say about the changes in my life that I'd completely forgotten, but I was distracted from that thought by another memory that was clearing in my head.

'I remember seeing you looking at those brochures,' I said. 'I thought you were planning a surprise for me. Oh God, I think I actually suggested we take the trip after Dee died and you freaked out, left that night.'

'Guilt,' he admitted. 'And grief. But mostly guilt. If it hadn't been for me she would still be here.'

'What do you mean?'

A pause and I could see it was killing him to go wherever his mind was taking him.

'She'd gone to the car to get her mobile because she knew I'd text her. Then she called me instead. She was speaking to me when it happened.'

For the first time since that day, my mind went back further than the sound of the grinding engine and the horrific thud.

Dee. Across the road. Smiling as she spoke. To Pete.

How could she have done that? How could the person I'd grown up with, who was closer than a sister, have gone there? Who was she? Didn't I know her at all?

I don't know what shocked me more. The revelation or the fact that, for the first time in our lives, I saw that he was crying.

My anger was instant. Crocodile fucking tears. How dare he? His treachery, her treachery, both of them... they'd wrecked all our lives for some cheap, tawdry, cruel affair. Their lies had killed her. And he was going to have to live with that.

'I'm sorry Jen, but I loved her,' he spluttered.

He was pathetic in every sense. If I didn't know him and I was hearing him speak now, for the first time, I'd think he was a broken man. I didn't feel a shred of sympathy, but seeing his guilt, his suffering, realising that torture would be with him for the rest of his days, made my fury pull back like the pale blue waves that were crashing around us.

'All this time I thought it was Arya,' I said, the fight draining out of me.

'It is now, sometimes. Has been for a while. But it's nothing serious. Friends with benefits,' he shrugged, and I tried not to react to his cavalier nonchalance.

How had I lived with this man for fifteen years and never seen this side of him? Since we were fifteen, I'd shared his life, watch him grow, change, mature, and I had absolutely no idea.

His turn to ask the questions. 'Why are you here?'

'Dee wrote the name of this place in her diary for this week. I saw it and decided to come.'

'She wrote it in her diary?'

That's when I saw it, right there, in the curve of his mouth and the light in his eyes. He was happy that she'd done that and he couldn't help showing it, even in front of me. No heartfelt apologies. No hint of remorse. All he could think about was what could have been instead of what he destroyed in the process.

The crashing noise in my ears didn't come from the waves. It was yesterday, crumbling to dust.

'You disgust me,' I said, quietly. I wanted him to hurt. To feel pain. To pay. But what more was there to say? 'She was seeing someone else.' It was out before I could stop myself and I could see it hit the target.

'What? No. She wasn't.' He was aghast, horrified, yet even in his shock, I could see a glimmer of belief.

'She was. Had been for years. So you see, the "thing" with you and her? Not that special. You were just one of many.'

His head fell back, eyes closed, as if bracing his body to accept the pain, flinching under torture.

Good. I'd never wished another human being hurt. Until now.

Time to go.

He wasn't getting another beat of my heart, another moment of my time.

I got up, and walked away, across the sands.

And if I could have had my way, I'd have kept on walking all the way to the rest of my life.

44

Luke

I'd been dreading coming home and now that the cab was pulling up outside the front door, the heaviness in my gut made it feel like it was lined with lead. I'd made the decision while I was in London – time to leave here. I couldn't do this anymore. Couldn't live in a shrine to the incredible wife and the great life I once had. Couldn't face empty rooms and empty hours. Couldn't go to pick up the phone a dozen times a day to call Jen and then remember that our friendship – or more – had been damaged. There was nothing here for me now. Matt and Callum were both making a great life for themselves in London and there was nothing to stop me joining them. Our agency had an office there, so a transfer would be painless. It would be a fresh start – no looks of sympathy, no casual avoidance because people didn't know what to say to me, no Callie rolling her eyes when I walked into the office because I'd flaked out on her and wasn't up for a repeat of that night.

Not her fault. She wasn't Dee. She wasn't Jen.

My holdall made a thud on the floor as I dropped it, deciding I'd unpack later. First, a beer and something to eat, then a flick through the pile of mail that was waiting on the dining table. Josie must have been here. The place was spotless and there was a whiff of some kind of polish. I must remember to buy her something nice to thank her and say goodbye. Unless of course I could persuade her to pop down to London once a month to keep the new place gleaming. If I could tie it in with anything to do with Tom Jones, the Rolling Stones or an Elvis tribute, I might be in with a chance.

In the kitchen, the fruit bowl had been filled, there was a French loaf on the counter and when I opened the fridge I saw that there was fresh milk and cold meats. So Val had probably been here too. Whenever Dee and I had travelled, Val always stocked up for us coming back. God, I'd miss her and Don. My own parents were great, but I'd been living in Val and Don's pockets for so long they felt like my family too. Telling her I was leaving was the thing I was dreading most. Well, that and saying goodbye to... I didn't want to think about it. See! This made my point. I was back in the door ten minutes and already I was thinking about her. This was why I needed to leave.

I twisted the top off the bottle of Budweiser and headed across the lounge. Dee was the one who'd wanted this big open-plan space because she said it was great for parties. She was right, but my days of partying here were done. Time to sell up and keep on going.

It was the faintest light that caught my eye when I walked past the doors leading out on to the balcony. More of a glow, like the one from the screen of a mobile phone. Christy Almighty, what now? Neighbourhood kids? Someone casing the house? How the hell had they managed to get up to the first floor?

I changed my grip on the beer bottle, making it more of a weapon than a drink, then slowly opened the door, stepped forward and...

Jen.

Sitting with her back to me on the chair that she always claimed as hers.

She heard me and turned. 'Hey,' she said softly.

I don't go in for all that romance stuff, but I swear my stomach flipped and there was suddenly a big daft grin on my face. I wanted to hug her. Was that OK? No idea, so I didn't. I just stood, leaning against the wall, looking at her, thinking how much she'd changed in the last year. Her hair was longer, her smile a little sadder, and she just seemed, I don't know... wearier. Before this year we had no worries, no stresses, just a great group of family and friends and a whole lot of good times. It was like a spark had been extinguished for all of us – yet when I looked at her – bugger, I was coming over all sentimental again – it was like the light was back on.

'Hi,' I replied, grinning like a fool but trying desperately to keep the laid-back, don't gush all over her vibe. 'Are you my welcome-back party? Or are Val and Josie hiding behind the sofa?'

'Just me,' she said, 'I hope that's OK?'

'More than.'

I moved forward and sat in the seat next to her, about a foot of distance between us. I'd never wanted to reach out and touch someone more but immediately a pang of guilt kicked in. Oh God, I'm sorry Dee. I'm so sorry. But these feelings are here and they'd never have grown if you hadn't left, but now they have.

'So how was London?' she asked, voice still quiet, calm. This felt surreal, to be sitting here with her again, the way we'd done so many times when she'd stayed here.

'Good. Actually, really good. Matt and Callum were asking after you.'

'Bet it was great to hang out with them again.'

'It was.' I took a sip of my beer to buy time, and thought about sticking with small talk, but what was the point? It would only be putting off difficult conversations until later. I ended up just blurting it out. 'I'm going to move down there, Jen. To London.'

In a way I was grateful for the way her eyes widened, as if this was something she didn't want to hear.

'Why?' was all she said.

I sighed. 'Because I can't stay. All this reminds me too much of Dee,' I said, gesturing behind me, back into the house. 'Our lives here have fallen apart. It was different when it was Dee and I, and you and Pete, and everything was great but now...' I got stuck for a minute, hating saying this, but sure it was right to tell her now. 'Now there's nothing left.'

'You've got me,' she said.

Ah, don't do this. Don't make me say it.

'Come on Jen, we both know I don't. The only thing that comes even close to the pain of losing Dee, is the pain of staying here and not being able to love you.'

She went to speak, and I realised immediately what she was going to say, so I cut her off at the friend-zone pass.

'And please don't say we'll always love each other as friends because you know that's not enough for me now.'

'Or me.'

It took me a minute to catch up.

'What?'

'Or me,' she repeated, but still I wasn't entirely clear what was happening because two huge tears were rolling down her cheeks.

'So...' I didn't want to hope. 'You think we could...' I left that hanging, determined not to make a complete fool of myself if I was getting it wrong.

'Be together,' she said, two more tears now, but also a smile I hadn't seen for a long, long time. A real one. Not forced. Not half-hearted. Not tinged with sadness.

'Are you sure?' Even as I said it I was on my feet, then in front of her, then pulling her up to me.

I stopped waiting for an answer when she kissed me instead.

45

Jen

It was strange opening the door to Val's house and hearing voices and laughter and life again. I passed the picture of Dee in the hallway and touched it, saying hello. It had taken a while. Seven days in the Maldives, doing nothing but staring at the ocean and thinking, making plans and sawing through the ties of the past. In the end it came down to a simple decision. Was I going to be grateful for the lifetime of love she gave me, for the fact that she made my life so much better than it would ever have been, or was I going to wipe out all those years and only remember what I learned since she left us?

Forgive or not? Love her or not?

I chose to forgive and love her.

She didn't sleep with him, didn't follow her wild crazy heart, so I know that there was a loyalty there. And yes, it could have been stronger, but if I had the choice of a life without Dee, or a life with her, making one mistake, I'd take Dee every time.

So I'd decided to live with it.

Maybe naïve, maybe too forgiving, but it was what I was choosing because look where I was now. Luke and I had a love that was unlike anything I'd had before.

When he'd told me how he felt, I'd backed away, crippled with guilt that I was stealing Dee's life. That had changed now that I knew it wasn't the life she wanted. If she truly wanted Luke, to stay with him and have his children, she wouldn't have been fooling around with Brad, or sharing intimacies with Pete.

Luke never truly had her heart, which meant I felt no guilt about giving him mine.

Once again, I'd spent a long time agonizing over whether I should tell him about Dee and Pete, but I knew I wouldn't. Nothing should taint her memory. This was a truth for me to keep. Dee might have taken Pete, but she'd given me Luke.

Our relationship was more than I'd ever had and I knew it would survive anything.

Even today.

I'd been putting off telling Val for weeks, but it needed to be now. It would soon be Christmas, almost a year since Dee died, and I wanted to be here for her, not watching what I said and being anxious not to look at Luke the wrong way in case our feelings showed.

'All right, love?' Don boomed, when I opened the kitchen door. He was sitting at the table with Mark and Tara, all of them buoyed up as if they'd been discussing something that amused them before we came in. I'd only met her a few times, but I was already a fan. She had that laid-back energy that was completely in sync with Mark's, and from Don's cheery disposition, it seemed that he agreed.

'I'm great, Don,' I said, giving him a hug, then Mark and Tara. I was so delighted for them, they deserved every moment of this happiness. I was only sorry that Dee would never get to meet her beautiful niece.

'Is Val out?' I asked.

'Upstairs with the wee one,' he said. 'Go on up. Claudie was sleeping but she should be awake by now.'

Claudie. A beautiful name that suited her huge brown eyes and shock of chestnut hair.

When I climbed the stairs, I heard them in the room Dee and I once shared. Val was singing to a gurgling audience, the sound of their happiness banishing the ghosts of Dee's absence that had haunted the house for so long. When I pushed the door open, it was like stepping back in time. The same two pine single beds, the same matching wardrobe and bedside tables with white lamps on them. We had an old TV in the corner that took up the whole of the top of a chest of drawers, and the carpet was a deep purple, a replacement for the bubblegum pink one that had got ruined when Dee slapped on blue hair dye then fell asleep on the floor. Val had hit the roof over that one. The walls were still pale blue, although the Ricky Martin and Backstreet Boys posters had long since been taken down. Other than that it was exactly as Dee and I had left it when we'd moved out to go to college. A wave of emotion rose, but I forced it back down. Today wasn't about the past.

Val was lying on Dee's bed, next to a tiny Claudie, the baby's eyes fixed on Val's face as she sang the 'The Wheels On The Bus'. I wanted to stand and watch them, to take in Val's obvious joy. I hadn't seen her like that for a long time. God, Dee would love this. Shaking off the sorrow, I flopped down on my old bed.

'Thought I'd come see where the girls were hanging out,' I announced, laughing.

Val blew me a kiss with one hand, the other protectively around Claudie, to make sure she didn't roll over. Val was wearing make-up again, her hair newly cut into a sharp blonde bob that framed her face. The black circles under her eyes were still there but she was like a different woman to one that had struggled to breathe under a shell of grief. We knew now about the late night supermarket visits, the conversations with Wilkie's mother. I wished she'd told us, but I think we just all retreated to cope with the destruction of our worlds in our own ways.

'I can't stop looking at her,' she said, then cooed to the baby. 'Because you're perfect aren't you? You're just granny Val's little angel and you're perfect.'

Claudie responded with a toothless grin that would melt any heart and Val smothered her little cheeks in kisses.

'You staying for dinner, my love? I've a steak pie in the oven.'

'Thanks, Val, but I'm going to look at a house. One of the new flats they're building on the edge of the river.' They were only about ten minutes from here – two bedroom apartments on the site of an old woollen mill. I'd thought about moving into Luke's but it was too much. We needed a fresh start, somewhere that was just for us. 'I just wanted to come over and talk to you about something first.'

Either the words or the fact that the thudding of my heart must surely be filling the room got her attention. Her gaze met mine, and despite having rehearsed a dozen different versions of this moment, my mind went blank and my mouth went dry. How could I tell her this? But then, how could I not? Words. Use. Words.

'Are you going to tell me about you and Luke?' she asked gently.

In none of my scenarios did she already know. 'But how...'

'Josie told me.'

Ah. Judas.

She went on, 'Don't be upset with her. It was a good thing, Jen. Gave me time to get used to the idea.'

'I'm so sorry if it upset you. We didn't want that to happen. To be honest, we didn't want anything to happen between us either.'

Claudie watched both of us in turn, her gaze following the voices.

'I know. And I can't say I was happy about it at first, but then... You deserve happiness, Jen. And Luke does too. I was worried we might lose him down south there for a while, and I'm guessing he's staying now.'

I responded with a nod.

'So it has to be a good thing. And you know, I think our Dee would get that. She always was one for following her heart and she loved you both, so she would have wanted you both to find someone. In a way, I'm glad it was each other.'

Gratitude, love, relief, each one of those emotions propelled me across to her and I wrapped her in a hug, Claudie nestled in the middle.

'I'll never be able to thank you for everything you've given me Val,' I told her, truthfully.

'Having you was thanks enough my love. Your mum would be so proud of you. Our Dee would too.'

More tears, this time from both of us.

'You're sure about Luke? And do you think Don will be too?' I checked, holding my breath, in case she changed her mind. I couldn't bear the thought. Now that Luke and I were together and committed to a future, we desperately wanted Val and Don's blessing. 'Because if not, please tell us. We'd rather know and we'd understand.' We'd understand, but we'd be totally crushed. These people were like parents to us and we couldn't bear the thought of that ever changing.

'I'm sure,' she said with such conviction that I knew she meant it. 'And I've discussed it with Don, love. He feels the same as me. If Dee's death taught us something it's that you have to make the most of every minute of the day because you don't know when it'll be over. This year has been more heartache than I ever thought I could bear, and I'll miss her every day of my life, but we have to keep going, Jen. Dee would be bloody raging if we didn't.'

I knew she was right. And that Dee would understand, more than anyone, that you just had to follow your heart.

46
Val

I stood in front of the gravestone, little Claudie in the pram at my side. She'd been here before so she didn't need any introduction. Mark had headed back offshore for his next stint, but Tara had decided to stick around and get to know us rather than heading back to Australia to wait for him there. Her mother had passed away a few months before, and in some ways I think she needed us as much as we need her. She'd have tracked Mark down eventually, but I was so grateful that his Australian mobile phone didn't work here so she'd had to come all this way to find him. I only hoped she would decide to make it permanent because every moment with this little girl was pure happiness and I was sure her arrival was down to Dee. The rest of them thought that I was crazy, but I had an overwhelming feeling our Dee had orchestrated that because I knew she was still here, still with us, still part of our lives.

'He got sentenced yesterday,' I said, my gaze on the stone. 'Six years. He'll be out in three if he behaves. It's not enough, is it? But I thought you'd like to know. Sleep tight,' I whispered, 'I'll pop back again soon.'

I gave the stone a quick polish with the arm of my jacket.

She'd passed away the day after he was found guilty. Her other kids hadn't had the money for the stone, so Don and I had paid for it. She was in the same cemetery as Dee, just a few hundred yards away. Every time I came here I'd sit with Dee, then pop down for a quick chat with Margo.

I took the brake off the pram and set off for home. Don would be out for the rest of the day, so it was just Claudie and I now that Tara was working part-time in the shop, a couple of days a week. We split it between us. She did two, I did three, and whichever one of us was off had Claudie. It was enough, especially now that I was doing two nights a week at the food bank, sorting out donations and restocking the shelves.

Don didn't mind. We were going out again at the weekends, and we'd already booked a fortnight in Tenerife for the summer. We'd found each other again – although I had threatened to suffocate him in his sleep if he didn't get something done about that bloody snoring.

At home, I gave Claudie the bottle Tara had expressed that morning then took her upstairs for her nap. Tara had moved into Dee and Jen's room now as it was bigger than Mark's old room, with more space for a cot. I laid Claudie down to sleep, and then, as always, I lay on the bed next to the crib and talked to her in a soft, low voice until her eyes closed.

'Auntie Dee would have loved you, my darling. She was just like you. Beautiful, and strong, and had a fair set of lungs. And she grew up to be the best daughter a Mum could have. That doesn't mean she was always perfect. She made me heart-sore many a time and we won't even talk about the times she sneaked out at night to go and meet some boy or other, not realising that I always knew. There will never be a day that goes by that I don't miss her, or a night I won't go to sleep hoping I'll see her face in my dreams. But I sleep now, knowing that she loved us and we loved her back and that's all you can do in life, just like we'll always love you.'

There was a tiny snuffle as Claudie closed her eyes.

'Sweet dreams, my darlings. Both of you.'

Epilogue

'Ida at three o'clock, Ida at three o'clock. Take evasive action,' Josie hissed, while Luke, Mark, Tara and I fought to keep straight faces under the prospect of the Ida ambush.

'Och, doll, she's a stunner! A stunner!' Ida proclaimed. 'Definitely looks like our side of the family. I think she's got my eyes.'

Tara, utterly gorgeous in a pale yellow, floaty dress, had the good grace to agree. She'd been warned about Ida so she was fully prepared to hand over her daughter's spotlight to the woman in the purple dress, with a lilac hat the size of a coffee table.

The christening had been beautiful, and Claudie Dee Murray had slept peacefully through the whole affair.

Luke and I had been surprised and delighted to be asked to be godparents, yet another link that would tie both of us to Dee and the Murrays. Not that we needed anything more than what we already had, two parents who might not be related to us by blood, but treated us like we were. Don had even offered to give me away if we ever got married. Maybe one day, but not any time soon. It was enough that we were living together, planning a future, and they were supporting us.

I could see Val and Don now, holding hands as they chatted to the humanist who had conducted the ceremony.

There were moments over the last year that I wondered if they would get through this but of course they had. If Claudie Dee Murray ever needed a role model for marriage, it was her grandparents. However, if she needed a role model for the position of CIA spy, then the spiky-haired woman standing to my right was definitely the best candidate.

'What's up, Josie?' I asked, spotting the fact that she was scanning the room like a NASA radar.

'I've lost visual contact.'

'With who?' I asked, confused.

'With...' she started, but was interrupted by a brief squeak as the speakers in the corner of the room came to life.

Oh dear Lord, no. Not again.

On the stage, the self-appointed entertainment had arrived.

'Ladies and Gentlemen, for those of you who don't know me, I'm Claudie's great-aunt Ida. I think she's got my eyes.'

Josie raised her eyes heavenward. 'Dee, I'm begging you – send me a catapult, right now, and I won't tell your mother you borrowed her Dolce & Gabbana bag and wrecked it. She still thinks it was me.'

Luke and I were trying and failing to hold back howls of amusement.

Ida tapped the mike to make sure it was loud enough, before she went on. 'We have a tradition in our family...'

I could see Val and Don shaking their heads in rueful wonderment.

'And that is that I give you a wee song at every gathering. Today, I'd like to sing a number that was very special to me and another member of the family. Claudie, this is now your song too.'

And what could the rest of us do, other than laugh, cry, and join in on the chorus of 'My Girl'.

Acknowledgements

I owe a huge thank you to Sheila Crowley and Caroline Ridding, whose faith, inspiration and words of wisdom guided this book from an idea to a reality.

To the teams at Curtis Brown and Aria, much gratitude for everything you do to support my novels.

Thanks, as always, to my family and friends, who never complain when calls go unanswered and coffee gets cold because I'm locked away finishing the next chapter.

To my guys, John, Callan & Brad, and to Gemma – I know how lucky I am to have you.

I heart you all. Yes, I do.

Love, Shari xx